PRESIDENTIAL AFFAIR

LOVE, LIES and LIAISONS

PRESIDENTIAL AFFAIR
LOVE, LIES and LIAISONS

BY

LES COCHRAN

www.bookstandpublishing.com

Published by
Bookstand Publishing
Morgan Hill, CA 95037
4249_7

ISBN 978-1-63498-077-7

Library of Congress Control Number: 2015935114

First Edition

Printed in the United States of America

CHAPTER ONE

Standing in front of a full-length mirror, the President of the United States unzipped her dark green evening gown and, letting it curl to her feet, admired her shapely body. She removed her cultured freshwater pearl torsade necklace and matching earrings, and placed them on an end table. Unhooking her bra, Janet Stetson ran her hands around her breasts — *a full-size larger than in college and as firm as ever.*

Sensuously, her hands slid over rounded hips — her smile turned down. *I can't believe I've added pounds there. That's always been the least of my worries.*

She turned toward him. "What do you think, darling?"

"You look fabulous," Steve said. "Every red-blooded man in the country voted for you. Who could ask for more?"

"That was two years ago." Turning back to the mirror, she murmured, "I need to lose a couple of inches off my hips."

"They look fine to me," he said, motioning for her to step closer.

She strolled his way, locking a sultry stare on his soft brown eyes. As she grew closer, her gaze took-in the graying at his temples and the barely visible five o'clock shadow. *He's so sexy and distinguished looking; I could mount him right now.*

She stopped a few feet in front of him.

He loosened the gold braided belt on his blue velvet robe, slid his legs off the chaise lounge, and planted his feet on the soft carpet. Beckoning her near, Steve spread his legs and pulled her between his knees.

"What are you doing?"

"I'm researching."

She scowled prettily, tingling at the touch of his hands around her hips. He slipped his fingers under the elastic of her bikini panties. Wrapping his hands around her cheeks, he pulled her stomach against his lips and nibbled her waist.

"That's more like searching. I know where you're heading."

"Seriously, I'm checking the size of your hips."

She pursed her lips in a half-fake pout. "Sure, you are."

"No, really, I can tell — you need to lose an inch-and-a-half."

Bristling, she pushed his head away. "Get out of here. I know what you're after."

He leaned back and gave her a sly smile — thought it best to change the subject. "How about a drink?"

"That'd be perfect. I'll slip on my robe."

She walked slowly to the bathroom, her wobbly gait revealing her extreme fatigue.

Not noticing, Steve scurried around the bedroom — dimming the lights, turning on Smooth Jazz 105.9 and prepping the bed. He filled two Old Fashioned glasses with ice, added three olives and Tanqueray to his, took a short sip, and filled hers with Jack Daniels.

Heading for the Duncan Phyfe coffee table, he admired its smooth curved legs and gilt-brass feet then placed her glass on a crystal coaster and took a long sip of his drink. He quickly returned to the small bar, added a splash of gin then rushed back to the lounger and kicked back.

He thought about the year they'd had traveling around the country — it'd been at a whirlwind pace — laying her on the seaside balcony in Miami, the pounding surf muffling her moans and groans. It was ecstasy, almost like doing it on the beach. Then that night in Dallas when she'd had three orgasms for the first time. *I thought she was going to lose her mind. And how could I ever forget that night in San Diego's Coronado Hotel when she'd tied my hands to the bedpost and stripped me naked? She'd teased and fondled 'til it blew my mind. God, I still can't believe it!*

Hearing the bathroom door crack open, he turned his head to watch her enter the room. She stepped into the doorway, a goddess vision, in a loosely tied purple silk robe. She slinked his way, the plunging neckline of her negligee beneath revealing more than a hint of her deep cleavage. *Brains and beauty, no wonder she's been elected twice. They ought to change the law so she can run again.*

Taking a couple of steps toward him, she gazed across the shadowed room. Flickering candles lead her eyes to his square shoulders and two-hundred-and-ten-pound frame. Quite a specimen for a guy in his mid-fifties, she thought. *George Clooney couldn't compare to him.*

Picking up on the beat of the smooth jazz, she moved her hips in sync with the sounds then looking around, asked softly, "What have you done? This looks like a love nest."

"Only the best for the president," he said, his eyes twinkling.

She grinned and still a few feet away, leaned over, showing off everything but her nipples.

His desires perked. "I do have a request," he whispered lustily.

Seemingly surprised, she asked, "What's that, dear?"

"Next time could you have Secret Service provide scented candles and Champagne?"

She straightened. "At least you could get the functions of people around me correct."

Steve wrinkled his brow, not understanding.

"The Secret Service protects me. The Usher's staff provides all of the household services."

He winked. "Got it."

Janet laughed, picked up her glass, and slid onto the wingback chair across from him. "Did you do anything special while I was out?"

"Not really, I read mostly ... watched part of the Academy Awards."

"Gosh, I forgot all about them." She took an extra-long sip. "Did *Titanic* win?"

"Best picture and a slew of other Oscars. Jack Nicholson won best actor."

"I figured he would. I loved his performance in *As Good as It Gets.*"

"Helen Hunt won the best actress award too."

"Understandably. The two of them seemed to feed off each other."

Steve changed the subject back to her. "How did the reception with the European prime ministers and presidents go?"

"Quite well. They're about ready to agree on the Euro as their single currency. That'll be a big step forward." She winced as she stood to refill her glass.

"You okay?"

"My feet are killing me." Sitting back down, her wrinkled brow smoothed quickly again. She gave him that sexy look and winked. "You know what would help me feel better. Would you be so sweet as to rub my feet?"

I thought you'd never ask. "It'd be my privilege." He jumped up and headed for the bathroom. "I'll get the lotion and a hand towel."

"Do you want me on my stomach or back?"

"Your stomach will be fine."

When he returned she was face down on the bed — her rounded ass inviting him like never before. His psychic senses flipped into gear. Having done his routine countless times on numerous women, he smiled, anticipating what lay ahead.

He eased his rear onto the foot of the bed. *Move easy. Take her to the top then ease her down. Take your time, make her squirm — have an orgasm — then make her squirm again.* He filled one hand with lotion then rubbed his hands together to warm it.

Starting with her right ankle, he stroked gently working his way down her foot, caressing every bone. He watched her unwind as if he'd released the air from a balloon.

She moaned. "Oh Steve, that feels wonderful."

"I've saved the best for last," he announced.

"I can hardly wait."

He grinned to himself, knowing what was next. *Before I'm done, she'll be putty in my hands.* He moved to her toes, gently massaging each one several times, slowly, sensually.

Janet moaned with every touch.

Adding a dab of lotion to his hand, he tenderly massaged her left foot and again watched the tension flow from her body. Sliding onto the bed, Steve inched his fingers up her calves to the backs of her knees. His hands moved slowly, rhythmically, gliding soothingly up and around the back of her legs. Her body sank further into the thick comforter.

"Perfect," he said under his breath. *Time to get down to business.* He slipped his fingers under the elastic band of her short negligee bottoms. Slipping them off, he doubled a pillow under her pelvis. Purposefully, he ran his fingers around, then between, her perfectly-shaped cheeks, and smugly watched their tightening reflex.

Her soft moans and increasing body thrusts let him know she was getting close — her cheeks moving in concert with his fingers, sliding up and down between her cheeks. He slowed and teased her private parts; her body rose then slammed against the bed. She called out, "Please Steve, I can't hold off any longer."

Grinning, he honored her request, fondling her G-spot gently watching her ass bounce out of control. "Oh my God," Janet screamed into her pillow.

Gasping, she melted like warm butter.

Knowing she was capable of another, he waited for her to relax and cool. Timing it perfectly, his urges fired unwilling to delay any longer. He pulled himself on top of her, caressing and fondling, fingering her private parts.

Again, her cheeks moved in tandem with his touch. *Oh my God, he's going to do it again. I can't believe it!*

Steve grazed his erection between her cheeks then eased it, ever so slowly, inside. The two locked and fell into a slow, easy rhythm.

It didn't take long for her to lose control. *Oh my God. Oh my God.*

He quickened the pace.

Janet's body tensed. "Please, Steve." She panted. "Fuck me … fuck me."

***

A year and a half earlier, Senator Kennedy (D) had convened the Health, Education, Labor and Pension Committee. After his introductory remarks, he looked across the room at Steve. "It is my privilege to welcome one of the nation's foremost educators — and President Stetson's designate for Deputy Secretary of Education —

Steve Schilling. His turnaround efforts of universities in Arkansas and North Carolina are well documented, as is his KidsStyle program — an impressive public school model for helping students deal with bullying and character development."

The senator speechified his long-standing commitment to education then commended the president for making the reform of education her highest priority. He paused, gathered his thoughts, and then said, "I yield to my colleague on the other side of the aisle."

Senator Enzi (R) from Wyoming nodded and delivered equally laudatory comments citing Steve's leadership and fundraising successes. Following his oratory, Chairman Kennedy welcomed Senator Dale Bumpers (D) from Arkansas who introduced the esteemed Dr. Steven Schilling. He, too, touted Steve's many accomplishments at Eastern Arkansas University before turning to him. "It's a privilege to present my good friend, Steve Schilling, the next Deputy Secretary of Education."

Steve shook his colleague's hand, closed his folder of notes with a flourish, and further earned his colleagues' praises with an impeccable presentation. Making eye contact with each member, he connected his comments with the accomplishments of each senator — making the proceedings sound more like an ol' boys' club than a confirmation hearing — the senators sat in awe as he extolled their endeavors.

An hour later, Senator Kennedy acknowledged Steve's sterling performance. "You've obviously done your homework, Dr. Schilling. That kind of attention to detail will serve you well as the next deputy secretary."

"Thank you, Mr. Chairman."

Senator Kennedy raised the gavel. "The committee will recess until the Q and A session tomorrow at ten o'clock."

Senator Bumpers stood and shook his hand. "Congratulations, Steve, you're home free."

Senator Kennedy motioned for Steve to approach the dais then leaned over, and said, "I've heard lots of speeches over the years … none better." He pressed his hand on Steve's shoulder and whispered. "Whenever you want something, remember I'm only a phone call away."

Steve raised an eyebrow. "Thank you, Senator ..."

He winked. "It's Ted ... call any time."

"I appreciate that," Steve said, then turned and walked toward the smiling faces waiting for him behind the table.

Department staff members spilled into the empty area. "I can't believe it," one said. "You didn't use a single note."

Steve gave the team a megawatt smile. "You briefed me ... what'd you expect?"

A cute young intern with black bangs pushed herself firmly against his side. "You connected with each of the fifteen senators here today. How did you keep them straight?"

He gave her a Cheshire grin. *I know what she wants.* "A trade secret."

The group laughed.

Sherry Holmgren, the Secretary of Education's personal assistant, who'd been assigned to guide him through the confirmation process, tugged on his hand. "It's time to go. We have to prepare for tomorrow."

Steve nodded and followed her to the door. Feeling a burst of adrenaline, he walked briskly from the Dirksen Senate Building to Constitution Avenue. Turning, he saw Sherry struggling twenty-five feet behind on her high heels, trying to balance a briefcase and an armful of files.

"I'm sorry," he said, rushing back to grab the files. "I was fired up."

"For good reason. You did an outstanding job."

He grinned, stepped onto the street and waved for a taxi.

Traffic buzzed by.

A traffic light a block away turned and another pack of cars approached. They too, streamed past Steve still waving to no avail.

Sherry stepped to his side. "Here, hold this," she said, handing him the briefcase.

Grabbing it, Steve froze, looked at her, dumbfounded.

She bolted to the center lane and waved, placed two fingers in her mouth, and let out a shrilling whistle.

A cab heading in the other direction slammed on its brakes, made a U-turn and wheeled between the two of them. She jumped in the backseat on the driver's side. Steve slid in on the passenger's side.

"Where to?" the cabbie asked. Steve fumbled to close the door. "Hey buddy, I don't have all day."

"I'm starved," Steve said, turning to Sherry. "How about a quick lunch?"

"Where *to* buddy?" the driver asked again, impatiently.

"The Wall Street Deli is right next to our office building," Sherry said.

Steve wrinkled his nose. "I walked past there the other day. I was thinking of something a little nicer."

"Hey buddy, I don't have all day."

She shrugged. "Capital Grill and 701 are upscale restaurants on our way back."

Steve glimpsed in the rear-view mirror. "Whataya think, buddy?"

The taxi driver turned and eyed Sherry, looking terrific as usual in her business attire. "The Capital Grill for business. An attractive lady — 701."

She blushed.

"701 it is."

***

Checking in with the hostess, Steve lagged behind, watching Sherry's gait — *nice ass.* Following her through the maze of tables, he gazed the hanging shaded lamps that filled the ceiling, said, "Great choice. It has the warmth and ambiance of a private club."

"I agree."

Dressed in black long sleeves and a muted-burgundy vest, the hostess stopped at a white-clothed table for two. Steve pulled out Sherry's chair and slid onto the chair across from her.

"The black and gold accents add a touch of class. It looks pricey," she said. "Let's go Dutch."

"No way," Steve said. "You worked your tail off, it's my treat."

She gave him a questioning look.

"I insist," he emphasized.

"Just this once. It's Dutch next time."

"I need a drink," he exclaimed. "How about you?"

"I usually don't drink at ..."

Steve cut her off. "C'mon, this is a big day."

"Cocktails today?" a slender waitress asked.

"Yes." He pointed to Sherry. "You first."

She hesitated. "I'll have a Manhattan, straight up, light on the vermouth."

The waitress turned to Steve. "And you, sir?"

"Tanqueray on the rocks, three olives."

Sherry grinned. "I know ... you drink gin for the olives."

Steve gave her a quizative look. "What made you say that?"

"My dad always said, he 'loves olives and orders gin just so he can eat them.' I just thought it was funny."

"It's true for me too ... that's why I drink Tanqueray."

"Sure." She looked him in the eye then changed the subject. "You were fabulous today."

"Me? Your team made it happen."

"I can't believe how smooth you were. It's like you knew what questions were coming up."

"Thanks again to you. I felt like I did."

She smiled broadly, showing her perfectly-shaped white teeth. "I've been at this awhile."

"Tell me about your career," he said. "Where are you from? Where did you go to college?"

"I grew up in Steubenville, Ohio."

"Where's that?"

"On the state line between Ohio and West Virginia — it's the finger area that divides Ohio and Pennsylvania."

"That's a big industrial area, isn't it?"

"It used to be — coal and steel. Now, it's part of the rust belt."

"I bet you were popular with the guys."

"Not really. I was a cheerleader and honor student. Didn't leave much time for anything else."

Steve laughed. "None of the cheerleaders I dated were honor students."

"Ha, that was my problem. I was on a mission to change the world. Went to Youngstown State and graduated with a 4.0."

"Wow, a four-point. The only one I ever had is when I added my first two semesters together."

She giggled. "I'm positive you did better than that."

"Not much." He stared into her bright blue eyes. "Did you go to grad school?"

"Yes, Ohio State. I received a law degree there and headed for Washington."

"What's happened since you've been here?"

She finished her drink. Steve ordered another round over her mild protest.

"I had several offers, ended up taking a position in the Office of Inspector General for the Department of Education, twenty-two years ago. I was there until I moved to the Secretary's Office."

"What does the Inspector General Office do?"

"They conduct internal investigations for fraud and inappropriate actions."

"I bet you've seen it all."

"Sure have," she agreed.

Steve took a long sip then turned his attention. "Anything I should be thinking about for the Q and A session tomorrow?"

"We covered almost everything yesterday. Senator Enzi is a stickler for details. He submitted ten questions. Staff has prepared a twenty-five page response."

"Twenty-five pages?" Steve wrinkled his nose. "Too long ... I want two pages."

"We can't do that. The introduction is three pages."

"Forget about the introduction — two pages. Tell them to start with the phrase 'since we agree on 80 percent of the issues, I'll focus my comments on the other 20 percent.'"

"Steve ..."

He cut her off. "Just do it. I read that phrase time and time again in Chandler's hearings; it'll shock the hell out of him."

"Okay."

"Anything else?"

"Senator Hatch will ask several budget-related questions. It'd be a good time to mention your leadership in the financial turnaround at Mountain State and how frugal your mother was."

"My mother?"

"They like to hear about your mother — what you learned from her, the values she instilled in you. They'll eat it up."

"You sure?"

"Positive."

He took a sip of his gin. "Do you mind if I ask you a business question?"

Sherry glimpsed at her watch — 2:10. "We're on government time."

"The Secretary has asked my opinion about naming you as my Senior Advisor. Why are you interested in the position?"

Sherry tensely wet her lips.

"You don't have to respond if you don't want to."

"No, I'll tell you." She took a moment to compose herself. "I'll never lie, cover up, or tell you something just because I think it's what you want to hear. I'll do my best and tell you what I think. After that, it'll be your decision."

"I appreciate that."

"To your point." Sherry brushed her blonde-streaked hair to the side. "Whether it's me or someone else, the naming of the Senior Advisor for Educational Reform is the most important internal decision you'll make."

Steve cocked his head. "Why do you say that?"

"Two reasons." She sipped her Manhattan, warming to the subject. "Senior Advisors are part of The Secretariat."

"The Secretariat?"

"That's the Secretary's immediate staff — they have his ear twenty-four hours a day. It's composed of his Chief of Staff, the Senior Advisors and the Liaison to the White House."

"How many Senior Advisors are there?"

"Four; with the addition of educational reform, there'll be five."

"And the second reason …?"

"Senior Advisors have department-wide responsibilities. They speak on behalf of the Secretary at department meetings. The Senior Advisor will be your lead person in communicating with all forty-five hundred staffers."

"Wow, there's that many employees in the department?"

"Probably more ... that's the official count."

Steve raised his brow. "Sounds like that person would have considerable power."

"It isn't about power. Think about it as your right arm. You'll have plenty to do representing the president, attending meetings, and making speeches across the country."

"So you'd be running internal operations?"

"Not really. I'd rather say I'd be your agent."

Steve paused and stared at her. She fidgeted, not knowing what else to do or say.

"Well then," he said, "if you're going to be my Senior Advisor we better get started."

"Really?" Her face glowed. She reached across the table and touched his hand. "You're really naming me?"

"Yes." He clasped her hands. "Congratulations."

She paused then gave him a questioning look. "You knew all the time, didn't you?"

He glanced down; when he looked back up a sly smile parted his lips. "The Secretary and I talked — we agreed."

"You ratfink, I'll get even with you."

Steve finger-combed his dark hair. "Ready to order?"

"Yes, but I'm also ready to explode. You'll have to excuse me." She straightened her ruffled blouse and tugged on the back of her red and gray tweed jacket.

"Of course."

She stood and walked toward the restrooms.

Steve eyed her red high-heels then zeroed in on her tight-ass skirt. *Holy shit, I can't remember when I last saw a piece of ass like that!*

CHAPTER TWO

Steve walked into room 430 of the Dirksen Building for the second day in a row, took the same chair and opened his notes. Nervously rubbing his hands together, he noticed the unfamiliar green tablecloth, and looked down at the Navy blue carpet covering the chamber floor. *I must have been out of it yesterday.*

Glancing up, he saw a dozen photographers positioned around the base of the half-mooned dais, television cameras stationed along the back wall, behind a row of black executive leather chairs. He turned to Sherry, and whispered, "Were the reporters and cameras here yesterday?"

She smirked. "They're always here, why?"

"I don't remember them at all."

"You were focused, yesterday. Did you notice the large brass sconces around the room?"

He looked up at the light casting up from them and shook his head. "Nope."

"I'm not surprised." She fluffed her frosted hair. "You were cruising in another world. I've never seen a performance like that."

"You made it happen."

She leaned over and whispered. "Do you recall the cute dark-haired staffer with bangs who pressed her body against you?"

"Yes. That I recall."

She gave him *the look* then giggled. "At least you're alive."

The two laughed then looked up from their conspiratorial huddle as the senators filed in.

Senator Kennedy nodded to Steve and called the meeting to order.

Praising President Stetson's commitment to reforming public education, the senator pontificated about the ills of education then highlighted his long-standing pro-education voting record. Twenty minutes later, he glanced to the side. "The chair yields to the senator from Wyoming."

Senator Enzi smiled. "The two-page summary that's been shared with all answered my questions. I yield to the senator from Utah."

Taken by surprise Senator Hatch (R) stared with a blank look. "Ah ... yes." He shuffled through his papers and turned hesitantly toward Steve. "You have an outstanding record of fiscal reform and accountability. I'd like to hear more about that."

"Yes, Mr. Senator. Growing up poor in the coal fields of Kentucky, I learned early the importance of frugality from my mother. She took in laundry, sewed, did whatever it took to make ends meet. She always said, 'We're not poor we just don't have any money.'" Steve paused, letting it soak in, then went on to describe the changes he had engineered at Mountain State, using his mother's philosophy.

Senator Hatch nodded throughout Steve's comments. "Sounds like your mother taught you well. No further questions."

Surprised by the lack of questions and cross examination, Chairman Kennedy's face flushed. He paused and stammered. "Are ... are there any further questions?"

He looked at the Republican minority.

No one moved.

"Well then, the chair will entertain a committee motion to support the nomination of Steven Schilling as the next Deputy Secretary of Education."

Sherry watched as the committee followed its parliamentary procedures. And then shook her head as each of the senators cast a vote for Steve.

"Motion passes, unanimously," Senator Kennedy announced. "This hearing is adjourned."

Staff members rushed around Steve, congratulating him.

Sherry watched from the rear.

When the celebration ended, she walked up to him. "I'm buying today."

14

"Sounds good to me — 701."

Her eyes twinkled. "You got it."

***

Minutes later Sherry led the way into the restaurant and motioned to the receptionist. "A table for two where we can talk, please," she said.

Standing beside her, Steve glanced at the contemporary décor. *It's far more inviting than I recall — teal flowered fabric on the booths, matching teal armchairs and soft carpeting.*

The hostess motioned to them and Steve followed Sherry to the table then pulled out a chair for her. "How did the session go?" he asked before settling in.

"That was the shortest Q and A session I've ever seen. The minority jumped on board without asking a substantive question. Six senators who voted against the Secretary, voted for you."

"Do you think he'll have his nose out of joint?"

"You're damn right he will. He'll make fun about it but it'll gnaw at him. He has an ego that won't quit."

"Should I say something to him?"

"I wouldn't. Let it ride, act like nothing happened. If you don't, he'll get defensive as hell. And then … all hell will break loose."

Steve nodded; his eyes brighten.

The waitress appeared, and asked, "Would you like a drink?"

Without looking up, Sherry ordered their usual.

Steve stared at her. "Are you upset about something?"

She glanced at him with a disgusted look. "Yes, I'm perturbed."

"About what?"

"We prepared forty pages for Secretary Chandler's confirmation and you gave them two pages. It doesn't make sense."

"Sorry … I don't understand the issue."

"Why did you only want two pages?"

"I had a gut level feeling."

"Gut level?" She interrupted. "There had to be something more than that."

Steve grinned. "Really, it was a hunch."

Giving him a questioning eye, she squinted. "You're in a confirmation hearing and you're playing a hunch. It had to be something more than that."

"Well … maybe." He picked up his gin and tipped it to her.

She clinked his glass and took a sip.

"Here's what happened," he confessed. "After reading the Secretary's testimony, I decided to answer the questions in as few words as possible."

"Why did you to do that?"

"Senator Enzi nailed him on each of the points in the Secretary's written responses." Sherry's eyebrows knitted together. "On three different occasions the senator referenced the importance of working together on the 20 percent on which we disagree. The Secretary didn't pick up on it, so I decided to try a different approach."

"That makes sense."

"The senator is from Wyoming. He's practical and down to earth so I figured I'd be the same way."

"That's quite insightful," she said. "Want another drink?"

Steve took his first sip then looked at her empty glass. "Did you inhale yours?"

"Sorry, I was hyped up."

He signaled to the waitress. "We'll have another round."

Sherry stared, without emotion. "So what's next on your list?"

Steve shrugged. "Looks like I'll have to find a place to live."

Her eyes lit up. "I have a friend who's a real estate agent. I can have her call, if you want?"

"That'd be perfect. I don't have a clue where to start."

"I'll ask her to call you as soon as she can. Anything else?"

"Yes, as a matter of fact there is. I'd like to name an assistant, you know … someone who can help carry the ball. A doer, someone who knows the place."

Sherry shook her head.

"Is that a problem?"

"A doer … around here? You've gotta be out of your mind."

"Why's that?"

"The Secretary assigned twenty-seven individuals to serve as your staff."

"Yes, I know … which one could do the job?"

She gave him a blank stare.

"Well?"

Sherry hesitated. "The Secretary didn't do you any favors."

Steve stared, a crease lining the length of his brow. "What does that mean?"

Her face reddened. "They're a bunch of malcontents, misfits … do nothings."

"I don't understand."

"Each of them has had a problem of one sort or another. Rather than firing them over the years, they've been shuffled from one place to another to mitigate their difficult behavior."

"Ha." Steve chuckled. "And all these years I thought tenure was the worst possible employment practice." He took a long sip, reflecting on her earlier comment. Leaning back, he grabbed a thought. "With over forty-five hundred employees in the Department, there must be one strong person who can be freed up."

Sherry raised her eyebrows. "Hmm, there is one but he's not in your group — Art Wallhollister."

"Who's he?"

"An old-timer tucked away in compliance. He knows the place upside down."

"Why is he over there?"

"He's outspoken, says his piece. The higher-ups don't like that."

"Has he been off-base?"

"He's always on target."

Steve paused. "How would others react if I named him?"

"It'd raise a lot of eyebrows." She took another sip. "But I'd admit it'd make a strong, positive statement."

"How would Will react?"

"He wouldn't be happy, but … probably wouldn't say much. He knows you're wired with the president."

"Any other liabilities?"

She shook her head. "Can't think of any."

"Good. Set up an interview with Art."

***

Steve plodded wearily into the Holiday Inn adjacent to the Department of Education at half past nine. *I'm wiped out. The president's announcement of my appointment followed by the press conference, the office celebration party, and all the hoopla, was exhausting. I'm gonna grab a quick bite and hit the sack.*

Crossing through the lobby, he stopped at the entrance to the restaurant and glanced inside. A few patrons sat quietly; he caught the eye of the lone waitress.

"Is a booth okay?" she asked.

He nodded then followed her to the end booth near the rear.

"Can I bring you a drink?"

"A Tanqueray on the rocks with three olives."

The middle-aged waitress scribbled on her pad and handed him the menu.

He glanced around the tired restaurant; three ceiling lights were out, dishes were stacked on half of the tables. *Guess this place won't receive a number one rating.* Skimming down the menu, he wasn't impressed. *Looks like the standard stuff. Maybe I should order the house specialty.*

Returning with his drink, the waitress asked, "Have you decided, yet?"

"I'm not sure. Anything look good to you tonight?"

She winced, hating to answer that question. "The veal parmigiana is always good."

"That's one of my favorites," he said with relief. "I'll have that, a Caesar salad and an order of onion rings."

She gave him a pleasant smile and hurried off then returned quickly with his salad, a plate of Italian bread and several pads of butter.

The remaining restaurant patrons left.

Steve glanced at a dark-haired woman sitting at the bar — recalled Dr. Benderman's advice — "Avoid situations where your addiction can go to work, mind your p's and q's."

Steve looked away and finished his salad.

The waitress reappeared and picked up his empty bowl. "Can I get you another Tanqueray?"

He nodded. "Sure."

The over-weight server motioned to the barmaid then stepping closer whispered something in her ear.

The barmaid glanced at Steve, leaned over the bar, and said something to the busty, dark skinned woman sitting on the bar stool. The hussy smiled and returned a comment.

The bartender giggled, picked up a towel and wiped the bar.

The woman slid off the barstool and paraded to the restroom, her large cheeks rubbing together. Steve fantasied. *I haven't seen meat and potatoes like that in a long time.* He poked himself. *What's wrong with you? She's a prostitute.*

Getting back to business, he downed the veal parmigiana without looking up. Satisfied, he ordered coffee and a piece of cherry pie. He took a deep breath, relaxing for the first time all day. His eyes wandered, ending up on the dark-haired woman's ass.

Back on her barstool, she returned his look and turned to the side. His desirous eyes fixed on her tight sweater. She smiled, slid off the stool and sauntered his way.

He recalled the doctor's words — *avoid the situation.*

Flaunting her assets, she leaned over the table and presented her voluminous breasts.

His eyes zeroed in on her cleavage. *Holy shit!*

"I'm sorry to bother you, sir ... but aren't you the person who was named to that big governmental position today?"

He smiled. "Yes, Deputy Secretary of Education."

"That's what I told the barmaid. You were on the six o'clock news with the president. Mind if I join you?"

I was hoping you would. "That'd be fine," he said, trying to sound uninterested. "Want a drink?"

She nodded.

Steve motioned to the barmaid then ordered a round.

The broad gave him a sexy smile. "A big day like this ... you ought to be out celebrating at some hot spot. Why are you here?"

"We had an office party. I figured I'd had enough, so I walked back over here."

"Had enough?" She reached a hand across to his, displaying her breasts prominently on the table, and rubbed his fingers at the same time. "Is there something else you'd rather be doing?"

"Ah ... no," he stammered, his addiction shouted. *You're damn right there is. You know what I'd rather be doing. Let's go for it.* Steve ignored his inner thoughts. "It was a long day. I'm tuckered out."

He glanced at her large brown eyes. Their eyes connected.

"Are you positive?"

Steve looked around, recalling the doctor's warning. *Avoid situations ... keep focused ... don't let your addiction grab the upper hand.* "I don't ..."

A bolt of lightning flashed, followed by an instantaneous thundering crash. The lights fluttered. Rain pounded the window.

"Looks like you're in luck," she said.

He glanced away. *Shit, I've always been lucky.*

"I'll give you a special deal."

"I can't ... I've never ..."

"You've never done what you wanted to do," she interrupted.

"No, it's not that."

Her sultry eyes gave him a seductive look.

Steve swallowed hard. "I-I don't think I can ..."

"$300. I provide condoms and a sanitary wash, take credit cards, too."

He stared at her beckoning breasts.

"C'mon, I'll throw in a blow job."

Reaching across the table, she placed her hands on top of his, showing off everything but her nipples. "C'mon, whataya say?"

He hesitated, knowing he wanted her, and couldn't say no.

She cast her eyes out the window at the continuing downpour then looked his way. "Look, it's nasty outside. I'm not going anywhere. $200."

"I've never paid for it ..."

She cut him off. "Look at it this way. Being together with someone on a rainy night is better than being alone, watching TV and jacking off."

Steve knew she was right. He shifted uncomfortably, balancing his addictive thoughts with his therapist's advice.

"Look, this is the last offer. All night ... that'll beat anything you can come up with."

Steve stared, unable to form the word "No."

"Give me your room number and I'll be up ten minutes after you leave."

Unable to resist, he looked at her one more time. "632."

***

The next morning Steve rolled over and squinted at the clock radio — 10:12 — then picked up the ringing phone.

He flopped a foot on the floor and answered. "Steve Schilling."

"Dr. Schilling. This is Margo Feliciano ... Sherry's friend ... the real estate agent."

"Oh ... yes, she said you'd be calling."

"I have an apartment to show. Do you have any time this afternoon?"

"Sure, pick a time."

"How about two?"

"Great. I'll meet you in front of the hotel."

Steve took his time, enjoyed a long hot shower, shaved, dressed for lunch, and boarded the elevator.

The restaurant seemed more cheerful than the night before — his thoughts of the broad still lingered — the tables were clean and covered with white tablecloths.

He took his time enjoying a Cobb salad and downing two glasses of white wine. He paid the tab and headed for the door.

Precisely at two o'clock a new, dark blue '97 Cutlass pulled up. A woman opened the window and waved. "Dr. Schilling."

He grabbed the door handle, slid inside, and extended his hand. "Hi, I'm Steve."

"Nice to meet you, I'm Margo," she said, shaking his hand then slapping the car in gear. "Tell me about yourself," she said as she squealed out of the driveway.

Steve rambled about his career; not bragging, just telling the facts.

Speeding across town, she smiled and chattered about her many sales records.

Gazing at the historic sites, his eyes brightened as they approached a high-rise.

"Here it is," she said, pulling up in front of a tall contemporary building. "This is one of my favorite places. I live two blocks from here."

"This looks great."

"Better yet, it's in the middle of the price range Sherry gave me." Margo took off her sunglasses, revealing her hazel-green eyes. "Wait until you see the inside."

Parking in a visitor space, she jumped out and led the way inside. Steve glanced at the contemporary art sculptures and paintings then followed her past a large bubbling fountain to the elevator. The door opened and she hit twelve.

When it stopped, he followed close behind watching her small, firm ass sashay down the hallway. She opened the door to the corner apartment and motioned to him.

He took three steps inside and paused. "It's fabulous ... nothing like this in North Carolina."

"It's furnished, as is." Her cell phone rang. "Look around. I have to take this call."

Steve took his time wondering through the two-bedroom apartment, ending up gazing out the sliders in the master bedroom.

"Whataya think?" she asked from the doorway.

"I love the contemporary furniture ... the view, I'll take it."

"I knew you'd like it."

She grabbed his hand and led him to the dinette table. "Here's the contract. I've placed an "X" on the places you have to sign."

Steve sat down, glanced at the price, signed in the designated locations and wrote a check.

She pulled a bottle of Champagne from the fridge. "Want to celebrate?"

"Sure, why not?"

Seeing her start to uncork the bottle, he stood and grabbed it. "Here, let me do that."

He popped the cork, filled their glasses and handed her one.

"Here's to your new apartment," she toasted.

He clinked her glass. "And here's to you. The best real estate person I know."

She gulped it down and handed him her empty glass. "Would you refill it please?" Her flitting eyebrows said more. "There's a signing bonus today."

"Sounds good." He laughed.

She picked up the Champagne bottle. "Follow me."

Steve trailed her into the master bedroom.

"Would you close the blinds, please?"

"Sure." He took his time pulling the cord then turned — stopping cold in his tracks — he swallowed hard. He watched her kick-off her heels, slip out of her slacks, and unbutton her blouse revealing her slender body and red pushup bra.

His imagination shifted into action; his addiction shouted for more. *Go for it!*

She flipped the bedspread back and slipped under the sheet. "Care to join me?"

You bet your sweet ass I do. He hurriedly stripped to his boxers and slid in next to her.

Wasting no time, she climbed on top and kissed him wildly, her hands running over his hairy chest then heading south. Finding her target, she stroked his erection.

Steve kissed her passionately and ran his fingers through her bleached blonde hair, his urges firing on all cylinders.

The two intertwined, searching each other, alternating being on top. Taking charge, she flipped off her panties and tugged on his boxers. He slipped them off. She climbed on top, slipped on a condom, and straddling his pelvis, pushed him inside. Going to town, she pounded him relentlessly.

Steve gasped trying to regain control. He ran his hands down her sides, around the small of her back, gently pulling her tight against him. Margo's body fell into his rhythmic motion, her fingertips running lightly over his lips and across his chest.

He increased the pace. Her burning urges heated up; her pelvis slammed against him again and again. "Please Steve, I can't hold off any longer," she murmured breathlessly.

He smirked and ignoring her plea, inhaled a deep, calming breath and slowed. "I bet you can."

She shot him a look as if unable to believe his words then closed her eyes. Steve took his time, eased her off her peak and took charge of her body, moving slow and easy — her body at his command. Feeling her throb, he pressed with increasing rapidity.

She arched her back and heaved once more then shot wildly.

Laying in ecstasy, Steve held her tight. Still panting, her body went limp.

Margo caressed him for a few minutes then jumped out of bed, grabbed her clothes and headed for the bathroom. "Take a nap ... I have to run."

Unable to move, he closed his eyes and dozed off.

It was dark when Steve opened his eyes again. Gathering his senses, he slipped on his shorts, slid out of bed and splashed his face. Walking toward the kitchen, he noticed a slip of paper laying on the countertop. Picking it up, he read:

Steve,

Thanks, for the wonderful afternoon. Your copy of the contract is on the dinette table. There's a bottle of wine in the fridge. Your dinner is in the freezer. Take it out of the foil and bake it for forty minutes.

Freddie and I are having a Super Bowl Party next Sunday. Bring a six-pack and have a good time.

Give me a call for directions.

Margo

CHAPTER THREE

Walking down the third floor hallway of the Department of Education Building, Sherry paused in front of Steve's office, and then glanced at Art. He nodded. She poked her head inside the door. "Ready to meet with Art?"

Steve looked up. "Yes, come in." He pushed his executive chair back and moved quickly around his dark oak desk.

Art stepped toward him and extended his hand. "Dr. Schilling, it's a pleasure."

"A pleasure." Steve chuckled. "I haven't heard that word for a while."

"I'm not joking. It's an honor to meet someone who has really done something. You've had an impressive career."

"Well, thank you." Steve gestured toward four armchairs clustered around a small coffee table in front of a large picture window then followed behind. The two took their positions. Sherry settled in the middle chair, facing the window while the two men sat on either side of her.

Art rubbed his jaw. "I want you to know, I was serious about the compliment."

Steve tossed him a grin. "I appreciate that."

"Not many people around here have done much of anything."

Steve raised his eyebrows. "Is that why Sherry's comments about you are juxtaposed to the letters in your personnel file?"

"Guess you nailed it. Being candid has been one of my biggest problems."

"Want to talk about it?"

Art shrugged his shoulders. "I wouldn't know where to start."

"Let me help you," Steve said. "The first seven years of your record looked like a young exec on the fast track to the top. Then something happened — thirty-two years of crap."

Art hesitated. "It's hard to explain."

Steve leaned back in his chair. "I have all day."

Art looked him in the eye. "Your career started with a positive mentor, right?"

Steve gave him a questioning look. "Yeah, Bill Thornton."

"Well … I wasn't that fortunate. I had four asshole supervisors in a row." He paused, for emphasis. "It doesn't take much to set off an insecure person."

"But, you've been outspoken about a lot of people."

"Everyone around here is a career something. Career politician … career civil servant. Not much difference; one talks out of his ass, the other covers his ass."

"I like that." Steve mused. "Here's the point, Art. I'm looking for an assistant to help in the educational reform effort."

Art chuckled. "An assistant? You need an army …"

Steve interrupted. "Dealing with Congress, school officials and unions will be a bear."

"I'm not talking about that. I'm referring to making changes inside the department."

A crease wrinkled Steve's brow. "How is that a problem?"

"The assholes here have never done anything. All they can do effectively is what they've been doing. And that won't get you anywhere."

"Shit Art, we don't have a choice."

The older man gave him a questioning look. "Good luck."

"I'm serious, Art. I'm going to make it happen."

Staring at Steve, Art paused. "You really think you can pull this off, don't you?"

"You're damn right. And if you don't think so, I'll get someone else."

"It's not that … you'll need a small dedicated leadership core."

"We have twenty-seven …"

Art talked over him. "You have twenty-seven out of forty-five hundred, that's less than six-tenths of a percent. Besides, not one of them ever accomplished a thing. A bunch of shitheads if you ask me."

Steve belly laughed.

"What's so funny about that?"

"I'm sorry, Art." Steve continued to laugh. "My former wife used to call me that."

"Guess that doesn't put me in good stead."

"Not a problem." Steve pressed his lips. "How do we shape up our staff?"

"We, kemosabe? *We* haven't agreed to anything."

"Okay then." Steve paused. "Would you serve as my assistant?"

Art frowned. "What do you expect?"

"Dedication and loyalty."

"Blind loyalty?"

"Not exactly. You can speak your mind, argue, debate ... throw a tantrum. I don't care, tell me to buzz off. That's fine! But after the final decision is made, I expect total support. No undercutting, backstabbing, eye rolling — a total commitment."

"And if I can't deliver that?"

"It's back to compliance and the gray roast beef."

"Fair enough. When do I start?"

"The office next door is vacant."

"Just like that?"

"Any reason to delay?"

"No, it's that most people in government don't move that quickly."

Steve's eyes narrowed, "Well, this unit is not going be like other parts of government."

***

Steve flipped to page 510 of the proposed education reform bill. Hearing his computer chime, he glanced up — an email from the Secretary — "Hi Steve, the president wants your assessment of the proposed education bill. Twenty-five pages max, ASAP."

Shit, I hate computers. I'm just down the hall. Why can't he stop by and ask. Steve turned the page then gave the Secretary's email a second thought. *Chandler is probably still pissed about those six Republicans who voted for me. Serves him right, he's a dork anyway.* Steve turned a couple more pages. *I might as well eat a little humble pie and see if there's anything he wants me to emphasize.*

He pulled himself out of the executive chair and trudged down the corridor. Stopping at the Secretary's administrative assistant's desk, he asked, "Is he available?"

She gave him a "who cares" shrug.

Steve ignored her and stepped into the doorway. "Anything you want me to emphasize?"

Secretary Chandler glanced up then lowered his eyes. "No. Give her your candid assessment."

"Do you want me to send you an advance copy?"

"No, just copy me in on the final report," Will said, without looking up.

Steve turned and walked back to his office.

Pouring through his notes on the proposed legislation, he tried to identify two or three themes he might build upon. *Two or three themes? Hell, I can't come up with one catchy point.* He read his analysis again. *There's nothing new in this bill. It's a rehash of the past — a bunch of crap if you ask me...*

He stood and paced his office, ending up at the small corner window. His eyes wandered floor to floor at the stark steel and glass across the way and recalled his mother's favorite saying, "You can't make a silk purse out of a sow's ear."

He slammed his notes down. "It's crap ... that's the best way I can explain it."

Steve eased behind his desk and pulled out a yellow pad, and scribbled a couple of points. Ripping off the sheet, he crumpled it up then tossed his second and third starts into the wastebasket, after it. He stared at a new page, and then printed CRAP on it. He did the same on a second, third and fourth sheet — an idea flashed.

He called his administrative assistant. "Connie, would you come in here please?"

A large woman with baggy pants and top appeared. Steve ignored her casual attire, "I'd like a standard report cover page with the title — A Personal Assessment of the Proposed Educational Reform Act."

"Yes, sir."

"On the twenty five pages inside I want you to type the word CRAP in increasingly larger font until it consumes the entire last page."

"Ah … that's it?" Steve nodded. "Who should I send it to?"

"The president and participants in next Wednesday's briefing."

The administrative assistant stared. "Sir, I don't want to sound …"

Steve laughed then cut her off. "The president will understand."

The aide raised her eyebrows. "I hope so."

***

Secretary S. William "Will" Chandler walked briskly down the hallway, Sherry Holmgren close on his heels. The fiftyish, tall, gray-haired egomaniac bolted into Steve's office.

"Who in the hell do you think you are?" he shouted.

Sherry frantically closed the door behind her.

Steve placed the phone's mouthpiece on his chest and covered his lips with his index finger. "Sh … I'll be with you in a minute." He put the phone back to his ear and swiveled halfway around, facing the window.

The Secretary bristled.

Steve continued to listen, nodding several time. "Yes, thank you … I'm pleased to hear that. Yes, thank you Bradley."

Steve turned back, facing Will. "Yes, he's right here. Would you like to speak with him?" Steve grinned, shaking his head. "Fine. I'll give him your regards."

Leaning on Steve's desk, the Secretary pulled his brows together menacingly. "Who was that?"

"Chief of staff Bradley Welton."

"What'd he want?"

"He said the president read my report last night at Camp David and got a real hoot out of it. She's looking forward to hearing my presentation."

Chandler's face flushed. "Oh." He turned and marched out.

Sherry stood dumfounded watching the exchange, then closed the door and drew a chair in front of Steve's desk. "Bradley couldn't have called at a better time."

Steve burst into laughter. "He didn't call. I made it up."

Sherry's eyes opened wide. "You what?"

"It was a sham."

"You mean ..."

Steve cleared his throat. "I had my finger on the receiver OFF button all the time."

"Wait till he finds out ... he's going to be pissed."

"Who's going to say anything? Do you think he's going to ask Bradley? I don't think so."

"I can't believe it." She stood up and headed for the door then turned. "You're crazy."

"Maybe so." Steve rose, stepped into the doorway and watched her walk away.

***

Arriving early for the Wednesday meeting, Steve stepped into the Roosevelt Room, across the hall from the Oval Office, and smiled, recalling the meeting two months ago when President Stetson had introduced him as the Deputy Secretary. He gazed at the historic pictures from the era of the two Roosevelt's as if he'd never seen them before.

His eyes followed the buff walls and white trim to the curved wall at the end — two huge doors stood on each side of the fireplace. Seeing the chief of staff standing by the fireplace, he strolled his way. "How have you been Bradley?"

He glimpsed at Steve without a smile. "This better be good. She's not happy."

Out of the corner of his eye Steve glanced at Secretary Chandler standing on the other side of the fireplace, stoic, glaring at his every move. Steve nudged Bradley. "Smile you're on candid camera."

He gave Steve a partial grin. "What are you talking about?"

Steve leaned closer and whispered, "Everyone here thinks the president is in on it."

"In on it?"

"They think it was a setup so the president could get the group's attention."

Bradley glanced around at the others, his grin broadened into a smile. "Really."

Secretary Chandler smirked and looked away.

"I'll tell you more when we're alone."

"Good. I want to hear all about this."

Dressed in a sharp blue suit President Stetson appeared in the doorway. Eyes shifted toward her. Conversations ended. Everyone stood.

She took her seat at the head of the table, the chief of staff to her right.

"Please take your seats," Bradley said.

The president looked Steve in the eye. "Dr. Schilling, would you expand on your twenty-five pages of CRAP?"

Looking sternly at him, a hush fell over the room.

"Yes, as you know I'm new at this …"

She cut him off. "And I'm a country lawyer."

Unshaken, Steve sat upright. "During my confirmation hearing, I was impressed by Senator Enzi's comment about passing the 80 percent we agree upon and working on the rest."

Steve noticed Secretary Chandler's sneer across the table from him. "That started me thinking about how we might gain bipartisan support for the education reform bill."

The president raised her brow. Bradley gave him his full attention. High-ranking staffers seated around the perimeter slid to the edge of their chairs.

"I'd suggest we scrap the entire omnibus bill. It's an approach of the past … besides it's more of the same — CRAP."

A collective gasp flew across the room. Steve's colleagues looked at each other. He continued, "I recommend we replace the archaic, kitchen sink approach with a more simplified, streamlined process composed of several smaller bills."

The president cocked her head. "I'm not sure of your point. Could you explain that?"

"My pleasure," Steve said, reeking with confidence. "The first bill I'm suggesting would include the standard operating procedures, continuing authorization, definitions, etc. It's Senator Enzi's 80 percent principal with half of the rhetoric that cuts out the dated, duplicative sections. It would reduce the bill by 250 to 300 pages. It'll contain basic policies and procedures everyone agrees upon."

"Really." The president nodded.

"And it'll break the logjam. Give each side something to vote for."

"I like that," she said.

"Second, the members across the aisle have it right." Steve didn't look up at her foreboding face. "Not only is there excessive paperwork and regulation, we're paying hundreds of mid-level governmental managers to do clerk-level work."

"Madam President," Mr. Chandler interrupted.

"Quiet Will. You'll have your opportunity to respond when he's finished."

Secretary Chandler slid back in his chair.

"You may disagree," Steve took a breath then continued, "but we ought to shift all of the 'CRAP' to the states. It'll free up billions of dollars, maybe as many as a thousand positions."

"A thousand positions? That's 20 percent of the department," she announced.

"And, most important those are dollars that could be used to fund the reform effort. It's money that could be spent on kids."

"I'll have to give that some thought." She pursed her lips then glimpsed at Bradley's smiling face. "Continue, Dr. Schilling."

"My last point comes from my mentor. He always said, 'you have to deal with process before you can handle policy and procedure.' The point being, if you haven't dealt effectively with the process, whatever you're proposing will go down the tubes."

"You need to expand on that," Bradley said.

"Sure, here's a simple example. The reform package I'm working on has five major components. If you put them in one bill the entire package is doomed. The Republicans will pick it apart. They'll rally twenty no's on this issue, fifteen on that idea and before you know it, we'll down the tubes."

"Makes sense," the president said.

"That doesn't mean the ideas were bad. We simply haven't dealt with the process." Steve glanced around the table at the nodding heads. "Keeping the issues separate, in five smaller bills, would make it more difficult for the Republicans to defeat any one of them."

Bradley glanced at his watch then stood. "Madam President, we have to move on."

"Yes … Dr. Schilling, we need to talk further about your thoughts." She stood. "We're adjourned."

Secretary Chandler led the way out.

The president beckoned to Steve. "Dr. Schilling would you join me in the Oval Office?"

Looking her in the eye, he got the message; he hadn't seen that look before. *Shit, here comes the other shoe … looks like it's my time in the woodshed.* He swallowed hard and followed her across the hallway.

She closed the door, walked slowly to the front of her desk and then eased onto the edge. Leaning back, she spoke bluntly. "I was not impressed by your stunt. You embarrassed the Secretary and made a mockery of the process." Her eyes shot daggers. "Need I say more?"

Steve studied his black wing-tips then glanced up. "No."

"Good." She fluffed her short black hair. "Bradley tells me you have more to say about today. You have two minutes," she said curtly.

Steve told her about his scheme and his assumption that others around the table thought she knew all along.

She cast him a Jonas eye. "Maybe so … but never again."

She motioned Steve to the wingback chair on the left side of the fireplace then pulled a chair on the right toward him. "That aside, I like your plan to streamline the department. There are a lot of people over there doing nothing. And, if all goes well, we could use it as a model."

"Don't worry about it working," Steve said, with unwavering confidence. "It'll be a no-brainer."

"Segmenting the legislation into five smaller packages … that'll shake up a lot of people."

"It'll do more than shake them up; it'll provide an opportunity for productive change."

"Productive change." The president cocked her head to the side. "I like that phrase."

"You can have it." He snickered. "I just made it up."

She brushed her hair aside. "Let's keep the thought of delegating authority to the states between the two of us. I'll need a trade-off from the Republicans for that. "

Steve pressed his finger over his lips. "My lips are sealed."

She eyed him. "I can see now we're going to need more time together. I'll have Bradley set up monthly meetings so I can keep on top of this."

"Sounds good." Steve paused. "How should I handle that with Chandler?"

She paused, giving him an unwavering look. "I'll invite you, Will and his wife over for a private dinner."

Steve smirked.

"What's wrong with that?"

"He'll pee his pants." Steve spoke softly. "And you better order an extra dinner."

The president wrinkled her brow. "Why?"

"His wife is quite large."

"Steve, I can't believe you'd say that."

"Sorry, it's the truth."

"I'll order large portions." She giggled then stared at him for the longest moment. Turning sharply, she walked briskly around her desk and slid her hand along the inside panel.

The side door opened and her secretary poked her head inside.

"Yes, Madam President."

"When do I have to leave for the reception tonight?"

"6:10."

"An hour and a half from now. Good, Steve and I are going to chat."

"Yes madam." The secretary closed the door.

"Tanqueray and three olives as I recall."

He hesitated. "The Omni in Charlotte, two years ago ... good memory."

"How could I forget? The Webster's gave me a million dollars that night." She paused and gazed into his eyes. "I remember, too, how Lizbeth looked at you. I thought the two of you would be married by now."

"Things change."

"Maybe for the better." She stepped toward him. "Would you like to have a drink?"

Steve's eyes bugged, knowing that had to mean in the White House residence. "Yes ... of course."

She stood and headed for the door to her secretary's office. Motioning for Steve to follow, she laid a report on the secretary's desk and said with a smile, "I'm slipping out early."

Her secretary didn't say a word. She glanced up at Steve as he followed behind.

The president opened the French doors to the Rose Garden and stepped out. Walking briskly down the walkway, she turned right onto the west colonnade and led Steve inside. Within minutes the two were inside the White House elevator. Zipping to the second floor, she thanked the staff member at the door then led the way to the living room.

"Make yourself comfortable," she said. "I'll fix us drinks and open a can of mixed nuts."

"Can I help?"

"No," she said, kicking off her heels and rubbing her feet across the peach-colored area rug. "They don't let me do much around here. I'll be right back."

Steve looked around the small square room she'd converted into a compact working den. Noticing the large desk, he recalled the news story about her restoring Reagan's desk and the backs of the two chintz chairs that go with it — now with multicolored peach-tone flowers — matching the rug perfectly. Between the chairs, a dark colonial coffee table.

The chandelier above cast a warm cozy glow.

Janet walked in and placed a tray on the table — two Old Fashion glasses filled to the brim, with a small crystal bowl full of nuts next to each. "I hope this will tide you over," she said, raising her glass to clink his.

He picked up his glass. "Here's to you, Madam President."

She grinned. "You're always proper, aren't you?"

He blushed. "I try to do the right thing."

"I bet you do," she said, giving him a sly look. Taking a long sip, she collected her thoughts. "What was it like being a university president in North Carolina?"

Hitting a point dear to his heart, Steve grabbed a handful of nuts then rambled for several minutes. She listened attentively before moving to her real agenda. "Tell me about Lizbeth."

Caught off guard, Steve looked her in the eye. "What do you want to know?"

Janet didn't mince words. "At the fundraiser in Charlotte the two of you seemed to be hot and heavy. What happened?"

Conjuring up his thoughts, Steve took his time. Rubbing his jaw, he started his yarn. "I didn't think it would ever end. She was perfect … we hit it off like gangbusters and planned to be married."

"And then?"

"We worked hard, adjusted our schedules so we'd have more time together, but … for some reason she continued to be a CEO and I went on being a college president. And then, we agreed on a new resolve — 'life is too short' — we tried harder and for a while everything was golden." He sighed, looking somber.

"Why didn't you get married?"

Steve responded slowly. "We were headed that way …" He gulped and wiped his nose with a handkerchief. "Her daughter was killed in an automobile accident. She couldn't cope with that. Finally, we agreed it'd be best to go our separate ways."

"That must have been hard on you."

"I guess. All of my thoughts were with Lizbeth and the issues she was dealing with."

"That's very understanding of you, Steve."

He gave her a half smile then downed the last of his gin.

Glancing at her watch, she smiled sympathetically. "I have to dress for the reception tonight. I'll take you to the elevator and one of the Secret Service agents will show you out."

CHAPTER FOUR

Steve introduced himself to the security guard in the main lobby, watched him check off his name on the guest list then followed directions to the bank of elevators. Taking the express to the top floor, he waited outside the penthouse suite for the party-goers to disappear inside. At the double-doors he peered over those standing in front of him. People stood wall to wall.

Spotting Margo in the center of the room, he decided to catch up with her later, and headed for the bar off to the right.

A tall, skinny guy with black curly hair and dark pencil-thin mustache caught his eye and waved. "Steve, over here."

He nodded and made his way to him. "You must be Freddie," he shouted.

"Until a better opportunity comes along." He laughed, eyeing a busty blonde to his left then turning back. "Ever see a pair like that?"

Steve's eyes bugged. "Not that I recall."

Freddie leaned closer. "Ten to one they're not real."

"I'd like to find out." Steve handed him a two-bottle bag of wine. "Thanks, for the invite."

Freddie pulled a bottle of Caymus Cabernet Sauvignon part way out. "Expensive." Looking around for the broad, he shoved the bag into Steve's hand. "Tell the bartender to put these with the good stuff, I'm going hunting."

Walking toward the bar, Steve glanced at the hanging fireplace and glitzy contemporary light fixtures. He couldn't recall ever seeing such opulence in a personal home. He glimpsed over his shoulder at Freddie, hitting on the blonde, and shook his head. *How did a sleaze-*

bag like him hook up with a woman like Margo? It must have been a dark night.

Slipping in at the end of the bar, he caught the barkeep's eye then sat the bag on the countertop. "Freddie said to put these with the good stuff."

The heavy-set bartender's eyes darted at him. "Whataya have?"

"Tanqueray on the rocks, three olives."

"A man after my own heart," he said. "You been in town long?"

"A couple of months. My first time here."

He leaned over the bar. "Most of the stuff is available. Pick one and go for it."

"You positive?"

He winked. "Been working this gig for five years, had several of them come on to me."

"Thanks." Steve grabbed his glass and worked his way through the boisterous crowd. Reaching the balcony railing that wrapped around the corner of the building, he caught his breath and gazed at the skyline. *The city looks like a fairyland — lights twinkling, the street lights crisscrossing a giant grid-work — it looks quiet and peaceful.*

A four-piece combo cranked up behind him.

He glanced at the mass of humanity then shook his head. *That's the best looking group of stuff I've ever seen — there are short ones, tall and slender ones, busty ones, whatever you want.* He laughed to himself. *If they're not careful they'll gyrate right out of their tops.*

Steve turned, and leaning over the railing, spotted a black limo parked below. Sucking on an olive, he felt what seemed like a large pair of boobs pushing into his back — *they had to be at least forty-fours* — two arms draped over his shoulder.

"I'll give you a half hour to stop," he jested, then turned around.

Looking him straight in the eye, the busty woman flaunted her breasts against him just in case he hadn't noticed. "Freddie said you won."

Steve furrowed his brow. "Won?"

"They're real." Her smile grew as she took his hand and ran his fingers down her cleavage.

"No doubt." He grinned.

"Freddie's hands were all over me as he explored their authenticity. I told him I'd let you prove it."

"Thanks for the privilege."

"Anytime." She slid a business card into his pants pocket. "I'm Deb. Give me a call."

Their eyes connected.

The band started to play, striking the bouncy chords of "Hot, Hot, Hot."

"That's my cue."

She turned and hurried toward Margo in the center of the living room. Joining the human-chain of flesh, she waved to Steve. *My God, any one of them would be worth a weekend stay.*

Placing his elbows on the railing, he leaned back and watched. Margo led the parade of women snaking through the suite, singing "ole ole, ole ole," each waving a pair of silk panties over her head.

The music stopped.

Margo continued dancing, a few of her friends following behind. The train stopped in front of Steve. She pulled herself around his neck and planted a wet kiss on his lips. "Sorry, we haven't had time to talk," she whispered. "I'll make it up some afternoon."

I can hardly wait.

Sliding down off her tiptoes, she turned to the girls behind and pointed. "Here he is, Steve Schilling."

He flashed his patented mega-smile.

"I want you to meet four of my best friends," Margo said. "This is Mary Ann." The cute short blonde turned side to side showing off her full cleavage, more than he'd ever hoped for. His eyes widened; he made a mental note of her bust size.

Faye was next in line, tall and slender, sexy as hell. She slid close and placed her lips on his ear, then whispered, "Give me a call. I'll show you a good time."

"Will do." He grinned, knowing within thirty seconds he'd have a full-fledged hard-on.

Margo pushed her away. "Get it on your own time." She giggled then turned to the next one. "Here's my very best friend, Jan."

She looked up at him with soft blue eyes, looking like the girl next door. Their eyes connected. "What do you do?" he asked.

"I'm a nurse. I can take care of any problem you have."

He wanted to say, I bet you can, but thought better to play it safe. "Give me a call some time and we'll have a drink."

Looking up at him, her eyelids fluttered. "I'd like that."

Margo stepped between the two. "I want you to meet, Deb."

"Yes, we've already meet. I won a bet." Steve paused, realizing he shouldn't say any more.

Margo frowned, with a questioning look.

Steve laughed. "It's a long story. I tell you some other time."

Deb winked. "Don't forget to call me."

His mind whirled, with hope and excitement. Margo raised her eyebrow, and her entourage turned to join the party.

Leaning on the railing, Steve gazed into the night, his mind drifting — it was always the same — thoughts about his mother, his dad had never given her a thing; a vision of his sister standing in her Sunday dress after being raped by their father. Perspiration ran down his sides. He wiped his brow.

"Want to dance?" a sexy voice whispered in his ear.

He turned, coming face to face with Faye. "Ah." He felt an urge. "How about we do the slow one later."

"Got it." She gave him a sexy smile and walked away.

"You need break," he heard in broken-English.

Steve turned and stared at the most striking woman he'd ever seen — sparkling brown eyes, shining long black hair with perfectly cut bangs, a glowing light-tan round face.

"You need break," she repeated.

Steve grinned. "I certainly do."

She pointed to the small table in the corner. "I have Tanqueray with three olives for you."

He paused wondering how she knew that then followed her, not sure how to react. "How did you know about the Tanqueray?"

She smiled, showing off her pearly white teeth. "I watch you and the beautiful women ... how you say, 'hitting on you.' I thought you'd like to relax."

"You're right about that." He took a sip. "What is your name?"

"Kim."

"Where are you from?"

"The Philippines. I'm the Administrative Liaison for the Ambassador at the embassy."

"Sounds impressive. Do you plan activities?"

"I coordinate his activities, arrange schedules, plan meetings ... do whatever is needed."

"It sounds like you are very busy."

"Yes, there not much time for anything else."

"Do you travel much?"

"No, most our activities ... in city."

"Do you go home often?"

"Once or twice a year. My father banker in Quezon City. He was very successful until the Kuratong Baleleng robbed his bank."

"Kuratong Baleleng?"

She hesitated. "It like your mafia. No want to talk about it." She smoothed her hair to one side, and changed the subject. "Are you big football fan?"

"Today I am. The Green Bay Packers are my favorite team."

"They ahead of Patriots thirteen points at halftime. Brett Favre make three touchdowns."

Steve grinned to himself. "Do you watch much football?"

"No. Freddie explained it when I came in. He big New England fan."

Margo leaned over Steve's shoulder, pressing her modest breasts into his back. "Could I borrow him for minute?" she asked her. "I have a friend who'd like to meet him."

"No problem." Kim's silky smooth face saddened.

Tugging on his arm, Margo pulled Steve up.

"We'll talk later," he said over his shoulder.

Kim smiled politely; her eyes twinkled.

God, she's hot!

Margo nodded toward the bar. "I'd like for you to meet Charisse. She's standing over there."

"The short blonde?"

Margo assured him. "You got it."

His heart rate rocketed. "God, she's something else."

"She asked to meet you."

"Sounds good to me."

Margo introduced the two. Their eyes connected automatically. "Do you come here often?" he asked.

"Occasionally, most when they have Sunday parties. That's my day off."

"What kind of work do you do?"

She paused. "I'm a housewife, raising two girls."

A line crossed Steve's forehead. "Did I miss something?"

She seemed uncomfortable, complex. "It's a long story."

"I'd like to hear it."

"Really?" She gazed up into his soft brown eyes; he recognized more than general interest. "Maybe you will. I have to leave now." Charisse turned and headed for the door.

"I'd like that," he called, loud enough for half of the room to hear.

The bartender gave him a thumbs-up.

Steve lingered, hoping she'd turn around, then walked toward the balcony and stared at Kim's empty chair. "Damn, zero for two. How could I let her get away?"

***

Steve sat in the Department of Education cafeteria at a round table the following Monday, kibitzing with four staffers about the game. Knowing he was the only Packer fan, he listened to the easterners pontificate.

"I don't understand what happened in the second quarter. The Packers scored seventeen."

"Hey, they came back and cut it to 27-21 in the third period."

"That ninety-nine yard run by Desmond Howard broke our back."

"At least they made it to the finals. The Ravens didn't do anything."

Steve felt a tap on the shoulder and looked up.

"Do you have time to talk?"

"Sherry, of course. Want a cup of coffee here or in my office?"

"It's not too busy here." She pointed. "Let's move to that table by the windows."

"Perfect. I'll grab a sweet roll. Do you want anything?"

"No thanks, I'm on yogurt all week."

Steve returned a few minutes later, unloaded his tray and plopped down across from her. "What's on your mind?"

"It's spinning like crazy." She took a sip. "You created quite a stir last week. How'd you even come up with the idea of cutting a thousand positions?"

"I've been checking around the department and listening to conversations, just like I was when you came in."

She looked at him in a doubtful manner. "You made it up, didn't you?"

"It was a little more scientific than that."

"You'll have to convince me of that."

"Whenever I walk past here I see the same people, sometimes they're in here for an hour, maybe two. Others have told me most of the people don't work hard."

"That's heavy. And now the president believes we can make a 20 percent cut."

"It's more than that. I made cuts like that at two universities. In each case, we cut nearly 25 percent of the employees and nothing happened."

"I don't understand. How could nothing happen?"

"There were the usual hassles. The newspaper editor wrote a column questioning how we were going to survive with such a loss of institutional knowledge. All of that was hogwash, sour grapes by those who didn't want to see any change."

"And that's it?"

"A few people fussed around. Next thing I heard was objections from the unions. The head guy came in and pounded the table, and said, 'Everyone is working too hard.' I scowled, said, 'I don't understand. Employees are expected to work hard during an eight-hour shift. How can they work too hard?' He looked at me, and said, 'you don't get it.' 'No,' I said to him, '*You* don't get it.'"

"How did it all work out?"

"A few months later it was business as usual. Cuts of 20 percent can be made in any bureaucratic structure."

"And just how do you propose to do it here?"

He flashed his trademark mega-smile. "I'm glad you asked."

Blood drained from her face. "Me?" She looked to be in shock.

"You're the Senior Advisor. You told me you have access to the entire department. It's your baby — work with the staff, develop a process, establish criteria, set up a timeline, and make it happen."

"You expect me to do that?"

"It'll be easier than you think. Listen to the people; you'll be surprised. They'll tell you the ways to cut the fat."

"Just like that?"

Her look gave him pause. "Put a team together and lay out a three year plan. Before you know it ideas will be flowing."

Sherry flopped back against her chair with her mouth open.

"Want another cup of coffee?" he jested.

She rubbed her jaw, trying to regain her composure. "Anything else you want today?"

He thought about ripping off her blouse. "Yes, as a matter of fact there is."

Her face flushed, waiting for the next assignment.

He laughed. "Relax. Are you going to Margo's first of the month party Saturday night?"

"How can I be thinking about a party? I have to cut a thousand positions."

"Well, are you going?"

"I hadn't planned on it. The place will be packed."

"I went to her Super Bowl party ... heard her Saturday night parties were even better."

Sherry spoke hesitantly, "Margo is a good friend and ... fun to chat with over lunch, but her parties are over the top."

"Over the top? How so?"

"People are fooling around on the sofa, looking to get laid. Margo has a key available for the guest bedroom in case someone can't wait."

"That sounds strange. Whataya think about her husband?"

"Freddie? He's a wacko, thinks he's God's gift to women."

"Did he ever hit on you?"

"Hit on me?" She contorted her face. "Whenever Margo looks away he has his hands all over me. No thanks, I'll pass."

CHAPTER FIVE

Steve stared at the two Secret Service agents admiring the paintings on each side of the White House elevator. *I know they're watching me. I bet they have eyes in the back of their heads.* He glimpsed at the walls. *They must have hidden cameras somewhere, probably mirrors too.*

"Ready to go?" the staff member on the elevator asked.

"Yes," Steve said, smiling at Will and Charlene Chandler as they strolled down the hallway. *That black dress may make her look smaller but that won't help us on the elevator.* Sliding inside, Steve held his breath hoping the overload buzzer didn't go off. And when the door opened for the second floor, he sighed to himself and started breathing again.

Standing in front of them, President Stetson gave Mrs. Chandler a welcoming smile. "My that's a lovely dress you're wearing tonight," she said.

Steve smiled politely, knowing Janet's real thoughts.

"I'm so pleased you could join us for dinner," she continued.

"It's our pleasure, Madam President," Will said.

"It's Janet, tonight." She led the way down Center Hall of the White House then turned to Charlene. "Have you been in the residence before?"

"No, I'm so excited," she said. "I understand you've personally directed much of the redecorating."

"Yes. I really enjoyed working with the designers. It's my one chance to create," Janet said, walking briskly. "Wait until you see the dining room." The president led the way through the West Sitting Hall then turned right. "Here we are. Don't you love the chandelier?"

"It's beautiful."

"It's part of the original décor Mrs. Kennedy installed in 1961. She acquired the Sheraton pedestal table and shield-back side chairs we'll be using tonight, too."

"Will ran his hand over the back of the chair. "They're in mint condition."

"Each presidential family since the Sixties has made changes in the wall coverings, paint colors and drapery but the room still has the influence of Mrs. Kennedy." Janet pointed to the chairs. "Steve, you can sit on that side closest to Will. That'll make it easier for Charlene and me to chat."

The four took their seats and wine was served.

Janet responded with delight as the guests took turns asking questions about the room. After a second bottle of wine, she paused. "Steve, would you share the key points of the reform plan with Will?

"Yes, of course."

The president looked at Charlene. "Would you be interested in a brief history of this room?"

"Oh, yes." Charlene bubbled. "That would be wonderful."

Janet obligated, relating her historical script while dinner was served — veal chops, twice-baked potatoes, asparagus, and a sliced tomatoes and onion salad.

After listening to Steve for most of the evening, Will folded his napkin. "Those were the best veal chops I've ever had."

"I wish I could take the credit but we have a wonderful chef. Would anyone like coffee?" She glanced around the table, as the hands popped up. "Make it four."

The waiter standing in the corner snapped to attention, making available cream and sugar, and filling their cups.

The president straightened, clearly in charge, and spoke firmly, "I'd like to summarize the points we've discussed tonight."

Steve leaned back.

Will's shoulders tightened against his chair.

"Making the types of changes Steve has described will require the highest level of professionalism. We have to come off as a seamless leadership team. Does everyone understand?"

She paused, extracting a nod from each of the men. "Good. The division of responsibility will be as follows: Will, you'll do what you do best — head up the congressional thrust. Your leadership in ushering the legislation through Congress will be critically important. Steve will develop the reform proposals, and the two of us will meet monthly to fine-tune the initiatives. When the time comes, I will lead our national campaign effort. Are there any questions?"

The president looked Will in the eye.

He nodded, not conveying his sense of disappointment.

"Good."

Subtly, she motioned to the waiter. "Let's hear the options for dessert."

***

With dark circles hanging under his puffy eyes, Steve filled his coffee mug and sauntered toward the conference table.

Art waited with a steaming mug. "Looks like you're enjoying the city life," he jested.

Steve mumbled, "The weekend was over the top."

Art didn't respond.

"I have a couple more ideas for the staff development plan we discussed last week."

"Perfect." Art gave him a partial grin. "I plan to work up a draft this week."

"I like the team building concepts you've talked about. In addition, I'd like to see more emphasis on activities that create ownership. Our team has never been a part of anything. We need for them to buy-in so they feel a part of the overall reform effort."

"Makes sense," Art said. "There are some games we can purchase that will involve them. I can think of two in particular that push participants to be open and make suggestions ..."

"Right on." Steve talked over him. "We need to find ways for them to provide input, make suggestions. And for us to accept their advice."

"Agreed." Art glanced at his watch. "It's quarter after ten. Wasn't Sherry supposed to be here at ten?"

Unaffected, Steve stood and refilled his mug. "I'll give her five minutes before I call her office."

Art gazed out the window. "Looks like another beautiful spring day."

Sherry rushed in, almost spilling coffee from the mug in her hand. "Sorry, the Secretary was bending my ear."

"About last Friday?" Steve asked.

"Of course."

"Let's hear about it," Steve said.

Sherry plopped down and took a long sip. "When I came in this morning the light on my phone was blinking. Listening to the tone of his message, I could tell he was pissed."

"What'd you do?" Art asked.

"I filled my cup with strong coffee and hustled down to his office. When I knocked on the door, he shouted for me to come in. Pacing like a cat on a hot tin roof, he was red-faced and chugging like a locomotive. For the first half hour I sat in front of his desk and listened — half of the things he said didn't make sense. Between fuckin' bastard, SOB, bitch, and a few other choice words, I figured out you were the root of his ire," she said to Steve.

"And then," Steve said, waiting with bated breath.

"Once in a while he'd say something like 'I can't believe the bitch would do something like that to me,' and then he unloaded on you again."

"Did he say anything coherent?" Steve asked.

"It all ran together — undercutting SOB, backstabbing bastard — it must have gone on for an hour. I thought he was going to have a heart attack. Finally he plopped down in his swivel-rocker, huffing and puffing, and looked at me. 'Why did she make me look like a fool? Why is she going to meet with him every month?' Before I could respond he went off again."

"And then?" Art asked.

"Finally he realized the type of behavior he was exhibiting. He stopped, walked sharply to the door and thanked me for listening. Before I had taken two steps down the hallway, I heard a loud crash. He either kicked or threw something."

"I can't believe he was that upset." Steve hesitated. "I'll have to find a way to make amends. We can't afford for him to be grousing. Any suggestions?"

Sherry shrugged, clueless.

"I'm the most experienced one for dealing with circumstances like this," Art chimed in. "My wife always says the best way to deal with uncomfortable situations is to confront them head on. Tell him that after reflecting you could see how he might have jumped to the wrong conclusion. Assure him that wasn't your intent ... something like ... I'm sure you didn't take it this way but in case you did, I want you to know that I had no intent of embarrassing you. I was simply following the president's directions."

Steve raised his eyebrows. "Whataya think Sherry?"

"I like it."

***

Steve smelled coffee then heard the sizzle of bacon frying. He slipped on his robe, tiptoed into the kitchen and grabbed Charisse. Spinning her around, he lifted her onto the countertop, angled her head to give his lips full access and planted a wet kiss on her.

"Steve." She shoved her hand against his chest. "Let me down before I burn the bacon."

Steve eased her down. "Want a Bloody Mary?"

"Yes." She giggled. "Make it extra hot like you."

Steve raised his eyebrows, "Coming right up."

He fixed their drinks and put them on the placemats. Sitting down in the small kitchen booth, he watched Charisse buzz around the kitchen like the queen in a swarm of bees. She placed two plates of scrambled eggs, hash browns and bacon on the table and then landed across from him.

Raising her glass, she toasted him. "Here's to the most exciting person I know."

Steve clinked her glass, not knowing how to react.

"I don't understand you; I just want to make you happy."

Steve's eyes bugged. "Now?"

"No, not now, silly. I'm happy being with you ... just looking at you makes me happy."

Their conversation bounced from one light topic to another. Steve fixed a second round of drinks. "Did you do anything special last night?" she asked.

"I went to Margo and Freddie's party."

She perked up. "I've gone to a couple of their Super Bowl parties. I've heard they're a blast."

"A blast? More like Saturday night fever — bodies gyrating, people making out — it was closer to an orgy."

"Poor baby. You had to rough it."

"I had a couple of drinks and sat in the corner."

"You must have had more than two Tanqueray's." Steve cocked his head questioning. "You were out cold when I arrived this morning."

"Now that you mention it I don't remember coming home. I need to make up for that." He jumped up, pulled her out of the booth and hoisted her on his shoulder — her arms and legs flaying.

"Steve, let me down."

Carrying her into the bedroom, he ignored her milk-toast plea, kicked closed the door and lowered her onto the bed. "You were saying?"

"You need to make up for this morning," she purred.

He nibbled on her earlobe and felt her body shiver with excitement. "Just how might I do that?"

She pulled him to her; her mouth found his. "You can start with my feet you're good at that."

***

Later that morning Steve rolled over and snuggled closer to Charisse. "You awake?"

"Daydreaming I guess," she said, turning toward him.

He kissed her lightly on the forehead and the tip of her turned-up nose, then ran his fingers around her face, mouth and left ear. "What are you thinking about?"

She gave him a questioning look. "Hmm, nothing, why?"

"I was wondering how you felt about me?"

She pulled her head back. "Whataya mean?"

"Right now, lying here beside me, how do you feel?"

She sent a smile his way. "I feel warm, like you're here for me." She wet her lips. "I can't remember the last time I felt this way."

Steve studied her lips as she continued.

"After sex I usually feel like I've gone through an ordeal."

"An ordeal? Even with your husband?"

"More so with him. I know he loves me. He's kind and gentle, a great father too; but, he doesn't make me feel attractive or desired. He uses my body for his pleasure, never has a thought about arousing me or nurturing our relationship."

"Give me an example of how he isn't nurturing your relationship."

"One? I could count a hundred. The worst is his lack of interest. After sex he rolls over and goes to sleep. I'm left hanging, looking at the ceiling, feeling empty. It's totally opposite than how I feel now."

"You give me a special feeling too," he said, circling his fingertips around her face. "Would you like to talk more about your feelings?"

"Hmm, I don't know … it's kind of scary … maybe another time."

"Whenever Charisse, you know I'll always be here for you."

"You're such a sweetie."

He snuggled closer. "How sweet?"

She pushed him away. "Take a shower. I'm fixing lunch."

Charisse jumped out of bed, slipped on a robe and headed for the kitchen. Steve slid out of bed and moseyed toward the shower.

It wasn't long before he was standing beside her in his bare feet wearing blue shorts and a white polo shirt. "What's for lunch?"

"Your favorite, BLTs and German potato salad."

"Sounds great. I'll put some pickles and olives in a bowl." He opened two Diet Cokes and poured part of each into glasses filled with ice.

Charisse placed the sandwiches on the table. "*Bon appetit.*"

He filled his plate and devoured half a sandwich before looking up.

She picked at hers.

Steve glanced up. "You okay?"

She laid her fork down and folded her napkin. "When you're finished, I want to talk."

"Talk about what?"

"Sex."

Steve fumbled his glass almost spilling his Coke. "Sorry."

She giggled. "I didn't mean to excite you."

"You startled me. I didn't expect you to say that."

"My life is all messed up."

"Whose isn't?"

"No, I'm serious."

Steve eased back, and gave her his full attention.

She stared at the tabletop then looked up. "This is not easy."

"Take your time."

"I have a compulsive behavioral disorder."

His brow wrinkled in concentration. "You mean ..."

She cut him off. "I'm a sex addict."

Steve's eyes widened in disbelief.

She took a deep breath. "I started masturbating when I was nine. As a teenager I used sex as a feel-good fix. In college I got an incredible boost from the men I slept with. Turning them on became a real ego-booster. I thrived on it ... that is ... until the high wore off, and then I felt ashamed."

"Ashamed?"

"It's a cultural thing. Women are supposed to be pure and nurturing. Males get laid, no one cares — they're praised for their sexual prowess. If a woman does half as much, she's labeled as being promiscuous, a whore or nympho."

"I never thought of it that way."

"Before I was out of college, I thought about sex all the time ... with my professor, the pizza guy, my best friend's boyfriend ..." She sighed heavily. "It wasn't long before planning, fantasizing and anticipating were more important than the act itself. I could moisten my panties without touching myself. My life was out of control."

"Wow, so where to now?"

"I finally found a therapist who I have confidence in, and am making progress."

"Finally?"

"It's like everything else — therapists are products of our male-oriented culture. It took a long time for me to find one who understood how I felt as a woman." She wiped a tear from her cheek. "I don't know. I'm going to take a shower."

Steve stared as she picked up her plate and set it in the sink on the way to the bedroom.

God, I can't believe the things she's gone through. I thought I had it bad. She's had a mountain twice as high to climb. I have to find a way to help her.

***

Studying Charisse's every move that afternoon, Steve leaned back in the booth. His mind reeled. She flitted from the fridge, stirred a pot on the stove then poured homemade batter into a baking tin. Dressed in red short-shorts, a red bandana in her hair and cutoff blouse tied at her mid-drift, she looked more like a hot teenager than the mother of two.

"Are you ever going to stop?" he asked.

She zipped past him without a glance. "I'm making brownies and a tuna casserole so you'll have something for the week. And then I'm starting dinner."

"Do you think you could take a break? I could cut the cheese and put some crackers on a plate. We could talk over a glass of wine."

Ignoring his comment, Charisse paused. "I was being a little compulsive, wasn't I?"

He chuckled. "I thought you were going to set a world's record for the fastest ever brownie prepping."

"It's part of my nature. I'm a compulsive shopper, a workaholic. If there was a casino nearby I'd be at the slots all day."

"How do you deal with all of this?"

She seemed uncomfortable and he wondered why. "Not very well. I'm up and down. Most of the time in I'm the dumps. My self-confidence and self-esteem are shot. I only hope it doesn't spill over to my kids."

"Come join me so we can talk. Red or white wine?"

"Red, it'll go with the steaks tonight."

Steve placed a plate of cheese and crackers on the table and opened a bottle of zinfandel.

She eased into the stylish booth, across from him. Flushed from the kitchen heat, her lovely face seemed even lovelier. "What are we talking about?"

He rubbed his five o'clock shadow. "It's time for a reality check."

"Reality." She laughed. "I don't have a clue about that."

"Who does?" He paused. "There's something I want to say."

Her body seemed to tense as if she thought he might probe further into her vulnerability.

"It's not about you," he reassured her. "It's about me and my problem."

She stared into his eyes.

"I'm a sex addict too."

"No." She shook her head. "You're not just saying that to make me feel better, are you?"

"No, I'm not. I've been one all of my life. I've hurt a lot of people and I don't want to hurt you."

"Steve, I ... "

He pressed his finger over her lips. "Let me finish."

She downed her wine. "Could I have another glass?"

"Of course." He filled it extra full then told her about his many affairs, his efforts to improve, his failures, and the ways he'd tried to cover up his philandering. I can't help it."

"Sounds like we're a couple of misfits," she said. The relief in her voice was evident.

"Do you have an idea about what we can do?"

"Ah ... commiserate together."

"How about we work on our problems together?"

She bit her lip. "Hmm, I don't know. I'll have to talk to my therapist."

***

Charisse left early that night.

Steve had a steak alone. He thought about the suggestion of the two of them working on their common problems. *Maybe that's not such a good idea. Maybe one of them would want to break it off.* "Ha," he laughed aloud. *Two sex addicts breaking it off — I don't think so.*

He put his dirty plate in the dishwasher and sauntered to his desk. *This is heavy. I have to talk to Charlie like we did when I was in North Carolina. He was a wonderful confidant — he always came up with solutions. I wonder if he would come up for a visit.*

He picked up the phone and called.

"McBride's," Charlie barked.

"Charlie, its Steve. You okay?"

"Been fighting off a cold for the last two weeks. How have you been?"

"I'm fine. The pieces are starting to come together."

"Good for you. I knew you'd shape things up."

"I remember Ellen talking about seeing the cherry trees. They'll be in full blossom between April 11th and 15th. How about you guys coming up? You could do the city and we could talk."

"I'd like that. I'll check our calendar and get back to you."

"Great." Putting the receiver down, he noticed the blinking light, knew he had several phone calls to return. He flicked through each call, jotting down the name and phone number, then started down the list.

Mary Ann was the first of five. "It's so good to hear your voice," he said. "This is Steve Schilling. I'm sorry it took so long to get back to you."

"Not a problem. I know how busy you are."

"I've been thinking about you," he fibbed. "Could we get together next week?"

"Wednesday would be good."

"Perfect."

He jotted her address in his pocket calendar then dialed the next woman on his list.

CHAPTER SIX

Steve stood on the balcony, sipping a gin, and watching the sun ease over the horizon. He thought about the number of times Ellen had talked about seeing the cherry trees in blossom. *Wait till she hears about the tickets I have for the Cherry Blossom Parade this Saturday. It'll be a dream come true for her.*

He downed his drink and walked inside just in time to hear the buzz of the building's intercom system. Pushing the button, he asked, "Charlie, is that you?"

"Yes."

"I'll be right down."

Stepping out of the elevator, he rushed toward Charlie, gave him a bear-hug then turned to Ellen and kissed her on the cheek. "It's been four months. How have you been?"

"We've been well," Charlie said. "Want to take our suitcases up now?"

"Let's do a load now. We can bring up the rest after we come back from dinner."

"Sounds like a plan," Charlie said, wiping the moisture from his bald head.

"Should I wear something special for dinner?" Ellen asked, as you might expect. Always prim and proper, at sixty-six, every strand of her silvery hair was in place and her outfits revealed the latest styles.

"No, it's a local restaurant down the street. Thai ... sorry Charlie, I know how much Ellen loves it."

"They'll have something else on the menu," Charlie responded.

"Come on up," Steve said, and then threw a hanging bag over his shoulder. Charlie pulled a suitcase from the trunk. Ellen grabbed an armful of smaller bags and followed the men inside.

"How many weeks are you staying?" Steve jested.

Charlie laughed. "I thought it was three days, before Ellen packed."

The three squeezed onto the elevator and chatted as they zipped to the twelfth floor.

Stepping inside his apartment, Ellen paused and looked around. "This is a wonderful place!"

"I like the contemporary motif," Charlie agreed.

"Thanks. You can put your bags in the guest bedroom. It's the last door on the left," Steve said, pointing down the hallway. "I'll fix some hors d'oeuvres."

"I can hardly wait to hear the latest," Ellen said over her shoulder, already halfway down the hall.

"You got it."

Steve placed a large platter of appetizers on the coffee table in front of the sofa then filled three glasses with merlot. Pulling a chair in front of the TV, he kicked off his shoes and grabbed a cracker.

Charlie and Ellen joined him on the sofa. Charlie eyed the blue cheese.

"Here's to the best of friends." Steve raised his glass in the air toward them.

"I'll drink to that," Charlie said. Ellen raised her glass with a smile.

The old friends took turns talking their way through the munchies. Being the politico-type of the group, Ellen asked about recent interviews by the talking-heads she'd seen on the Sunday morning shows. "Tell me about Madeleine Albright ... William Cohen. Have you met Janet Reno?"

Steve responded half-heartedly. Charlie squeezed in a few comments about the campus. Ellen made several positive comments about the president then shifted her thoughts. "Do you enjoy working for Secretary Chandler?"

"He's okay," Steve said.

"That doesn't sound like a ringing endorsement."

"I don't work with him much. The president has separated our primary duties. I meet more often with her than I do with him."

"How do you feel about that?"

"She's terrific, has given me plenty of latitude. She understands how to make things happen."

Ellen wrinkled her nose. "I don't trust Secretary Chandler."

Steve gave her a troubled look. "Why do you say that?"

"It's not so much his words. He's always politically correct. It's the way he talks down to people, his condescending look. You should keep an eye on him."

"Good advice." Steve finished off his wine. "Ready for dinner, Ellen?"

"I couldn't eat another bite," Charlie said.

"Speak for yourself, Charles. I'm having pad thai." She picked up a load of dirty dishes and headed for the kitchen. Charlie and Steve cleaned up the rest.

They took the elevator down and stepped outside. A soft spring breeze ruffled Ellen's hair. "I can smell the fragrance of the cherry blossoms."

"You've been smelling them since we left North Carolina."

"The restaurant is just two blocks away," Steve said, heading down the street. "Oh, I forgot to tell you, I have tickets for the parade on Saturday."

"You do?" Ellen sounded surprised. "That's wonderful."

"There'll be lavish floats, giant helium balloons and marching bands from all over the country."

"Sounds spectacular. Do we have to leave early?" Charlie asked.

"Nah, it starts at ten. We can take the Metro to Federal Triangle. From there, it's only a short hop, skip and jump." Steve paused and pointed. "Here we are."

He opened the door to the Thai restaurant. A large bronze Buddha greeted them solemnly.

Charlie looked at his bald head and large protruding stomach. "That's my kind of guy." He laughed.

"Charles!" Ellen said in a harsh whisper. She shook her head then followed Steve to a booth dimly lit by the hanging, shaded oriental lights.

The three sat down. "I can hardly wait," she said, spreading open the menu.

Each one had a small bowl of noodle soup. Ellen and Steve opted for the pad thai. Charlie ordered a burger. "I want to hear all about your confirmation hearings," Ellen said while they waited for their dinners.

"Ellen, you read about it in the paper and twice online," Charlie said, a little out of sorts.

"I know, but I want to know the behind the scenes stuff. Tell me about Ted Kennedy. How did you get the Republicans to vote for you? I want to hear it all."

Steve talked his way through dinner, highlighting the hearings. Charlie didn't say a word.

It was after ten when the three walked back into Steve's apartment. Ellen glanced at her watch. "Oh my gosh, I can't believe it's so late. I'm hitting the hay."

"Want a nightcap, Charlie?"

"Sure, a glass of port will be fine."

He filled a glass for Charlie and poured himself an amaretto on the rocks then kicked off his shoes and leaned back in the comfy recliner.

Charlie was ready with his list of questions. "On the phone you said you wanted to talk. How are things going in your personal life?"

Steve shrugged and took a long sip.

"C'mon, I didn't drive all this way to smell the cherry blossoms."

Steve gave Charlie a half-hearted smile. "It's a long story."

"It can't be that long, you've only been here four months."

"Well ..." Steve sighed. "Things are all messed up ... it's like being in a candy shop. The women around here won't stop. They're calling me all the time."

Charlie sat his glass down. "Okay, let's hear the facts. How many women have you slept with since you arrived?"

Steve counted on his fingers. "Eight."

Charlie took a deep breath. "And how many have you slept with more than once?"

"Seven," he said, without hesitation.

"How many are you sleeping with on a regular basis?"

"Regular? You mean on a certain day?"

"Forget it," Charlie said, then tried another attack. "Steve, you can't go on this way."

"I know. I'm at my wits end."

"Wits end ... that's bullshit! You can start by keeping your goddamn zipper up. Stop calling them back. You're going to screw yourself to death."

Steve laughed. "Seems like you've said that to me once or twice."

"Once or twice ... a hundred times. I have to sleep on this."

***

Sunday morning Charlie had an early coffee then poked his head back in their bathroom. "Are you dressed, dear?"

Ellen turned away from the mirror. "I'm finishing my hair."

"Come out here we have to talk."

"I'll be out in a few more minutes."

"You'll have to finish later. We have to talk, right now."

She peeked out the door. "Why? Is something wrong?"

"Come out and take a chair." He pointed to the small stuffed chair in the corner. "This is going to take a while."

Ellen stepped out of the bathroom, tied her robe and eased onto the chair. "What is it, dear?"

Charlie sat on the bedside across from her. "There's a blonde out there ... thirtyish, maybe five foot three. She's cute as hell with a pixie haircut and short bangs."

"Who is she?"

"Charisse. A friend of Steve's. He didn't tell me her last name, but she's the wife of a Baptist minister."

Ellen scowled. "The wife of a minister? What is she doing here?"

Charlie raised his eyebrows and shrugged. "She arrives around six o'clock every Sunday morning and stays until nine or ten at night, according to Steve."

"What does she do?"

Charlie raised his hand. "Wait, let me finish. Apparently, she dislikes the church."

"Can I ask something, now?" Ellen asked, impatiently.

He pressed his lips in disgust. "Okay, go ahead."

"What does she do?

"Everything."

"Does that mean ...?"

Charlie nodded his head. "Plus, she cooks, bakes pies and cookies, and prepares meals. And that's only half of it." Ellen's eyes opened wide. "When I was making the coffee this morning she came out of his bedroom in her nighty."

"Where was Steve?"

"In the shower." Charlie swallowed. "We chatted briefly. She filled two mugs and went back into his bedroom."

"And then?"

"A little later Steve came out and gave me the full scoop."

"The full scoop?"

"He screwed her earlier this morning. She gave him a blowjob while he was drinking his coffee."

"I can't believe that." She giggled. "I hope he didn't spill his coffee on it."

"Ellen, it's true. She screws him twice, sometimes three times every Sunday, and she fits in a blowjob when he's least expecting it."

A wrinkle appeared on Ellen's forehead. "He has to be putting you on."

"No, he isn't. The two of them were joking about doing it while I was on my second mug of coffee."

Ellen's jaw dropped. "How do I react to her when I go out there?"

"Treat her like a member of the family. She seems quite personable and has a dry sense of humor. You'll like her."

"Charlie, you need to talk to Steve about this."

"I know. From some of his other comments, I think he's worse than before."

"How so?"

"In addition to Charisse he's doing six or seven others! I don't know how he keeps track of them."

"Does he still treat them all the same?"

Charlie nodded. "He's just like always, fired up about making them happy — exceeding their expectations — turning them on, watching them squirm, and then doing it again, making them have a second or even third orgasm."

"He must be a miracle man."

"Apparently ... the women think so too."

Her eyes brightened. "Maybe you should take a lesson."

"Thanks a lot."

"Just joking." She laughed. "Really, you need to talk with him."

"I will. Tonight."

"Breakfast is served," Steve called.

***

It was almost ten o'clock that night when Charisse grabbed her oversized purse and said her goodbyes. At the door Steve gave her a man-sized hug and unloaded a wet kiss.

"Goodbye, everyone," she called.

"So long," Charlie and Ellen chimed in.

Steve returned to the living room. "So whataya think about her?"

Not knowing how to react, Ellen waffled. "She's ... very personable. How long have you known her?"

"Six weeks. I told Charlie all about her."

"Yes. It wore me out just listening."

"I like her," Charlie said. "She's a doer, seems to enjoy everything."

"I'm going to bed." Ellen stood and winked at Charlie.

"Sleep tight," Steve said.

Charlie leaned back on the sofa. "How about a nightcap?"

"Brandy on ice or a glass of port?"

"Brandy, will be fine."

"Sounds good." Steve filled two Old Fashion glasses to the brim. "Whataya think about Charisse?"

"I think you're fuckin' nuts."

Steve laughed. "You've told me that before."

"How did you meet her?"

"She's the friend of a friend."

"Let me get this straight." Charlie took a sip. "You're screwing Charisse on Sundays and sleeping with the others during the week. I suppose you have them on a schedule and you're in love with all of them."

"Maybe not in love but they're all special."

"That's hogwash, Steve. They're only special because they spread their legs. Do you remember Dr. Benderman's admonitions about multiple partners?"

"Yes." Steve spoke deliberately. "They're only feeding my addiction."

"Anything else?"

Steve fidgeted with his cocktail napkin. "It doesn't matter how many there are, I'll always crave more. I'm just like a smoker who wants another cigarette or the gambler who has to place one more bet."

"And you're supposed to ..."

"Be on guard, and avoid situations where my addiction gains the upper hand."

Charlie shook his head. "You sound like a parrot. You repeat the doctor's advice word-for-word but it doesn't have any meaning to you. You're not serious, Steve. You're playing games with yourself."

"Charlie, I've tried to avoid ..."

"Tried ... that's crap," Charlie cut him off. "You never called anyone or made arrangements to meet anyone. C'mon Steve. Is there any woman you've been with for a day or two that you haven't screwed?"

Steve hesitated. "One."

"One?" Charlie questioned, in disbelief.

"Sherry, she's just like the girl next door."

"I've heard that before too ... movin' easy, right? You're planning to seduce her eventually, aren't you? And then sleep with her on a regular basis. Steve, I've heard that before. It's only a matter of time."

"Charlie, that's not fair."

"Look me in the eye. You're planning to take her to bed, aren't you?"

Steve's eyes wandered around the room and then hesitantly said, "Yes."

"You can't go on like this. You need help."

"Can I call you?'

"Of course, but I can't run your life from North Carolina. You need someone here you can talk to. A confidant like I was for you. Someone you can talk to on a regular basis."

Steve scrunched his shoulders. "There isn't anyone like that here."

"Who is your therapist?"

Steve hung his head.

"You do have one here, don't you?"

Steve didn't look up.

"Jesus Christ, Steve. You can't continue banging one and then another. Sooner or later you're going to hurt someone."

"No, I'm not," Steve shouted.

"Look at me, Steve." Charlie waited until he had his full attention. "You've hurt people in the past — the list of women is a mile long. Sooner or later it's going to happen again."

Steve's eyes moistened, his mouth quivered.

Charlie stood and placed his arms around Steve. "I'll call Dr. Benderman and get a reference for you in D.C. You have to take charge of your life before it's too late."

"I will." Steve placed his hands over his face and sobbed, remembering the pain he caused before. "I don't want to hurt anyone."

CHAPTER SEVEN

For the third month in a row Steve leaned over the railing waiting at Margo's for the black limo to arrive. Seeing it slow and come to a stop, he watched Kim step out. Hurrying to the fireplace mantel, he pulled a red rose from the bouquet, rushed into the hallway and camped out in front of the elevator.

He waited for one group to unload then another. The doors opened and three guys shoved their way past him. His eyes zeroed in on Kim standing in the back — their eyes connected and the two stepped toward each other. Pulling the rose from behind his back, he handed it to her. "A beautiful rose for a beautiful lady."

Kim's eyes sparkled; her smile showed off her white teeth. "It perfect, Steve. Thank you."

He took her by the hand and led her through the maze to their corner table on the balcony. "The vodka and tonic on the right is yours," he said. "I'll be back as soon as I find a vase."

She smiled and took a sip.

Steve returned with a Heineken bottle full of water. "Sorry, this is the best I could do."

"How cute." She grinned and watched as he pushed the stem into the opening. "We only ones with centerpiece." She giggled.

"You're my centerpiece."

Her grin turned into a smile. "You always say right thing."

"How have you been?"

The joy of her face turned into a frown. "Not so good. We have big problems in my country."

"Problems?"

"It's Kuratong Baleleng. I mentioned before. They dreadful intimidate. Last year big shootout with police in Quezon City," she said in her charming accent. "People killed. Crime doubled; murders, drugs, prostitution, human trafficking ... they out of control."

"This is America ... you are safe here."

"Not safe anywhere. My family at risk." She paused and took a long sip. "I no want to talk about it."

Steve gave her a sympathy grin and gently squeezed her hand. "I'm your friend, you can tell me." She looked into his compassionate eyes. "If it makes you feel better I will listen."

Her lips cracked open slightly and in a hushed tone, she said, "I not talk about it outside embassy."

"You can tell me. I want to know everything about you."

"You so sweet." A partial smiled appeared. "It long story.

He glanced at his watch — 7:45. "I have all night."

She peered hesitantly into his eyes and then connected the dots. "Kuratong Baleleng formed by government in 1986 ... vigilante group to fight communist guerrillas. They extremely successful. Disbanded by government in 1988. That when it started."

"Started? I thought you said they were disbanded?"

"No military supervision ... they turn into organized crime syndicate."

"How did that happen?"

"They supported by powerful people who wanted control. Most from Christian Cebuano community. They close-nit ... protected by local officials."

"That's hard to believe."

Kim bit her lip. "They stole millions from father's bank. He had pictures of who did it. Local officials did nothing. He went to the federal government. They shook heads, said 'their hands tied.' He not give up, started protest movement. They kill my brother when he march in support."

"I'm so sorry to hear that."

"My father organize bank boycott in brother's memory. They march in several cities. Carry protest banners ... banks closed. There riots and protests against Kuratong Baleleng. Finally, government agree to bring them to justice."

"What happened?"

"It a farce; they arrested two or three low-ranking members, said it over."

"Wow."

"It got worse for us." She wiped a tear from her cheek. "They burn our house. Kidnapped younger sister. Make her prostitute. We never see her again."

"My God, I can't imagine the pain your family has experienced."

"It awful. My father ... broken man. He got me job in embassy to protect me."

Steve sympathized with her; his expression grew grim. "Oh Kim, I wish there was something I could do."

"You good man," she said, holding her glass up. "I have another drink."

"Yes, of course." Steve jumped to his feet and quickly returned with a glass in each hand. He slid his chair closer to her and spoke softly. "Do you have many friends here?"

"Only at embassy. I afraid to go out alone."

"Would you go out to dinner with me?"

Her eyes showed her vulnerability. "I want to be with you ... but I can't."

"There has to be a way."

"You want me?" she said, guardedly.

He smiled softly; his mood was optimistic. "Yes Kim, I want to be alone with you."

She gazed into his eyes for the longest moment. "You positive?"

Flashing his mega-watt smile, he caressed her hand. "Yes, I'm positive."

She stood, walked to the balcony railing and stared into the night then turned back and looked at him, as if she had a new resolve. "You stay here. I be back."

Downing his drink, Steve felt a surge, and wondered if her thoughts were the same. He looked up to see her talking to Margo across the room. Then Kim was gone.

A few minutes later she stood in front of him, grinning ear to ear. "I ready."

Steve pressed his lips, hoping his interpretation was the same. "Ready?"

She gave him a sly smile and extended her hand with a key dangling from a chain. "I ready."

Steve's brain clicked. He stood and hugged her. She grabbed his hand and tugged him through the masses and down the hallway. Unlocking the door at the end, she motioned him in. Steve took two steps inside and paused, burning incense perfumed the room. He squinted his eyes adjusting to the candlelit room.

She locked the door and stepped toward him. He wrapped his arms around her and held her tight.

Stretching on her tiptoes, Kim threw her arms around his neck and planted a kiss on his lips. Steve lifted her in his arms and kissed her passionately.

"I want you," she purred.

He eased her down and led her toward the bed, the top sheet folded to the side.

Kicking off her heels she turned for the bathroom. "You get ready. I join you."

Steve stripped naked and slipped into bed. His thoughts went wild. *I can't imagine the things she's gone through, her sister being forced into prostitution. Her brother, her dad. God, she's beautiful. I want her so much!*

He heard a light-switch click, the bathroom door opened and she slinked toward him. With each step the features of her silhouetted body became clearer — her long black hair hung freely over bare shoulders, her breasts bulged from the edges of her dainty yellow bra, her low-cut matching panties caressed her slender frame.

Pulling the sheet down to his waist, Kim eased onto the bed and slid next to him, her eyes admiring his body. Lightly, she trailed her hand down his hairy chest. Reaching under the sheet, she fondled him until his erection stood alone. She admired his size then pulled off her panties and jumped on top of him.

Straddling his legs, she unhooked her bra, unleashing perfectly-shaped breasts, larger than he'd anticipated — round and firm he thought — as she pushed against his erection. In the soft light, her dark brown nipples flashed like half-dollars.

She toyed with the hair on his chest then reached up around his face, running her fingers up through his dark hair. Gently she lifted his left hand and placed it over his head, then did the same with his right hand, locking his fingers together behind his head.

Smiling broadly, she said, "I make you happy, yes?"

He nodded, his eyes penetrating hers. "Yes."

Rising to her knees, she placed a condom on his erection and eased down on him. Feeling her sensual body consume him, Steve gasped and closed his eyes.

She pushed her hands against his shoulders, pressing him into the bed. Her pelvis moved slowly side to side then up and down, gradually picking up the pace. Steve cracked open a blurry eye — her breasts protruding over him, her body glistening with moisture — he willed himself not to come too soon.

Increasing the pace, he lost track of this thoughts, his body spontaneously responding as she increased the rhythm, up and down. Feeling suspended in time, he panted aloud. *Oh my God. I've never had a woman like this before. I can't believe her, she's going non-stop. I'm going to lose it.* His body jerked. Steve gazed into her eyes, knowing she was the best ever. *I've never screwed anyone like her… she lasted longer, took me up and let me down, then did it again.*

"You best man ever."

Steve tried to smile through his pleasure. "It's only … because … of you … you're the most … wonderful."

"I do better."

Steve shook his head and gasped. "You can't … I can't."

Kim eased back, wiped her brow with the edge of the sheet, and quickly reclaimed her place on top of him.

Steve lay helpless like never before. He felt her every move. *Oh my God, not yet. I won't last a minute longer.*

She moved more deliberately than before, taking her time. Sweat broke out on his forehead; perspiration ran freely down his sides. She hesitated slightly then slammed against him. Breathless, Steve glanced up, unable to speak, panting out of control. She arched her back and pressed with all of her might. He grabbed her ass and pulled her tight.

Their bodies locked as one.

By the time they returned to the party room, the crowd had thinned. Freddie winked at Steve. Kim slipped the key into Margo's hand, thanked her, and said goodbye.

Steve walked Kim to the elevator, turned to her and held her tight. The two kissed as deeply as before. She slid down off her tiptoes and hugged his waist one last time.

"I love you," she said, then turned for the open door.

"I love you too," he said as the elevator door closed.

Turning for the bar, Freddie stepped into Steve's path. "How was that piece of ass?"

Steve bristled, offended by his comment, then turned and said to the barkeep, "I'll have one last gin."

Freddie didn't follow up. "You leaving so soon?" He slurred, "the party has yet to begin."

"I have some dignitaries coming in tomorrow," Steve fibbed. "Have to hit the sack early."

"Guess that's why you're paid the big bucks." Freddie laughed. "Did you talk to Margo?"

"No." Steve shook his head. "She's been huddled with the broads all night."

"She wanted to ask you something." Freddie looked around and stumbled into the living room. "Margo, get your ass over here. Steve's about ready to leave."

She gave Freddie *the look* then headed for Steve. "You can't leave yet. I need your help."

"What for?"

"I'll tell you. Let's go out on the balcony where it isn't so noisy."

He followed her outside and propped himself against the railing. "Let's hear it."

Margo cozied up to him. "One of my best friends is coming to Washington in a couple of weeks. Freddie and I will be out of town the first few days. I'd like for you to take care of her."

"Take care?"

She grinned. "You know, have her over to your place and show her a good time."

"Geez, Margo, I'm really snowed. I-I don't ..."

"C'mon Steve, I've told her all about you. She wants to meet you."

He grimaced, unwilling to give her a hint of his true feelings. "Really, I ..."

Margo talked over him. "Hannah's tall with dark-brown hair and sophisticated as hell. Her old man, Saul, has a wholesale diamond place in New York. He'll be in Antwerp all week. C'mon."

Steve stroked his growth. "I can't, really ..."

She cut him off. "I'll make it up to you ... please." Her eyes as inviting as hell.

Steve stared blankly.

"I'll do anything you want."

His urges rushed. "Okay ... just this one time."

"Perfect." She slid her hand down and grabbed his ass. "Thanks, I'll stop by your place after work on Monday and pay you back."

***

Standing outside his apartment with a large sign in hand, Steve glanced at his watch. *She called from the airport forty minutes ago. She ought to be here anytime.*

Glancing down the street, he saw a taxi turn the corner. Holding a sign over his head — BAR HARBOR-SOUTH — he waved with the other hand.

The cabbie slammed on the brakes, stopping a few feet in front of Steve. He unlocked the trunk on his way to open the back door.

Steve waited in anticipation.

Her long slender legs slid out, one at a time, offering a flash of her black panties. Steve brought his head up and gazed into her beautiful green eyes.

Hannah stood before him, dressed to the hilt, completed by a large diamond necklace and matching dangle earrings. She zeroed in on the sign.

"How did you come up with that?"

"Margo said you had a summer place in Bar Harbor. The idea just popped out."

She eyed him. "You look just like she said you would."

"I hope that's good."

"It's better than good."

The cabbie sat her green and gray tweed bags in front of him and waited.

Steve gave him an extra ten. "Thanks," he said, picking up her bags and heading for the lobby door.

She ran ahead, opened the door then followed Steve in. "Wow, this is quite a place."

Steve ginned and rolled her suitcases onto the elevator. "Wait until you see my apartment."

A few minutes later, he led the way down the hall and unlocked the door. She stepped in.

"I love the contemporary furnishings and the view," she said, walking briskly toward the sliders. "You can see the entire city. Is that direction west?" she asked, pointing to the horizon.

Steve nodded. "I'll put your bags in the guest bedroom so you can spread out."

"If you don't mind, I'll slip into something more comfortable."

"Take your time. I have some special hors d'oeuvres for you."

"Sounds perfect," she said on the way to the guest room.

Steve popped the cork on a bottle of Treveri Cellars NV Brut, placed it in an ice bucket and carried it onto the balcony. Hurrying back to the kitchen, he made a mental picture of the four sections of the platter then placed blue cheese and crackers in one.

Pulling three containers out of a bag from the Jewish Deli down the street, he memorized the labels on each box as he filled the other sections of the platter with horseradish gefilte fish, goat cheese and spinach cakes, and salmon croquettes.

Placing the array, two small plates and a small stack of napkins on the table between the two chairs on his small balcony, he scurried to his bedroom to change clothes. By the time Hannah walked onto the balcony, he was lying on a lounger wearing white shorts, a purple polo shirt and sunglasses.

"What's going on?" she said.

He lifted his sunglasses and looked up at her with his sexy brown eyes. "That depends on you."

"You don't mess around, do you?"

"Mess around?"

She giggled. "I didn't mean it that way."

Hannah paraded in front of him on the way to the other lounger. Her black shorts showed off long tan legs, while her loose black-knit top extended over square shoulders and average-sized breasts. The sun outlined her slender silhouette as she passed by.

"This looks like something special, she said, looking at the spread on the end table.

"It's especially for you."

She picked up a round treat and took a small bite. "My favorite, goat cheese and spinach." Eying him again, she hesitated. "How thoughtful. Most men would never have done this."

"You can thank my mother," he said, encouraged by the hint of her smile. "She always insisted on doing something distinctive for special guests."

"Too bad more men don't have mothers like yours."

Steve smiled ear to ear. "Would you like a glass of sparkling wine?"

"That'd be wonderful." She slid onto the lounger and leaned back.

Steve handed her a full glass. "Here's to a beautiful lady."

She clinked his glass then gave him a sexy smile. "And here's to the next three days."

"I'll drink to that."

"I love the apricot flavor."

"There's a hint of peach too," he added.

Steve fixed her plate, describing each item as he had memorized them, then heaped his plate.

The two quickly fell into casual conversation, chatting like friends who'd been apart. Steve filled his plate for a second time. She talked about the places she'd traveled. Steve emptied the bottle, popped the cork on another and filled her glass.

Touching his upper lip with the tip of her forefinger, she said, "I want to tell you about my husband."

Steve shrugged knowing perfectly well he was interested. "You don't have to do that."

"I'd feel better if I did."

"Fine, go ahead."

"Saul and I have been married for nineteen years. He's sixty-six and travels to Antwerp three or four times a year to purchase diamonds. He's big in the cartel. I'm … positive he has a chickie there."

"Why do you say that?"

"When he comes home from a trip he treats me like he's never been gone — walks in like he's been at the office all day. Once in a while, you'd think he'd be horny and want something. It's always the same — nothing. I'm no dummy. So when he's gone, I do my thing."

Steve hesitated then stood. "Here, let me refill your glass."

"Thanks," she said. Switching hands to take a last sip before handing him the glass, she spilled the wine down her front. "Darn, it's the only lounging top I brought." She loosened the top buttons. "Do you mind if I take it off?"

"Of course not," he said, anxious to see more. "No one can see in up here."

She slipped off her top and handed it to him. "Please hang this on a chair so it can dry."

"Sure." His eyes racing across her bare breasts, each seeming more the size of a large orange. He picked up the bottle and refilled her glass. "Now don't waste this," he jested.

"I'll try not to do that."

She gave him a sly, sexy look then wiggled her index finger, gesturing for him to sit next to her.

He slid onto the lounger. She studied his virile body thoughtfully.

He took his time slowly drizzling the sparkly on her right breast then left. Her breasts seemed to enlarge. *They looked more like grapefruits.* He thought about his conversation with Charlie and hesitated.

"C'mon, we don't want to waste it," she encouraged.

Steve's engine roared to life. He ripped off his shirt and snuggled next to her. Circling his tongue around her left nipple, he paused to examine her sensual body. "Nice flavor." He laughed.

"Can you taste the apricot and peach flavors?"

He glanced up with a sly sexy smile. "That and much more."

She leaned back and locked her hands behind her head — her nipples perked up and aimed at him. "There's more to come."

Getting the message, he eased on top of her and licked her left breast again, then the right. She casually shifted, pushing the other one further into his mouth.

He sucked tenderly.

Beads of moisture formed under her nose. "You're really good," she said, pushing against Steve's stomach.

He eased up while she slipped off her shorts, picked up her glass and tipped it — sparkly wine splashed over her, running between her thighs.

Their eyes connected. She closed hers and spread her legs.

His mouth feasted.

***

Having tickets for *Chicago* the next night at the National Theatre downtown, Steve wondered all day how he'd top the afternoon on the lounger, and how she'd screwed him all night. *I can't believe her. I lost track of the number of orgasms she had.*

On the way home that night, the two chatted about the play they'd seen. She repeated the scenes about the gangster killings. "I loved the music."

"It was great," Steve said, still looking for a lead, some insight into how he might please her tonight. Stepping into his apartment, his mind was at zero. "Would you like a liqueur to unwind?"

"Unwind? I'm ready to go. I'll slip on my nighty and be down to your room in no time."

"Sounds good to me," he said, still unsure of a plan of action.

He lit candles, turned on the soft jazz station, opened the bed and fluffed the pillow. Stripping to his boxers, Steve eased into bed and pulled the sheet down to his waist.

Hannah strolled in, exuding sensuality, her black negligee barely covering her private parts.

"You look fabulous."

She smiled and turned from one side to the other, showing off everything she had. "What would you like tonight?" she said in a sexy, raspy voice.

"I was thinking about you ..."

"I was hoping you were. "How are you at back rubs?"

"I'm pretty good," he said, trying to sound modest. "I'm better when I start with the feet."

"Feet? I haven't had a foot massage in years."

Steve's trademark-smile erupted. "Would you like one tonight?"

"Yes, of course."

"How about naked on your stomach with a pillow doubled under you."

"Sounds interesting." She assumed the position.

Wanting her more than ever, Steve began his familiar routine.

An hour later — lathered head to toe and panting — he watched her lose control. She gasped, her head thrashing side to side, until everything slowed. Her head laid still on the pillow. "That was beautiful."

Kissing her on the cheek he said, "I'm only halfway."

Her eyes opened wide. "You mean ... I can't do any more."

"You don't have to do anything ... just enjoy."

Steve turned her over and slipped the pillow under the small of her back, propping the promised-land toward his mouth.

Her eyes drafted toward his, then connected. She laid waiting.

He didn't disappoint. His tongue circled and went to town.

CHAPTER EIGHT

Waiting for Steve to hang up the phone, Sherry reached toward the conference table and sat her coffee mug on the plastic coaster. She glanced at him, intensely involved in a conversation. *God, he looks good. He's personable, bright, and extremely articulate. Margo thinks he's the best and so do her friends. Women in the rumor mill are hooked on him. It's like there is some kind of Steve-a-mania. I don't get it; he's never made a move on me.*

Steve ended his conversation and looked her way. "How's Will doing? Has he accepted his new assignment?"

"I think so. He's been meeting with Congressional leaders like crazy. You'd think he was a life-long golfing buddy with Senator Enzi."

"That's good to hear."

"Did you have a good meeting with him?" she asked.

"Yes, I did everything Art and you suggested. I told him I had second thoughts about my strategy and hoped I hadn't offended him."

"How did he react?"

"He looked at me in a puzzled way. I said, 'I had no intent to embarrass you and hoped it didn't come off that way.'"

"How did he react?"

"He seemed warm and fuzzy ... well, warm and fuzzy for him. He said he'd thought about it too, but since the president was in on it, it all seemed kind of funny."

"He said that?"

"Yep, I said, 'regardless, you can be assured it won't happen again.' Then he extended his hand with a smile, and said, 'Matter over and done, subject closed.'"

"I can't imagine him saying that."

Steve rubbed his jaw. "It was a dumb thing to do. I'm really having second thoughts. Guess I was lucky."

"Lucky? I'd say you were shrewd."

Steve sat down in the chair across from her. "How are your staff meetings going?"

"Amazingly well. At first they were leery. They thought it was another hairbrained idea. No one was really serious about it. When I told them you had mentioned it to the president, ideas started to pour in. I'm positive we'll produce cuts that will exceed your 20 percent goal."

"Terrific. I told you it was possible."

"I know; but I'm shocked."

"People in the trenches know where cuts can be made. I can't wait till the president hears about your projection."

"Have you met with her yet?"

"Yes, we're having our second meeting next week."

"In the Oval Office?"

Steve nodded.

"Weren't you nervous the first time?"

"Nervous?" He laughed. "I was scared shitless."

"Really?"

"No, but it did cause me to pause."

"I would have peed my pants."

"You would have done fine." He looked her in the eye and changed the subject. "How'd you like to have dinner next Thursday night?"

Finally. She bit her lip. *I can't believe he's asking me.*

"If you have plans that's okay."

"I-I don't," she stammered. "That would be very nice."

"How about I pick you up at seven? There's a good restaurant not far from your place."

She cocked her head. "How'd you know where I live?"

He gave her his mega-smile. "I checked it out some time ago."

She grinned. *Can you believe it? He's been thinking about me for some time.*

***

Steve stopped on 36th Street in Georgetown. The valet ran around his dark blue Caddy and opened the door for Sherry.

Steve trolled around the front of the car, grabbed the valet's ticket and took her by the hand. She noticed him glimpse at her cleavage out of the corner of his eye. *Just because I wear business attire all day, doesn't mean I don't have anything to show off.*

Steve opened the door to the 1789 Restaurant and followed her in. Waiting behind another couple, he whispered in her ear. "This is supposed to be a quintessential Washington dining experience."

With a questioning look, she turned on her tiptoes. "What did you mean by that?" she whispered.

He laughed softly. "I read it in their ad and looked it up — it means nearly perfect."

"I'm glad to know that."

"They have six dining rooms each one decorated differently. I hope you like the one I picked."

"I'm sure it'll be fine."

"Right this way," the hostess said.

The two followed her to a small room. Sherry turned toward Steve. "This is delightful. It's so quaint, reminds me of an English pub."

"Funny that you mention that," he said, pulling out her chair before taking the chair across from her. He pointed toward an old clock hanging on the wall. "That's a Parliament clock. It dates back to a time when English pubs installed clocks after Parliament enacted an unpopular tax on watches."

"How do you know that?"

"I was a history professor in a former life."

"Really. I'm a history buff. I minored in history when I was in college."

"Any particular period?"

"Antebellum South."

"Interesting, my specialty was the Civil War."

"Sounds like we could have some interesting conversations outside of our work topics."

"I guess so." He picked up the wine list. "Would you like a glass of wine?"

"White would be fine. You pick it ... I'm not much of a connoisseur."

He glanced at the list of white wines then laid it aside.

The waiter appeared. "Something to drink before dinner?"

Steve looked at her. "Would you like a cocktail?"

"Wine will be fine."

"I'll have a Tanqueray on the rocks with three olives. And we'll have a bottle of the Pinot Grigio from Italy, Bin 006."

"Yes, that's a fine light-bodied white; the lady will enjoy it."

Steve gave him a half grin then looked Sherry in the eye. "Twenty years. I bet you've seen a lot of changes in the time you've been here."

"Lots of activity; not many changes."

"How about the chances for implementing our educational reform measures?"

"At first I said here we go again." She cracked a partial smile. "It's like my dad used to say, 'same chance as a fart in a windstorm.'" She giggled. "Then you pulled off the coup with Senator Enzi and finessed Will with the president. I started thinking maybe, just maybe, he can pull it off."

"And now?"

The waiter sat Steve's drink on the table and offered him a taste of the wine. When Steve declined, he poured a half-glass for Sherry. Steve raised his glass of gin. "Here's to a most enjoyable evening."

"Thank you." She clinked his glass.

"And now?" he repeated.

"I'm more confident. Streamlining is a done deal. That'll be a real bargaining chip for the president. And ... your goal of implementing standardized competence testing in grades one through three is doable."

"Doable? Is that all? C'mon."

She shrugged. "Who knows ... I'd say you have a 25, 30 percent chance of pulling it off."

"25 percent?" he questioned in a high pitch. "That's not very encouraging."

She grinned. "I was giving you the benefit of the doubt."

"Thanks. I appreciate that." He ran his fingers through his hair. "Enough of that. Tell me about Sherry Holmgren."

"You know all there is to know; growing up in Ohio, going to college and coming out here."

"I'm interested in the Office of Inspector General and how you got to your current position."

"I really enjoyed my experience in the Inspector's office."

"You mentioned the Inspector's Office does investigations for fraud — tell me more."

"It conducts independent audits, inspections, and investigations of possible fraud, waste or misconduct in the Department of Education. They're an internal watchdog group."

The waiter freshened her wine. "Another Tanqueray?" he asked.

"Sure," he said, keeping his focus on her. "What did you like best when you were there?"

"The variety of assignments and learning about behind the scenes operations."

"Did you find any steamy stuff you can share?"

She gave him a light shrug. "No but there's plenty of it. Unless it got really nasty we stayed out of it."

"How did you move from there to the Secretary's office?"

"I've asked myself that several times. I wasn't looking to go anywhere. One day the Secretary called me into his office and asked me to apply for the opening."

"How long ago was that?"

"Last year."

The waiter picked up Steve's empty glass. "Are you ready to order?"

His glance across the table caught Sherry's nod. "Yes, and I'll have wine now."

Sherry had a salad and scallops. Steve ordered a Brussels sprout salad with toasted pine nuts and pork loin. Handing the menu to the waiter, he turned to her. "It's interesting they listed the location where each entrée was from."

"I noticed that too," she said. "I've been in places where the source of the mussels and salmon were listed but I've never seen the location for every item mentioned in the menu."

The two settled into a leisurely dinner, each asking questions about the other's interests — where they'd traveled and things they liked to do. Every response seemed to generate another topic. *Steve seems so interesting and sincere.* Sherry felt comfortable with him, but still held back a little, playing it safe. *I hope he gets the message — I'm not a one-night stand. If that's all he wants, he's barking up the wrong tree.*

***

Over the next few weeks, the two fell into a pattern, going out for a lunch on Wednesdays at one of the "in places" on the hill, where they talked mostly about business. She guarded her comments and kept a close eye on their intimacy. Each meeting produced more reassuring feelings; he never made an inappropriate comment. She was impressed.

On Saturdays through the summer, they regularly attended a Baltimore Orioles game, enjoyed one of the many museums, or took in a matinee. *He's a perfect gentleman ... always walks me to the lobby of my building and says goodbye.*

By late summer she had seen enough and was looking for more. He paused at the elevator and hugged her gently. She unloaded a firm kiss. *He's really hot. I wonder if he'd like to come up.* Looking up at him with yearning eyes and hoping he'd gotten the message.

"Would you like to go back to 1789 for dinner Friday night?" he asked.

Oh well, it's better than nothing. Her eyes sparkled. "Yes, I'd like that."

"Would seven o'clock work?"

"That'd be perfect."

The week buzzed by and before she knew it, he was standing in the lobby of her apartment, extending his hand. "Is the pub okay?" he said.

"It'll be wonderful; it's so quaint. She leaned his way, giving him more than a hint of her cleavage. He didn't take the bait. She wondered if she'd done something wrong. He barely said a word as he drove to the restaurant. Stopping in front, he grabbed the ticket from the valet, gently took her by the arm and in they strolled.

"Dr. Schilling," the hostess said. "Your table is ready." She guided the two to the table in a secluded corner.

Sherry slid to the end of the cushy bench-seat, all the way next to the wall. He eased in beside her.

"Cocktails tonight?" the well-endowed waitress pleasantly asked.

Sherry looked at him. "The wine I had last time would be fine."

Steve ordered a bottle of the Italian Pinot Grigio and his usual. "How about we share a cheese plate?"

She nodded in agreement.

The two chatted briefly about work before ordering. Sherry chose monkfish and Steve ordered red snapper. He had another Tanqueray and motioned for second bottle of wine.

Finishing her fish, Sherry sipped her third glass of wine. "I can't eat another bite." Noticing her wooziness, Steve slid closer, pinning her in the corner. She giggled to herself then realized his right hand was halfway up her thigh. *When did he do that?*

She didn't move.

The waitress appeared. "Dessert or coffee?"

"I'll ..." Sherry cleared her throat. "I'll have coffee."

"Make it two," Steve added, his hand gently caressing.

She swallowed hard and gazed into his soft brown eyes. *I know what I should do ...*

He smiled as his fingers inched higher. She started to speak then glanced away. Steve kissed her on the ear; his fingertips touched the edge of her panties. Trying not to show any emotion, she sighed and took a deep breath. *I have to say no ... ask him to stop.*

Not a word came out.

His fingers slid along her crotch.

She gulped. *Oh my God. I have to tell him to stop.*

He placed his fingers lightly on her private area.

Oh shit, I can't believe ...

Trying to shift her thoughts, she stared at the fireplace across the room, in a hazy trance.

He didn't stop.

Coffee was served. Giving the waitress a fake smile, she covered her face with her hands, trying not to reveal her erupting pleasures. He continued, gently fondling.

Closing her eyes, Sherry muffled a gasp and panted inconspicuously. Not wanting him to stop, she bit her lip and swallowed hard. Finally, her emotions spun out of control and she lost it, her insides somersaulting.

He gave her space then placed his arm round her shoulder and pulled her tight. She snuggled close, unable to do anything more.

Steve took his time paying the bill, letting her regain her composure, and then kissed her on the tip of the nose. "Would you like to go home now?"

Looking into his eyes, she nodded. "I want you."

***

Holding hands, the two lovebirds walked slowly through the lobby of her apartment building. She eagerly tapped the elevator button then stepped in. He followed as she pushed number seven, then turned and pressed against his chest — her heart pounded a hundred beats a second. Grazing her hand over his five o'clock shadow, she glanced up. *He's as sexy as hell. I can't wait to get him in bed.*

The elevator door opened and Sherry pulled him down the hallway into her apartment — city lights filled the room, crisscrossing with a stray moonbeam.

Before she could flip the light switch, he eased behind her and slid his hands around her waist. "Thanks, for a wonderful dinner," he whispered. "I really enjoyed being with you."

Dinner? I can't remember what I had to eat. My panties are still moist. "The atmosphere was lovely," she purred.

His lips grazed the right side of her neck then kissed her on the ear. Goosebumps raced down her arms. He slid his hand down her side, loosened a button and ran his fingers inside her blouse, tracing the bottom edge of her bra. Her stomach lurched with a tingle. Swallowing hard, she felt her knees weaken. *I can't wait. Take me, please.*

She gasped then turned around and kissed him wildly. Groping at him like she'd never touched a man before; she tugged on his shirt, pulling on each button. Urgently, she pulled his shirt off, tossed it to the side and snuggled her head against the soft tendrils on his chest. Sliding her hands down his side, she grabbed his cheeks and pulled his bulging pants into her stomach.

They pressed together.

I can't wait. Grabbing his hand, she pulled him into the bedroom and shoved him onto the bed. Climbing on top, Sherry smothered him with kisses, then jumped up, stripped to her bra and panties, and eased back in bed. Steve unzipped and removed his pants, flipped them toward the side chair and snuggled next to her.

He's like a dream come true. I want him so badly. I don't want tonight to ever end. Sherry pinched herself unable to believe she was really lying beside him. Climbing on top, she groped his erection, slipped on a condom and pulled him inside. She tried to go slow, but it was too late for restraint.

CHAPTER NINE

After pouring a second mug of coffee, Steve sat in his office Monday morning doodling on a yellow pad; his mind stuck on the wild weekend — it had started Friday night when he'd seduced Sherry at the restaurant. He made love to her the rest of the night and most of the next morning. *I can't wait till we're together again. She's the most giving, loving person I've ever met. She likes to do everything I do — go to ballgames, concerts and plays — I could to talk to her all day about the Civil War.*

He took a long sip of coffee as his daydreaming continued. A vision of Sherry naked flashed into mind. *I had no idea she had a body like that. Who would have thunk it?* He mused a little longer about their night. *I wonder how many orgasms she had. At least four, maybe five or six. And then when she turned the tables, I thought I would lose my mind. God, she was good!*

His mind wandered to Saturday night when he'd been standing by the railing at Margo's thinking about Kim. A warm body had pressed against his back and before he could turn around, a hand dangled a key in front of him.

Turning around, he came face to face with Deb. He'd been out with her a couple of times and she was no slouch — each time seemed like a totally different experience. She had pulled him against her, placed an insistent kiss on his lips and announced, "Margo said your oriental friend isn't coming tonight. She's gone to see her father who's ill." With that she grabbed his ass and ushered him into the guest bedroom. "I have something that'll take your mind off her."

His desires fired on cue; his mouth raced over her face in rapid kisses. She shoved him on the bed and took time teasingly stripping to her panties. He flipped off his shoes, and then tugged at his pants, shirt and sox. She smirked and gestured for him to take off his boxers.

Steve flipped them in the air over his shoulder and laid down. His erection stood tall and firm.

She smiled smugly. "Spread eagle … this is my night."

"Sounds good to me," he recalled saying.

She stretched on a condom and was on him before he could say more. Time passed in a blur — the fast, furious rhythm of her hips gloriously sapped his energy. She continued, hot and heavy, slamming against him, again and again.

Fighting for a breath, he knew he had to retain control. He eased his mouth from hers. *Savor the closeness. Take her to the top then slow down and do it again.* He worked one hand down her back, his fingers finding her soft cheeks. The other hand joined in, fingers caressing at first, then probing deeper. She stiffened noticeably. He felt her hesitation, then an eruption of juices. Her head sagged onto his chest.

Steve smiled to himself, knowing the night was only half over.

On Sunday, like always Charisse was there, bounding around in her normal fashion. *She must have been on a mission. We ended up in bed most of the day. She probably made it a half dozen times.*

Art poked his head in the doorway. "Ready for our meeting?"

Steve's mind snapped back to reality. He nodded, stood and walked toward the conference table.

Sherry and Art strolled in and placed their mugs on the plastic coasters with the departmental seal. "How was your weekend?" Art asked.

Steve glimpsed at Sherry's smiling face. "Perfect. It couldn't have been any better."

Her smile said more than words.

Steve asked, "Who wants to go first?"

"I do," Sherry popped. Steve winked at her. "Our staff has finished the reduction plan. It looks like we'll end up cutting 23 percent of the employees over the next three years."

"That's terrific."

"After legal counsel's review, I'll start working with the legislative staff so it'll be ready to incorporate into the next budget bill. The entire package will be finished within the next few weeks. We'll be ready to go whenever the president wants to announce her plans."

"Sounds great. Anything new to report on Will?"

"He's about finished with the core legislation bill. It looks like Kennedy and Enzi will co-sponsor the bill."

Steve turned his attention. "Art, how's our staff development effort moving along?"

"It's been a little slow. People are using up their vacation time, so we've slowed to one training session per month. In September we'll crank it up again."

"Excellent. I'll be interested to see how your retreads preform."

Art grinned. "I think you'll be surprised."

"I hope so."

Art changed the subject. "How are your meetings with the president going?"

"Couldn't be better. We've agreed on the basic concepts. All we have to do is flush out the campaign strategies."

Sherry shook her head. "How's she going to finesse the Republicans? They won't compromise on anything."

"That's where your reduction model comes into play."

"The Republicans will eat that up," Art chimed in.

"I think so ... I've learned not to question her political instincts. When she believes she can pull it off, it's a done deal."

"That'd be something," Art said. "Watching the size of the federal bureaucracy dwindle. A lot of unneeded heads will roll."

"That's for sure," Steve said, smugly. "Anything else we need to cover today?"

His two aides looked at each other, shaking their heads.

"Good," Steve said.

Sherry picked up her mug and walked out; Art lingered by the door.

"Is there something else, Art?"

He gave Steve a half grin then closed the door. "Are you doing Sherry?"

Steve wrinkled his brow. "Why do you ask?"

"I saw how her eyes were glued on you. She stared at you throughout the entire meeting. And when you winked at her, I thought she was going to wet her pants. I just figured something is going on."

"You're grasping for straws, Art."

"Hey, I'm not on your case. Half the guys in the department have hit on her without luck. I was starting to think she was a lesbian."

Steve leaned closer to him. "She's not a lesbian."

Art's eyes bugged out. "My lips are sealed."

***

Charisse slid off Steve, fluffed her pillow and propped herself up against the headboard. "Wanta talk?" she asked.

Steve perked up. "Ah … sure, of course."

"Maybe I shouldn't say anything."

"C'mon, we have to be honest with each other."

She hesitated. "My therapist said it would not be good for us to try to help each other."

"Why not?"

Charisse laughed. "She said it'd be like the blind leading the blind. If we got into anything substantial we'd lie to each other and cover things up just like we've done all of our lives."

"I hadn't thought about it that way."

"She said we could talk about sex, then emphasized 'never try to help each other.' I told her I felt better about myself since I've been seeing you and that I've stopped seeing other men."

"How'd she react to that?"

"She was adamant, then pointed her finger at me and said 'don't deceive yourself.' Sooner or later you'll hurt me — that's what addicts do."

"I'd never do that to you, Charisse."

"My therapist said you'd say that. You know as well as I, addicts hurt the ones closest to them. We lie and cheat, use delusional thinking to rationalize our behavior. We do whatever it takes to make things work out the way we think they should be."

Knowing she was right, Steve stared off into space. "Can we talk about things in general?"

"Of course, why not?"

"All of my therapists have said my chances for getting better are practically nil," Steve said. "Did yours say why it's so hard to change?"

"She's shared some very good examples; she explained there are three aspects of the brain — thinking, doing and being. Actions occur when there is an interaction between the knowledge in the mind and experiences of the body. They form a sense of being."

"I've heard the same thing but that's as far as I've gotten."

"I didn't even get to that point, my first time." Charisse leaned closer and pecked him on the cheek. "Emotions and feelings come from experiences. When this happens there's a chemical reaction, like a rush of adrenaline when you're scared. These chemicals are highly addictive. If it continues for a short period of time it's called a mood. If it goes on for months it's referred to as your temperament. And if it extends for a year it becomes a personality trait."

"You sound like an expert."

"I don't know that much but it makes sense to me."

"It sounds simple when you say it. I don't know why my therapist makes it sound so complex."

"One last point," Charisse said. "After a period of time habits are formed and the experiences of the body tell the brain it knows more than it does."

"Sounds kind of crazy to me."

"It did to me at first too."

"So when a person says it's only logical, what they really mean is it's logical based on their experiences."

"Right."

Not liking logic that separated him from his desires, he clarified, "Then based on my experiences something may be logical to me, but based on your experiences the same thing may not be logical to you."

"Exactly. So guess what happens when you take that kind of thinking one more step?"

Steve threw his hands in the air. "Who knows? You're the expert."

"Think about it, Steve. Society says we should only love one person at a time, right?"

"Yes." Steve nodded. "I've heard that a thousand times."

"That's part of our mores, customs and religious beliefs."

Steve scowled. "But how does that make being in love with more than one person wrong?"

"Hmm, not quite. It's wrong in terms of our morals, ethics and values, but based on its experiences your body may not think it's wrong."

"Let me see if I have this right." Steve paused, pondering the concept. "Since both of us have had multiple partners, our bodies are saying it may be logical for them but not for us. Love one, two or three, the more the merrier."

"Exactly. Love one …our body keeps telling our brain they're dumb as hell."

"So the chance of changing is practically nil," Steve said.

"Right. You tell your mind 'I want to change.' Your body reminds the brain of the ninety-five times you've gotten laid — ninety-five chemical rushes — there's no chance of changing."

"Wow, that's really insightful."

"Ham and eggs or a piece of ass?"

Steve pulled her tight and laid a big smacker on her. "Ham and eggs to start."

She laughed again. He grinned back and said, "I thought you were going to say both, at the same time."

"I've never done that."

Steve smiled and tweaked her nipple impishly. "That's your problem. Maybe we ought to try it. Who knows maybe we'll get a chemical rush!"

***

The summer heat hit Washington and the city slowed. When Steve stepped into Margo's place the crowd was half its normal size. The sliders were closed.

Grabbing a Tanqueray for him, Margo rushed to his side, shoved the glass into his hand and began to babble.

"Slow down," Steve pleaded then took a slug.

"I'm hearing good things about you. We need to talk."

"Seems fine to me," he said, unsure of her agenda.

"Tell me about Sherry."

His brow revealed his dismay. "Sherry, what are you …?"

Margo cut him off. "Going out for lunch, seeing Orioles games, taking her to the theater, dinners at upscale restaurants."

"You've covered it all ..."

"C'mon Steve, she has the hots for you. She's even thought about cancelling her annual month-long stay with her parents, so she could be with you."

"I told her she had to go. With Congress on their August recess, it'll be a perfect time for some R & R."

"I know she finally agreed." Margo gulped down her bourbon. "So tell me about her."

"It sounds like you already know it all."

"There must be more. She's never acted this way before. You've taken her to bed, haven't you?"

Steve bristled at the thought of discovery. "It isn't like that."

Getting a sense of his feelings for her, Margo changed the subject. "What did you do to Hannah?"

"Do? Nothing, we did the town like you asked."

"You did more than that. She's raving about you, too — special Jewish hors d'oeuvres and ... lapping up the wine — she'd do anything to see you again. How about it?"

"I don't know." Steve shrugged, trying to make both relationships appear casual. "It'll soon be Labor Day and after that everything cranks up in the department."

"Hannah told me Saul has to make a special trip to Antwerp toward the end of August. If she sends their jet down, would you fly up to Bar Harbor for a few days? She's hoping you will."

"Ah ..."

"C'mon, I know you won't regret it."

Hearing Hannah's name produced an instant surge in Steve's pants. "Okay, tell her to give me a call and we'll work out the details."

***

Steve stepped onto the tarmac at Hancock County-Bar Harbor Airport and picked up his bag. Hannah ran out to greet him with a firm hug, then motioned her driver to stow his luggage in the trunk. She pulled Steve into the backseat and welcomed him with a heavy kiss.

"I'm so glad to see you. I could hardly wait another minute."

Steve gasped, overwhelmed. "I can't believe it's only been six weeks. It seems more like six months. I've really missed you," he fibbed.

"The help will be at our place for another two weeks so I reserved a suite for us at the Bluenose Inn. The driver is taking us there now. I left my car there so I can spend the night."

"Perfect."

"How is Margo doing?"

"Fine, she has a hundred and one projects in the works."

"Sounds like her."

"When will your husband be back?" Steve asked.

"Friday. He's attending a special meeting called by their headquarters in the Netherlands."

"I thought his meetings were in Antwerp."

"Oh yes, sorry. He's meeting with the Bilderberg Group."

"Bilderberg ... that's a highly powerful group."

"They're powerful has hell. Saul doesn't talk about them much. Maybe you should forget I mentioned their name."

"My lips are sealed." He smiled as he ran his fingers over his lips in a mock zipper motion.

"Here we are," she said. The car stopped in front of the Inn. "My things are already in the room so we can go directly to the elevator."

"Sounds like you have thought of everything."

"Maybe not everything but I have a few plans."

"I thought you might," Steve said, giving her his patented smile. He followed her through the lobby and up to the room. Hannah unlocked the door and stepped in. Steve pulled his suitcase in, set it on a luggage caddy and walked to the windows.

"Great view," he exclaimed, then opened the French doors and stepped out onto the balcony. A steady breeze blew across his face. He took a deep breath and exhaled slowly. "I love the smell of the ocean air."

"You can leave the doors open if you want."

"Okay." He turned as she laid her slacks and sweater on the chair. Getting the message, he stripped to his boxers and slid into bed next to her.

She climbed on top and French kissed him. The cool breeze teased their hot caresses.

***

Bedraggled by the Bar Harbor sex marathon, Steve took off the Thursday and Friday before Labor Day. With nothing planned for the long weekend, he poured himself a tall gin, leaned his head back on the recliner and reflected on the last eight months.

The confirmation hearings seemed like an eternity ago. Art had shaped up the staff. Sherry had miraculously surpassed the staff reduction goal. And he was on the right track with the president — things couldn't be better.

A vision of Sherry naked appeared before his eye as he daydreamed — she was more than he'd ever expected. *God, I miss her. I can hardly wait till she's back from her parents. And Charisse, it's only three more days until I'll be with her again.*

He tossed out the last of the ice in his empty glass, threw a handful of olives in it with fresh ice, and filled it with gin. Taking a slug, he thought about Hannah. *I've never experienced anything like her. She's unbelievable.* Visions of the other women he'd been with flashed through his mind. Counting them on his hands, he ticked off each finger then added four more. *This place is better than college. I've never had it so good.*

Steve stood and marched deliberately to the bar. *How's that for walking a straight line.* He laughed, poured another gin and staggered toward the balcony doors. Opening a slider, the Saturday afternoon hot summer air blasted his face. "Shit," he said, closing the door. "Who needs that?"

Continuing on to his lounger, he picked up a *Hustler* magazine from the rack next to it and settled in to read the lead story. His urges fired and before he knew it he was fondling himself. Downing his gin, he flipped on a porno movie and then watched another. Masturbating during the last one, he fell limp in the recliner and dozed off.

A bright light flashed across his face. Turning away to shade his eyes, he wiped his brow trying to find relief from the morning sun. "I feel like shit … ugh … I think I'm going to vomit."

He heard the front door open and close. "Are you up, Steve?"

"I'm over here," he called. "By the fireplace."

He heard a rustling sound then a hand landed on his shoulder. "Are you okay?" Charisse asked.

He coughed. "I've been up all night."

"This place smells like crap; there are empty bottles all over. How long have you been drinking?"

"Does it matter? Nobody seems to care."

"I care. If I didn't I wouldn't be here."

He looked up through blurry eyes. "Why are you here?"

"Why? It's Sunday morning."

"Sunday?"

"How long have you been like this?"

"I-I." He belched.

"That's gross. When did you last go to work?"

"Last week … I was on a trip the first part, took off Thursday and Friday."

"You've been in a stupor three days?"

Steve threw his arms in the air. "What can I say?"

"You look pathetic." Charisse shook her head and picked up some of his debris strewn around the living room. "And to think you wanted to help me … you can't help yourself."

He closed his eyes.

"You're not sleeping while I'm here. Get your ass up and take a shower. I'm making coffee."

He didn't budge. "If you're not up by the count of three, I'll throw cold water on you."

"Okay, okay." Steve pulled himself up and stumbled to the bathroom.

***

Charisse took a sip of coffee then plopped down at the kitchen booth. Placing her elbows on the table top, she propped her head up. *I can barely cope with my problems, how can I help him? I can't let him drag me down; I'll be in the pits again.* She coughed and wiped her eyes, swollen from her tears. She didn't move when she heard the bedroom door squeak open behind her.

Steve filled a mug and walked slowly toward her.

She looked up with a sad smirk. "Don't come near me."

"Okay." Dejected, he pulled a stool from the kitchen bar and sat down on the other side, across the room from her.

Neither said a word for the longest time.

Steve drained his coffee and headed to the pot for a refill. "I'm sorry Charisse. I didn't mean for you to see me this way. Want some more coffee?"

She shoved her empty mug across the table. He filled it and walked toward her. "May I join you?"

Continuing to scowl, she looked away.

He slid onto the bench seat across from her and reached for her hand. She pulled it away and gave him *the look*. "Don't touch me."

Steve backed off and gave her space.

Charisse looked him in the eye. "I can't handle this, Steve. I've worked hard. I've stopped seeing other men. I started feeling good about you. You don't care about me. You'll hurt me just like my therapist said you would."

Steve raised his hand. "Can I say something?"

"You look dreadful. I don't want to hear anything from you. You're not trying to get better. Your friend Charlie gave you a doctor's name in April; five months ago. Have you called?"

Steve looked up sheepishly. "No."

"Have you avoided situations where you might be tempted — no — how many times in the last six months have you missed Margo's Party?"

He hesitated.

"Well, how many?"

"None."

"You're getting laid by multiple women every week. I know you're banging Margo and Deb, probably others during the week. And now you've added Sherry to your list — one more notch on your belt — you don't care about me. All I'm doing is feeding your addiction. I bet you've screwed a dozen or more women since you arrived. You don't give a shit about any of them. It's all about getting laid."

"That's not true ..."

Charisse cut him off. "I'm the one person you can't fool. I *know* what it's like. One little negative in your life and you're on a downer.

Look at you, a Ph. D with no self-control, smashed out of your mind ... such a pity."

"That's not true, Charisse. I know I can do better."

"Better? Is that all you can say." She bristled and slammed her coffee mug on the table, spilling the dregs. "Better is not good enough."

She ran into the bathroom and a few minutes later returned with an oversized purse looped over her shoulder. "I'm out of here. And don't have Margo contact me," she shouted as she flung open the door.

"It's over!" The door slammed with a bang.

CHAPTER TEN

Steve spent Labor Day sitting in his recliner thinking about Charisse' comment. *She was right. I haven't tried. If I don't change I'll go down the tubes like before. I have to get help!* He walked over to the desk, opened the center drawer and pulled out the slip of paper with the doctor's name Charlie had scrawled on it — Dr. Frank Pritts — *I'll call him in the morning.*

Three days later at 6:30 p.m., the receptionist escorted Steve into the doctor's office. Stepping into the walnut-paneled room, he eased into a brown leather stuffed chair.

A few minutes later a short balding man with Dr. Peepers-type glasses walked in and extended his hand. "I'm Frank Pritts. It's nice to meet you."

Steve shook his hand. "I'm glad to meet you too. And thanks for squeezing me in."

"No problem. Dr. Benderman is an old classmate. He sent your file some time ago and yesterday we went over it on the phone. Sounds like you've been through a lot."

Steve gave him a half grin. "It's been a struggle for a long time. Every time I think I'm doing better something happens. Next thing I know ... I've had a relapse."

The old doctor grinned. "It's not a relapse, it's part of the process — two steps forward and one back — real progress comes when you're able to deal with adversity and move two steps forward and stay there."

"I haven't done that very well."

"Why do you think this time will be any different?"

"Ah ... I'm here. I want to be better."

The doctor rubbed his jaw. "That's not good enough."

Steve's eyes widened.

"You have to make a strong commitment. If not, you're wasting our time."

Steve looked bewildered.

"I'll see you next week, Thursday at four o'clock; then we'll decide if it's worth going any further. In the meantime, give my question more thought, and return with a decisive answer."

***

"Well, have you decided anything?" Dr. Pritts asked on Thursday.

Steve straightened in the overstuffed chair. "Yes, I thought about it and I'm ready to commit. I can't go through the rest of my life the way I am. I bounce from one extreme to another — one week I'm on a high, the next I'm in the dumps, smashed out of my mind."

"Good, recognizing the problem is a positive start." The doctor opened his pad. "How many women did you sleep with last week?" He looked up from his pad at Steve.

Steve glanced down then looked back at the doctor. "Three."

"And the week before?"

"Four."

"You missed one, why?"

"She dumped me."

"Dumped you ... why?"

"She's a sex addict too. Charisse is her name, and she said ..."

Dr. Pritts raised his right hand. "A sex addict stopped seeing you?"

"She was getting better, said there was no way she was going to let me pull her down. I'd only end up hurting her."

"Good for her. Sounds like she's made a lot of progress. How did you feel about that?"

"At first I was shocked. I didn't know how I felt. After a while, I was pleased for her."

"Pleased? Why did you feel that way?"

"Hmm, it made me feel good about her. She had turned the corner and was really trying to be as normal as possible. I thought about her a lot. That's why I called you."

Dr. Pritts nodded and ran his fingers through his short, white pointed goatee. "Do you think you can do the same?"

"I have to. Being with her helped me understand why I'm like I am. I don't like myself."

"You don't like yourself? Have you ever said that before?"

Steve's brow furrowed in thought for a moment. "Not that I recall. Doc will you help me?"

The old doctor paused then nodded. "Yes, as long as you stay committed."

"Don't worry. I'm committed. I'll follow through."

"Good. I'll lay out a plan and we'll meet every week to discuss your progress and determine how well you're doing. We'll start by taking small steps. Are you willing to do that?"

"Yes, I have too."

"Okay, in our next meeting we'll assess your week and discuss the next objective. It's imperative that you're truthful with me and yourself. If you're not, you're only fooling yourself. Agree?"

"Sounds good to me."

"Okay, I have to get up to speed. Tell me about all of the women you've slept with since you've been in Washington, D. C."

"All of them?"

"Yes, starting in January."

Steve began with the prostitute the night he'd been appointed Deputy Secretary then ticked off another dozen or so, ending up with the past week. "Friday night Sherry and I had a wonderful dinner and spent the rest of the night at her place. I met Deb at a party on Saturday night and took her back to my place. Wednesday, Margo stopped by my place after work."

"Do you have the same feelings about all three?"

Steve gave her a questioning look. "I never thought about that."

"Steve, I know you've thought about it. I want to hear the truth."

Shifting uncomfortably in the cushy chair, Steve hesitated.

Dr. Pritts looked him in the eye. "I'm waiting."

"I-I," Steve stammered. "I think all three are great."

"Great? Great lovers? Great conversationalists? Great women? The kind of a woman you'd want to marry?"

Glancing distractedly around the room, Steve cringed at the doctor's questions.

"Steve, look at me. They're not all the same are they?"

Steve ran his fingers nervously through his hair.

"You know what's going on, Steve. Admit it. You're addiction is saying they're all the same. They're not; your brain knows better. Now, tell me."

"Sherry is different," he mumbled.

"Say it louder. I didn't hear you."

"Sherry is different. She's like the girl down the street. The one your parents would like to meet. I love her. She's bright, capable, and fun to be with."

"How about Deb and Margo?"

"They're fun to be with."

"Fun? Sounds more like they're fill-ins."

"What do you mean by fill-ins?"

"Someone who is used to feed your addiction, but you don't have feelings for."

"They're not like that."

"So you love both of them, too?"

Steve nodded.

"Hmm ... if you had to, which one would you give up?"

Steve's eyes strayed toward the window then settled back on Dr. Pritts. "Would you ask the question again?"

"Never mind. You've already answered."

Steve stared blankly at him. "What else do you want to know?"

Dr. Pritts pursed his lips. "Would you marry Sherry?"

"Marry her ... I-I ..."

"Just as I thought." The doctor laughed. "Do you know why you stammered?"

"Steve pouted. "Ah ... no."

"We're back to your addiction. You responded with a hesitation. Your body knows getting married would cut off your sex supply. The non-response was automatic."

"God, I can't believe it. So where do we go from here?"

"It's back to our plan. One step at a time."

Steve slid forward in the chair. "What's the goal for this week?"

"You say no to everyone else and pledge you'll *not* sleep with anyone but Sherry."

"I have a date with Mary Ann."

"Cancel it."

Steve looked him in the eye. "Just like that?"

"Just like that. You have to start sometime. Will you do that?"

"How about we wait a week?"

The doctor stood, walked toward the door then turned toward Steve. "Wait a week and I'll relinquish you as a patient."

Steve sucked in a deep breath. "Okay … I'll do it."

"Good. I'll see you next Thursday."

***

On the receptionist's cue, Steve strode into the doctor's office. He flopped down in the familiar chair and took a slug of water.

"Well, how did it go?" Dr. Pritts asked.

"I cancelled my date with Mary Ann, told her I had to represent the Secretary at a reception."

"And?"

"I had a couple of opportunities but I played it cool."

"Excellent. How did you feel about that?"

"The first few days it was really difficult. I kept looking at boobs, saying to myself, forget it, you've seen hundreds. Then, I realized there was only one day before I'd be with Sherry."

"Do you think you could do that for a month?"

"A *month*? Couldn't we take a smaller step, maybe two weeks?"

"Would you feel more comfortable with that?"

"I think so."

"Okay, you're on your own for two weeks. We'll schedule our next meeting after that."

Steve's face flushed. "You mean we won't meet next week?"

"Two weeks. You're on your own."

***

The secretary's driver presented his credentials at the West Wing security gatehouse then dropped Steve off at the entrance. He stepped in and took a deep breath.

Stepping up the stairs to the main floor, he passed several Secret Service agents — each standing as if they were invisible. He walked slowly down the hallway to the presidential secretary's office. Glancing at the two agents dressed in regular suits, one standing on each side the large door, he noticed their bulging pockets and telltale earpieces.

The president's secretary confirmed Steve's appointment and directed him toward a chair in the reception area.

Within minutes the door opened. The president stepped out. All eyes shifted toward her. Steve stood and the president motioned to him. Extending her hand, she gave him a soft smile. "It's good to see you again, Steve."

"Thank you, Madam President."

Leading the way, she stepped inside and closed the door behind him. Steve stood in awe, as he did each time he entered her office. She directed him to one of the wingback chairs located by the fireplace, settling into the one across from him.

"How's it going?" she asked.

"Extraordinarily well. Will is on board. The streamlining process has picked up steam. I'm confident we'll be ready when the time is right."

She looked inquisitive. "Tell me more."

"We've finalized the 20 percent reduction plan. Turns out we'll probably be cutting closer to 23 percent of the employees in the department."

"Really. Are you positive?"

"Absolutely. We've sent the plan to legal counsel and then it'll be ready for legislative staff. The savings should be freed up over the next three years."

"Perfect." She stood and strutted around the office like a peacock. "We'll win the budget cutting debate and have money left to invest in the reform effort. God, I'm excited about that."

"It'll be a real feather in your cap."

"I'm more interested in making the reforms." She glanced at Steve. "Last time we talked, you mentioned the five-point plan. How's the first piece coming along?"

"It's almost done. I'll be ready to send you a five-page synopsis by the end of the week. That way you'll have plenty of time to think about it."

"I like that."

"The focus will be on demonstrating basic competencies in grades one through three. It'll be a major shift in public school policy — if a student doesn't pass the competency test at each grade level, he or she will not pass to the next grade — it'll end social promotion!"

"That'll be a big issue on the local level. Some parents will go bananas."

"It's a tradeoff. Current practices have significantly weakened the public schools. Sure, a few mommies and daddies will be upset … one time. I can assure you the next year little Johnny will pass with flying colors."

The president crossed her shapely legs. "You're right about that."

"We'll have some backup procedures — summer school, computer-assisted instruction and retesting — so you'll be home free on that count."

"I can still see them ranting about their little babies."

"Maybe so," Steve agreed without conviction. "There are a couple of big issues you'll have to address before I put the final touches on the proposal."

She uncrossed her legs and leaned forward in the chair. "What kind of issues?"

"It depends on which way you go."

"I want to hear your preferences."

"The first question deals with the applicability of the program. Shorthand — should it be extended to all students?"

"You're talking about students in voucher programs and charter schools."

"Yes, if the school received any federal dollars will they be included."

"That's a hotbed … let me think about that. Next."

"Who administers the program — the states or the feds?"

"What do you think?"

"I'm betting on the states."

She twisted her hands in her lap. "At least that's a battle inside the party. Anything else?"

"Nope, that's it."

The president stood and paced the room. "Okay, go for the whole thing — all students are covered and it's administered by the states."

"This might be the time when you raise the 20 percent reduction plan."

"Perhaps." She stepped his way and leaned over the back of the sofa next to his chair. "I'd like to celebrate the reduction plan. Would you have a drink with me?"

Steve's eyes widened. "Ah, sure."

Janet drifted toward the public entrance then turned a doorknob he hadn't notice. Pushing the door open, she motioned for him to follow her through the opening, then closed the door behind them.

He looked around, flabbergasted. "Has this always been here?"

"Yes. Most people think it's simply another door to the hallway, but it goes to this private study."

"Amazing."

"There's a small fridge in the corner. Would you get the olives? I'll fix you a Tanqueray."

"Sure." He pulled the jar from the fridge and handed it to her. Janet pulled two glasses from a small cabinet. "Have a seat." She pointed to a small settee in the middle of the room.

Gawking around, Steve eased down on the small sofa. "So, is this room part of the original building?"

"From the beginning." She handed him a gin then poured herself a Jack Daniels on the rocks. Joining him on the loveseat, she clinked his glass. "Here's to our success."

He raised his glass. "And here's to you."

"Are you enjoying D.C.?"

"Yes. I have a terrific apartment and … the pieces are coming together at the office."

"Good for you." She took a sip then looked him in the eye. "Have you heard from Lizbeth?"

"Not a word," he replied quickly. "Did I mention her daughter's accident before?"

"Yes, she was very emotional when I heard about it and called her." Janet took a long sip then held her glass up. "Would you fix me another, please?"

"Of course." Steve headed for the tiny sink.

She slipped off her tweed jacket and hung it on the back of a straight-back chair. Easing over to the center of the sofa closer to where Steve had been sitting, she loosened the button on her Mandarin collar of her blouse and leaned back.

Steve handed her the glass filled to the brim. "Careful, I added too much ice."

She steadied the glass and leaning over it carefully, took a sip. "I may not be able to go back to work."

"Sounds good to me," he jested.

Their eyes connected. "Where do you go in your spare time?"

"Spare time? I've been burning the midnight oil. I have this boss ..."

She talked over him. "Careful now. I bet there are other reasons why you're up at night."

"Why would you say something like that?"

She gave him a peck on the cheek. "I've seen how you've looked at me."

"Geez, can't a guy look?"

"Not that way." Contrary to what she was saying, she loosened a button on his shirt and slid her hand inside.

He pulled back. "What kind of a guy do you think I am?"

"I've given that some thought." She pulled him close and kissed him on the lips. Steve wrapped his arm around her and kissed her gently for an extended time.

"How would you like to get together sometime?"

"Me?"

She gave a fake glance around the room. "I don't see anyone else."

Steve stared into her eyes for a long moment. "Would you mind if I asked you a question?"

A furrow parted her brow. "Okay," she said, hesitantly.

"I'd like to know more about your husband," he said, already knowing her history.

She cocked her head to one side. "You're the first man to ask. Is that important?"

"Kind of ... I don't want to be caught with my pants down."

"Fair enough. Jeb and I met after I won the Miss America title. I fell for him hook, line and sinker. Later I learned I was his trophy. I gave him everything except the kid he wanted."

"And then?"

"He picked up some floozy and got the son he wanted." Steve's eyes widened, not knowing that aspect of the story. "He wanted a divorce. I said no way; but told him, here's the deal, you can do your thing with anyone, as long as you pay for what I want. Money means nothing to him so he said, 'Fine.' He paid for my first gubernatorial race in Texas and I was on my way."

"Do you ever see him?"

"Nah, once in a while the chief of staff will hand me a news clipping about him being seen with some broad in a faraway place."

"And the media says nothing."

"You probably noticed, I got beat-up in my first race; after that our relationship became old news."

"So I won't get caught with my pants down?"

She giggled, and planted a firm kiss on him. "Only by me."

***

Dr. Pritts welcomed Steve with a bottle of water and motioned him in. "Well, how'd it go?"

"Fine, couldn't have been any better."

"Was Sherry the only one?"

Steve paused slightly. "Yes."

A frown crossed Dr. Pritts's face. "You're positive ... no sex, no urges?"

Steve's mouth quivered at the corners. "I had an urge."

"Wanta tell me about it?"

"I can't."

"You mean you won't."

Steve shook his head. "No, I can't."

"Can you describe the circumstance?"

"We were sitting on the sofa and she kissed me. I felt my pants move."

"Did anything happen?"

"No, that was it."

"You're going to have experiences like that. It's important to keep reminding yourself — those urges are your addiction calling. You need to stay in control."

"I know Doc, but she's not an ordinary woman. She's powerful, sexy, and bright as hell."

"I don't care if she's the President of the United States. You can't expect your dick to make a logical decision." He chuckled. "It has one eye and only sees one thing — a pussy!"

Steve laughed. "Good point."

"Sounds like you're ready for the next step."

Steve's eyes brightened. "O-okay."

"You're going for a month this time, and you're not going to Margo's party."

"Doc, that's a lot to ask. Could we phase up to that?"

"It is the phase-in. Spend every weekend with Sherry. I don't want you to be with another woman. Deal?"

"I-I …"

"Steve, is that a deal?"

He gave the doctor a positive nod. "Yes."

***

FBI — Clarksburg, West Virginia
Criminal Justice Information Services Division

A young staffer looked at the computer flashing ALERT. "It looks like the new program is working."

"Which one?" her supervisor asked.

"The one that identifies anyone associated with TWO or more subversive or questionable groups."

"Let me see it."

She handed him the report. "Do you know him?"

He skimmed the report:

Name:	Steven Schilling	
Previous:	None	
Possible Contacts:	Kuratong Baleleng	Philippines
	Bilderberger	Netherlands

"The name sounds familiar. I'll have to check him out."

CHAPTER ELEVEN

Steve followed Dr. Pritts's advice for the next two weeks, spending most of the weekends with Sherry. Nothing could have been better. The two fell into a pattern as young lovers might — laughing and joking, doing crazy things — their feelings deepened. *I can't believe how much I love her. We're a perfect pair. It's like she's the girl of my dreams. And being with her in bed, she's unreal, more of a woman than I've ever had.*

The third weekend was a challenge. Sherry was gone with girl friends for a weekend getaway that had been planned for six months. Steve insisted she go and then realized Saturday was the first of the month when Margo had her party. At first he thought nothing about that. Friday night he went to a movie and had a later dinner out. Feeling exhausted from a busy week, he checked into bed early and woke up Saturday feeling refreshed.

The day started out fine, with regular chores around the apartment, vacuuming and straightening up. Having an unusual burst of energy, Steve cleaned the sliders then went grocery shopping to replenish his supplies.

Ready for lunch, he made a BLT, grabbed a bag of chips and plopped down in his recliner to watch the Cardinals and Dodgers baseball game of the week. The screen came alive with a glaring message, "Game Delay, Rain. Stay tuned."

"Shit," he said to himself. Irritated, he flipped the set off. "I need to find something to do."

Stirring around aimlessly for another hour, he washed the towels and sheets, rearranged the can goods in the pantry, cleaned the fridge and flipped the TV back on — "Game Postponed."

"Crap!"

Opening his briefcase, he pulled out a handful of reports and dug into work. Reading the last one, he glanced at his watch — four o'clock. "Got any more ideas?"

A vision of Deb at Margo's party flashed though his mind. Dr. Pritt's advice followed close behind. *Avoid the situation. Mind your p's and q's.* He plopped three olives into a water glass of ice and filled it full of gin. Setting the glass on a cork coaster on the side table, he sank into his recliner. *I can't believe how difficult it is to avoid an opportunity. Jesus Christ, if Dr. Pritts only knew.*

He thought about putting on a porno film. "Goddammit, put on your thinking cap, Schilling."

Reaching into the magazine rack, he pulled out the latest issue of *Hustler,* skimmed through the boobs and butts, and tossed it aside. "You crazy bastard." A thought about Charisse giving him a blow job warmed his thighs. He wished she'd be coming over tomorrow. *I need her so much. I'm calling Margo to see if she'll ask Charisse to stop by.* He reached for the phone then caught himself and stopped. *Christ, what's wrong with you?*

Steve downed his gin then sucked on the last olive. A vision of Deb's naked body flashed across his mind again. Margo, Hannah and the others he'd recently enjoyed, also appeared. A cold sweat ran down his forehead. His hand slid down into his blue jeans, and he fondled himself. "Crap," he shouted then jumped up and paced the room. Unable to stop playing with himself, a firm erection formed. He started to stroke then stopped and bolted for the bathroom.

Throwing off his clothes, he slammed the shower door behind him, and lathered up. One hand then the other then both, he stroked. *God, that feels good. Take your time … make it last. His mind went blank as he shot out of control.* Gasping and panting, he wished there was more.

Exiting the shower and quickly drying everything but his hair, Steve flopped on the bed. Still breathing hard, he closed his eyes and dozed off. It was after ten when he stirred again. "Too late to go now," he said to himself.

Sunday morning brought no relief. He wished he had called Margo about Charisse. *Now there was nothing. Alone, like always.*

Nothing. How can I manage? Staring at the television, he fell into his old routine — a glass of gin, the *Hustler* magazine — flipped on a porno tape, masturbated then drifted into a stupor.

***

Walking slowly into his office on Monday morning, Steve noticed the blinking light. He picked up the pace, headed for the phone, flicked the button and listened.

"Steve, this Bradley Welton, the president would like to talk with you ASAP. Call me."

He picked up the phone and dialed direct.

"Steve," he heard, "thanks for calling back. The president would like to discuss her thoughts on the phase one campaign. Can you come over at five?"

"Of course. Should I bring anything?"

"No." Bradley hung up.

Steve closed his door, filled a mug with steaming coffee and eased onto his swivel-rocker. *Is something wrong? Damn, I can't imagine anything being that urgent.* Unable to come up with a response, he went through the motions the rest of the day.

At 4:40 the secretary's driver produced his credentials at the West Gate, dropped Steve off at the White House, and a few minutes later he was waiting outside her office in the reception area.

Precisely at five o'clock the president stepped in the doorway and motioned to him. Steve stood and followed her, walking double-time. She closed the door and pointed to a large chair on the left side of the fireplace, picked up a pad from her desk, and slid onto the chair across from him.

He sat erect, wondering if he'd done something wrong.

"Thanks, for coming over on such short notice," she said without a smile.

"No problem." Steve forced a partial grin.

"The game plan for the phase one campaign came to me over the weekend. There's not much time so I wanted your reactions as soon as possible."

Steve sighed inside. "Fine, fire away."

"On Friday Will told me the skids were greased for passage of phase one — we have a deal."

"Terrific." Steve opened his pad.

"We'll control the tests, collect the data and establish norms and cutoff points. The states will administer the program and may change up to 10 percent of the questions. Competency testing will not exceed four days per school year."

"Does it apply to all students?"

Janet nodded, her expression optimistic. "Everyone ... charters, voucher programs and the like — any student that's in a school that receives federal dollars."

"Wow, how did you pull that off?"

"When I mentioned the possibility of state involvement, the Republicans went nuts. They wanted state control at almost any costs. When we agreed, they wanted more. I said, 'Look you have your nose in the tent.' They got the message that I'd be open."

"How will you handle the debates?"

"We'll pound away like usual. They'll act like they're having a tizzy — go bananas to please the right — then the leadership will swallow hard and vote for the inclusion of charter-school programs."

"Makes sense in Congress. Do you think the public will get stirred up?"

"I assume we'll have a real dogfight on our hands. We have to come up with a strategy to head that off."

"How do you plan to do that?"

That's exactly why I wanted to talk with you. I'm planning to host a Governor's reception around the Christmas tree lighting, but I haven't thought about anything beyond that."

"Great idea. With the Governors involved you'll have fifty advocates just like that." Steve snapped his fingers.

"That's what I figured. Any thoughts about additional steps we might take?"

"That'd be a great kickoff." He ran his fingers across his lips as if pondering the concept. "After that I'd suggest you take the media roadshow to Tennessee."

"Tennessee? Jesus Steve, I want national exposure. Why would I go there?"

"Three reasons."

She slid onto the edge of her chair, poised to write in her tablet. "Okay, let's hear them."

"First, Tennessee is light years ahead of the rest of the country on competency testing. Governor Alexander introduced testing for math, science and computer education in 1983. You can tell them we'll use their tests in the first three years."

"Hmm, I like that," Janet murmured as she jotted a note.

"The whole state will eat it up. If you can get Lamar Alexander on board it'll be a piece of cake. You could jointly host the event at his home in Nashville."

"I like the idea of joining hands across the aisle. But ... Nashville, how will we get the media to notice?"

"I know how to get the males interested." She looked confused as he continued, "We'll have Dolly Parton sing the national anthem. She's from Nashville; that'll get their attention."

"Steve, that's perfect. I can't believe you. I've been fretting about it all weekend. That'll be a perfect way to gage public support. After that St. Louis, Atlanta, Orlando and Dallas, the rest will fall into place."

He flipped his palms in the air. "What can I say?"

She strutted around him like she'd made a great discovery. "You could say you'd like a drink."

Steve leaned close to her as she stopped in front of him, and whispered, "How about a drink?"

Grinning, she eased toward the doorframe. Running her hand onto the doorknob, she opened the door opened, motioned him in and closed it.

"I need to unwind," she said. "Would you fix the drinks?"

"Of course." Steve walked over to the small bar, filled two glasses with ice and completed them with booze. Turning with a drink in each hand, he froze.

Standing in a red bra, bikini panties and red spike heels, her index finger beckoned him. Steve's eyes searched her perfect body — not an inch extra on her waist or hips. She took her glass and pointed toward the straight-back chair she'd slid to the middle of the room.

He followed her signal.

"Whenever I find a solution like this, I get a rush, and feel like dancing."

Steve's eyes brightened.

She took a long sip, moved her feet to the beat of her campaign theme song then turned on the tape for "These Boots are Made for Walkin'."

Steve sipped on his gin, taking in every move as she paraded around the room. Stopping in front of him, she shoved her empty glass toward him. "Would you fix me another?"

He accommodated, then eased back onto the chair. She downed half a glass, set the drink on the end table and slow danced in front of him — her hands moved sensuously around her breasts then down her sides, caressing her hips.

Stepping closer to him, she flicked the top button of his shirt and pulled on his belt. "Take them off."

His urges fired, an erection made Steve fumble with his pants.

She ripped off her panties and tugged on his boxers. He pulled them off and tossed them aside.

Janet slid onto his lap and pushed against him. Grasping her hot body, Steve pulled her tight. They continued the throbbing rhythm until she rose and slid a condom on his erection. Clamping her hands on his shoulders, and wasting no time, she eased him in.

Locked as one, Janet increased the pace then slammed against him. He tried not to come too soon. *Inhale, take a calming breath. Be patient, take your time. Let her desire build.* Try as he might it wasn't long before her intensity overwhelmed him. "Oh my God," he called out.

She smiled smugly, arched her body and shoved one last time. Fire burning in him, he went lightheaded. Gasping, every breath left their bodies.

***

Standing in line behind two Governors and their wives, Steve looked to the far southeast end of the White House's East Room — George Washington's 1797 portrait, rescued from the 1814 fire hung on the right. A companion portrait of Martha on the left. In the center a small raised stage and podium was flanked by two American flags.

118

Mr. and Mrs. Alexander stood at the right garnering the attention of most of the new governors and their wives.

Governors George Bush and Frank Keating, along with their wives, took their seats near the front of the room. Laura Bush pointed to the crystal glasses and goblets, then the elaborate chandeliers, noting they were from the same era. Pete Wilson from California and Jim Edgar from Illinois eased into chairs at the adjoining table and chatted about the unique centerpieces of red, white and blue flowers.

Making his way toward Leslee, Lamar's wife, Steve worked the crowd as he had done hundreds of times. He waited for the right opportunity then turned toward her and extended his hand. "Good evening, I'm Steve Schilling."

"I'm pleased to meet you, Dr. Schilling. Lamar has been impressed with your leadership initiative."

"Thank you, I've read all of his papers. His insights provided direction for the entire competency-based testing movement."

She raised an eyebrow. "How nice of you to say that. He'll be pleased to hear your comment."

Steve stepped closer. "The president is so pleased with his willingness to play tonight."

"Lamar's thrilled with the opportunity. He's an accomplished classic and country pianist, I'm sure everyone will enjoy it."

"I remember growing up to the 'Tennessee Waltz.'"

"That's his favorite. Tell the president he's honored by her request."

"Will do." Steve winked.

Following a five-course dinner featuring filet mignon and lobster tail, the president approached the lectern. A hush fell over the room. She reminded the group of her governorship in Texas and stressed the important leadership responsibilities they shared. The governors ate it up as she piled on the praise.

Pausing a moment to let her words soak in, she glanced at Steve then looked back at the audience. Reminding them again of her role as governor, she praised them for their sustained leadership, and moved into her script. "We are finalizing legislation for the elementary competency-based testing program. Its foundation comes from the sterling work Lamar did as governor of Tennessee." She paused to acknowledge him. "It is his example that gives me confidence all of you could do the same. The longer I've been in Washington, the more convinced I am that programs of this type cannot be run effectively from here." She looked around the room while they waited for her to continue. "With that in mind, I am pleased to announce that the competency-based program will be administered by the states."

Suddenly every eye in the room looked up. Dazed at first, soon a loud roar echoed through the room. The standing ovation that followed was like none she'd ever heard.

Letting the group bask in their glory, she raised one hand. The cheering and applause continued. She stood with a smile, soaking it in, then repeated her hand signal and finally, raised both arms over head.

The group took their seats.

"And in case you're wondering," she continued. "You'll have the capability to tailor the tests around the needs in your states."

The group interrupted with another resounding ovation.

"Thank you, thank you." She hesitated, waiting for the governors to be seated. "And now we have one more highlight for the evening."

They were spellbound, with all eyes on her. She winked at Lamar then pointed to the specially designed Steinway supported by three large gilded eagles. "Lamar, will you do the honors?"

He stood and walked like a peacock to the piano bench and flipped his imaginary tails.

The crowd chuckled.

He stretched his fingers and flawlessly played the "Tennessee Waltz."

Standing at the conclusion, his former colleagues gave him a thunderous round of applause and cheered. "More ... More!"

Stepping onto the stage, the president waved her hands, spurring them on, and then pointed to the grand.

Lamar flicked open his suit coat, settled in on the bench and played the "Flight of the Bubble Bee."

The group clapped and cheered bringing a fitting closing to the party.

Secret Service agents watched as the attendees made their way into Cross Hall then out the door. When most of the crowd had departed, the president stepped closer to the tall, square-shouldered agent standing next to her. Nodding toward Steve, she whispered in Tony's ear — not a facial muscle moved — she smiled up at him.

Agent Petrarca walked across the room, stopped by Steve's side, said a few words then led the way down Cross Hall. Near the end, the two turned to the right and waited for the elevator.

When the door opened, he motioned Steve inside. A staff member nodded. At the second floor, the staffer signaled for Steve to leave. "The president will be up shortly," he said, as the door closed.

***

President Stetson rushed into the living room. "How'd it go?" she asked.

Steve looked up from the sofa. "It couldn't have gone better. You were terrific."

"Thanks for chatting with Lamar's wife."

"No problem. She understands the process. She was a former staffer for John Tower."

"Oh yes, I had forgotten that." Janet wiped her brow. "I'm going to take a quick shower. You can open the Champagne. It's in an ice bucket in the bedroom."

"I can handle that." Steve followed her into the bedroom, slipped off his clothes and put on the robe she'd laid out for him. He popped the cork and moved the ice bucket between the two wingback chairs on the left side of the fireplace.

Janet paraded toward him, looking as sexy as hell.

He filled their glasses then toasted. "Here's to the best president ever."

She clinked his glass and took a sip. "At least the best female one." She laughed.

The two chatted for over an hour, debriefing each other on the various segments of the event. He poured the last of the Champagne then opened another bottle. "Ready to dance?"

She leaned back with a frown.

"I thought maybe you got a rush from events, too," he said with a grin.

"Dreamer. I get a rush when I come up with a solution to something that's bugging me."

"I'll have to remember that." He laughed.

"Forget the dancing. Let's move to the main agenda." She stood and took him by the hand.

***

Dr. Pritts sat in his leather chair waiting for Steve to settle in across from him. "It looks like you're on a roll," he said. "Passing the Education Operations Bill with a two-thirds majority was a real coup."

"It's part of the president's strategy to break the gridlock."

"Sounds like more is coming with her proposal to delegate control of the competency-testing program to the states. She doesn't sound like a Democrat."

"She's very practical, has common sense, and knows the end game is more important than the insignificant turf wars."

"Too bad we don't have more politicians like her." The doctor laid Steve's file aside. "Well, how'd the month go?"

"It couldn't have been any better."

"No glitches at all?" His eyebrows shot up.

"Hmm, well there was one two weeks ago. Sherry was out of town, and the usual Saturday night party was on."

"Did you go?"

"No, but I went through hell, and acted like I have before." Steve shook his head remembering the frustration.

"None of that is important, Steve. You coped. Fact is you didn't go. Anything else happen?"

"No," he lied.

"Steve, the road to recovery is not going to be a straight line. There'll be twists and turns, ups and downs. You'll be tested again and again. You need to stay the course. Most importantly, you must be truthful to yourself and with me. We can't afford to let things slide. Do you understand?"

"Yes, of course."

"Good. Next time we'll talk about the difference between making love and being *in* love."

CHAPTER TWELVE

Talking on the telephone three weeks later, President Stetson paced behind her desk in the Oval Office. Catching the eye of Bradley Welton standing in the doorway, she motioned for him to move the wingback chairs forward. He picked up her hand signal and slid the two chairs in front of her desk.

She continued her phone conversation.

Bradley motioned to Ira Magaziner, her senior adviser for policy and planning, to take the chair on the right. Easing into the other chair, he struck up a quiet conversation with Ira. He probed to learn all he could from the world-renowned business consultant, whose tenacity was out-shone only by his brilliance and creative solutions.

The president started to wind down her half-hour conversation. "Yes, and thank you again, Lamar. I really appreciate your help and thanks too, for opening your home. It couldn't have gone better." Listening for several more moments, she nodded repeatedly. "Yes, thanks again; and please give my regards to Leslee."

She hung up, eased down into the executive swivel-rocker and looked up at the two. "Do you have the campaign figured out?"

Bradley turned to Ira then back to the president. "Just about," he said. "I still like the plan we discussed earlier. Stops in St. Louis, Atlanta and Orlando should give us a good measure of the center of the country. St Louis is one of the most conservative big cities in the country, so we'll learn quickly how it'll play with them. Atlanta is a strong urban area and Orlando should give us a good sense of the feelings of seniors."

"Dallas should go well; I've always had a strong following there," she said.

"Right," Bradley continued, "and then we'll head west — Denver, L.A. and San Francisco. We should be in good shape by then. If need be, I'll add Chicago, Cleveland, and New York City on the way back."

"Sounds good to me," she said and looked at Ira. "Do you still want Dr. Schilling to do the whistle-stops in the Midwest?"

"Yes," Ira answered, nodding his head. "He really hits it off with the small-town folks."

She looked away from Ira. "Any other suggestions, Bradley?"

"Sounds like you have it covered. But, we don't have a backup."

"Don't worry, I'll be fine." She stood and shook hands with each of them. "Thanks, again for your leadership."

***

On Air Force One, President Stetson sipped a Jack Daniels then closed her eyes. After briefing the press corps, Bradley Welton eased onto the seat across from her. "How did we do?" she asked.

"They were gentle today but one more day like this and we're in deep trouble. The Save Our Schools folks are better organized than we thought. They're planning a rally in Atlanta at the same time as your speech. Rumor has it that they're hoping for three thousand in attendance."

"Wow, anything we can do?"

"Stay the course and keep hammering away."

***

ST. LOUIS POST-DISPATCH

TESTING GAINS LITTLE SUPPORT

SAVE OUR SCHOOLS PROTEST DRAWS 1500

St. Louis — President Janet Stetson made the case for competency-based testing in grades 1 through 3 as eloquently as possible. Charter school representatives were unimpressed. Later in the day a Save Our Schools protest drew over 1500 angry parents.

Two days later the headlines read:

THE ATLANTA JOURNAL-CONSTITUTION

SCHOOL PROTEST OUTSHINES PREZ

PROTESTORS DRAW 4000 IN PARK RALLY

Atlanta — President Stetson's centerpiece program for educational reform took another hit today as support in the polls for the competency-based program fell to 38 percent.

The following day support fell to 35 percent as the *Orlando Sentinel* editorial blasted the initiative. On Air Force One that night, Bradley told the president several Senate votes were wavering. "Without their support the Elementary Competency Testing Bill will be dead on arrival."

Looking pale and tired, she downed a second drink. "I have a strong base in Dallas. I'm positive I'll turn the tide."

Bradley seemed less than optimistic. "We have to hit them with something that will catch them off guard."

"Let me know if you come up with something. I'm taking a nap."

***

The Secret Service agent stepped aside. Bradley knocked softly on the door. Hearing no answer, he rapped harder, and heard a rustling inside the plush Ritz-Carlton suite. A weak voice followed, "Who is it?"

"It's Bradley, Madam President."

"Just a minute."

He waited patiently until the door opened. Standing in a robe, without makeup, her hair uncombed, Janet motioned him in.

"Are you okay?" he asked.

She pointed to her throat. "I can't talk. I have laryngitis," she murmured. "The doctor is on his way up."

"Would you like some hot tea?"

"No," she whispered.

Following a light knock, the door opened and her personal physician walked in. He took one look inside her mouth. "Yes, it's laryngitis. I want you in bed, right now."

Looking tired and drawn, with dark circles under her eyes, she shook her head.

The doctor glared, led her to the bed and tucked her in. "Take at least a week off, maybe more. I'll be back with your medication." He turned for the door then paused in front of Bradley. "Cancel the rest of the tour, she's exhausted."

Bradley walked to her bedside. "You heard it. I don't have a choice."

She shook her head sharply, side to side. "No, no, no," she mumbled. "We'll lose it all."

Bradley gave her a consoling smile. "There's no choice."

Janet motioned him closer. "Have Steve do it," she croaked out.

He questioned. "Steve Schilling?" She nodded. Doubting the option, he asked, "Have you heard him speak?"

The president motioned toward a notepad on the night stand. Bradley picked it up and handed it to her. She reflected a moment then jotted a few words down and handed it to him.

Steve is extremely articulate. He's a former university president and has given hundreds of speeches. You've seen him perform in cabinet.

Bradley read the note. "He's excellent on his feet but you're talking a major speech in front of seven hundred people," Bradley lamented. "He could blow the entire plan. How about Secretary Chandler?"

"He's a turn off," she mouthed, stiffly. She motioned for the pad again, wrote a note on it and shoved it toward him.

I want Steve to do it. The vice president is flying to San Diego tomorrow. Have him pick up Steve and fly him down on Air Force Two.

"Has he started the whistle-stop tour in the Midwest?" She nodded. "Okay. I'll have him here as soon as possible."

***

Steve stood in the wings of the Ritz-Carlton ballroom. Bradley walked slowly to the podium, tapped the microphone, and cleared his throat. "Ladies and gentlemen, I'm Bradley Welton, chief of staff for the president." He paused. "President Stetson has laryngitis, and regretfully sends her regards."

The onlookers released a collective moan.

"Her doctor has ordered bed rest and suspended her activities for the next ten days." He hesitated. "Fortunately, Dr. Steve Schilling, Deputy Secretary of Education is present and will deliver her remarks."

A courteous applause sprinkled the room.

Steve stepped to the podium and acknowledged the group.

Following the president's script, he spouted the facts: "If you start out behind in the first three grades, you'll never catch up … Nationally, only 18 percent of low-income children are proficient in reading by the fourth grade. The US has fallen from first to twenty-fifth in academic achievement, out of the world's thirty largest industrialized nations."

Sensing the crowd was not with him, he paused then threw the speech in the air, papers scattering across the dais. The audience let out a collective gasp.

He removed the microphone from its holder and carried it in front of the podium. Slowly he raised the mike to his mouth. "Ladies and gentlemen, here's the message from the president."

The listeners rustled.

"First, the facts. There is a small group of citizens calling themselves 'Save our Schools.' They want to use federal dollars for lunch programs to pay for equipment, to build classrooms, and pay the heat bill." He paused, letting his words soak in. "But, they don't want their privileged kids to take the same tests or achieve the same scores as our kids and grandchildren. To quote my grandmother, 'That's a bunch of hooey.'"

Chuckles filled the auditorium.

"Point is they're not talking about our schools; they're talking about their schools — schools that cater to an elite few and often teach their own beliefs." Steve slowed, sensing the crowd's growing attention. "It's plain and simple: If you can't cut the mustard there's no hot dog for lunch."

Laughter filled the room. He lowered the hand mike then slowly raised it back up to his mouth and stated, louder. "If you can't cut the mustard there's *no free lunch*."

The audience shouted. "No free lunch."

Knowing he'd hit the nail on the head, he paused then shouted, "If you can't cut the mustard ..." Pointing the mike toward the crowd, they instantaneously finished the phrase.

"There's no free lunch," echoed through the hall.

Acting as if he didn't hear them, he cupped a hand around his ear and repeated. "If you can't cut the mustard ..."

"There's no free lunch!" rang out and then the crowd chanted, "If you can't cut the mustard, there's no free lunch!"

Steve waved to the standing crowd, turned, and walked smartly off the stage.

The crowd continued to chant. "If you can't cut the mustard, there's no free lunch. No free lunch!"

Reaching Bradley, Steve smiled broadly as the two embraced. "I can't believe it. You nailed it," his earlier doubter said.

The crowd emptied the auditorium, continuing to shout, "No free lunch."

"You were terrific," Bradley said. "I can't wait to see the morning paper."

"Me too," Steve said. "I'm starved. Do you know where there's a steakhouse?"

Bradley shook his head. A stagehand standing nearby said, "There's a Morton's down the street."

"Great." Steve motioned to Bradley. "Let's go."

"Go ahead and get a table. I'll catch up in a few minutes. I need to update the president."

***

Sucking on the last olive, Steve ordered another Tanqueray. *This is the best I've felt since I've been in Washington. I'm on a real high!*

Bradley slid in on the other side of the booth. "The president was elated. She listened to your speech on NPR. Here's a note she jotted to you."

Steve unfolded the small piece of paper.

Steve, you were terrific. I felt a rush!

Janet

Glancing at his watch, Steve tried not to give away the point.

"Do you understand the rush part?" Bradley asked.

Steve stammered, "Ah … I-I guess it's like a rush of adrenaline when you get it right."

"Makes sense." Bradley looked around at the restaurant's dark rich woods and dimly-lit octagon-shaded lights hanging above. "This place is pretty spectacular."

Steve held up the large leather-bound menu. "Wait till you see the steak selections."

Opening his, Bradley's eyes widened. "Looks like eeny, meeny, miny moe."

"I'm having the peppercorn rubbed strip, and onion soup."

"Sounds wonderful. I think I'll stick with a New York strip and a Caesar salad."

"Can't go wrong with that," Steve said.

Bradley gave Steve a questioning look. "How did you come up with that slogan?"

"It just kind of happened."

"Things like that don't 'just happen.' C'mon, give me the straight scoop."

"No, really." Steve flashed his Cheshire smile. "Coming down on the plane, one the reporters said, 'sounds like they want to have their cake and eat it too.' That got me thinking ... school lunch programs popped in my mind, then hotdogs and mustard. I jotted down all kinds of phrases on the plane — nothing worked. It didn't come together until I actually said it at the podium."

"It's a winner I'll tell you that."

Steve mused. "Who'd ever thunk it?"

***

Ten days after Steve's euphoric speech in Dallas, he walked into his apartment, tossed his sport coat on the chair and flopped down in the recliner. His mind still swirling after six speeches — *one high after another* — it'd been a whirlwind experience.

He glanced at the blinking light on the phone, clicked through the messages then listened to three again. "Steve, it's Mary Ann, give me a call." He pressed the button. "Steve, it's Deb. Let's get together." He clicked. "Steve, it's Margo, thought you'd like to know Kim will be at the next Saturday night party."

Steve's face glowed with urgent memories. *It's been five months since I've seen her. I don't care about Dr. Pritt's advice. I have to see her.*

The week passed in a blur and before he knew it, Steve was standing in his usual position on Margo's balcony, staring down at the front entrance. He waited impatiently for the black limousine to appear. Seeing her step out of the limo, his heart pounded. He ran to the elevator and waited.

Kim peeked out as the door slowly opened then rushed toward him. Steve grabbed her by the waist and twirled her around then put her down and kissed her repeatedly on the cheeks and nose.

"It good to see you," she said. "How you been?"

"I've been great. How about you?"

Her eyes saddened. "Father's heart failed."

"I'm so sorry to hear that."

"He happy to see me. We visit many times … had long talks. He broken man; no reason to live."

"How are *you*?"

"I happy to see you."

He had missed her quaint accent. Steve's heart pounded in anticipation. "I've missed you a lot."

"I want talk with you."

"Sure, I'll get us a drink and meet you at our table."

She nodded and disappeared.

Steve sat their drinks on the table and waited. Kim slipped up behind him, kissed him on the cheek, and eased onto the chair across from him.

He searched her large brown eyes as he placed his hand on hers. "You're the most beautiful woman I've ever met."

She blushed. "You handsome man."

The two talked quietly in the corner. Steve fetched another round and moved his chair next to hers. She slid her arm around his waist and the two snuggled, his hand gently stroking and caressing her thigh.

She stopped talking and gazed into his soft chocolate-colored eyes.

Steve felt the tingle of their connection.

Leaning closer to kiss him on the cheek, Kim said, "I think about you every hour since my father pass away. I want to make you happy."

He smiled. "I want to make you happy too."

"No, it different." She shook her head. "In my country when two people in love, it woman responsibility to make man happy."

Steve gave her his mega-smile.

"It okay for me to make you happy?"

"Of course, you can make me happy any time."

Her starry eyes twinkled. "I make you happy now?"

Steve raised his eyebrows. "Sure."

She reached into a small black purse and held the key in front of him. "Maybe an hour or two. That okay with you."

Liking nothing better than to be with her the rest of his life, he extended his arm around her and held her tight. "You make me happy now."

With a shy smile she looked up, eyes glowing with her desires. She stood up quickly and yanked on his arm. He gladly let her tow him toward the bedroom.

***

Sunday morning, Steve rolled over, awaking to the pleasure of a hand fondling him.

He cracked an eye, saw Charisse's smiling face. "What are you doing here?"

"What's it feel like?" she said, starting to stroke.

"I've missed you so much," he said, in spite of his better judgment.

"Not as much as I've missed you." She slipped off his boxers and climbed on top, kissing him passionately.

Steve grabbed her cheeks and pulled her tight. The two took their time, exploring each other like it was the first time. Charisse slowed and raised her head. "Margo told me you hadn't been to her place for a while. I figured you had finally made a commitment to get better."

He interrupted. "I haven't been fooling around. The last time I was there I turned down two offers. I thought that was really good."

"That's terrific. I'm proud of you." She kissed him on the cheek then slid her leg over his waist and straddled him. Sitting upright, she eased a condom on him and pushed him in. Moving deliberately, she brought him up to a rapid pace.

Steve panted, ready to unload. She slid up and down on him relentlessly, then slowed.

"He gasped. "Don't stop ... now."

She reassured him. "Don't worry, honey. I'm not close."

Steve looked up through blurred eyes. "You gotta be shittin' me."

Her index finger crossed his lips. "Relax, sweetie."

***

The smell of sausage filled Steve's nostrils when he woke again. Rolling out of bed, he headed for the bathroom to splash a little water on his face and brush his teeth. Stepping out of the door, he made a beeline for the coffee pot then watched as Charisse flitted around the kitchen — opening the pantry door, closing the fridge, peeking in the oven.

"What are you doing?" he queried.

"I'm making Scotch eggs, toast and fruit." She paused. "Did I wake you?"

"Mmmm, the sausage did. How do you make Scotch eggs?"

"You boil the eggs, peel them, press a sausage patty around the outside and roll them in crumbs. And bake. They'll be ready in about five minutes."

"Why is today so special?"

"You are. Wait till you read the *Post.* The editorial is all about you."

"Me? Let me see it."

"It's on the table with your V-8."

"Thanks." Steve slipped onto the bench seat and opened the paper to the editorial page.

THE WASHINGTON POST

PRESIDENT PULLS ONE OUT OF THE HAT

A month ago it looked like President Stetson would be home free on her Kennedy-Enzi Competency Testing Bill — the Senate and House were lined up. Then she started a ten-city campaign to further bolster public support. The bottom fell out.

Led by a coalition between Catholic bishops and Protestant ministers, Save Our Schools held protests in several cities. Poll numbers of support fell to 35%.

Confined to her bed with laryngitis, President Stetson called in her top lieutenant, Dr. Steve Schilling, Deputy Secretary for Education, to save the day. Using his now famous slogan — "If you can't cut the mustard, there's no free lunch" — he turned the numbers around. And now, our numbers show the legislation will easily pass the Senate on Tuesday. Kudos to President Stetson and her rising star, Steve Schilling.

Steve laid the paper aside.

Charisse sat his plate on the table. "Pretty good, huh?"

He nodded then told her how he'd come upon his catch phrase. The two laughed. Charisse reached across the table and squeezed his hand affectionately.

"I'm always amazed at how things happen. Like there is some big master plan up in the sky." She crunched on her toast as her mind drifted. "Do you ever think about being intimate?"

Steve's brow furrowed, not understanding. "We're intimate all the time."

"We're not intimate. We just have sex."

"How is that different?"

"This morning I felt *intimate*. Close to you, like you were a part of me."

"And that's different than before?"

"It was more than touching, hugging, kissing and doing it." She took a sip of coffee. "Has your therapist ever gone into detail about intimacy?"

Steve hesitated. "No ... not really."

"It's more than the physical act. There's emotional, cognitive, and experiential intimacy. These are feelings that are shared by two people — building trust, forming personal bonds, exchanging ideas and displaying mutual respect. You've never felt that way, have you?"

"I never thought about it."

CHAPTER THIRTEEN

Bradley Welton sat across from her desk as the president signed a stack of letters. After two or three more, she looked up with a half-smile. "Don't tell me there's another crisis."

"No, no crisis. I've been thinking about those protests and imagining another scenario."

"Another scenario?"

"Can you imagine a series of events had Steve not turned things around? Save Our Schools folks could have seized the opportunity. All hell could have broken loose."

"Like how?"

"Protests could have erupted nationwide. We'd have more concerns than ever about your safety."

"Nothing we haven't been concerned about before. I don't know where you are heading."

Bradley bit his lip in troubled hesitation. "We have to revisit the double idea."

Janet gritted her teeth. "How many times have I told you, Bradley. No double. I don't like the idea. I've never been a fake or phony. I stand for who I am."

"Janet, this is not about you. I'm concerned about the president of the United States, who happens to be Janet Stetson."

She acted as if he'd rang a bell never tolled before. "I never thought about it that way."

"Does that mean I can do it?"

"I'm not sure. Let's talk about it." She thought for a moment and gave him a questioning look. "When would the double come into play?"

"That'd be your decision. We could do events when you're off in the distance, like the lighting of the Christmas tree, or when walking alone in the park."

"Hmm, I don't know."

"Would you at least give me a shot with it?"

Her eyebrows pulled together, as if still unsure.

"Let me do some research for a stand-in. If you don't like my choice, I'll stop. Regardless, you'll have the final say."

She wrinkled her nose. "How long will it take?"

"I can't say, maybe a couple of weeks, a month, who knows."

"Okay, I'll give you a trial period."

"Fair enough."

***

Sitting in the bathroom, Janet finished applying her eyeliner and looked closer in the mirror. She blinked at her image in a double take. "What the …" She turned around and stared. "Who the hell are you?"

"I'm Janet Stetson, the President of the United States."

Janet stood and walked around her, checking every inch of her body. "Stand here in front of the mirror and face me."

The double did as she was told then turned and looked in the mirror at the president.

"What are your measurements?" Janet asked.

"38 - 26 - 36."

"I can't believe this. Let's go into the sitting area so we can talk."

The woman followed Janet and sat down in a wingback chair next to her.

Eyeing her again, the president shook her head. "Where are you from?"

"Lubbock, Texas. I graduated from Texas Tech and received my law degree from the University of Texas at Austin. During my reign as Miss America I met Jeb Stetson and we were married a year later. You know the rest of the story."

"Anyone could have researched that. How do I know you're really the president?"

"Would you like to see the tattoo on my right cheek or the birthmark on my left thigh?"

136

The president shook her head. "When I was governor, what was the senatorial vote on the abortion bill?"

Brushing back her short black hair, the double hesitated. "Seventeen to fourteen, you won!"

Janet raised her brow. "How did you get up here?"

The double winked. "I walked in and took the elevator like always."

"How did you pass through the security checkpoints?"

"Bradley set it up with Tony Petrarca. I simply followed your normal routine, winked at the agent at the desk, like always, and walked in."

"Where did Bradley find you?"

"Ah … our chief of staff." She giggled. "He did his research. I've been a longtime admirer of yours."

The president leaned back in her chair. "Are you finished now?"

"If you want me to be."

"Yes, you may go."

The Janet-double stood and walked out of the bedroom door. Catching her breath, Janet grabbed the phone and called Bradley's cell.

He picked up and before he could say hello. The president said, "I want you in the Oval Office, ASAP." .

Janet hung up and rushed downstairs to the West Wing then waited for Bradley to appear.

Minutes later, he popped his head in the doorway of the Oval Office. "Well … do you approve?"

"Close the door," the president demanded.

Bradley did so then eased gingerly onto the chair in front of her desk.

She paced around him, ending back behind her desk — face red, hands trembling. "Where did you find her?"

"Lubbock, Texas," he jested.

She gave him *the eye*. "That is *not* funny."

"Sorry. The computer picked her out of our pool. She's a quick study."

"I guess … I felt strange when I looked at her … kind of eerie."

"I think she's perfect."

"Too perfect." The president rubbed her neck. "Where do we go from here?"

"We try her out a couple of times and see how she does."

"Try her out? Where? How?"

Bradley scrunched his shoulders. "We'll go for a car ride. Take her shopping at one of your favorite boutiques. Attend some events where's she's seen off in a distance."

"And then?"

"We'll give her a bigger challenge, at one of the state receptions where the two of you can exchange places."

The president looked hard. "How will we do that?"

"You'll go into the bathroom and she'll come out."

"Just like that?"

"Don't worry. The two of you will be wearing the same dress. She'll pass through the room so quickly no one will notice."

Janet wrinkled her nose. "But ..."

"No problem. I'll show her off to a few dignitaries and we'll see how she handles it."

"What am *I* supposed to do?"

Bradley chuckled. "Sit on the toilet."

"Thanks a lot." She fretted, still not okay with the concept.

***

Charlie and Ellen waited in the baggage claim area of the Asheville Airport. Spotting the familiar five o'clock shadow, Ellen waved. "Over here ... Welcome to North Carolina, Steve."

His mega-smile spread as he reached out and hugged her. "Thanks for inviting me to spend Christmas with you folks."

"It's the least we could do. We couldn't imagine you sitting alone in your apartment for a week," Charlie said.

"Besides, I have a lot of catching up to do," Ellen added.

He kissed her on the cheek. "I have plenty of fodder for you."

"I can hardly wait."

Charlie fumed. "At least you two could wait until we have the bags in the car."

Steve chuckled and reached for his bags. "I can handle those. Lead the way."

Charlie pointed, and then walked briskly toward short-term parking. Ellen and Steve lagged behind, chit-chatting along the way. Motioning to Steve, Charlie opened the trunk. "Think you can take a break long enough to put your bags in the trunk?"

Steve smiled at his friend. "I think I can handle that." Sliding in the front seat with Charlie, he asked, "How are things going at the university?"

"Quite well. Carl picked up the reins when you left and hasn't missed a beat."

"I'll have to call him so we can get together for lunch."

"I've taken care of that," Ellen said. "The five of us are having dinner at the Beaver Creek Inn Wednesday night."

"Perfect." A memory of Bev's last night alive flashed through his mind. *Why didn't I wait until the storm was over? We could have gone back to my place rather than risk driving down that ice-covered hill. Bev, I'm so sorry.*

Ellen placed her hand on the front seat and leaned forward. "I can't believe it's been almost four years since the state's vice chancellor was killed."

"Funny you mention that. I was having the same thought about Beverly Harrington. She was highly instrumental in us receiving that commendation from the chancellor for our fiscal turn around."

Charlie turned toward Steve, winked and looked quickly back to the road, "Quite a looker too." Steve remembered the conversations he'd had with Charlie about his affair with her. The conversation ended; they rode in silence as Charlie drove in the darkness toward Midville.

***

The next morning Charlie brewed a pot of coffee while Ellen put the final touches on an egg-sausage-mushroom casserole and placed it in the oven.

Steve staggered down the stairs. "It's almost ten. I can't recall sleeping that late in ages."

"Good for you. At the pace you've been going I figured you'd sleep till noon," Ellen joked.

"Something smells really good."

"A casserole." She lifted her brow. "I have a list of questions. I don't know where to start. Are you ready?"

"Geez, Ellen let the poor guy have a cup of coffee first."

"Okay," she said reluctantly, then glanced out the window. "Looks like that storm is about here."

The three watched the trees bend as the fluttering flakes turned into a heavy snowfall.

"Doesn't look like we're going anywhere this morning," Charlie noted.

Ellen handed Steve a plate with a double helping and two slices of toast. "That's fine with me."

"Wow, this looks great ... sausage and mushrooms."

"You bet, nothing better on a brisk winter morning."

Steve dug in and was half finished before he said a word. "This is wonderful. How do you stay so trim, Charlie? I'd be two hundred and fifty pounds if I ate like this every morning."

"So would I." Charlie rubbed his rounded stomach. "Fortunately, casseroles only come on Sunday."

"It's a good thing."

Steve cleaned his plate and pushed way from the table. "Well Ellen, where do you want me to start?"

"I haven't read much about the Competency-Based Testing Bill passing Congress and its signing by the president."

"I want to hear about cutting the mustard," Charlie said.

"Okay," Ellen said. "Let's start with that."

"There's not much more than what I told you on the phone. I'd been giving a modified version of the president's speech on my junket through Ohio and Indiana. You know Charlie, I never give the same speech twice. I was trying to come up with a catchy phrase but nothing worked. After the speech in Fort Wayne, Sherry said 'They can't have their cake and eat it too.'"

"Sherry?" Ellen questioned.

"Sherry Holmgren. She's my senior advisor; really smart and savvy too. Anyway, that phrase stuck with me, kept bouncing around in my head — no free lunch, hot dogs, mustard and relish — nothing connected. Then I got a call from the chief of staff."

"Bradley Welton," Ellen spouted.

"My brain went numb and my thoughts shifted to her speech. Before I knew it I was in Indianapolis boarding Air Force Two with the vice president."

"Air Force Two? Tell me about it," Ellen directed with piqued interest.

"It's nothing special. The one we were on was a Boeing C-32. There are different planes. Air Force Two doesn't refer to a specific plane. It's the call sign used by traffic control — it's simply a designation for any plane carrying the vice president. He was on his way to San Diego; they changed the flight plan so I could hitch a ride to Dallas."

"Sounds exciting," Ellen said.

"The entire experience was unreal."

"Tell us about the mustard," Charlie requested.

"Like I said, you know how my brain works when I'm at the podium."

"You're telling me." Charlie laughed. "Carl and I have talked about your performances many times. No one better."

"The first time I said something about cutting the mustard and hotdogs. Then it just popped out — 'If you can't cut the mustard, there's no free lunch.' The place went wild."

"How'd you feel going to all of those other cities?" Ellen asked.

"It was a real high. I can't explain it — red carpet treatment, press interviews, banquets. I felt like a king."

"Or maybe the president?" Ellen ventured.

"Hah, there's too much that goes with that. She's under the microscope, twenty-four-seven. It's ten times worse than when I was university president, here."

Ellen aimed a sarcastic question at Charlie. "Can I ask about the legislation *now*?"

Charlie looked away without responding.

"Whataya want to know?" Steve asked.

"Who were the movers and shakers?"

"When it comes to politics there's no one better than President Stetson. She did the arm twisting, must have had a hundred sidebars. By the time the vote came around she had everything orchestrated.

She knew the outcome in both the house and senate before the votes were cast."

"How'd Will Chandler do?" Ellen asked.

"Quite well. He knows the political arena, and how to deal with congress."

"I still don't trust him," Ellen reinforced her comments from their earlier visit.

"He showed his stripes on this one."

"Can you tell us about the second phase of the reform package?"

"Ellen, the guy is going to be here four more days. Give him a break." Charlie stood and gazed out the window. "Looks like the snow didn't last. I have to pick up a couple of tools at ACE and grab some beer at the liquor store. Want to ride along, Steve?"

"Yes. It'd be good to get some fresh air."

***

Late that afternoon Charlie poured three glasses of merlot then helped Ellen place the hors d'oeuvres on the half-moon bar in the kitchen.

"Once again it looks like you've outdone yourself," Steve said to her.

"I still have plenty of questions."

"Of that I have no doubt." Steve grinned, picked up his glass and toasted. "Here's to the best friends ever."

"I'll drink to that," Charlie said.

Steve cast an eye to Ellen. "Phase two of the reform package is next. Right?"

She smiled, didn't say a word.

"It'll build on the early elementary component; competency testing in grades four through six. And, again, if a student fails to reach the minimum cutoff score, he or she will not advance to the next grade."

"I really like that," Charlie said. "It puts real teeth into the program."

"And it makes parents and students understand schools are about academic achievement."

"If a kid is held back, he or she will adjust and move on. Only the parent's ego will be affected," Charlie emphasized. "And that's likely to occur only once."

"By the time a kid reaches middle school, he or she should have the basic skills needed for a successful life," Steve said.

"How about that young boy who's growing facial hair and can't cut it," Ellen asked.

"They're a challenge. We're adding special funding for school districts to establish programs for kids like that. They'll be expected to cover the same competencies as students in other classes, but they'll do it in a more applied manner."

"That's like some of the classes I had in junior high," Charlie added.

"For some students, art or music might be the driving force. For another student, it might be drama, computer technology, or construction skills," Steve added.

"That's terrific," Charlie said. "I like the idea of gaining basic competencies through multiple approaches. We lost the applied concept when we starting pushing everyone into college. It shouldn't be either/or; we need different ways to help kids learn."

"I like that," Steve said, "'help kids learn.' Somehow we've forgotten about learning."

"Here, here," Ellen chanted.

***

On the last night of Steve's visit, Charlie poured their favorite liqueurs — amaretto on the rocks for Steve and port for himself. Ellen went to bed early.

"Once again, we've solved all of the world problems." Charlie paused with a chuckle. He took a sip and queried Steve. "How are you doing?"

"Things haven't changed much."

"How are the sessions with Dr. Pritts progressing?"

"He's extremely insightful. And I like him a lot ..."

"But you're still involved with several women on a regular basis, right?"

"For two or three months I made great progress. Sherry and I were really hitting it off; then it happened with another one."

"Happened? Sure ..."

Steve cut him off. "No, Charlie. It really just *happened*. I had no idea it was coming."

Charlie twisted his mouth into a frown.

"Then a friend returned from a trip. I hadn't seen her in months and before I knew it we were in bed. Next thing I knew, I woke up the next morning and Charisse was back."

"You're back to four?"

Steve looked down at his house slippers. "It all happened in two weeks."

"Shit Steve, when are you going to learn? You can't have your cake and eat it too."

He grinned. "I've heard that before."

"It isn't funny. Sooner or later you're going to hurt someone again."

"I'm not going to hurt anyone. I've told you that before."

"You said that about Lizbeth, Brooke, Bev, Kate, and all the other ones in Arkansas."

Steve hung his head.

"Will Sherry be next?"

Steve's eyes brightened. "I love her, Charlie, I really do. She's smart, works hard, everyone in the office thinks she's terrific ..."

"And she's attractive and has a nice ass. I know ... I've heard it before."

"She asked me to spend Christmas with her at her parents' place in Ohio."

"Why didn't you go?"

"I told her I had longstanding commitment with you folks."

Charlie scowled in disbelief. "Longstanding? We just called last week."

"I fibbed a little. I didn't know how to deal with it."

"You know why you didn't go, don't you?"

Steve shook his head.

"Steve, we talked about it before. It'd be like making another level of commitment." Charlie gave Steve a look of frustration. "Just like the woman you got pregnant in college and didn't marry?"

"Rhonda."

"You didn't want to make a commitment because it would limit your sex supply. Same thing now. Your addiction was talking — that's why you made up the story — you knew it lessened the number of opportunities. You're repeating the same things that happened in the past." Charlie rubbed his bald head. "Tell me about Charisse."

"She's making real progress and has stopped seeing other guys. She broke it off with me for three months and now she's back. The last time we were together she talked about intimacy."

Charlie cocked his head. "Does that mean anything to you?

"Ah ... no."

"C'mon Steve, intimate feelings means she gone beyond just having sex. It's a good sign for her but it means she's vulnerable — the greater her feelings for you, the higher her potential for being hurt. Doesn't that bother you?"

Steve took a deep breath and ran his fingers through his hair. "I never thought about it."

"Shit Steve, you never *thought* about it? Does your dick do *all* of your thinking?" Charlie bit his lip in exasperation. "I don't want to hear about the other ones."

***

FBI Headquarters
935 Pennsylvania Avenue NW
Washington, D.C.

Buried three floors below ground level in the J. Edgar Hoover Building, two staff members discuss the printout from information services.

"Steve Schilling? Is that the same guy who came up with the 'can't cut the mustard' slogan?"

"I don't know," the long-term staffer said. "Let me check."

Less than a minute later, he said. "Sure enough, he's the one."

"What kind of contacts did he have?"

"Hold on," the old man said. "He's been seen with the daughter of a banker in the Philippines whose bank was robbed by the Kuratong Baleleng. We've had her under surveillance for some time."

"That's nothing," the new female staffer said. "How about the Bilderberger's?"

"Just a minute." He hit a few keys on his computer pad. "Here it is; he was spotted three times in Bar Harbor with the wife of one of their members."

"How'd that happen?"

"We've had a tail on her and her husband for some time. Maybe it's diamond smuggling, maybe it's just the Bilderberger's, I don't know, but something is going on."

She grinned. "Sounds more like a romantic getaway than a clandestine operation."

"Agreed. There's no reason to send this up the ladder."

CHAPTER FOURTEEN

Steve walked briskly into Dr. Pritts's office, grabbed a bottle of water from the counter and picked up a *People* magazine. Sitting down in a straight-back chair, he leafed through a few pages then tossed it aside. *Last time Doc said he wanted to talk more about intimacy. Charisse told me she had intimate feelings for me. And Charlie mentioned the hazards of becoming more intimate. Could all of this be a coincidence?*

Dr. Pritts walked by and caught his eye. Steve stood and followed him into his office. "Did you get away for the holidays?" the doctor asked.

"Yes, I spent most of a week with good friends in North Carolina."

"Good for you. Can't beat a little R and R," he said, laying Steve's folder on the table. "It's been more than a month since your last visit. How are things going with our little experiment?"

"It was going fine ..."

The doctor leaned forward on his desk. "And then?"

"It happened with another woman."

"Steve, I've told you before it doesn't just *happen*."

"No Doc, it did. I was fixing drinks and when ..."

"Fixing drinks?"

"Yes, I turned around and she was stripped to her bra and panties, coming on to me."

"Just like that?" he said, in a questioning manner. "Tell me about it."

"Ah ... I can't."

"Steve, you've agreed to tell me everything."

"Honest, Doc, I didn't plan anything. You have to believe me."

Dr. Pritts sighed. "Have you been with her since then?"

"Yes, a couple of times."

"And you're still seeing Sherry, too?" Steve nodded. "How about the sex party?"

"I went last month."

"Jesus, Steve ... two steps forward and three back. Can you tell me about *that*?"

"I hadn't attended one for some time, then I learned Kim was going to be there."

"Kim ... you never mentioned her?"

"She'd been gone for five months. Went to see her father in the Philippines. He passed away. She's a terrific person. I had to see her; I love her."

"Back to square one ... you're seeing Sherry, Kim, and the mystery woman ... I suppose you're in love with all three."

Steve hung his head. "Charisse came back too."

"Four!" The doctor rubbed his hands over his face. "Okay, let's try another approach," he said, pausing a little longer. "How many times have I told you there is a difference between making love and loving a person?"

Steve shrugged and looked away. "Twenty-five, thirty."

"At the end of our last session, I mentioned the topic of intimacy."

Steve perked up. "Yeah, you won't believe it, Doc, intimacy popped up in two different conversations since then."

"Did you learn anything?"

"Hmm." Steve finger-combed his hair. "The more intimate you feel toward a person the greater your vulnerability."

"That's good. Anything else?"

"Um, nothing we haven't talked about."

"I want to ask you a few questions. Maybe that'll help you get the message, okay?"

"Fine, have at it."

"On a hundred-point scale if you're strongly in love with a person, how would you rate that?"

148

Steve looked up at the decorative molding over the window. "Ninety-five to hundred."

"Most people say that." The doctor shifted in his chair. "Vulnerability is one of four measures I use to define intimacy. I'm going to ask you four questions using words like vulnerability." The doctor cleared his throat. "Picture the woman you spent the most time with last month."

"Okay, I have it — Sherry."

"Think about her and the word vulnerability. If you were to go three months without seeing her then learned you'd never see her again, how disappointed would you be? On a ten-point scale, with ten being the highest, rate your feelings."

"Ah, maybe a four."

"Next, when it comes to dialogue with her, do you have open conversations? Do you share ideas and opinions freely?"

"At work or when we're alone?"

"When you're with her, totally."

"Eight."

"Next is transparency. How candid are you with her? Do you share everything, never lying, fibbing or trying to hide anything?"

Steve scrunched his shoulders. "Two."

"The last word is reciprocity. On a personal basis do you have open exchanges and do things cooperatively?"

"Eight."

"Let's see, four plus eight, plus two, plus eight. Twenty-two out of forty possible points. By multiplying your score by two and a half, I can translate it onto a hundred-point scale."

"Fifty-five," Steve responded, almost instantly.

"Right, good math."

"Fifty-five out of a hundred. That isn't good, is it?"

"Remember, it's only a thumbnail score."

"Fifty-five!" Steve rubbed his chin stubble. "That means I don't love her, doesn't it?"

"It's a real eye-opener."

"Yes." Steve shook his head. "I can't believe ..."

The doctor spoke over him. "That's why I've been saying all along that you can't be in love with two women at the same time. That kind of thinking is driven solely by your addiction."

"No one ever explained it to me like that before — fifty-five — I still can't believe that."

"Like I said, it isn't scientific."

"Even so — fifty-five — it sheds a whole different light on things." Steve looked him in the eye. "Where do we go from here?"

"I have a couple of things in mind. I want you to think about how you affect others."

"Others, why?"

"Addicts are more self-centered than the general public. They lie and cheat more often. Basically they'll do anything to cover up an action to make things look good from their perspective. That's why they end up hurting people. And most of the time, it's the ones closest to them."

"I've hurt a lot of people." Steve said, studying the tassels on his shoes. "I don't want to do that anymore."

"No one does, but it happens more often than not. When you go home tonight I want you to apply the four-way intimacy test to each of the women you're seeing. Next, I want you to answer a page of questions. It'll help guide you through this process."

"Should I write down my responses?"

"Absolutely. Writing is a thoughtful process. It'll make you think about your actions. For example, when you're alone how do you feel about each woman? Do you fantasize about her? Do you masturbate while you're thinking about her?"

"Should I do a separate page on each one?"

"Yes. It'll make it easier for us to talk about each one."

"Is that it?"

"No. There are several questions I want you to apply to yourself. I'll give you a list so you can think about them in advance. For example: Are you happy with your personal life? If so, why? If not, how would you like to change it?"

"Sounds like I have a lot of homework."

"You must give more thought to who you are. And why you're that way. A few sentences for each question will be fine. I need to hear your basic thoughts."

"Anything else?"

The doctor stared across the room, in deep thought. "You can't go through long periods without talking to someone. You need a confidant to share your feelings with on a regular basis."

"There's Charlie in North Carolina."

"Yes, you've mentioned him before. It's best though, to have someone here. Talking to an old friend once in a while is nice, but you need someone here. Someone you trust … a good thinker. A person you can talk to on a regular basis, and preferably a man."

"Geez, I don't know. I'll have to think about that."

***

On Monday Steve joined Art and Sherry at his conference table. Glancing at her he smiled to himself. *It's a good thing I didn't go to see her parents in Steubenville. Fifty-five, my God. How could I be so far out of touch with my feelings?*

"Who wants to go first?" Steve asked.

"I will." Art popped his hand up. "The staff training is complete for now. We're all on the same page and I think everyone is working in an effective manner."

"Effective," Sherry chimed in. "They're a real team. There's a tangible sense of camaraderie. If we had the same attitude across the department, we could eliminate several more positions."

Turning to Sherry, he asked, "How's it going with you?"

"Unofficially I've implemented the plan. When there's a vacancy our supervisors are automatically moving pieces around. We're ready to announce, when the president is ready."

"Good. I don't see any major hurdles in passing phase two of the reform package. We'll likely do a short roadshow to test the waters; if there're no problems we'll be ready to take it to Congress. The president wants to hold off as long as possible on the staff reduction plan. She'll need all the capital she can muster on phase three. It'll be loaded with controversial issues."

"Did you say loaded with mustard?" Art jested. "I can't believe how lucky you were in Dallas."

"Lucky?" Steve laughed. "It was a calculated strategy."

"Sure it was." Art laughed then the other two joined him.

"Anything else?" Steve asked. He eyed each one, generating head shakes, and then said, "I have one more informational item. On February 6th Washington National will be renamed, Ronald Reagan National Airport."

"Yeah, I read about that last month in an up-and-coming column," Art said.

"On the evening of the 5th President Stetson is hosting a major bipartisan reception for the Reagans. She's building her base for the spring when we tackle phase three."

"Can you say much about your plans for phase three?"

"It's still a concept in my head. Basically we'll combine high school graduation, public service, and the military in one big swoop. Once I've drafted a few pages I'll share it with the two of you. I'll need plenty of help."

"I look forward to that," Art said. Sherry nodded and picked up her mug. Art led the way out. Steve's eyes glued on Sherry's gait on her way to the door. *Nice ass. I can't wait until Friday night.*

***

Public officials and fifty dignitaries with their spouses, from each side of the aisle, gathered in the East Room. Once again, President Stetson had outdone herself. A fountain by the west wall spouted red and blue streams of water. Patriotic banners and flags, vintage and new, filled the walls. Around the perimeter white table-clothed, high top bistro tables with colorful Uncle Sam centerpieces, surrounded brightly decorated banquet tables.

Twenty-five servers dressed in red, white and blue striped outfits, each wearing a blue or red stovepipe hat, carried silver platters loaded with heavy hors d'oeuvres. Everyone mingled in a festive mood, chatting, telling jokes, and poking fun at each other. Within minutes of former President Reagan's arrival, he was back in his element, hobnobbing and glad-handing as if time had stood still.

Nancy and Janet chatted near George Washington's portrait. "Have you had any hors d'oeuvres yet?" Janet asked.

"I had a couple of the seafood items. They were wonderful. Ronnie said he'd had beef 'something.' He thought it was terrific. I haven't had any beef yet."

"I'll give you a hint." Janet grinned. "The servers with blue hats are serving beef. The ones in red have seafood."

"Great idea. I'll have to remember that."

Nancy squeezed Janet's hand. "I want to thank you again for hosting tonight's event. Ronnie has been talking about it ever since you made the proposal. Look at him. He's back in his element like nothing has changed."

Janet smiled. "Looks like he's still in office."

"I'm so proud of him."

"For good reason. He made a difference. His leadership will have a lasting impact."

Nancy's eyes twinkled. "It's nice of you to say that."

Janet leaned closer. "I hope you'll help me out with one thing tonight."

"Of course." Nancy nodded.

"When the Marine Band plays 'The Wind Beneath My Wings' that'll be my signal to dance with President Reagan — it'll be a real photo op — the first time ever two presidents have danced together."

"Ronnie will love it."

"At the end the band will continue to play and then phase into 'Nancy (With the Laughing Face).' That'll be your sign to come forward and dance with him."

"Perfect, being in the spotlight, dancing to his favorite songs, Ronnie will eat it up."

"I thought he would like that."

Nancy gave her a gentle hug. "Thanks so much. We won't forget your special efforts."

"You're so welcome." Janet grinned, sincerely. "Enjoy the evening."

Nancy winked then headed toward her husband.

Janet walked over to Steve and pulled him aside. "It's all arranged. When Nancy comes out to dance with President Reagan, I'll motion to the group to join in and you can dance with me."

***

After the reception that night Steve joined the president upstairs as had become a normal practice for major events. An usher staff member escorted him to the elevator.

Arriving on the second floor, Steve slipped on his robe and waited in the wingback chair by the fireplace.

Janet popped in. "I'm taking a quick shower."

"Perfect, I'll pour you a drink."

It seemed like only seconds when Steve glanced up from the TV and saw her parading his way — black bra, panties and matching high heels — rather than the robe she normally wore.

Steve looked startled. "What's happening?"

"I feel like dancing."

"Did you have a rush?" Steve asked, hoping his comment wasn't taken in jest.

"No ... I just didn't have a chance to dance all night."

Steve sounded confused. "You mean, I don't count?"

She ignored his question and continued to slink around. "You'll never believe what happened," she said, running her hands over her breasts and down her sides.

Steve rubbed his hands together. "Can we talk about that later ..."

"Not until that thing under your robe settles down."

Steve adjusted himself.

She started to explain, "Everything was perfect until ... the dancing started."

A puzzled lined Steve's forehead. "I don't understand."

She contorted her lips into a mock grimace. "I missed the best part."

Steve picked up her glass from the end table and held it out. "Here, you need a drink."

Grabbing it from his hand, she gulped it half down.

"You okay?"

154

She giggled then sat down with the rest of her Jack Daniels. "Pour me another. This is going to take a while."

He did as told, refreshed his gin then eased back into his chair. "Okay, let's hear it."

"You're not going to believe this."

"Try me."

She wet her lips on the drink. "I was on the crapper when you danced with *her*."

"On the crapper? When I danced with her …"

Janet laughed. "I don't know where to start."

"You better start at the beginning on this one."

"Okay … no interruptions."

Steve nodded and gestured for her to start. Janet described the bathroom scene when she exchanged places with the double. Dumbfounded, Steve's mouth dropped open.

"How did Bradley pull that off in such a short period of time?"

"Don't ask me. All I know is that she's just like me. It's kind of creepy."

"Creepy? It's downright scary."

"Scary? For all you know she may be me right now."

"Jesus Christ." Steve's face froze with the thought. "Are you her? I mean is she you?"

She slid her hand under her panties and pulled them halfway down. "Can you tell?"

"C'mon, this is not funny."

"Funny? Wait until the early edition hits the streets tomorrow. A picture of two US presidents dancing together for the first time in history … and it isn't true … it wasn't me. It was the phony me."

"Fake or not. It'll go down in history as a memorable shot."

He refreshed their drinks. "How did the screw-up occur?"

"It's crazy. We made the exchange in the restroom as planned. I was sitting in the stall waiting for her to return. All of sudden I heard the band strike up 'The Wind Beneath My Wings.' I looked at my watch. It was an hour early. The director must have gotten it wrong."

"That's hard to imagine."

She laughed. "The Secret Service agents went nuts. Everyone scurried around to make sure the photos focused on former president Reagan and only showed her profile."

"Did it work?"

"I guess. They had me back in the room in no time." Janet paused. "Is she a good dancer?" Steve gulped. "C'mon, is she?"

He raised his brow. "I thought it was you."

CHAPTER FIFTEEN

Sitting in his lounger with a tall glass of gin, Steve reflected on Dr. Pritts's assessment. *Fifty-five for Sherry. I can't believe it's that low. I love her in so many ways. But ...fifty-five, how can that be?*

Hearing the phone, he turned and picked it up. "Kim, what a pleasant surprise. You usually don't call during the week. How are you doing?"

"I doing better. It take long time to adjust to father being gone."

"Things like that take a long time. It's one step at a time."

"You right." She hesitated. "You doing anything tonight?"

"No, want come over?"

"I hoping you ask. Would half hour be okay?"

"Perfect. I'll meet you in the lobby."

Steve hurriedly freshened up and took the elevator downstairs. Exactly a half-hour later, the black limousine stopped in front of the door. Kim stepped out, then leaned back inside and said something to the driver before she headed toward the lobby.

Steve stepped out the front door. Kim ran toward him and threw her arms around his neck. They held each other for the longest time.

He took her hand and stepped inside. Strolling toward the elevator, the two swung their arms like two lovebirds.

"You look terrific as usual," he said.

She blushed. "You always say right thing."

Inside the elevator, he pulled her tight and gave her a long, firm kiss. Gasping for breath, she gazed up at his soft brown eyes and smiled.

The elevator door opened. Steve pulled her toward his apartment and motioned her in. "Would you like a drink?"

"A Sprite be fine."

"No problem." At the fridge he filled a glass with ice, poured her a soda and walked toward the fireplace where she waited. He gestured toward the sofa then placed her glass and can on the coffee table. After refreshing his gin Steve joined her on the sofa and leaned closer, gently caressing her thigh. "I was surprised you could come over during the middle of the week."

"It works for me," she said. "We have events every weekend."

He flashed his trademark smile. "Maybe we ought to do it more often."

"I like that." She snuggled closer. "I want to be with you much as I can."

He kissed her lightly on the lips. "I've missed you too."

Their eyes connected. "I make you happy."

"Sounds good to me." He lifted an eyebrow.

"You not understand. You make me go out of control; it make me want you more."

"I-I …"

She pressed her lips on his then unbuttoned the top of his shirt. "It okay with you?"

Steve double-nodded, knowing nothing could be better.

Her warm smile revealed more than a hint of what was coming. She loosened his shirt and pulled it out of his pants. Pushing him onto the sofa, she ran her finger across his hairy chest then climbed on top, straddling his waist.

Steve's soft, sexy eyes slid down her body. She pushed her right breast into his mouth, and closed her eyes as if drifting into her own fantasy world. Sensing her desires, Steve moved smoothly, sliding his fingers slowly across her midriff and down her sides to unhook her slacks. His firm erection pushed into her crotch.

Kim eased up, slipped off her slacks and panties and tossed them aside. Steve jerked off his pants, threw his boxers to the side, slid back on the sofa and tugged her gently back on top of him. Her legs tightened on his sides; her pelvis pressing against his tool.

Taking charge, she rolled on a condom and slid him in, moving slowly in a rhythmic fashion; then pushing more rapidly. He placed his hand on her hips and pushed against her, joining the pace. Feverishly she slammed against him again and again. Her breaths shortened and she gasped, panting out of control.

"Relax, sweetie," he said. "Take a deep breath."

"I want you so much."

"You can have me any way you want … just take it easy."

She pulled her shoulders back and took a deep breath, filling her lungs.

He rose up, placed his mouth around her right breast and tongued her nipple. He felt her body tense, her heartbeat pounded, faster than before. Her body jerked wildly, her long, black hair flying in all directions.

"Oh Steve, I love you," she cried.

Steve pulled her quivering body tight and pushed with all of his strength. Her body exploded; her arms and legs thrashing.

Still gasping, Steve took her in his arms and held her tight. Her arms fell limp and she collapsed on his chest. He caressed the small of her back gently, easing her down slowly.

***

Rolling over in bed the next morning, he reached for Kim. Not feeling her, Steve stretched his arm to the side of the bed. Nothing. He raised his head and glanced toward the open bathroom door — the room was dark. *Where is she?* He stood and made his way to the living room then spotted her naked image on the balcony. Slipping up behind her, he slid his arms around her waist and pulled her close. "Are you okay, sweetie?" he asked.

"I am now. Having you near me make trouble disappear. I warm all over."

"It's the same for me, darling."

She turned and kissed him lightly on the chest then slid her arms around his neck, and stretching on her tiptoes, kissed him firmly on the lips. "You're just like the man my father said I'd meet," she said, easing down on her feet.

"Do you think of him often?"

"All the time." She gazed up into Steve's eyes. "I love you."

"I love you too, more than anyone in the world." Steve slipped his arm around her. "Would you like to talk about him?"

She shrugged, seeming uncomfortable.

"Come inside. I'll fix some hot tea and we can talk."

"You thoughtful."

He took her hand and guided her to the booth in the kitchen then put a kettle of water on to boil. He set cups and saucers on the table and poured the hot water. Giving her a peck on the cheek, Steve slid in across from her. "I can tell," he said, "there's something else on your mind."

She bit her lip then gazed into his eyes. "Father had box of evidence on wrong-doings of Kuratong Baleleng. I delivered to High Tribunal upon his death."

"What kind of evidence?"

"He has times, dates, pictures, eye-witness signed affidavits, the whole thing ... had the leaders of the Kuratong Baleleng dead to rights. He documented their involvement in bank robberies, killings, kidnapping, drug and human trafficking."

"How did he collect all of that?"

"After they took sister, he dedicated life to catching them. He work night and day. It kept him alive. He walk me through the material. I knew it only a matter of time before he passed."

"Are you worried about your safety?"

"Very much. Kuratong Baleleng evil. Have connections all over world."

"Here too?"

"Absolutely. I have driver, Felix, who take me everywhere and Rodrigo, my personal bodyguard, watch over me."

"Where are they now?"

"Felix took car back to Embassy. He pick me up at eight. Rodrigo watch building. The two talk before limo stops."

"I can't imagine the agony you've gone through."

"Nothing I can do about it. I live my life; I not going to give in to them."

"Good for you. Do you want an early breakfast?"

"Maybe later. You made me happy twice last night. My turn make you happy," she said, with an impish grin, then grabbed his hand and pulled him toward the bedroom.

"I'm already happy."

160

***

Without realizing it, Steve had fallen back into his old pattern — Kim on Wednesdays, Sherry on Friday and/or Saturday, and Charisse on Sunday — rain or shine he was always on time. He'd filled out the questionnaires on the three women and mailed them to Dr. Pritts. Three days later he cancelled his next appointment.

Waiting for Kim to call on the fourth Wednesday in a row, he sucked on an olive then downed the last of his Tanqueray.

The phone rang.

He glanced at call waiting then answered, "Hi Kim."

"Hi sweetie, I sorry I late. Rodrigo check out places you mentioned. Either works. You want to go to the Blues Alley or Clyde's? He case place one more time before we arrive."

"I've been stopping by the Blues Alley on a regular basis. How about we have dinner at Clyde's at seven."

"Perfect. I meet you there. We go back to your place after."

Within the hour Steve had shaved, put on a flashy purple and teal sports shirt and tan slacks, and was standing in front of Clyde's when the limo came to a stop. Rodrigo appeared out of nowhere to assist Kim.

Steve took her hand and guided her into the traditional upscale eatery and bar.

The owner looked up. "Table for two?"

"Schilling, we have reservations for a booth."

"Yes, Dr. Shilling. Right this way."

The older man stopped halfway down the bar. "How's this?"

"Fine," Steve said, looking up at the tiffany lamp that hung over the leather seats.

"This fancy neighborhood bar," Kim said. "How quaint."

"I thought you'd like it. They have great burgers."

"Sounds good." Kim grinned then glanced down to the end of the bar at Rodrigo having a beer.

"Anything new with your father's court case?"

"They start preliminaries. Kuratong Baleleng drag out case long as possible." She brushed her long black hair aside. "They start harassing my mother."

"Harassing?"

"Yes, little things. At first seem like nothing then she realize too much going on to be coincidences."

"Can you give me an example or two?"

"Three weeks ago mother's car had flat tire. Then battery died. Next, air conditioner for house went out. Then dog killed by car. That way they work. If you don't give up, they turn up heat."

"Isn't there anything the police can do?"

Kim shook her head. "They all connected."

The waitress stopped. "Something to drink tonight?"

Steve looked at Kim. "I'm having a beer. Want to try one?" She nodded. "We'll have a couple of Yuengling's."

The waitress made a note and quickly returned with two tall drafts.

Steve picked up his glass and clinked hers. "I hope everything works out."

"Me too."

Steve ordered onion rings, a burger and fries. She had a steak salad. Throughout the meal they chatted about Washington, D.C., and things they'd like to do together. Kim placed her hand on his. "You wonderful man. I never met anyone like you ... so considerate and understanding."

"Being with you makes it easy."

She gazed meaningfully into his eyes. "I ready to go home."

"No dessert?" he jested.

Not sure if he was joking, she asked, "You want brownie sundae?"

"Not tonight. I'd rather have you."

She blushed then smiled. "Tonight my treat."

***

Friday night Steve picked up three chunks of cheese, two bottles of cabernet and two heart-shaped boxes of chocolates. He hit the elevator button at Sherry's apartment with his elbow while balancing a box of candy and a bag of goodies. Unlocking the door to her apartment, he poked in his head. "Happy Valentine's Day, sweetie."

"Come in," Sherry called from the bedroom. "I'll be right out."

Hurriedly, Steve placed the chocolates at her place-setting on the dinette table and unloaded the wine and cheese in the kitchen.

Sherry strolled out wearing red high heels, a matching mini-skirt and red bow in her hair. Steve zeroed in on the plunging neckline of her tight white sweater. "What's going on?"

She turned from side to side, showing off the full impact of her new pushup bra. "I thought you'd like a Valentine treat."

"Treat ... hell." He gawked at her tight-ass skirt as she paraded around the apartment. "Where did you come up with this idea?"

"I saw the way you looked at that jazz singer the other night at Blues Alley, and said to myself ... 'go for it.'"

"She doesn't hold a candle to you."

"I wanted to make sure you realized that." Sherry smiled. "Want to open the wine while I cut the cheese?"

"Yes, I'll grab some crackers too."

"You can set the glasses on the coffee table. I'll join you on the sofa in a minute."

Steve did as told then watched her strut around the kitchen. *Holy shit, I feel like jumping her right now. Hell with the hors d'oeuvres.*

She leaned over the coffee table, taking her time positioning the plate of appetizers in front of him. Steve stared at her cleavage. "If you're trying to seduce me, you're doing a great job," he said, adjusting himself.

"I wanted to see what was most important to you."

"Forget about the wine and cheese." He started to rise.

"Sit down." She laid her hand gently on his shoulder and giggled. "You'll get yours later."

"Mercy." He flopped back down against the sofa and wiped his brow.

Sherry filled her plate and turned to face him. "How did your meeting with the president go this week?"

"Who wants to talk about that?"

"C'mon, I'm interested."

"It was fine. She's wrapped up phase two, has the votes in the house and senate, and is strategizing about phase three. That'll be a biggie."

"Based on the outline you shared with Art and me I'd say ... catastrophic. Good thing it's a single piece of legislation. It wouldn't have a chance if it was bundled with something else."

"That's why we segmented the plan into a series of bills."

"It'll take a lot of heavy lifting on everyone's part."

"You can say that again." He laughed. "He looked at the nearly empty wine bottle. Want me to open another bottle of wine?"

She pulled her shoulders back and gave him a come-on smile. "Maybe later."

***

Sunday morning Steve was up early, placed a red tablecloth on his dinette table, and added white napkins, a red rose in a crystal bud vase and a box of chocolates. Fixing two Bloody Mary's before Charisse's normal arrival time, he eased back in the recliner and loosened the belt on his robe, exposing his hairy chest.

He heard the door open and watched Charisse tiptoe toward the bedroom.

"Happy Valentine's Day," he shouted.

"Shit." She turned his way. "You scared the crap out of me," she said. "Happy Valentine's Day to you, dear."

Steve blew her a kiss. Charisse stepped in front of him and loosened the buttons on her coat. Flinging it open, she stood naked and posed; then pointed to the red heart hanging against her bare breasts — BE MY VALENTINE.

"You're unreal." He jumped up and hugged her.

She looked down with a mock frown. "They're real."

"No, no ... I meant you not them."

She ran her hands over his chest.

Steve flipped his robe off and standing naked too, asked, "How would you like to celebrate?"

She looked at his partial erection then picked up the glass and laughed. "I'll have a Bloody Mary."

***

Later that morning, Charisse propped her head up on a pillow. "Do you know what I love about you?"

Steve glanced down at his naked body.

"No, not that. After sex we snuggle and talk. That's special for me."

"It's good for me too. After talking with you I feel like I don't have a worry on my mind."

She paused as if contemplating a comment then changed the subject. "How did your last meeting with Dr. Pritts go?"

Steve wrinkled is brow. "Are you a mind reader? We talked about being intimate; had practically the same conversation you and I had the last time you were over. He talked about a four-way test for intimacy."

Charisse butted in. "I know that one! Did you score over sixty?"

"Sixty … ah, no. How did you know?"

"My therapist gave me the same test. I didn't score in the sixties either."

Steve gave her a questioning look, didn't respond.

"Do you think …" they both started to say, then laughed.

"Go ahead," he said.

"I think it's strange how we've allowed our bodies to play games with our minds."

"I don't understand how that happens."

"I don't either but now I realize why it's so hard to change." She paused as if pondering how to couch the next statement. "Take you as an example."

"Me?" He leaned back.

"We have sex multiple times on Sundays. That's probably more than most men get all week. I assume you're screwing another one or two during the week. Think about what your body is saying to your brain."

He stared blankly at her before exclaiming, "I still don't get it. There's nothing wrong, being with two or more women. Why can't I be in love with more than one person? The doctors are crazy, probably envious."

"Maybe." Charisse smiled. "That's exactly how I used to feel."

"How did you get beyond that point?"

"It's hard to know … but one day I just said, 'If I want to change, I have to do it myself.'"

"Wow, that's a big step. I don't think I'll ever get to that point."

"I used to say that too." She grinned. "Someday you will, just wait and see."

"I sure hope so," he said, though not in a convincing manner.

CHAPTER SIXTEEN

Knowing phase three would be the most controversial and complex of all, President Stetson called Bradley Welton into the Oval Office. He sat in the wingback on the left side of the fireplace, and paid strict attention.

"You'll need to sharpen your pencil on this one," she opened. "It will require all of our political capital and then some."

"You're telling me. I've already heard rumblings about some of the pieces. There's a growing buzz in the rumor mill."

"Is it negative?"

"Mostly, and a lot of misinformation."

"Sounds like the same ole same ole."

"We need to get the facts out as soon as possible."

The president nodded. "We'll have our hands full finding a way for the military to bend, and shepherding it through Congress."

"Winning the battle in the court of public opinion may be the toughest part. Any one of the pieces can do us in. How do you plan to proceed?" he asked.

"I want to pull together our best thinkers and find ways for the key players to become involved. We need them to buy-in as soon as possible."

"Makes sense; any thoughts on who should be around the table?"

"There are some obvious ones — Steve Schilling, Will Chandler, Sherry Holmgren ..."

"Any thoughts about Congress?"

"George Mitchell for sure. As the Majority Leader in the Senate he'll have his hands full."

"How about the other side of the aisle?

"I like Chuck Nagle, the new Republican senator from Nebraska. He has a sound military background and a good head on his shoulders."

"We can't bypass the minority leadership. We can't afford pushing anyone's nose out of joint."

"Right, and how about the Joint Chiefs of Staff?"

"I'm leaning toward the Secretary of Defense, William Cohen," said the president. "I've also been thinking about adding a politico or two. I'll be crisscrossing the country, giving speeches. It's time for you to put on your thinking cap."

***

Steve paused outside the Roosevelt Room admiring the bust of Abraham Lincoln, then followed Sherry and Will Chandler in. Bradley greeted them and the other committee members at the door, and took a seat next to the vacant chair at the head of the table. He glanced at his watch — ten o'clock.

Straightening in his chair, Bradley looked up. "I'd like to thank you for your willingness to serve on this special committee. President Stetson will join us in a few minutes. She asked me to start the meeting so as not to waste your valuable time." He gave the group a fake smile. "Since the original memo went out, we've added three members." He pointed to the nameplates — Marilyn Atwell from the American Council on Education; Ira Magaziner, a business consultant; and House Majority Whip, Tom Delay.

The members beamed with their acknowledgement and brief introduction.

"You are a diverse group representing varying views. The president respects each of your perspectives — that's why you are here. She asks that you speak frankly and freely. Be assured, what's said here stays here. Are there any questions?"

He scanned the room looking for a nod from each member.

"I'll be the spokesperson for the group. So if you're asked, you know nothing until you receive the press release. Does everyone understand that?"

Again, he extracted a nod or smile from each one. "Good. Steve would you walk us through the plan?"

"Yes, thank you, Bradley." Steve pushed his notes aside. "In the earlier pieces of legislation, we established the principle of 'go, no go' competency-testing in grades one through six, with major diagnostic components at the end of grades three and five." He glanced around the table to make sure the team was on board.

All eyes focused on him.

At that moment the president stepped through the door. Everyone rose.

"Please continue," the president said, gesturing for the members to take their seats.

Steve nodded and took up where he left off. "The planned bill will extend competency testing through grade twelve with more elaborate testing at the ends of grades nine and twelve. The first question for today is what do we call the final product? A high school diploma? Certification of Excellence? Or, something else?" He paused giving time for the questions to sink in. "Who wants to start?"

Chuck Nagel raised his hand. "I'd stay away from the term diploma. It's ingrained in our society, like local control. It'd be like tampering with motherhood and apple pie."

Heads nodded.

"Absolutely." Ira agreed. "You're already taking on two-thirds of the establishment. No reason to needlessly create an issue."

"If there's any federal intrusion into education, the bill will be dead." DeLay said. "It's important to keep the focus on student competencies."

"Anything we can accomplish in this area will be a milestone," Secretary Chandler piped in. "Over half of the students who enter college today have to take one or more remedial courses in math, reading or writing."

"That's hard to imagine," the Secretary of Defense commented.

"Worse yet," Will continued. "Half of the coursework for many college freshmen is composed of remedial or developmental courses."

Secretary Cohn shook his head over the issue.

"I think we should add a special certification to the transcript and the diploma. Maybe we could come up with a logo that states certified for college," Sherry said.

Steve raised a hand in agreement. "I like that. It'd be like a USDA stamp of approval."

The group laughed.

"Great concept." Senator Nagel stood for emphasis. "Being from Nebraska, that's very important to me. When Steve mentioned USDA we all had an image of high quality. That's the goal."

Everyone around the table agreed, as the senator took his seat.

"Sounds like we have a consensus," the president said. "I'll instruct staff propose a supplemental certification that can be added to high school transcripts and diplomas. Does that make sense?" She looked around the table. "Good. In two weeks Steve will walk us through the public service component. Steve, would you distribute your one-page handout?"

He nodded and shuffled the handout around the table.

"Again, I'd ask that you not share this with anyone." She garnered a glance from all. "Good. Meeting adjourned." The members stood and filed out.

The president motioned to Steve. "Could you stop by my office for a moment?"

"Of course."

Steve lingered, chatting with a few stragglers, then followed her into the Oval Office. She closed the office door, opened the door to the private area and motioned him in.

Stepping into the middle of the room, he paused and turned. She threw her arms around his neck and planted a wet kiss on his lips.

Steve stumbled backward.

She pushed him onto the sofa and climbed on top, kissing him again and again; his erection pressed against her pelvic area. "I've missed you so much," she gasped then fondled his protruding slacks. "We must find a way to be together more often."

"And for a longer time," Steve gasped. "We need four or five days, alone."

"Sure ..." She snickered. "And how do you propose the president of the United States be disposed for a week."

"A week? This is sounding better all the time."

"Okay, big talker, tell me how we're going to do that?"

"I'll have to think about it."

"Fine, you have two weeks," she said, then pulled her skirt up and flung her panties aside. Steve tossed his pants and shorts. Climbing on top of him, she slipped on a condom and pushed him inside.

***

Bradley called the meeting to order as the president walked in.

Everyone stood, then settled into the leather chairs. The president nodded to Steve. "Give us a quick overview of the public service components."

"Part one is simple: Students who graduate from high school will be required to give two years of public service to their country. I'd like to require it before they go to college but that's probably not feasible. These students will be paid minimum wage or earn two free years of college. If they go to college first, the debt for the first two years will be cancelled after their public service is completed." Steve paused, waiting for their reactions.

"Plain and simple. I like that," Ira said. "What if they or their parents pay their way?"

"They get a two-year credit to complete their degree or to use in graduate school."

"Perfect. That's an excellent motivator for the go-getter."

"I like the idea of public service," Senator Mitchell kicked off a discussion. "My grandkids weren't ready for college at eighteen. Two more years of growing up would have been very helpful." He paused. "However you handle it I'd ask that you keep exceptions to a minimum. We don't need to be inundated with appeals."

"Good point," the president interjected. "Does anyone have a problem with the concept?"

"Conceptually, it's fine," Will Chandler said. "Several foreign countries have similar programs. We can probably pass that in

Congress; the real challenge will be to find a way for the American public to buy in."

Heads around the table nodded.

"Anyone else?" she asked. No one said a word. "Let's hear about those who don't graduate from high school," the president continued.

"That'll be our biggest challenge," Steve said.

"Hell, they're a big challenge now," Ira spouted.

"And a real drag on our economy. Welfare costs are killing us," DeLay said.

"Go ahead, Dr. Schilling," she directed.

"Non-high school graduates will be required to serve four years in the military ..."

"Four years?" Secretary of Defense interrupted. "How do you expect us to handle that?"

Steve agreed. "That's the challenge."

"Are you talking about *all* dropouts? The bum off the street?" Will Chandler pressed.

Steve nodded.

"Christ, we're not miracle workers," Secretary Cohen said.

"No." Steve grinned. "But you're the best we have."

Cohen flopped back in his chair and shook his head.

"Before we go further, I think we should lay out our budget plans," the chief of staff said.

"Agreed." The president sat upright. "I will propose a 20 percent cut in the personnel portion of the Department of Education."

A hush fell around the table.

"Sherry Holmgren, to my left, is the architect of the plan; she'd be glad to explain how we're going to accomplish that."

The president looked around at a roomful of solemn faces. No one looked her in the eye. "And in the following budget year, I'll ask that the same requirement be applied to all other agencies ..."

"Madam President," the Majority Whip interrupted. "I respectfully disagree with this tactic. The house will never approve a 20 percent reduction in the military."

"You're absolutely correct and ... I'd never propose that. The same requirement will be applied to all other agencies except the military. Who has a problem with that?"

"You'll never pull that off," a member protested.

"It isn't possible," another chimed in.

"Fine," the president announced. "I'll shut Washington down."

"You can't do that, Madam President. The country will be up in arms."

Looking around the table, she smirked. "To the contrary. Every family in this country has been hit by hard times. You mean to tell me that Joe Six Pack will oppose a 20 percent reduction in the size of government? That's hogwash, I'll shut it down and save even more!"

Silence filled the room. No one looked up.

The president waited, daggers shooting from her eyes. Steve thought an eternity passed.

Secretary of Defense Cohen broke the ice. "What would you expect of us?"

"In exchange for no cuts, I'd expect you to assume an expanded charge."

He swallowed. "And how might we do that?"

"We'd expect you to design a multi-tiered program. For the bum off the street, place him in your traditional boot camp program where he'd stay until he decided to shape up. For the young woman who's pregnant or already had a child, we'd expect you'd show compassion to help her complete a GED and prepare her for a job, so she could raise her child with dignity."

Mr. Cohen stared without making a response.

DeLay jumped in. "How do you expect the military to achieve such laudable goals within existing dollars? They're already in trouble, closing bases to meet existing demands of the Balanced Budget Act."

"That's because they're acting like ostriches — they have their heads in the sand," the president retorted.

Secretary of Defense Cohen bristled.

"They're projecting the past into the future," the president continued. "Times have changed."

"Yes, of course, Madam President, but ..." he stated.

She prickled. "That's the second time you've cut me off." Her eyes bored into him, "I find that condescending."

"Sorry, I ..."

Her glare continued as she snatched a folder lying in front of Bradley. Leafing toward the back, she held up a single page. "Let me read from the latest congressional report. We have three times as many aircraft carriers as the Soviet Union — that's assuming they could sail out of port." She paused for affect. "We can destroy the world ten times more easily than any other country. The Chinese have one tub that floats. We have fleets all over the world."

She took a breath then hammered on. "And now, you're about ready to pass a bill that will authorize the construction of a thousand more tanks. There're over three thousand state-of-the-art tanks parked in Arizona's desert that we don't need and can't sell. Don't tell me there's no room for the military to play a role in addressing America's most pressing problem — education. All of us need to tighten our belts and face a better future."

"Madam President, you are right," DeLay interjected. "But look at the jobs that would be lost if we cancelled all of those contracts."

"They're a bunch of leeches," she shouted. "Cut off the lifeline in one area and they'll move to the next dollar source. They'll survive, maybe even thrive. Put out a RFP to train America's most disadvantaged kids and you'll be inundated with proposals."

She looked at the group.

No one made eye contact.

The president stood. "I'll see you in two weeks. Put on your thinking caps. We *must* educate America!"

***

Steve followed her into the Oval Office and waited for her to open the private door. Pushing him inside, she shoved him onto the sofa and paced around him. Looking up, he wondered if he'd done something wrong.

"Okay smart guy, just how do you propose to pull it off?" she demanded.

Steve hemmed-and-hawed.

"C'mon, I don't have all day."

Realizing she had shifted agendas, he raised his hand. "Easter is coming up and you always go to Camp David for a little R and R, right?"

"Of course, I go there every year."

"I was thinking about being with you for a week."

Janet wrinkled her nose. "I can see it now. We play tennis in the morning, go horseback riding in the afternoon and watch a couple of movies every night. The staff will go bananas and the media will have a field day. They'll be all over my ass. My credibility will be shot. I won't be able to pass anything."

He laughed. "I had my own thoughts about being all over your ass."

"Funny. Funny … so how do you propose to be all over my ass?"

He gave her his patented Cheshire-smile. "I was going to propose Aruba."

"Aruba … no way."

"Yes, I know. Tony Petrarca gave me a lesson of the various protocols, hotlines, and prohibitive number of people that would be involved. Obviously, it wouldn't be a secret getaway. He said if you really insisted on going someplace that you consider the Greenbrier Resort in West Virginia."

"Hmm, not bad. That's where the bunker was built in case of a national emergency."

"So? There's over a hundred and twelve thousand square feet of space built underground."

"It became public in 1992 when *The Washington Post* exposed the whole thing. Even so, there are countless things we can do, and all of the secret service protocols are in place." She mulled the idea.

"He could arrange off the record movement for us," Steve said, with tentative hope, "and the double could go to Camp David. It's your call."

A smirk started then she broke into laughter. "Yes! Let's do it."

CHAPTER SEVENTEEN

Everyone stood when President Stetson walked into the Roosevelt Room. She smiled, motioned for the group to be seated and without delay, went into her agenda. "Any reflections or second thoughts about the topics we discussed at our last meeting?"

Heads turned toward each other. No one said a word.

"Do I need to use a crowbar?"

Senator Nagel spoke up. "The public service concept has a lot of appeal. How do you rationalize the military being a major player?"

"Twenty-five years ago I wouldn't have been able to make this case — securing peace for the American public required a large, highly trained military force armed with the latest equipment and technologies." She paused with a grin. "At that time, those capabilities were essential ... times have changed. The battlegrounds of the past have shifted to our front door. Guerrilla warfare and terrorism both home and abroad, have become our greatest enemies. We face challenges to our freedoms from inside our country, as well as those outside our borders. Bottom line — we can't afford a 30 percent dropout rate — those youngsters are easy prey for the evil forces who want to destroy our way of life."

"Good point," Secretary Cohen agreed.

"I like the concept," Ira said. "It's proactive rather than reactive."

"I like the idea of high school certification, too," Marilyn Atwood said. "It avoids an inevitable fight while accomplishing the same goal. Ten years from now your certification will be the new standard for high school graduation."

Heads nodded, the mood was optimistic.

"Not much has been said about the economic impact of addressing the dropout problem," Senator Mitchell said. "Our economic power grows with each dropout we eliminate, and the welfare rolls go down — it's a win-win situation."

"Yes, I like that," DeLay agreed.

The Secretary of Defense placed his arms on the table. "I like the idea of us having a public service role. And Madam President, I buy into your description of the changing character of our adversaries. Still, I'm struggling with how you expect us to reallocate 20 percent of our workforce."

"Mr. Secretary, you know your budget better than I, but since you asked, I'd suggest you carefully review the billions of dollars projected for equipment expenditures. How many more tanks, battleships, fighter jets do we need? As I recall, attrition for the military runs around 5 percent a year. With final implementation off six years, 30 percent of your current staff will be gone. How many of them must be replaced? And how many of the new people will be doing the same thing as those they're replacing ... not many, I'd venture to say."

She glanced at Sherry then paused, setting up her question, "Ms. Holmgren, where did the largest amount of your costs savings come from?"

"From the top."

"There you have it, Mr. Secretary. Look at the gains you could make if 20 percent of the personnel located in the Pentagon were shifted to productive positions?"

"Madam President," Mr. Cohen objected.

"Comment withdrawn," the president said. "Point made."

Smugly, she eyed the group. "Well, you've heard the proposal. Who has a better idea?"

Everyone around the table looked at each other. No one said a word.

"We need to flush out the details. The question is ... is the concept a go or no-go?"

Steve swallowed as she looked around at them for feedback. Obtaining a yes or a positive nod from each member, she smiled. "Good. Now let's talk about our strategies." She turned to her political guru. "Mr. Magaziner."

"Thank you, Madam President. And thank you for allowing me to witness this dynamic process. While the toughest part is still ahead, all of you should be pleased with the consensus you have achieved."

"Enough of that," she said, impatiently. "I want to hear your thoughts."

"I like your division of responsibility. Secretary Chandler knows the hill. You and Steve are great at the podium. Having him in the smaller minor markets while you're in the big cities makes sense." Ira paused. "And if need be the two of you can team up if the heat gets too hot."

"That'd be fine with me," she acknowledged.

"The real challenge will be how we deal with the military. You have thousands of VFW's who are going to be stirring around. They see the purpose of armed forces from their perspective — win the war. And they have preserved our freedom. They're wonderful men, some women too, with conservative views. Asking them to embrace a black thug for the betterment of our country will be a stretch."

"Not all of the young people we're talking about are black or thugs."

Ira released an exaggerated sigh. "Doesn't matter, that's the perspective you're up against."

"It isn't only the veterans," Secretary of Defense Cohen chimed in. "It's a view shared by many inside the military. I can lean on them and most will give a lip-serve commitment, but it won't be easy to generate broad-based support. Ira you're right ... that's where we need to focus our attention."

She tossed a questioning look at the Secretary of Defense. "How do we do that, Bill?"

"To start I'd like for you to appear before the Joint Chiefs of Staff. It's critical that they understand your vision and the role you see the military playing in the decades ahead."

"Done. Bradley will make it happen," she announced.

"Next, I'd suggest Dr. Schilling present the entire reform package to them. Each one of them is a detailer in his own right. They need to understand the integral role the military plays in the overall success of the plan."

"I'm ready whenever you call," Steve said briskly.

"And Miss Holmgren, I'd like for you to outline the 20 percent reduction plan that's being applied to the other federal agencies. It's important for them to understand the alternative. That'll help them look at the challenge in a more constructive manner."

Genuinely delighted, Sherry smiled. "Yes, I'll be pleased to help in any way I can."

"Good," the president said. "Anything else for today?" Janet glanced around the room.

No one responded, but the mood was lighter.

"We're adjourned. Happy Easter."

***

Janet tugged on Steve's shoulder. "Wake up dear, we're almost there."

He rubbed his eyes and glanced out the car window at the dark roadside flashing by; off on the horizon he spotted a white glow. "Is that Greenbrier?"

"Yes, the driver said we should be there in ten minutes."

Steve squinted at his watch. "It'll be close to one o'clock, right on schedule."

"Right, Tony said there shouldn't be anyone in the lobby at that time of the morning."

"He's on top of everything, isn't he?"

"He's the best. He's thinking about retiring after my term is over."

"I can see why. I can't imagine the kind of stress he and the other agents are under, twenty-four-seven."

"It must be unreal."

"How did you make all of the arrangements for us to slip out of the White House and travel two hundred and fifty miles without anyone knowing?"

She smirked. "There are plenty of people in the chain who know. It's just that the media isn't in the loop."

"How do you do that?"

She smiled. "I don't. Tony takes care of the details. It's called off the record transportation."

"Huh, it must take a lot of coordination."

"It does. Once in a while the media gets wind of it, but they usually let it slide as long as we don't take undue advantage of the procedure."

"Interesting ..."

"We're almost there," the driver announced.

"Could you turn on the dome light so I can put on my wig?"

"Yes, of course." The light popped on.

She made the final adjustment then turned to Steve. "How do I look?"

He eyed her décolletage. "You look fabulous."

"Not that silly, my hair."

A sly smile crossed his lips. "Oh, that's nice, too ... *Hope*."

"Thanks, for the reminder."

Grinning, the driver glanced in the rearview mirror. "I'll slow when we approach the entrance. The lighting at night is spectacular."

She had no more than thanked him when the car slowed and the rear window on her side rolled down.

She gasped, "Look at that, Steve."

He gazed at the huge white edifice. "Did you ever see anything like that? Look at those huge white columns. It looks like the white house; it must have a thousand rooms."

"Seven hundred and ten to be exact," came from the front.

***

The two slept in the next day, catching up on some much needed rest. It was nearly nine when she snuggled against Steve's shoulder. "You awake?"

He cracked an eye. "I am now, *Hope*. How does it feel to be on your own?"

"Hope?" She lifted her brow and grinned, remembering she had taken an alias. "It's kind of weird. I guess it'll take some time to get used to this."

"How about we order breakfast in?"

"Fine with me. Before or after?"

Her mouth turned down in thought and she giggled. "Let's have breakfast in between. That way we can do it both times."

"Wow, sounds like you're relaxed already."

She jumped out of bed. "Waffles and sausage or eggs benedict?"

"Hmm, how about both. With that much activity I need to keep my strength up."

"Sure." She tied her robe and walked toward the phone. "I'll order double for both of us at ten."

"Great, I'll be in the shower."

Before he knew it she was in the shower rubbing against him and lathering his back. "I love the way your fingers work, Hope."

She dug her nails into his back.

"Ouch, I didn't do anything."

"I'm not sure if I like the tone of that."

"Why don't you get in front of me so I can do your back?" Knowing that was her favorite position, he could hardly wait until she had slid around him.

"I hope that makes you happy."

He kissed her on the side of the neck and behind her right ear then whispered, "I was thinking more about making *you* happy."

"You devil, you." She rotated her hips, wiggled her butt and put her ass into overdrive.

Steve placed his hands on top of her shoulders and gently massaged. He lathered her back, sliding his fingers slowly down her vertebra and around her shoulder blades.

"Oh Steve, that's so relaxing … I don't know when I've felt better."

You think that's good … wait till I take you out of your mind. His hands headed south caressing her hips and pelvic area. He could tell his touch gave her an instant feeling of anticipation; she inhaled a deep, calming breath.

He pressed against her back and whispered. "Step closer to the shower and put your hands on the wall."

She did; the hot water streamed down her back. His hands caressed her cheeks then fondled her private area. She moved her ass in concert with his hands. "That feels wonderful, Steve."

He pushed his erection between her cheeks and pressed in. At first moving slowly, she picked up the pace. "Please, don't stop, Steve, I want you."

He eased back and slowed.

Arching her back, she gasped. "Please, don't tease. Fuck me … *fuck me.*"

***

Much later that morning after a hearty breakfast and another round of sultry sex, the president scanned a list of preapproved activities for the trip.

Steve lay exhausted in the center of the bed; his eyes barely open after she had taken every privilege once and sometimes twice. Reveling in the moment, he recalled how she had climbed on the foot of the bed and worked her way up his legs and thighs. Reaching his crotch, her mouth had consumed him, kissing, licking, sucking. He had done everything possible in his power to avoid coming too soon, enjoying her antics. That is, until she climbed on top of him and unleashed all her sexual prowess that had rendered him helpless.

Unaware of his reverie she skimmed down the list of activities preapproved by the Secret Service. "How would you like to take a walk on the grounds and a carriage ride? It'd be a good way to get acquainted with the place."

"Sounds good." Steve peeked through his squinted eyelids. "I'd like to take a nap first. How about we leave around two o'clock?

"Perfect, that's what I was thinking." She picked up the phone and called the agent on duty. "We'd like to take a walk and a buggy ride around two. Can you work out the details by then?"

"Just a minute," he said, and then moments later responded. "Yes, we'll meet you in the lobby then."

The two lovebirds spent a relaxing afternoon touring the facility.

"How about we get a drink in the bar when we return," Steve suggested.

"I'd like that. I can't recall the last time I sat at a bar watching other people."

"Yes, we'll do it."

***

After tipping the carriage driver, the two casually wandered into the Lobby Bar — a small, quaint place with a dozen or so green padded chairs clustered around a glossy oak bar with heavy dark-green leather below.

"Let's sit on the end so we can see the action."

"Perfect." She readjusted her blonde wig knowing she felt more natural when disguised.

"What do you want to drink?"

"I'm having a Mint Julep; they're supposed to make the best around."

"Sounds good to me."

The barmaid placed a bowl of mixed nuts in front of them. "Whataya have?"

"Two Mint Juleps," Steve replied.

"Two for one."

"Hell yes," Hope said. "Let's go for it."

Steve glanced at a reflection in the mirrored wall behind the bar, spotting an oriental man on a cellphone. His mind scrambled. *Could that be … Kuratong Baleleng? Nah, it's not possible.* He turned to Hope then glanced back. The stool was empty.

Steve turned around and surveyed the room, nothing. *You're overly paranoid. There's no way anyone could know I'm here.*

"What are you looking at, Steve?"

"Ah, nothing special, I was admiring the southern flare in the décor."

"Isn't it wonderful? There's a warm, comfortable feeling."

"I have a warm feeling too."

"Steve." She gave him the eye. "I haven't even finished my first drink yet."

***

Returning home Wednesday afternoon, Steve checked his messages. "Hi sweetie, it's Kim. I'm running a little late. I probably won't be there until seven-thirty. Let's eat in. Love you."

He clicked through three marketing ads then heard a garbled message. He clicked and played it again. "When are you going to tell Kim about Hope?"

Steve dropped the receiver on the sofa. *Who was that? No one knew I was going to be there with Hope. How could anyone come up with that?* He wiped the beads of perspiration from his forehead. *Is it the Kuratong Baleleng? But why would they be following me?*

He set the phone back in its cradle and poured himself a double gin. Settling into the lounger, he thought about his last conversation with Kim. *She said they were evil and had subtle techniques. Why would they be harassing me?* He took another slug of his drink. *It doesn't make sense. I'd never hurt Kim. I love her.* His brow exposed his concentration. *Maybe that's why. They think I would hurt her … maybe they … No, I can't tell her about Hope.*

He closed his eyes and dozed off.

Hearing a ringing in the distance, he tried to shake the cobwebs from his head. He picked up the phone, and slurred. "Hello."

"Steve, its Kim."

"Sorry, I must have fallen asleep."

"I leave embassy now. Be there in fifteen minutes."

"Perfect. I'll be waiting outside."

He took a quick shower, shaved the stubbles and slipped on his loungers. On the way out the door, he grabbed the bud vase with the red rose he'd picked up on the way home.

Waiting outside with the vase behind him, he watched the black limo pull up and stop. He stared at the long gouge extending along the passenger side. Rodrigo jumped out, his eyes ice cold. He inspected the building and surrounding area then walked toward Steve. "Are you alone?"

"Of course, I'm waiting for Kim."

"There's no one inside?"

"No. You can come in if you want."

"It's okay, I trust you," he said, motioning to the car.

Felix opened his door, then moved to the back door on his side. He held Kim's arm and guided her around the limo toward Steve. She was shaking, tears streaming down her cheeks.

Steve reached for her. "Kim, are you okay?"

She threw her arms around him. He could feel her heart pounding on his chest. "I explain later. We must go in. Rodrigo has work to do."

Steve nodded to Rodrigo and hustled her inside. Reaching the elevator, he punched his floor button and stood still, not knowing how to react.

She pulled the vase from his hand. "You so sweet. I love you."

"I love you too." He hugged her with all of his might.

At his floor, Steve fished out his key with one hand and held her tight with the other arm. He unlocked the door and pulled her toward the sofa. "Sit down, sweetie. I'll pour a glass of wine."

She sighed. "Thank you."

Steve placed a full glass of chardonnay and his usual on the coffee table and snuggled close to her. "Take a sip. You'll feel better once you relax."

She gave him a fake grin and took a long sip.

Several minutes later, she took a deep breath. "I thought I going to die."

"Why? What happened?"

Felix noticed a car following us. He sped up. They ram back of limo. We fishtail, I thought we crash — somehow he kept going. I thought we in clear then car came out a side street and sideswiped us. It awful."

"Poor baby, are you okay?"

She looked up with glassy eyes. "Being with you make me feel better."

"Do you think it was the Kuratong Baleleng?"

"No question. They tossed a firebomb into my mother's house last week. They're escalating activity. I'm extremely concerned about her."

"Is there anything you can do?"

"No. They will be relentless until they win."

CHAPTER EIGHTEEN

Feeling refreshed from the recent trip, Steve walked into his office, grabbed a mug of coffee and plopped down in his swivel-executive chair. *I've never had a week like that. Janet is the best ever.* He dug in and attacked a stack of mail from the inbox. Halfway through the pile he picked up a small international envelope. Checking both sides, he noted there was no return address and that it had a Manila, Philippines, postmark. Wondering who it was from, he sliced it open and slowly unfolded the single sheet of paper. He read the two sentences:

She's sucking you in.

Drop her before it's too late!

He read the note again then flipped it on his desk. *Who could have sent this? Drop her … what does it mean? Is it a subtle warning from the Kuratong Baleleng? Is it even about Kim, or someone else?* He placed his hands over his face and tried to think. *I don't get it. Shit, I don't need this. I'm trying to sort out the rest of my life.*

He closed the office door and paced the room. Refilling his mug, he eased back into his chair. "Why me? I don't know anything about this kind of stuff. Who can I ask? Sherry … no." *What about Art? He'd knows about everything … but I'd have to tell him about Kim. And that would lead to the others. Crap.* He sipped his mug dry. *Dr. Pritts said I have to find a confidant. I trust Art; he has a good head. Maybe I should ask him.*

Steve went through the day as if nothing was wrong; yet, every free moment thoughts about the letter flashed through his mind. *Does it have something to do with Kim? Is it connected with the Kuratong Baleleng? Why me? There's no connection with me. Maybe they think I'll pressure Kim in some way? How? Why? I don't know anything?*

It was after four when Steve's last appointment ended. He rubbed his eyes, still wondering what he should do. His mind scrambled. *Dr. Pritts's advice; Kim, Charisse, Sherry and Janet; the Kuratong Baleleng.* "I wish Charlie was here so we could talk. I have to talk with someone. He picked up the phone and dialed Art.

"Art Wallhollister."

"It's Steve, do you have a minute?"

"Of course, I was just straightening my desk. I'll be right down."

Steve was sitting at his conference table when Art arrived. "Close the door, if you don't mind."

Art did so and joined Steve. "Whataya want?"

"Some advice."

Art grinned. "I have lots of that. And it's free."

"How's your time?"

"I have plenty of that too. The wife is at her mother's for the week. Fire away."

Steve hesitated, unsure of where to start. He flipped the envelope on the table. "Read this."

Art opened the envelope, read the two sentences then studied the outside of the envelope. "I don't understand."

Steve took his time telling Art about his relationship with Kim, the Kuratong Baleleng, the recent phone message, and the limo incident. Then he went into his relationships with the other women.

Art bit his lip ingesting all he was hearing, then looked Steve in the eye. "Who's Hope?"

"Another woman I'm seeing."

"Did Sherry and you break up?

Steve shook his head. "That's part of the problem."

"Problem?"

"There's another one, too."

Art mentally counted. "Four women?"

Steve ignored the question, seemingly weighing his options. "I'm a sex addict."

Art didn't blink. "How long has this been going on?"

"All of my life." Sweat broke out on Steve's brow. "My doctor said I should find someone to be a confidant. Someone who I trust. You're the only one who fills the bill. Would you help me?"

"Geez Steve, of course, I'll help." His eyes narrowed. "But … I don't have any expertise."

"It isn't necessary. It's important to have someone with a good head on his shoulders, who's willing to listen."

"Okay, if you think so. I'm your guy."

"Thanks." Steve wiped the moisture from his temple. "It started when I was a kid growing up in Kentucky," he opened the book on his personal history. A half hour later Steve stopped. "Anything else you want to know?"

"Wow. I don't think I can handle much more today."

"Have any thoughts about the letter?"

Art shook his head. "I'll have to give that some more thought. She could be the problem."

"Kim? Nah, that's not possible."

"You can't make a snap decision like that. The jury is still out in my mind."

"How can you say that?"

"I'm an outsider. I'm looking at the facts, without bias." Art hesitated. "You wouldn't be the first guy sucked in by a blow job."

"That's not funny, Art."

"Steve, we have to keep all options open and explore each possibility."

"I suppose you're right." Steve looked at his calendar. "Have any time later this week?"

"Thursday … four o'clock."

***

Art walked in on Thursday with a handful of papers.

"What's all of this?" Steve asked.

"My homework. I've read every article on addiction I could find. I was surprised to learn the amount of similarity among the various types of addiction. It doesn't matter whether it's smoking, drinking, gambling, sex, whatever, those affected face the same challenges."

"Absolutely. And if you have one type, there's a good likelihood you'll have increased tendencies for one or more of the others."

"Do you have other difficulties?"

"I hit the bottle when I'm overly stressed. I've had several week-long binges."

"Any since you've been here?"

"Last Labor Day weekend."

"How about the other areas?"

"I'd gamble every day if I could."

"It looks like you've put on a few pounds."

"That's another problem. I snack constantly, particularly when I'm alone."

"Hmm." Art rubbed his jaw. "When is your next appointment?"

Steve grimaced and glanced down at his scuffed shoes. "I don't have one. I cancelled the last two."

Art's eyes darted across the room at Steve. "How can I help you if you're unwilling to help yourself?"

"Things were going so well, I thought I could handle it. Then instead of better, they got worse."

"I'm not a Ph.D. but you ought to work on those other tendencies too." Art paused then continued, "Sound body, sound mind — cut down on the drinking, lose some weight, go to a fitness center."

"There's one in our building."

Encouraged by Steve's response, Art added, "Put yourself on a regular routine. A little discipline in your life."

"Makes sense."

"And call the doctor."

***

Charisse ran her fingers through Steve's hair, gave him a peck on the cheek, and turned onto her side. "You're better every time we're together."

He popped a mega-smile. "It's you. You were fantastic."

"Don't try to butter me up ..."

His fingertips caressed her lips; he whispered platitudes. She seemed uncomfortable and he wondered why.

"You're not going to butter me up." She rolled on her back. "Want breakfast now?"

"Maybe later, I feel like a nap."

Sliding her feet to the floor she muttered, "I'll call you in an hour or so."

Steve turned on his side and pulled the sheet over his head.

It was slightly before ten when he staggered out of the bedroom in his boxer shorts.

Dressed in a matching purple and green outfit with not a hair out of place, she stared at him. "I'm not eating breakfast with a person looking like that."

Steve turned with his tail between his legs and took a quick shower. Returning in a new black and silver sweatsuit, he strolled toward her.

"That's better. You really look spiffy."

She sat two plates of Belgium waffles and sausage on their placemats. "How are things going in your personal life?"

"I'm making progress."

"Progress?" Her eyes opened wide, as if surprised. "Give me a couple of examples."

"A colleague at the office agreed to be my confidant. He put me on a new regimen. I'm cutting down on the amount I eat and drink, and working out every day. After three days, I'm already feeling better."

"That's good. All of that fits together."

"Next week I'm meeting Dr. Pritts again."

"Good for you." She smiled. "I've noticed your name in the paper a couple of times last week. How's it going at work?"

"It couldn't be better." Steve hesitated then looked her in the eye. "That reminds me, next Sunday I'll have to take a rain check."

She wrinkled her brow. "Why?"

"I'll be on *Meet the Press* with Tim Russert."

"Tim Russert? That's terrific."

"I about crapped my pants when I heard he was on the phone."

"I would have too." Chewing on her last piece of sausage, her eyes drifted down his sweatsuit and back to his eyes. "Maybe that would be a good time for me too."

Steve looked confused. "A good time?"

"A good time to stop seeing you."

"Why would you do that?" he said in an elevated tone, his eyes opening wide.

"My therapist says it's time for me to break it off. I haven't been with anyone else for six months and my feelings for you are growing."

"Something wrong with that?"

"In a way it's good — I haven't had real feelings for someone in ages — but we have a dead-end relationship. Sooner or later one of us will dump on the other. That's how addicts act."

"Are you positive that's the best thing for you?"

"No, but ... it's a shot I have to take. Maybe I'll find a flicker of light between my husband and me. I have to try."

Steve pressed his lips, his eyes glazed. "I only hope I'll have the same feelings someday."

"You will. You're a good person. It'll come someday for you."

***

Ellen waved her arm in the air. "Hurry up, Charlie. *Meet the Press* is coming on."

The sweet rolls aren't quite done."

"Sh, it's starting."

Charlie tiptoed in and sat his coffee cup on the end table next to hers.

Ellen's eyes stayed zeroed on the television screen.

The oven buzzer went off. Charlie rushed into the kitchen and returned with a plate of cinnamon buns.

Ellen didn't look up.

During the commercial break Charlie refilled their coffee as Ellen commented, "Charlie, can you believe it? We know someone on *Meet the Press*. Steve looks great."

"Yes," Charlie agreed. "Looks great. And sounds like he's running the show."

"Sh, here it comes again."

Ellen munched into her second pastry, mesmerized by the screen. "Ask him about the shithead," she shouted to the television.

"Shithead?"

"Shithead Chandler. I don't trust him."

"Dr. Shilling, what's it like working for Secretary Chandler?"

"We're a great team. For the most part we work independent of each other. His primary focus is on the hill. I work on the actual legislation and promote it. We're both committed to making President Stetson successful.'"

Ellen fumed. "Bullshit, Steve. He's an asshole and you know it."

"Relax, dear, it's politics."

The program ended. Ellen jumped up and headed for the kitchen.

"Did you hear Russert's last comment?" Charlie asked. "He said next time he's out of town, he's going to ask Steve to host. That's the ultimate compliment he could make."

"I have to call Steve."

"Ellen, he's in the studio. Give him an hour or two."

"Oh, yes, I forgot."

***

Dr. Pritts shook Steve's hand. "I was beginning to worry about you until I saw you on *Meet the Press*. You acted like you've known Tim Russert all of your life."

"Thanks. There's something about being on television or at the podium that turns me on. I was on a real high. I felt like I was chatting with an old friend."

"You came off like an old pro. The people at the *Post* thought so too. I don't think the president ever received such glowing comments."

"I'm sure she has. There's no one better in front of a camera."

"You missed your last couple of appointments. How's it going?"

"A colleague has agreed to be my confidant. I'm working out every day and watching how much I eat and drink too. I feel better."

"The physical discipline is good, but four women ..."

Steve interrupted. "Actually, it's only three now. Last week one stopped seeing me."

"She stopped seeing you?" Steve nodded. "How did you feel about that?"

"At first I felt sad, kind of lonely, then I realized it was a good thing for her. That made me feel better."

The doctor opened his pad. "Tell me about her."

"She's the sex addict."

"Oh yes, I recall — Charisse."

"She was doing better, and her therapist said it was time for her to take the next step. She hadn't slept with any other guys for six months and her feelings about me were growing. But she knew our relationship was a dead end."

"How did that make you feel?"

"It made me think … then I realized she was right."

"That's a good lesson for you. And a brave step for her."

"She's trying to rekindle things with her husband. I'm really proud of her. I hope it works out."

"Seeing someone else's joy can be helpful to you."

"I've never seen anyone so happy about the unknown."

"Put yourself in her place. An unknown future may be better than a terrible past."

"Hmm, I never thought about it that way." Steve took a deep breath. "Where do we go from here?"

"I want you to plant her smiling face in your memory banks. It ought to be something you strive for."

"That'll be easy. She really seemed happy."

Dr. Pritts paused. "Next time, I'd like to meet with your confidant. What's his name?"

"Art."

"Tell him about the incident with Charisse, and how you feel about her."

"Okay," Steve said, hesitantly.

"I want him to see that side of you. It'll be good for the two of you to talk about a positive relationship. And, it'll give you something to work toward."

***

FBI — Clarksburg, West Virginia
Criminal Justice Information Services Division

A computer flashed "ALERT" then printed:

Name:	**Steven Schilling**	
Previous:	**Kuratong Baleleng**	**Philippines**
	Bilderberger	**Netherlands**
New Information:	**Suspect seeing Kuratong Baleleng-associated woman on a regular basis. Last month two Kuratong Baleleng operatives were killed in Washington, D.C. on the same night the two were together.**	

The old staff member in the bowels of the building held up the printout. "Sharon," he called, to his assistant. "Have you seen the latest on our hotdog man?"

"No."

"Come over and have a look-see."

She pulled a chair up beside him, plopped down and grabbed the printout. Glancing at the first line, she smiled. "Steve Schilling. He's not a hotdog. Every woman in town is talking about him."

"Looks like he's doing more than talking," the old-timer laughed.

She read the new information then read it again. "I don't like this."

"Sounds like he's out on the town, having a good time."

"Maybe so. Sleeping with the wife of a Bilderberger is one thing. But ... being involved with a Kuratong Baleleng woman is something else; they have a 'take no prisoners' philosophy."

"Whataya think we should do?"

"There's no choice. We have to send it up the ladder," the head man said.

"I agree. I'll take care of it right away."

CHAPTER NINETEEN

Steve's fingertips circled Sherry's breasts, his lips following close behind. She sighed, turned onto her back and stretched her arms above her head to give him full range. He didn't miss the opportunity; his urges shifted into action. *Move easy. Take her to the top then watch her shoot out of control.*

Following his script to a tee, he kissed her gently around her face and ears, running his fingers around her lips down her neck and over her shoulders. She closed her eyes and pulled her shoulders back, inviting his touch to her heaving breasts. His lips accommodated her desires, sucking one then the other.

His right hand slid down her side, lightly circled her belly button with one finger, then caressed her stomach. Heading south, he fondled her private area. Beads of moisture popped from every pore; her body moved in concert with his hand — up and down, and around. Breathing heavily, her head flopped side to side, her body gently jerking.

"I can't hold off any longer," she gasped.

Steve raised up and smiled, watching her body twist and turn. Running his tongue insistently around her right nipple, he teasingly paused, then sucked on her left nipple. Sherry's body shot out of control. "Oh my God, Steve, I love you so much."

"I love you too, sweetie," he said, pulling her tight and kissing her tenderly.

Gently easing her down, he held her firmly as her body fell limp. And the two dozed off.

***

It was afternoon when Sherry kissed Steve on the cheek. "Are you going to sleep all day?"

His eyes fluttered at the sound. "Only if it's with you."

"I can't believe it." She poked him in the chest. "How can you think of that so fast when you're barely awake?"

He liked nothing better than being with her every night. "It's easy when I'm with you."

Seeming preoccupied, her indecision didn't last long. "We ought to team up."

"Team up?" He studied her thoughtfully.

"I've been thinking about my meeting with the Joint Chiefs of Staff. Maybe it'd be better if the two of us meet with them together."

Somewhat surprised, he stammered, "O-okay. Let's talk about it after I take a shower."

"Fine. I'll fix an omelet while you're getting dressed."

"Perfect, I'm starved."

Within minutes Steve had shaved and showered. Parading into the kitchen, wearing a new pair of silk loungers she had bought for him, he asked "How do these look?"

"Terrific. If I wasn't so hungry, I'd jump you right here."

He felt a surge and wondered if her thoughts were the same. "Well ..."

"Forget it, I'm having breakfast."

The two downed their omelets and toast while skimming the morning paper. Sherry refilled their coffee mugs and plopped back down across the dinette table from him. "Well, whataya think?"

He gave her an unconscious shrug.

"About meeting with the Joint Chiefs of Staff together," she said, impatiently.

"Why are you so antsy about it?"

"I googled them. Their conference room is called *the tank*. It really looks intimidating."

"Tank ... why do they call it that?"

"Their original conference room was built in 1942, in the lower level of a building. The flight of stairs went through a portal that gave the impression of entering a tank. When they moved to the Pentagon the nickname stuck."

"Interesting. Why does the room seem so intimidating?"

"It isn't just the room. It's the entire atmosphere; meeting with a bunch of generals on their turf. There's a large glossy, mahogany conference table in the center of the room. It must be four inches thick; and it's shaped like a rounded-off arrow. There are four chairs on the two sides and two at the rounded end. I assume it's the place where we'll be interrogated."

He unfolded his hands and gestured. "Your imagination has gone haywire."

"Around the room are additional chairs, probably for fifteen or more generals. I'm scared shitless."

"I'll change my schedule, no big deal. And I'll let Bradley know that we can save them time by the two of us meeting with them concurrently. It might be better; we can double team them."

"That'd be wonderful," she said, giving him a peck on the cheek. "You're so sweet."

"I thought a decision like that would be worth more than a kiss on the cheek."

She gave him a sly look out of the corner of her eye. "You don't miss a beat, do you?"

Thoughts of again exploring the secrets of the night exploded. "Well?"

Smiling seductively, she pulled her shoulders back, her breasts rose up and she loosened her blouse, revealing a braless top. "Only if I can be on top."

His eyes burned hotly with desire for her. "Works for me."

Sherry jumped up and chased him into the bedroom.

***

Stepping out of the car's back seat, Steve looked up at the young captain walking smartly toward Sherry and him. "Dr. Schilling, I presume."

Steve paused, examining the man's spit-shined shoes and flawless uniform.

"Ms. Holmgren." The captain acknowledged her. "Follow me, please."

Walking briskly, the captain ushered them through the Pentagon's security then headed to the second floor. Sherry took a double-step to keep up. Softly, she asked Steve, "Do you know where we are going?"

"Corridor 9 in the E ring."

She contorted her face. "Where's that?"

"There are five rings around the building. They're alphabetized — E is on the outside — it's the power ring. That's for the big guys ... they have the windows."

"You might know."

The captain stopped in front of an open door. "Here we are. I'll wait for you out here."

"Thanks." Steve nodded to him then led the way into the room Sherry had described.

A general approached them and extended his hand. "Good morning, I'm General William Crouch, Chairman of the Joint Chiefs of Staff."

"A pleasure, sir. I'm Steve Schilling and this is Sherry Holmgren."

He gave Sherry a pleasant smile. "Follow me, I'll introduce you to the others."

Working their way around the table, Steve couldn't help from having the same feelings Sherry had anticipated. *This place is intimidating as hell. The flag of each chief was stationed in the front of the room. There must be a dozen generals standing around the room's edge.*

He glanced over his shoulder and Sherry joined him at the interrogation end of the table.

General Crouch formally welcomed the two, then made a few comments about the role of the group. "President Stetson and Secretary Cohen were here two weeks ago with an outline of your plan. You've come up with an interesting public service concept."

His words stirred enthusiasm. "Thank you, sir."

"I'd like for you to provide a fifteen minute overview of the educational reform package. Then we'll open the floor for questions."

"Thank you, Mr. Chairman." Steve walked the group through the salient aspects of the plan then shifted to his selling points. "The armed forces play an extremely important role in the overall success of our plan. Without your endorsement and guidance our country will be unable to maintain our leadership role."

He paused to make sure the message was heard then commended each member of the group for his dedication and service. "In closing, General Crouch, I'd like to draw upon your own experience as a student of history." The general's eyes refocused on Steve. "History teaches us that at certain times leaders are called upon to make a difference in the future. We're at that point in time."

Again, Steve paused to let his words soak in.

"We can no longer allow a large segment of our population to be uneducated. It puts the entire country at risk. The military is the only hope we have to correct this weakness. Without your leadership we risk our entire way of life."

"That's a powerful statement, Dr. Schilling," the chairman said.

"It's more than a statement, Mr. Chairman — it's the truth — without your leadership we're all at risk."

"I'd like to go around the table so my colleagues can ask a question then we'll open the floor for general discussion. Vice Chairman Ralston."

"I'm interested in the logistics of all of this. You're talking about millions of young people. How do you propose we manage such a challenge?"

"That's an excellent question. And exactly the type of question I'd expect from the guru of military strategic planning," Steve replied, collecting his thoughts to review the backgrounds of the others.

The general puffed up.

"First, we'll maintain all of the bases being considered for closure. Quite frankly, we must find places to accommodate the most troublesome youth. Second, the mandatory aspect goes into effect in 2004. We anticipant large numbers will volunteer in the coming years. Many will see the program as their only way out of the vicious cycle of poverty."

"I have a question, Dr. Schilling," Army General Reimer said. "If we accept this challenge, how do you see the military being capable of accomplishing goals that educators have failed to achieve?"

"The failure of our educators is the very reason we are coming to you. We need to change the rules." Steve smiled. "You'll be in charge, instead of some local school board running for reelection."

Smiles popped up around the room.

Steve took the advantage, "As a ranger you learned to cope. You took whatever actions were necessary to survive, right?"

The general nodded, clearly showing his pleasure, as Steve's eyes connected with him.

"In this case we're giving you all of the tools to work with these troubled youth. That's different from the teachers who 'got no respect' from their students. And teachers are not supported by their principals. I don't see that as a problem for you ... no problem for any of you around this table."

Hammering in another point, Steve said, "And parents think their child is perfect, and try to run the system. I wouldn't expect to see parents running any of your bases."

The general grinned, his expression radiant. "Point well made."

Admiral Jay Johnston asked, "Dr. Schilling, how do you see the military training such a diverse group of people?"

"Last year, I had an opportunity to spend a few days on an aircraft carrier. There were over three thousand young sailors on that ship. Their average age was under twenty-one — the ship ran like clockwork. I don't have the answer as to how. But based on my experience I know that if given the challenge, the navy will figure out the *how*."

"What is your perspective on our ability to address the challenges of such a massive group?" Air Force General Ryan asked.

"It's the same as you have done in the past, sir. In flying over a hundred missions, you learned how to delegate authority and make teams work. We're asking you to do the same thing you've done to ensure the success of each of your commands."

"All of this calls for a great deal of compassion," Marine General Krulak said. "Some of those kids have already been through hell."

"Absolutely," Steve agreed. "It's the same as when you personally deliver Christmas cookies to the people on your post. As I recall the eighteen pregnant women on your base were treated differently than the recovering druggies."

General Krulak's pride blossomed with more than a hint of a smile.

Lt. General Baca from the National Guard asked, "How do we cultivate a desire in these young people to learn, to have goals and succeed?"

Steve flashed his trademark smile. "You are far more qualified to answer that question than I. You grew up in a struggling working-class family. You saw, first hand, friends on your street fall by the wayside. We need to design programs that instill the same values your mother taught."

"I agree, Dr. Schilling, but the challenge is still enormous."

Steve held back his excitement knowing he had the group where he wanted them. "Agreed — but the size of the task is not a good reason for turning your back on the challenge. We can't afford to ignore the task."

"Touché."

General Crouch looked around the table. "Do we have any more questions before we move on to the second item?"

The room was silent.

"Good. Ms. Holmgren, would you provide an overview of the 20 percent reduction plan you initiated in the Department of Education."

"A privilege, sir." Sherry looked at the generals and admirals surrounding her then proceeded like an old pro. Twenty minutes later, she paused with a tone of confidence in her voice. "What questions do you have?"

"Where did you find cuts that produced the greatest savings?" General Ryan asked.

"Mid-management and at the top, sir. In terms of dollars per position the savings at the top were by far the greatest. Volume-wise the largest number of dollars was saved in the middle of the organization. We made few cuts at the lower level. Those employees are highly valuable; they provide direct services."

"Is that to say others aren't important?" General Crouch asked.

"No. These office workers are like your front line people. They provide tangible results. The question is how many people are required at the top to provide direction."

"How do we find the necessary people to staff the training programs you're talking about?"

Sherry bit her tongue to refrain from a "can't you figure that out yourself?" attitude. "Candidly," she said. "You begin with the people in this building. There are twenty-eight thousand employees in the Pentagon. 20 percent is fifty-six hundred — that sounds like a good start to me."

The ten generals sitting around the edge of the room stirred.

Still seeking specific direction, General Crouch countered, "How do you decide which positions are to be eliminated?"

Clearly in control, she sent a smile his way. "We assessed each vacancy as it occurred. We asked, 'Is this position essential? Does it add value? Is any part of the position duplicative? Can the work be done by someone else?' It didn't take long before we identified a large number of unneeded vacancies."

"Where did they come from?" Admiral Johnston asked. "Who gave you the advice?"

Sherry paused for effect. "The suggestions didn't come from people like those in this room. Honestly, people at the top are often overly protective of *their people*."

Several generals around the perimeter bristled, knowing they were often the guilty ones.

"Where did it come from?" General Baca repeated Johnston's question.

She spread her arms as if to include everyone. "From the staff. They know what's happening in the office. I'll give you an example. On the way up here today, we passed several offices. For discussion purposes, let's assume each one had twenty employees. If that office reported to you, sir, how would you know which employees are contributing the least? Who would you target for elimination or reassignment?"

"I look at their records and ask their supervisors."

"Performance appraisals are important but maybe the supervisor should go. We went directly to the staff members. They know who is working and who the slackers are. In some cases we eliminated half of the unit. In other cases we cut fewer than ten percent of the staff."

"Interesting." General Crouch looked around the table. "Anyone else?" His eyes grazed over his colleagues. Their heads shook.

The general's smile revealed his admiration. "Dr. Schilling and Ms. Holmgren, on behalf of the Joint Chiefs of Staff, I'd like to thank you for the excellent presentations. Your insights have been quite helpful."

***

Sherry could hardly wait until the car door closed. "How did you come up with all of those personal insights? It sounded like you've known each of them all your life."

"It's an old technique I learned from a longtime friend. She used to say 'You need to know where a person has been so you understand where they're headed.'"

Sherry wrinkled her brow. "I-I ..."

Touching her upper lip with the tip of his forefinger, his eyes softened. "I googled them, found out a few tidbits and sprinkled them out as I responded to each question."

"I still can't believe it ... you sounded like old buddies."

"That's the point. Once you're on the same page with a person, it's easy for them to think you agree with them."

Steve squeezed her hand; her lovely faced was even more adorable to him. "You did a great job."

"I could have peed my pants when I walked in. But ... watching you fired me up."

"I was impressed." He kissed her on the cheek.

"Where to now?" she asked.

"That depends on the chiefs. If they don't buy in then we'll have to go back with a series of one-on-one sessions. If they come around, we'll start planning our tour."

"Our?"

Holding off his unrelenting desire, he'd waited for just the right moment. "I told Bradley and Ira that I want you to come along so you could be my backup. They agreed. It looks like you'll be going to Paducah, Kalamazoo ..."

"That's great." She cut him off with a peck on the cheek.

"I hoped I wouldn't have to twist your arm," he jested.

"When would it start?"

"As soon as you return from your parent's place in August. Will has started working his numbers. He's short four or five more senators and seventeen members in the house. Not much else will be happening this summer. Ira wants us to test the water for the president. We'll be done by the time she cranks up, early October."

"Sounds exciting."

"I can't wait to spend that much time with you."

She slid close to him; her mouth found his. "Do we have to go back to the office right now?"

"Only to pick up our cars."

***

Steve pulled a stool up to the end of the bar in Blues Alley — the oldest jazz dinner/night club in the country — and only a short walk from his apartment. It was fast becoming his neighborhood hangout. The bartender winked and within minutes sat two Tanqueray's with three olives in front of him. "It's on the house," the sixtyish, gray-beard said.

"What's the deal?" Steve asked.

"Hey, you're our most famous regular ... being on *Meet the Press* ... I couldn't believe it."

Steve laughed. "Sometimes you have to be lucky."

"Lucky hell, you're one of the first ones up there to make any sense. Do you think you'll really be able to pull off those changes?"

"We're going to give it the old college try."

"It'd be great if we could educate the bums. That'd make a tremendous difference in this country."

"It makes sense but it'll be a long haul."

"Good luck. Let me know when you want to order dinner."

"Will do."

Steve turned his eyes to the stage as the first show began. *I love this place. First-class jazz every day of the year. You can't beat that.* He looked around at the nearby dimly lit tables. A group of five women caught his eye. *God lord, they all look like tens.*

He motioned to the barkeep then leaned over the bar. "Gino, have you seen those women before?" Steve pointed subtly.

"They started coming in a couple months ago. They buy tickets for the early show on the first Thursday of the month."

"A bunch of knockouts."

"Wait till you see the group leader."

"Why?"

The old Italian smiled. "You'll know when you see her."

"I'm having the Dizzy Gillespie Jambalaya tonight."

"Another round?"

"Sure with dinner."

Steve watched the next performance then dug into his jambalaya and cornbread.

Gino leaned over the bar and whispered. "So, what do you think of her?" He nodded slightly toward the group of hot women.

Steve turned, spotting the back of flaming red hair, perfectly sculptured around her head. "Can't tell much from here."

"I'll give you a signal when she goes to the bathroom."

Looking that way occasionally, Steve finished dinner then glanced her way. He watched her stand and head his way. *Holy shit.* Knee-high black boots and jeans stretched sexily over slender thighs. He couldn't stop staring.

She passed him by.

He leaned to the side and watched the tight-ass jeans beckon as she strode toward the back.

Gino walked to his end of the bar. "Whataya think?"

"Who in the hell is she?"

The bartender shrugged his shoulders. "Their waiter thinks they're a group of interpreters."

"Interpreters? From where?"

"Don't know." Gino reached to clean a glass. "Here she comes."

Steve glanced at her bulging sweater and shapely body then gazed into her golden brown eyes. As she began to pass in front of him he said, "Enjoying the show?" and mentally frowned for being unable to think of anything more creative.

"It's terrific, isn't it?" she said, a half smile parting lovely, full lips, as she continued on her way.

Steve kicked himself in the butt. *A chance of a lifetime and you blow it. You dumb bastard.*

CHAPTER TWENTY

On the first Thursday in July, Steve arrived early for the six o'clock show at Blues Alley. Staff members lit candles in the center of the tables. Technicians adjusted the lighting and sound systems. Pulling out his regular stool, he eased on to it and cast an eye to the table of importance — so far, it stood vacant. The lights dimmed and the tables filled.

Gino sat Steve's usual in front of him. "Early bird gets the worm, huh?"

It was almost six when she strutted in, dressed in Navy blue boots, matching stretch pants and a light blue sweater that wouldn't quit. *Look at those tits testing the strength of each fiber.* Greeting the others already in their seats, she pulled out the last chair at the table and eased down, her back to him.

Steve took a deep breath and ordered another Tanqueray.

Gino leaned his way. "Whataya think of those knockers?"

"Damn. Did you ever see anything like them?"

The old man glowed. "Sophia Loren's were bigger."

Still staring Steve ignored the comment trying to figure how he'd make a move. Dr. Pritts didn't even enter his mind.

A long-haired hippy type guy walked up and tapped him on the shoulder. "Is this seat taken?" the fortyish dude asked, then looked Steve in the eye. "Hey, didn't I see you on TV last month?"

Steve gave him a "who cares" shrug. "*Meet the Press.*"

"Yah, you're the guy who wants to put the bums in the military. Good for you. It's about time someone had some balls around here." He extended a hand. "I'm Patrick Ridelman, the backup drummer for the band."

"Nice to meet you. I'm Steve Schilling."

Pat shook his head. "I can't believe it. Wait till my girlfriend hears about this."

Gino handed him a Bud. "It's on the house."

"Thanks," he said, then gestured toward the redhead. "Whataya think about *her*?"

Steve glanced her way. "She's something else. I'd like to know more about her."

Pat leaned closer to Steve. "See the blonde next to her?" Steve nodded. "She has the hots for drummers. I've screwed her several times."

Steve turned with growing interest. "Can you tell me anything about the redhead?"

"Wanta buy me a beer?"

Steve motioned to the barkeep. "Gino, my friend wants another Bud."

"Coming up."

Leaning toward Pat, Steve said, "Let's hear the scoop."

The musician took a slug. "She's Russian, drinks vodka, her name is Elena something or other. She's an interpreter."

"Do you know anything else?"

"She loves jazz."

Overhearing the conversation, Gino leaned into Steve. "I have an idea."

Steve lifted a brow. "Let's hear it."

"Wait a minute." The bartender slipped to the backbar, pulled open a drawer under the cash register and took out a piece of paper. Walking back like a proud peacock, he handed it to Steve. "Here's an upcoming program for two weeks from today."

Reading the names, Steve shrugged his shoulder. "So?"

"Simon Nabatov is the top jazz pianist in Russia. He's performing with Nils Wogram, a topnotch German trombonist. We've been sold out for months."

Steve scrunched his shoulders. "Sorry to be so dense."

"I have two tickets for the two stools you guys are sitting on."

Steve asked. "How much?"

Gino laughed. "You get her to come and we'll talk about it." Steve took a sip. *How in the hell am I going to do that.* He brushed his fingers through his hair then glanced at his new buddy. Pat was all smiles. "What's with you?" Steve asked.

"I figured you'd ask Gino how in the hell am I going to do that?"

Steve admitted, "That's what I had in mind next."

"It's simple," Pat suggested. "Give her waiter five bucks and have him tell Elena you'd like to buy her table a round of drinks."

"You think that'll work?"

His new found expert grinned. "Of course, it works every time." Pat downed the last of his beer. "She'll have to come over and thank you."

Steve's eyebrows shot up. He ordered his buddy another beer and asked Gino to follow through with the waiter.

Out of the corner their eyes, the two watched the waiter walk over to Elena and say something. She turned and smiled at Steve then nodded to the waiter. A buzz went around their table. One woman said something to her friend then gestured toward Steve. The two giggled and one by one the rest of the group looked his way.

"Looks like you made a hit." Patrick hesitated. "I think one of them recognized you."

"How can you tell?"

"The way they looked at you and giggled. That's how women react when they're out on their own. You'd think they were a bunch of teenage girls."

"Should we do something?"

"Just wait … she'll probably come over during the next break. That'll be your chance so don't blow it."

Steve ordered another round then took a sip. *What do I say? How do I make the pitch about the upcoming show?*

Pat turned toward Steve. "Just strike up a brief conservation then ask if she's aware of the show in two weeks."

"Are you a mind reader," Steve jested.

The seasoned pro fumbled with his paper napkin. "I've done this a few times."

The soloist ended her song. The audience stood and cheered.

"Sit down. She's on the way over," Patrick whispered.

Steve eased onto his stool, fiddled with his drink coaster and waited. She tapped him on the shoulder. Steve turned and stood, *trying not to look at her tightly stretched sweater.*

"Thanks for the round of drinks. That was very thoughtful."

"You're welcome," he said, pushing his stool under the counter. "Your group seemed to be having a lot of fun so I said why not."

"You're Dr. Schilling, aren't you?"

"Yes, how did you know?"

"One of the girls saw you on TV. She'd like to meet you. Would you be willing to come over to my table?"

"Of course ..." His friend kicked him. "First I'd like to ask you something."

She stiffened noticeably.

Steve picked up the program. "Have you heard of Simon Nabatov?"

"Simon Nabatov!" she exclaimed. "He's my favorite pianist. I tried to buy tickets. They've been sold out for weeks."

Steve held up the program. "How would you like to attend with me?"

She stepped back. "Do you have tickets?"

Steve pointed to the two stools. "Right here."

She gave him a questioning look. "Are you putting me on?"

I'd like to. He motioned to Gino. "Where are my seats for the Nabatov performance?"

Gino looked at her then pointed to the stools. "Right there."

Elena stood frozen then pecked him on the cheek. "Yes, I'll be here."

"Perfect." Steve winked at Pat. "Let's go see your friends."

She grabbed his hand and towed him to the table.

***

Kim and Steve chatted in the lobby of his apartment building waiting for the limo to appear. "We ought to get away sometime for a long weekend," he said.

She snuggled closer. "I love to do that."

"There are several flights from here to Bermuda. Have you ever been there?"

"No. Any place with you would be wonderful."

His engine roared. "How about sometime in the first part of August?

"Super."

Seeing the limo pull up, Steve led her toward the door. They froze mid-step as several shots rang out. The lobby's front window shattered. Steve pushed her under a table and covered her with his body.

The front door flew open. Rodrigo rushed in. "Kim, are you okay?"

"Yes," she called meekly.

"Stay where you are, don't move." He slammed the door and ran for the car. Minutes later he returned, his shirt blood-soaked. "Felix was shot twice in the head. Go back up to Steve's apartment and don't come out or let anyone in. I'll call you as soon as I can."

Steve helped Kim up and the two scurried for the elevator. He held her tight until they arrived at his floor then rushed her into his apartment and bolted the door.

Easing onto the sofa, he took a deep breath. "It's going to be okay, sweetie. Try to relax."

"It won't be okay. It never be okay. Kuratong Baleleng never stop."

"I won't let them harm you," Steve pledged.

She hugged him. "Sooner or later they come after you. I cannot let that happen."

He held her tight, wondering if he should tell her about the call and the letter. *The timing sucks. Maybe I should wait. Hmm, I can't hide anything from her. I love her too much.* He turned her face toward his. "I've already heard from them."

Her face flushed. "No, that not possible. Tell me."

Steve took his time, telling her the details about the message on his answering machine and the letter he'd received. "We talked about contacting the FBI but decided not to unless there was another incident."

"There be more threats. They crazy."

"I am more concerned about you."

"You not worry about me. Rodrigo protect me. There no one to protect you."

Having never thought about his own danger, Steve paused, beads of perspiration laced his upper lip. "Want a drink?"

"I have beer. I hungry … you have frozen pizza?"

He nodded. "A supreme. Want hot peppers on it?"

"Double."

Staying away from the windows, Steve opened two cans of beer and sat them on the coffee table in front of her. A few minutes later, he pulled the pizza from the oven and sliced it. Slipping on a pair of padded gloves, he carried hot tin to the coffee table and eased it on the ends of his gloves. The two snuggled on the sofa and finished off the pizza. She jabbered nervously.

"I love you, Kim, more than anyone." Steve kissed her lightly on the cheek.

"You my man. I love you too."

The phone rang. Steve stood and picked it up.

"Dr. Schilling, this is Rodrigo may I speak with Kim?"

"Of course." He handed her the phone and mouthed "It's Rodrigo."

"Yes," she said, sounding stronger.

Kim listened and nodded then blurted, "No, I won't." The conversation continued. "You don't understand." She brushed a tear from her cheek. "You can't make me." She wiped another tear and sniffled. Steve handed her his handkerchief. She wiped her eyes and sobbed, the phone plastered to her ear. Continuing to listen, she sighed, then took a deep breath. "Okay, I will."

Kim replaced the phone in the cradle, looked at Steve and broke into tears. Unable to talk, he held her for a long time. She closed her eyes and laid her head on his chest. Slowly, ever so slowly, she composed herself. Taking a deep breath, she raised her head and looked him in the eye. "I must go."

"Go? Where? Why?"

She bit her lip. "My government made arrangements. I fly out of Dulles tomorrow morning at eleven."

"No, you must stay."

She shook her head. "Decision made. Rodrigo is only one to protect me here. In my country there hundreds of agents."

"When will I see you again?"

"I don't know." Her eyes welled. "Maybe never."

"No, I can't let that happen. I love you. I want to marry you."

"I want to be with you forever." She smiled, lovingly. "That not possible. Rodrigo is coming in morning."

***

Arriving early at Blues Alley, Steve ordered his usual and a Ruskova vodka — the best Russian vodka on hand at the bar — on the rocks for her. She arrived before the drinks, wearing burgundy knee-high boots, black skin-tight pants and a vintage cowl-neck, white cotton top with an embroidered burgundy design. Steve looked her in the eye, trying not to stare at her cleavage in full sight.

Gino placed their drinks on the bar in front of them.

"Vodka, as I recall." Steve slid a glass toward her.

She looked fabulous; didn't need makeup. He'd been walking on air since he first saw her. "Here's to the most attractive woman I've ever seen."

"Thank you." She took a sip and licked her lips. "Ruskova! Excellent choice."

"It's the best they have."

"It's in the top two or three by any measure in Russia."

"I bet you are too."

Her eyes drifted up to his. "I think you're getting a little ahead of yourself."

Receiving the message loud and clear, Steve swallowed hard.

"Do you know much about Simon Nabatov?" she asked.

Steve searched his memory banks. "Let me see," he said, buying time. "Simon Nabatov is the premier jazz pianist in Russia. He began playing at three and had his first composition at six. Then he studied at Julliard."

"Stop." She raised her hand. "You're either a jazz aficionado or you googled him."

Steve looked up sheepishly. "I googled him."

"Nothing wrong with that ... at least you took the time. I'm impressed."

"Want to order dinner now or later?"

"Let's wait. I want to enjoy the performance."

"Sounds good to me."

The two watched Nabatov and Wogram perform as if they'd played together forever. At each break, the crowd cheered and shouted. Steve ordered a round, then another. The two performed an encore; the crowd called for more. They performed another duet.

Steve slid closer. She placed her hand on his leg.

The performance ended. Steve and Elena stood and cheered with the room, then settled back on their stools. "I'm starved," she said.

"Me too," Steve picked up the menus and handed her one. "Let's order."

"Anything look particularly good to you?" she asked.

"I've had the jambalaya and crab cakes recently. You can't go wrong with anything, though."

"Hmm ... I'm having Nancy Wilson's Shrimp Etouffee," she announced.

"Sounds wonderful. I'm trying to cut down; going for a bowl of seafood gumbo."

The two settled into a comfortable conversation, and before he knew it, his bowl was empty. She looked at him casually. "I want to thank you for a wonderful evening. It was much more than I anticipated. Could I pick up the tip?"

"No way. Tonight was my treat." He rubbed his five o'clock shadow. "May I see you again?"

"I'll be here with the group on the first Thursday of August. You can join us."

"Terrific," he said, knowing he had other thoughts in mind.

***

Steve took off early Thursday so he could unwind before going to the Blues Alley. *I'm concerned about Kim. Why would the government call her back? Her family must be very important. I wonder how she's doing.* After a quick shower and shave, he sat

down at his desk and opened his calendar. His eyes bugged —
August was blank. *Kim and Charisse had split. Sherry was with her
parents in Ohio. Move easy on Elena, she's really hot, but she's still
skittish.*

Arriving at the club a few minutes before six, Steve eased onto
the high-back chair next to Elena. He didn't want to interrupt her
conversation with the women next to her, so he glanced around the
table. *Boobs galore.* He tried not to stare.

Elena turned; her smile warm, stirring an instant feeling of
anticipation in him. "Thanks again for the ticket and dinner last
month."

"My privilege," he said. "Where do you work?"

"We're interpreters at the American Center for Communications.
Each of us specialize in a different language. This is our chance to
taste a little of your culture."

"Interesting. I can't think of a better place," he said, then ordered
a chicken Caesar salad and joined the conversation. There was a
constant buzz around the table the rest of the night. The group asked
about Steve's job, working with the president, making speeches, and
traveling on Air Force One. He enjoyed being the center of attention.

On the way out, he eased closer to Elena. "How about dinner
Saturday night?"

Her large brown eyes twinkled. "I'd like that."

"Do you have a special place you like?"

"La Chaumiere is not far from where I live. We could meet
around seven thirty or eight."

"Eight sounds good. I'll make the reservations and meet you
there."

***

Steve stepped into the French restaurant and gazed at the
romantic atmosphere. Elena slid up behind him and nudged him in the
back. "Hey Mr., would you like to have dinner with me tonight?"

Glancing over his shoulder, he tossed her his trademark smile.
"I can't think of anything I'd rather do."

She winked. "You're quick on your feet, aren't you?"

"One has to be nimble when it comes to a beautiful woman."

"Sly too." Her green eyes sparkled.

The maître d' asked, "Table for two, sir?"

"Yes. It's under Schilling."

The man's pencil-thin mustache quivered as he glanced at the pad. "Of course, thank you, right this way."

The maître d' lead them to a small corner table. She eased in on one side. Steve slid in on the other, and glanced around. "The plastered ceiling and wooden beams give it an authentic French feeling. And look at that massive fireplace in the center of the room."

She shot him a sensual look that took his breath away. "The food is even better."

"Would you like a drink?"

"Hmm, maybe a glass of white wine."

Steve scanned the wine list and motioned to the waitress to take their drink orders, then glanced at Elena. "I'm having sauvignon blanc. If you like I'll order a bottle."

"That'd be fine."

The two chatted over the menu. "The Fricassee du Pecheus sounds wonderful," he said.

"Mmm … Good choice. It's a delicious fish stew."

"I'm ordering that."

She laid the menu down. "I love their marinated duck breast. I'm having the Magret de Canard."

The two lingered over dinner. He asked about her job and plied her with countless questions about growing up in Moscow, where she had gone to school. She countered by asking about his childhood days in Kentucky. "Do they still wear those funny looking fur caps there?"

Steve restrained himself with a chuckle. "You mean the coonskin caps. They wore those back in the old pioneer days."

They talked about his job and the travel plans for selling phase three. Feeling comfortable, he placed his hand on her thigh and inched up as he had done so many times with other women. "Would you like some dessert?"

She glanced down at his fingertips. "If you're searching for a zipper there's not one there."

Steve pulled his hand away uncomfortably.

218

Her smile grew. "How about dessert at my place?"

Taken aback, Steve struggled to find the right word. "Really?"

She gave him *the look.* "I assume that's what you were interested in." He hemmed-and-hawed. She voiced what both were thinking. "There's a big difference in our cultures."

"I guess so," Steve said, feeling like a greenhorn. He masked his embarrassment by paying the bill.

Grabbing his hand, Elena guided him down the street to her flat and pulled him inside. She didn't waste any time, stripping to her panties and parading around her bedroom lighting candles — her breasts pointed like beacons showing the way.

She turned on a soft jazz tape and dimmed the lights.

Steve stripped naked and slid under the sheet. His erection already stood tall.

She smiled at his size tenting the sheet, then reached under it and fondled his tool. Throwing the sheet off, she slipped lower, and sucked. While Elena was having her way with him, Steve gasped and twisted from one side to the other. She groped him relentlessly.

Unaccustomed to not being in control, he tried to psych himself out. *Relax. Don't come too soon. Move easy … take your time.*

She eased up, slipped off her black bikini panties. Pulling on a condom, Steve tried to catch a breath. She was relentless pushing him inside and banging against him again and again. He closed his eyes trying to hold off. Picking up the pace, she pounded harder.

Steve struggled to keep up then faltered. "I can't hold off any longer," he cried out.

She didn't stop. Moisture filled her cleavage, dripping on to Steve's chest and running down her sides. Her body whaled against him. She gave a final heave. "Oh my God," she screamed.

Unable to believe what had happened, the normally clear thinking and in control guy wilted under the furious pounding of her slender hips. He wanted her more than anyone before — the ache was huge — he had to see her again.

***

FBI Headquarters
935 Pennsylvania Avenue NW
Washington, D.C.

A month later three staff members buried in the bowels of the J. Edger Hoover building reviewed the latest computer printout:

Name:	**Steven Schilling**	
Previous:	**Kuratong Baleleng**	**Philippines**
	Bilderberger	**Netherlands**
	Unknown woman	**Russia**
New Information:	**Suspect seen with Kuratong Baleleng-associated woman. Two months ago two Kuratong Baleleng operatives killed in Washington, D.C. on the same night the two were together. Another KB agent was killed this month under the same conditions.**	
	Suspect involved with Russian woman, possible spy. They've been seen together several times in the last month.	

"Maybe he's a stud, but being seen with three different women on our suspect list is more than I can take. There is no way this can be a coincidence," the assistant director said.

"Hey," the female intern said. "There's no evidence these women are threats. Maybe they just happened to be in the wrong place."

"Could be but that's not for us to say," said her mentor. "We have to send it up the ladder." People are getting killed. I don't like that."

His assistant nodded. "We can't ignore his access to the president. Maybe he's being used as a pawn," she said.

"Doesn't matter, I'm showing it to the boss.

CHAPTER TWENTY-ONE

FBI Headquarters
935 Pennsylvania Avenue NW
Washington, D.C.

September 1, 1998

In a small conference room on the sixth floor five mid-level managers pulled their chairs up for the monthly meeting. Placing a large coffee container in front of him, Mitchell Blake called the meeting to order and distributed the eight-point agenda.

"Looks like August was another busy month," he jested. "Item 1 — Hot Spots in the US. Who wants to go first?"

By eleven fifteen the group had reviewed forty-seven situations. "Moving on to item number eight — New Situations," Blake said, and handed out a small file to each person. "Staff has culled four suspicious activities out of almost four hundred cases. Let's take a short break before we review them."

Three agents stood and stretched their legs. Another refilled his coffee mug. One read each word before the group reassembled. He raised his hand when the last agent returned to his place. "Let's start with the Schilling case."

"Sounds good to me," an old-timer said. "Let's take a minute to read it so we're all up-to-date."

A couple of minutes later, the studious one said, "I don't like the smell of this. It has the potential of being a major security breach."

His associate to the right agreed. "On the surface it looks like it's he's on the up and up, but with his access to the president is a potential problem. What do we know about the Russian woman?"

Mitchell flashed a picture on a screen of Elena standing in front a Moscow fountain.

"Holy shit," an agent across the table said. "Did you ever see anything like that?"

All eyes glued on her provocative profile. "Jesus Christ," the old-timer said. "We have a potential security breach … big time!"

"Flick that thing off," another agent complained. "I can't focus on the question. Other than a great body, what do we know?"

Mitchell picked up another file. "She's worked for TASS as interpreter for seven years."

The studious agent looked up. "Hmm, since 1991 when the KGB disbanded. Agents were dispersed throughout government; some were sent to the Federal Security Service. The rest went into their Foreign Intelligence Service (counterpart to our CIA) and their news agency, TASS — a perfect place to hide an international spy."

"Right." Mitchell agreed; several nodded their heads with him.

"Other than being the Deputy Secretary of Education, do we know anything else about Steven Schilling?" The inquirer raised several pieces of paper. "I googled him last night. He had a distinguished career turning around two universities — one in Arkansas and the other in North Carolina — he looks on the up and up to me."

"Mountain State? They upset Louisville a few years ago."

"Right, their coach, Bo … something, and he were on the cover of *Sports Illustrated*."

"You're right. Bo Willard."

"How does that connect?" Mitchell asked.

"It doesn't, sorry."

"However you cut it, this country boy is in some high cotton," Mitchell said. "I want him checked out. Have one of our field offices also check out the woman associated with the Kuratong Baleleng, and the one affiliated with the Bilderberger's. I want one of our teams on Elena."

"I'll sign up for Elena," the younger agent across the table said.

Mitchell laughed. "No thanks. We'll use a senior team to follow her. Anyone know where the two universities are located?"

"One's in Ruston, Arkansas. I think that's near Memphis."

"Instruct someone in our Memphis office to head to Ruston and find out everything they can about his activities while there."

"Mountain State is near Asheville."

"Request someone investigate him. I'm putting it on our October agenda. Anything else?"

"Did you see the scrap of paper in the back of Schilling's file signed EK?"

Mitchell paged through his file copy. "I don't have anything. Let me see it."

"Ed Kowalski is an old friend of Art Wallhollister," an old-timer said. "He's Schilling's assistants. Ed's meeting with them tomorrow to discuss a threatening phone message and letter Schilling received from the Kuratong Baleleng."

"That means the Kuratong Baleleng is closer than we thought."

"Who knows, maybe it's a smokescreen," the younger agent suggested.

"A smokescreen?" Mitchell questioned. "Or, Schilling might be covering his tracks to make it look like he doesn't know anything."

"I suppose ... at this point anything is possible."

***

Arriving home after a grueling sixteen-day road trip for the phase three campaign, Steve collapsed on his lounger. "I guess I'm getting old." He said aloud, and grinned to himself. "Living out of a suitcase isn't as much fun as it used to be."

He eased out of the chair, walked over to his bar and tiredly plopped two olives in his glass of ice and filled it up. Returning to the recliner, he propped up his feet again, and reflected on Sherry. *Being with her every night made the trip worthwhile. She's so easygoing and loveable, I could spend the rest of my life with her. When this gig is over I'm going to propose.* He sipped on his gin. *I haven't heard from Kim since she left. Wonder if she is okay. It's a little scary the way she talked about the Kuratong Baleleng being so evil and having no scruples. Not to mention our night of gunshots.*

His thoughts flashed back on Elena; he recalled the nights he spent with her before his trip. The first night after dinner at the French restaurant was unreal. The last two weekends were unbelievable. *She goes non-stop; must have had three or four orgasms every night, maybe five. Shit I lost count.*

The ringing phone jarred his fantasy. "Steve Schilling," he said automatically.

"Steve, it's Janet, how was your trip?"

"It went well. I missed you terribly."

"I've missed you too, sweetie. I've been at Camp David for the past three days but decided to sneak out and come home a day early. Any chance you could slip over tonight?"

"Of course." He rubbed his five o'clock shadow. "I'll take a quick shower and clean up."

"Save the shower. We can freshen up together here."

"Sounds better all the time. Would forty-five minutes be okay?"

"Perfect."

***

Flashing his credentials at the door, Steve walked past security then smiled at a staff member standing next to the White House elevator. He stepped to the rear and waited for the door to open on the second floor.

Janet stopped her idle pacing in the hallway when the elevator doors opened. They barely had time to close when she pulled him tight and planted a wildly wet kiss on his lips.

He grabbed her ass. "God, I've missed you."

"At least you've been out with people. I've been looking at the same four walls at Camp David for two of the last three weekends."

Steve was surprised by the number of times he'd thought about her on the trip. He now realized how much he'd missed her. They kissed until he was breathless with desire. "How much time do we have to shower?"

"Forty minutes. I just put the appetizers in the oven." Looping her arms around his neck, she felt him hard against her. "Will that be long enough?"

Feeling her rapid heartbeat, he winked. "I can handle that, can you?"

"Absolutely," she said, tugging him to the master bathroom. She stripped and was in the shower before he had his shoes off. "Are you coming?" she joked.

"Not yet," he zinged back. "I don't even have my pants off."

Steve slipped in the shower and his hands didn't hesitate as he caressed her gently and kissed her lightly on the neck and cheek.

"Would you do my back, sweetheart?"

Steve grinned, getting her message. He moved behind her and ran his fingers through her scalp then down her shoulders. She placed her hands on the wall, hot water gushing down her back. "God, that feels good," she said.

Knowing that she hadn't yet started to *feel good*, he gently massaged her neck and shoulders, taking his time, moving over each location two and three times. Slowly his fingertips worked down each vertebra. He could see the tension in her body release.

Steve clasped her cheeks and squeezed them tenderly, then began to fondle — around and between her cheeks. Her ass fell into the rhythm of his hands, seemingly moving on its own. She gasped as he fondled her vital parts. He forced himself not to hurry.

Longing with desire — heat against heat — fire burning in him, he moaned throatily. Her breaths shortened. Slamming her hands against the wall she uttered lewd remarks in between heavy panting.

"Do it. Do it," she cried out breathlessly.

Steve slid forward, his tool in his hand then stopped.

"Don't tease, Steve. Do it ... *do it*."

His mind swirled; an uneasy feeling came over him. *She's never said that.* He stepped back like a guilty teenager. *How can this be?*

Placing his hand on her shoulder, he slowly turned her around and stared into her eyes. He studied her face, thoroughly, unmindful of the water steaming around them.

"You're not Janet, are you?"

"What are you talking about?" she asked stiffly.

"Answer my question." Steve's face reddened. "You're not Janet, are you?"

She bit her lip then shook her head. "I'm Hope ... her double." She wiped her face. "But I can explain."

His eyes squinted, staring at her in a questioning manner, still wondering, not sure of what was happening.

She took a deep breath. "I've wanted to be with you ever since that first dance at President Reagan's reception."

Steve stood motionless, his voice quiet. "I don't understand."

"I enjoyed dancing with you. I could tell you liked it too."

"Yes, I did but ..."

Her forefinger brushed his lips. "I knew you thought I was Janet, but God ... what a feeling. It was like a chemical explosion. I wanted to jump you right then."

"Hope, that was months ago."

"I know. But, I can't count the number of times I've experienced my secret pleasures with you." She ran her fingers over his face. "I've dreamed of the opportunity. Just one time."

Steve sympathized with her. "I've had those feelings myself, but why tonight?"

"It seemed like a real shot so I took a chance."

"How is it you called me from the White House?"

She snuggled closer. "Since the president was supposed to work at Camp David tonight, I had the night off," Hope said. "Then she decided she was too tired to come back. I knew you were coming home tonight. So I said, 'Why not go for it?'"

"I can't believe you'd do something like that."

"How did you figure it out?"

Steve laughed. "When Janet loses it, she always says, "Fuck me ... fuck me."

Hope looked at him in disbelief. "You mean ..."

Ignoring the flowing water rivulets Steve angled her head and kissed her lightly on the cheek. "You said, 'Do it ... do it.'"

"That's it."

He gave her a lazy smile.

"So if I had said, 'Fuck me ... fuck me,' you would have?"

"Hell yes, and I would have never known the difference."

She pursed her lips. "Would you like to have a little secret just between the two of us?"

Steve cocked his head to the side, water dripping from his face.

"C'mon," she said, placing her hands on the wall and slowly moving as before. "Fuck me … fuck me."

He stared at her ass grinding and raised his eyebrows. She continued to gyrate.

"Fuck me … *fuck me*."

Steve hesitated, then pressed his hardness against her, his instincts firing on all cylinders.

***

Steve and Ira Magaziner waited outside the Oval Office. "I'm interested in hearing your report on your trip to the Midwest."

"It went very well," Steve said. "I picked up several ideas that will be helpful to the president."

"Do you think it'll be necessary for the two of you to team up on the presentations?"

"I don't think so. It'd be better for me to hit the VFWs while she's addressing the movers and shakers."

"In this case, the boys … and girls … in the VFWs might carry more weight."

Steve gave him a blank look. "You're the expert on that one."

The door to the Oval Office opened and the president motioned the two men in. Steve followed Ira, each taking a wingback on either side of the fireplace. Janet pulled a side-chair from her desk and placed it between the two, facing the glowing warmth.

"I'm hearing good things about your trip, Steve," she said. "How'd it go?"

"Really well. I'll have my report on your desk tomorrow."

"I look forward to reading it. What's next, Ira?" she asked.

"Steve and I have chatted briefly. I like the idea of double teaming the communities."

She wrinkled her brow. "Double team?"

"Yes, you speak to the business leader's downtown and Steve can meet with the commanders of the VFW posts. That'll keep the good ol' boys in the loop."

"I like that," she said. "We can hit the top and keep the grass roots folks involved." Ira nodded. "Have you identified the cities yet?"

Ira opened his smaller black folder. "Right now I have Tampa and Palm Beach in Florida; it's a swing state. We'll hit both Republican and Democrat strongholds. After that you could head for Atlanta, Chicago and Denver. Phoenix is a must. And either San Diego or San Francisco will do the West. We can add Richmond if we need it and wrap up the tour in New York City."

"Sounds good to me." She looked at Steve for his thoughts.

He shrugged. "The two of you are the experts. I'm going along for the ride."

Ira changed the subject. "Anything happening on the hill?"

Janet's smile visibly showed her pleasure. "Will has done a fantastic job. We're two votes short in the senate and ten in the house. Several of them are waffling, waiting for the polls and listening to the talking heads. If we can pick up momentum on the tour, we'll be fine."

"I'll have four or five additional cities ready if you want to add them."

"Good ... that's it?"

Ira nodded then stood and walked toward the door. Steve started to rise.

"Steve, could you wait for a minute. I have a couple of questions."

"Of course."

Steve eased back into his chair and lingered. Ira left.

Knowing the office was bugged, she closed the door and jotted him a note:

Tomorrow at eight, okay?

His desires instantly ignited his crotch. He gave her an assuring nod.

***

Central Intelligence Agency Headquarters
Langley, Virginia
September 10, 1998

The computer flashed: SECRET — SECRET

Name:	**Steven Schilling**
Previous:	**None**
Operative:	**Russian Spy**
New Information:	**Suspect seen with Russian spy Elena Vishneva.**
	Seven contacts in August, a romantic relationship is expected.

"Secret," we haven't seen one of those for a while," the computer operator said, handing the printout to his new supervisor.

She gave a questioning look. "Steve Schilling with no priors, why the alert on him?"

"It wasn't triggered by him; it's Elena Vishneva. Whenever her name pops up, it's 'Secret,'" the operator said.

"Let me see her profile," the supervisor requested.

He raised an eyebrow. "Are you serious?" The clerk asked, then laughed as he stroked the computer's keyboard. "Sorry, it's a guy joke about her shape."

"I don't understand," she said, waiting for the file to open.

Elena's beautiful face and flaming red hair filled the screen. "See what I mean?"

The plain-looking supervisor gulped.

The computer operator clicked. "Here's her profile."

Four photos of Elena — in various locations — rolled across the screen. She stared, unable to look away. "You're putting me on. That's not really her, is it?"

The computer operator laughed. "You said you wanted to see her profile."

"I didn't mean that ... turn those pictures off. I've seen enough of her big tits. I want to see her dossier. What do we know about her?"

"Lots." The operator grinned then clicked again.

A long list of assignments scrolled down the screen. The supervisor read each one. "She's one of Russia's top spies."

The operator nodded. "She works on top security assignments. That's why her name triggers the secret alert."

"Steven Schilling ... where have I heard his name?"

"He's the president's top guy on educational reform ... 'if you can't cut the mustard, there's no free lunch,'" he recited.

"Goddamn," the supervisor exclaimed softly. "With first-person access to the president — run everything you can find on him. And hand deliver it to my desk, ASAP."

CHAPTER TWENTY-TWO

Art and Steve waited in the leather chairs in Dr. Pritts's office. The balding doctor strolled in. "Steve, it's been awhile. How are things going?"

"It's been crazy on the hill."

"I can imagine. You did a great job on *Meet the Press*."

"Thanks, I really felt comfortable."

"It showed. My wife and I were on vacation most of September, travelling through the Midwest. I saw your name on several newscasts. Sounds like things are going well."

"It couldn't have gone better. Our mini-tour was a prelude for the president's circuit." Steve turned to his colleague. "I want you to meet Art Wallhollister; he's agreed to help."

"Congratulations, Art," the doctor extended his hand. "It's a real friend who's willing to be a confidant."

"I'm not an expert but I'm a good listener."

"That's all it takes," Dr. Pritts said, glancing at Steve. "Did you lose some weight?"

Steve grinned and pointed at Art. "It was his idea. He's read several articles on addiction, and has a good handle on the overall challenge. He's a big believer in sound body, sound mind."

"Good for him."

"I've been working out whenever I can. Art pushed me hard. I've lost fifteen pounds and cut my alcohol consumption in half."

The doctor turned to Art. "You're more of an expert than you may think."

Art grinned ear to ear with the compliment.

"How are you doing on the other fronts?"

Steve twisted his lips into a wry grin. "I've stopped going to Margo's parties. I haven't been there since the last time we talked. "

"That may sound like a small step but each sign of progress is important."

"I've thought a lot too about your intimacy test."

"Come up with anything?"

He shook his head. "Not yet. I can't believe I fooled myself so long."

"Let's go over things again for Art's benefit," the doctor urged. "How long have you been seeing a therapist?"

He raised his left eyebrow. "Six years, maybe longer."

"And how long have you had your addiction problem?"

"All of my life, since I was a kid in high school."

"In all of those years you were with a therapist, how many changes occurred in your life?"

Steve gave him a look of disappointment. "Not much; it seems like I'm always going over the same turf."

"Why do you think that's true?"

"I try hard, but something always seems to happen. Next thing I know I'm back to square one."

"You're problems are deep-seated. You need to do more than give lip service."

"I've tried, Doc ... I feel like I've worked hard ... it seems like nothing helps."

"You've told Art the chance of eliminating your problem is practically nil?"

"Yes, it's not very comforting but I knew he had to know."

"How many women are you seeing on a regular basis?"

"Three."

The doctor leafed through his notes. "Have you told Art about the one that recently dropped you?"

"Ah, no ... I forgot."

"I'd like Art to hear about Charisse, the sex addict."

Art's eyes opened wide.

"Did you feel happy or sad? Did you pursue her, beg her not to leave?"

"No, she felt like she'd turned the corner. That she was making progress beating her addiction. It was the best thing, so I encouraged her to go."

"You encouraged her to go?" Dr. Pritts repeated. "You didn't have any misgivings or thoughts about yourself?"

"Nope. I felt good for her."

"Have you ever had feelings like that before?"

He reflected for a moment. "No, I can't recall ever feeling that way. Or caring for long, one way or the other."

The doctor smiled. "That's an important step forward."

"Why?"

"You've demonstrated compassion for another person. For once, your first thought wasn't about yourself," the doctor said. "What do you think that means?

Steve shrugged. "I have close feelings for a sex addict?"

Doc grinned. "You're close."

"Close?" Not understanding, Steve shook his head.

"You have compassion for her because you understand, know how she feels."

"She's like me."

"Absolutely."

"Sounds like progress," Art noted.

"It's an important milestone." The doctor rubbed his jaw. "Let's go back to the three you're still dating. I want you to number them one through three according to the length of time you've been seeing them — one being the longest."

"O-okay," Steve said, not sure where the questions were headed.

"How would you feel if number three left and you'd never see her again?"

"God, I'd miss her."

"Why?"

"Being in bed with her; she's really something." A small smile escaped Steve's lips.

Dr. Pritts hesitated. "Anything else?"

With a blank look Steve said, "That's it I guess."

"How about number two?"

"Hmm, tough question. I've seen her much longer."

"Okay. If you never saw her again, how would you feel?"

Steve hesitated, not knowing how to respond. "I-I ..."

"Would you feel sick? Be depressed?"

He took a deep breath. "I don't know ... I guess I'd just go on."

"Would it be the same for number one?"

Steve thought for a few moments. "I guess so."

"What do you think that means?"

His expression went blank; Steve stared at the doctor.

"It says you may be good friends and like being in bed with all of them; but you don't have compassion or true feelings for any of them."

"I want to be with them," Steve insisted.

"That's because you want sex with them. There are no real feelings of affection because you don't have intimate feelings for them. Does that make sense?"

"Yes, I understand."

"Good." The doctor smiled then jotted down a note. "Another step forward."

Steve lowered his head then looked back up at Dr. Pritts. "How do I change? How do I develop those kind of feelings?"

"That's exactly where we are heading. We must reprogram the behaviors you learned as a kid. Rather than dwelling on your dad and all of those negatives, we need to shift your thoughts to your mother. It's the same thing your sister, Sally, had to do."

Steve stared without moving a muscle.

"You were traumatized when your dad raped her. Obviously, it didn't impact you the same way it did her." The doctor paused. "You reacted differently. That's part of the reason why you want to make women happy. Down deep, you're trying to make amends for things you couldn't contend with as a kid."

Steve wiped a tear, recalling the times his father had raped his sister and beat his mother.

"Your relationship with women is your way of trying to compensate for how your mother and sister were treated. It's all about pleasing women, exceeding their sexual expectations — you want them to experience multiple orgasms ... to thoroughly enjoy sex ...

the opposite of rape. And you'll do whatever it takes to accomplish that goal."

Steve covered his face, trying to hide his remorse.

"In the long run, you end up feeling empty because you're unable to develop intimate feelings. Does that make sense?"

"I guess, I-I … never really thought about it like that."

"Its complex, Steve, but I want you to know I'm really proud of you. I believe you can learn to feel intimacy." Dr. Pritts made a few notes on his pad. "In your upcoming sessions with Art I want you to do something."

Steve looked up.

"I want you to talk about your mother and Sally in detail. Will you do that?"

Steve fidgeted with his tie. "Do I have to?"

"Yes," the doctor said firmly. "You need to learn how to express your feelings about others so we can talk freely about *your* feelings."

Steve sucked in a deep breath then sighed. "Okay."

***

**FBI Headquarters
935 Pennsylvania Avenue NW
Washington, D.C.**

October 1, 1998

Mitchell Blake called the monthly meeting to order. "Item number one — Steve Schilling. "Who wants to start?"

"I do." The younger agent to his left raised his hand. "I have the report on Hannah Lieberman, one of the women in his file."

"Go ahead."

"I'm confident we can close the book on her. She's a former model who snatched one of the rich old boys. He's a member of the Bilderberg Group and is big in the diamond cartel. He travels to Antwerp four or five times a year, and has a chickie there. Probably smuggling diamonds, big-time, but that's a problem for another division. She's a liberated woman who has an occasional fling. There's nothing to connect Steve with the Bilderberg's."

"What about the Filipino woman?"

Another staffer popped up. "That's messy. Her mutilated body was found last week in an abandoned roadside park outside of Quezon City. Her two bodyguards had been decapitated. It doesn't appear there's a threat from that connection, though."

"Yuck." Mitchell wrinkled his nose. "Anything else on her?" The younger agent shook his head.

The old man of the group gritted his teeth. "The Kuratong Baleleng are nasty bastards. Smart, too. It wouldn't be unlike them to set up something like this to throw us off."

"What do you mean by that?" Mitchell asked.

"Well … they're devious … crazy. They don't think like we do. I'm not convinced we can close the book on them."

Mitchell nodded. "Fine … keep following them." He looked at the next item in Schilling's file. "What about Miss Hotsey Totsey?"

"Elena Vishneva. The CIA has her listed as a spy, likely a former KGB operative. So what's happening with her?"

"She was spotted with Steve Schilling seven times in August. Apparently she's fuckin' his brains out," the old pro said. "He was gone half of September and as soon as he returned, she had to be banging him nightly, like clockwork."

"What a way to go." the young agent quipped.

He attracted solemn stares from around the table and clamped his mouth.

"Anything about Steve-a-reno from Memphis?" Mitchell jested.

Another agent spoke up. "We hit the jackpot there. After a week of digging, the field uncovered a hussy who claimed she'd screwed Steve for three years. The agent coughed up $2,500 — she spilled the beans and told him about four other women."

"Do you think she's credible?"

"She had to be; she knew too much."

A wrinkle lined Mitchell's brow. "If we found all of this so quickly, the other side knows the way to his brain is through his pants."

Heads nodded around the table.

"Anything from Asheville?"

"Nothing that specific. Steve was engaged to an attractive millionairess. He travelled all over the state, but no one could connect him with anyone else."

"I bet there were more," the old agent said. "A tiger doesn't change his stripes."

"We ought to put him on twenty-four-hour surveillance. Does anyone disagree?"

Not a head moved.

***

"Steve, I'm glad you and Art could squeeze in one more visit before you take off next week with the president," Dr. Pritts said. "How did your sessions go?"

"We had some good discussions about his feelings for his sister," Art responded. "I think it was helpful. Most of the time he wanted to talk about his Russian girlfriend. He's head over heels in love with her."

"Anything specific I should know?" Art shrugged his shoulders.

Steve chimed in. "I've never met a woman like her. She goes non-stop."

"Non-stop?"

"You know, Doc, she's all over me from the time I step into her apartment till I leave."

"How do you *feel* about her?"

"Whataya mean? I love her."

"How do you think she would do on the intimacy test?"

Steve lowered his head. "Probably not very well."

"Just as I figured," the older man said. "I want to share some ways for you to start thinking about how you act."

Steve raised his eyebrows in question.

"It's going to be a slow and laborious process."

"Don't worry. I'll make it happen," Art said.

"Good. Reprograming a person's behaviors is a tedious process. Throughout your life your subconscious mind has saved all of the messages your brain received. There are millions of thoughts grouped into clusters — they form your beliefs, mindsets, and character traits. These learned behaviors are just like learning to walk or ride a bicycle. They're all there, tucked away, waiting to be used again."

"Like the Ragu spaghetti sauce ad," Steve jested. "It's in there."

The doctor chuckled. "Our challenge is to reprogram a small segment of your behavior by inputting and reinforcing new thoughts and actions."

"Sounds like a real challenge," Art said.

"That's why I like to start with a series of small steps. Once Steve starts thinking about his actions, we can start helping him to reshape and hopefully modify his behaviors."

"Fine with me, Doc, I'm ready," Steve quipped.

"The first step sounds simple, but it's probably one of the hardest. I call it reclaiming your power." The doctor paused letting the words settle in. "You're the only one who can control your actions. I want you to make a list of each action that triggers a sexual response. Recognize how you react when you hear a particular phrase or fantasize about a woman. Why do you put on a porno tape? What makes you think about masturbating?"

Steve gulped, realizing he'd never thought about "why."

"I want you to keep track of all these things."

"Jesus Doc, I don't know ... I'd need a pad of paper in every room."

"So be it. I want you to make a pact with me. Will you do it?"

He gave the doctor a feeble response, "I'll try."

"I need more than 'I'll try,' Steve. When you meet with Art I want you to share that list. Will you do that too?"

Steve's head nodded in agreement.

"Next, pay close attention to the sexual actions you take. There's always forethought — conscious or subconscious — before you take action. Focus on your thoughts before you take action."

"Do you want me to share that with Art, too?"

"Yes."

"Do you own stock in Weyerhaeuser?" Steve joked. "It's going to take a lot of paper."

"No, but you may want to buy some," Dr. Pritts rejoined.

Art mused. "Thanks for the tip."

"Ready for number three?"

Steve raised an eyebrow, not sure if he could do more.

"When your brain starts racing, I want you to slow down before your urges fire. Take a deep breath. Think about you mother, work, anything. Refocus your thoughts."

"Do I tell Art about those too?"

The doctor grinned. "I'll give him a reprieve on this one."

"Thank God," Art said.

"Don't forget, Steve. I want a list of every trigger."

"Like looking at Art's ass?" Steve zinged.

"I'm out of here," Art asserted and half-rose, pretending to leave.

"Not Art's ass, but … relaxing in your lounger, taking a hot shower, reading *Hustler.* After a couple of weeks, review your list and put alternative behaviors in place. It might be as simple as not picking up the bar of soap or opening a porno magazine."

Looking at the doctor, Steve hesitated, "Is that it?"

Dr. Pritts nodded. "Make a pact with Art to be open and honest. If you're not willing to do that you're wasting our time."

"Agreed." Steve reached over the end table between them and shook his hand.

"The two of you need to meet on a regular basis; pencil it in, make it a high priority. Maybe lunch on Wednesday or after work on the same day. It needs to become a ritual."

"Makes sense to me," Art closed.

CHAPTER TWENTY-THREE

Air Force One landed at Palm Beach International Airport. Brimming with excitement, Steve waited with the other staff members, watching the orderly procession unfold — Secret Service agents, the president, the chief of staff and more agents. By the time he departed the crowd had shifted to the front of the caravan.

Six members of the press corps slid into the last limo with him. The balding one looked Steve in the eye. "Is this your first trip on Air Force One?"

"No, but every time seems more exciting."

"For good reason." He laughed. "Are you going to pull another trick out of your hat?"

Steve took his red fedora off and held it in front of him. "This is the luckiest hat in the world. It works like a charm every time I give a speech."

The senior CBS political reporter winked. "From the things I'm hearing you're going to be wearing it for a long time."

"Hope so."

The conversation ended with Steve turning to watch the high-rises along the coast appear in front of them. He pinched himself. *I'm really in a presidential motorcade. Can you believe that? Mom would have been so proud. I wish my sister could see me now.*

After checking into The Ritz Carlton north of Miami, Steve opened the slider and peered down at the tropical garden below, framed by the U-shaped hotel. "Nothing like that in Kentucky or Arkansas," he said to himself. "I think I'll check it out."

He took the elevator to the lobby, checked for messages at the front desk and stepped outside. Strolling past the tropical plants and palms that lined a sizable pond, he slowed, watching ornamental Japanese Kio swim by — red, yellow, white, and blue — *not the type of carp you'll see in the Mississippi.* He laughed to himself then looked up at the humongous swimming pool. *It's longer than an Olympic-sized pool. My God, there must be fifty loungers on each side. Did you ever see so many bodies? Barely covered ones with red, yellow, white and blue patches — on display like the fish.*

Taking in the scenery at the tiki bar, he slowly downed a burger and chips then headed for his briefing meeting with Ira Magaziner.

He knocked on Ira's door. Hearing a call to come in, Steve pushed the door open. Light green carpet and matching drapes with painted, dark green ferns, jumped out at him. "Wow, this is really cheerful looking."

"You think this is something ... take a look out the window.

Steve walked across the room and pulled the drape back, his eyes searched for the woman in the yellow bikini lounging by the pool. Seeing her turn onto her stomach and unhook her top, his pants stirred. "Not tonight," he told his addiction. He turned around to see Ira pouring a tall Crown Royal on ice.

"Fix yourself a drink while I open a can of mixed nuts," the old pro said.

Steve headed for the bar and poured his usual. Taking a quick sip, he ambled over in front of a comfortable-looking chair across from Ira, kicked off his shoes and eased into it. "What's the plan for tomorrow?"

Ira opened his black notebook and handed a sheet of paper to Steve. "At ten in the morning I'll meet you in the lobby and go over the schedule one last time. Shortly after that a car will take us to the civic center in Boca Raton; it'll take about thirty minutes. In the meantime the president will leave for her speech in Miami."

"How come we're not staying all night in the city?" Steve asked.

"You see all of the stuff at the pool?" Ira gave him a wry smile. "This is an important trip. We don't want to break concentration."

Steve lifted his eyebrows. *Good enough reason for me.*

Ira laughed, knowing by Steve's expression what he had on his mind. "Also, this is where presidents stay. It's been cased a hundred times by the Secret Service. They like the place; it has limited access points."

"Dumb question I guess."

"Hey, we all have a first time." Ira picked up his glass and tipped it slightly toward Steve. "Here's to a successful speech, tomorrow."

"Thanks." Steve air-toasted Ira's glass and took a sip.

"After lunch it'll be your show. Anything special I need to know?"

"Hmm, not really, I've given the same basic speech seven or eight times. After my remarks I'll move in front of the table and sit on an angle with one leg draped over the edge. I come off a lot more sincere that way."

The consultant's brow wrinkled. "Hold on, let me check out the seating arrangement." He opened a second file and shook his head. "It's a head-table arrangement."

"Can you change it?"

"Probably. I'll call right now." Ira picked up the phone, heard a dial tone and called. After talking to three individuals, he finally nodded. "Good." Placing the phone in the cradle, he turned to Steve. "They've rearranged things so you'll have a table on the right for you to sit on."

"Super. How many do you expect?"

"There are roughly twenty VFW posts in Broward, Miami-Dade and Palm Beach counties. We asked each commander to bring a couple of carloads. I figure we'll have at least two hundred; knowing how some of them operate it may be closer to two hundred and fifty."

***

Feeling he'd hit the target, Steve reached for the shelf under the podium, pulled out his red fedora and slipped it on. Turning to the small table, he walked over and assumed his pre-planned casual position.

Chuckles filled the room.

Genuinely pleased, Steve picked up the handheld microphone as he propped a leg on the table. *I'm in my arena now … let the questions flow.* "You've heard my thoughts. Now, who has the first question?"

"What's with the red hat?" An old-timer in the back shouted.

Steve removed his well-traveled fedora and looked it over. "I've had this hat for ten or twelve years. I started wearing it to football games when I became a university president. Wearing it made people feel comfortable about approaching me. It was a real icebreaker. And, we won most of our games so it became a symbol of success. It still has the same ol' magic charm." He grinned and slipped it back on. "Next question."

"A lot of your comments make sense. There's one point that bothers me." The speaker, wearing a WW II veteran's hat, his face lined with experience, paused. "Why should the military be the one to carry out this mission?"

"Excellent question," Steve said, thinking he already had them eating out of his hand. "Would anyone disagree that our schools have failed?"

Listening to the grumbling, Steve knew they agreed with him. He stood and walked back and forth across the dais. "The schools have lost the discipline they had when we were there. Parents think they are in charge. Poor little Johnny can do no wrong."

"That's because he can't read," an old marine shouted. Everyone laughed.

"That's the point." Steve's face changed from jovial to somber. "We've implemented changes to correct that but it'll be some time before they're fully implemented. Even then we'll need alternatives for some of the youth."

Scattered applause sprinkled the room.

"Washington is gridlocked … quite frankly, the military is our last hope." He paused for effect. "Those of you here today have demonstrated the type of leadership and discipline it'll take to shape up the dropouts."

Everyone in the auditorium stood and clapped.

Steve looked around. "Who's next?"

A decorated soldier rolled his wheelchair into the aisle. "I'm proud to have served our country."

Steve stood and applauded. "We're all proud of you son. Thanks for your commitment." The crowd cheered.

The handicapped man continued. "It seems like cutting the equipment budget like you've suggested will lessen our ability to protect our country."

"That's an interesting point. I had the same reaction when I began my research. I've learned we have surplus tanks and fighters in storage. Still, we're no stronger than the weakest among us; we can't afford to have 30 percent of our youth unable to read."

"I agree with that," a woman veteran said. The auditorium rocked with cheers.

"The Secretary of Defense understands and the Joint Chiefs of Staff are on board. We need to eliminate our own failures before someone takes advantage of them." Steve looked around then slid off the table. "Any other questions?"

No one said a word.

Steve stood, saluted the flag then turned to the audience. "Thank you for coming today, and thank you for your dedication and service to our country. Our future is up to our youth. We must educate them so they'll have the same commitment to preserving our freedom that you have demonstrated." He saluted the audience. "Thanks again, for securing our freedom."

The veterans stood and gave him a standing ovation.

***

Art handed Dr. Pritts a list of activities for the last month. "Steve and I discussed these points in our Wednesday luncheon meetings," Art said, then joked about some of the words and actions that had triggered Steve's fantasies.

Enjoying the levity, Dr. Pritts laughed. "Where's the next stop for you and the president?"

"Tomorrow we'll be leaving on a ten-day swing through the Midwest — Chicago, Atlanta and Denver — and then out to the West Coast."

"Sounds exciting."

"I'll be doing my thing with the VFWs and she'll be hitting the movers and shakers. After Thanksgiving, she'll make her push on the senate. That'll give her December to work on the house. She wants to wrap it up before Christmas."

"Why Christmas?"

"The president is trying to keep the opposition off guard. If it goes longer the detractors have more time to pick up momentum."

"Makes sense," the doctor said, opening his pad. "Have you stopped seeing any of the women?"

Steve looked down at the glossy oak floors and pressed his fingers into his forehead.

"What does that mean?" the doctor asked in an elevated tone.

"Ah … nothing has changed."

Dr. Pritts gave him a stern look. "You're talking about your addiction problem over lunch. Art is working his ass off for you. And you haven't changed one iota?"

"Geez Doc, we've only been working on it for a month."

Clearly irritated, the doctor rose and paced the room. "Don't give me any of that crap, Steve. You're rationalizing. You've been in therapy for years. You don't *want* to change."

"I do, Doc, I'm working hard at it."

"You're not, Steve. We had a plan; you made a commitment — you've done nothing!"

"I need more time. I know I can do it."

Dr. Pritts slammed his pad on the desk. "If you're not willing to try, I'm not either. I quit!" He grabbed the door handle and motioned to Art. "Come on, we're wasting our time."

Surprised, Art followed him out the door. The doctor slammed the door then grinned at Art. "We'll see if that works."

"You think it will?"

"Hopefully. It's kind of like shock therapy. I've used it a few times as a last resort."

"Why do you think it'll work on him?"

"Steve has been a sex addict all of his life. He's been in various stages of therapy for years, and look at the results. Essentially nothing … he's made gains here and there then regresses to ground zero."

"And shouting at him and bolting out of the room will do what?" Art tried to understand the tactic's effectiveness.

"I'm trying to trick his brain."

"Trick his brain?" Art cleared his throat, still a bit confused.

"For years he's told himself he's working hard. His body has been winning the game — getting more sex — while he plods along. His brain keeps saying, 'I'm trying,' when in reality he's depending on me — or whatever therapist he's seeing — to keep the process going. As long as I keep appealing to his brain, he can keep saying, 'I'm trying.'"

"Tell me more about your strategy."

"He's been in therapy so long he's using it as a crutch. It's like a dependency; as long as he's meeting with me he can say he's trying. I told his brain 'I'm out of here; you can't depend on me.' Now the ball is in his court."

"How long are you going to let him sit in there?"

"There's no magic number. Right now his mind is having a debate with his body about his addiction."

Art wrinkled his brow.

"His addiction is saying wait, the doctor will come back in, and it'll be okay. The logical part of his brain is saying this is the end of the line. No more trying to fool this doctor, he's seen through your charade."

"Have you tried this before?"

"Ah, two or three times."

"Has the patient ever come out on his own?'

"That's a good question." Dr. Pritts scratched his head. "As a matter of fact, no."

"I think we should let him brood for a while."

"Fine with me," the doctor said. The two waited — eight, ten, and then twelve minutes passed. "It must seem like an eternity to him."

"Think we should go in?" Art asked.

"Let's give him another five minutes."

The two waited four minutes. Dr. Pritts stood, turned the doorknob and looked in. "Sorry Steve, I thought you had left," he said, then started to close the door.

"Wait."

The doctor poked his head back inside, but turned toward the waiting room. "Hold it Art," he shouted, as if Art was walking away. "Steve is still here."

"It's okay, the two of you can come in."

"Hold it Art," the doctor said. "He wants to talk."

"To both of us?" Art asked.

Steve shouted, "Come back in." The two men returned and sat down.

Steve looked at his shoe tassels then glanced up. "You can't quit," he said to Dr. Pritts. "I'm going to do it."

"Do what?" the doctor asked.

"I've decided. There's one woman in my future. And if she'll have me I'll never cheat again."

"That's hard for me to imagine."

"I've figured it out. You can't do it for me. If I'm going to change I have to do it."

"Just like that?"

Steve raked his hair. "Yes, just like that. My Russian girl friend is just that. She's a friend who I sleep with; she's feeding my addiction. I don't need to be with her."

Dr. Pritts stared into Steve's watery eyes. "That doesn't sound like Steve Schilling."

"It isn't. This is a new Steve Schilling. I can do it. I'm going do it."

"Are you going to make a commitment to Sherry?" Art asked.

Steve pursed his lips in thought for a moment. "She's a wonderful woman. We're a great team at work, but down deep I know she doesn't compare with the other one."

"Compare?" the doctor cocked his head to the side.

"Yes, I've compared her with the other one." Steve grinned. "I know I'll hurt Sherry, and it'll hurt me to tell her, but I have to. I don't have a choice."

Dr. Pritts gave Steve a sympathetic smile. "I'm glad you said 'it will hurt.' That's a good sign. Congratulations!" Dr. Pritts bent over and hugged him. "Do you want to talk about the other woman?"

"I'd like to but I can't. Maybe sometime later."

"That's fine. Whenever you're ready."

"I'm proud of you," Art said as Steve stood. He wrapped his arms around Steve. "I'll be there if you need a shoulder to lean on."

"Thanks Art, I know you will." Steve gave Art a bear hug.

***

Central Intelligence Agency Headquarters
Langley, Virginia
October 17, 1998

A young staff member carried a sealed brown envelope from the floor below, labeled TOP SECRET, to the director's office and waited for the director to appear.

The director opened the envelope and read the email that had been intercepted:

To:	**Elena Vishneva**
From:	**Family Member**
Subject:	**Кот выпущен из мешка. Проверь алфавит**
Translation:	**Cat out of bag. Check ABCs**
Meaning:	**Family Member has been decoded before. It is the Russian Foreign Intelligence Service. Their counterpart to the CIA. CONFIRMED — SHE IS A RUSSIAN SPY.**
	Cat out of bag means her cover has been compromised. Normally, that's a directive for agent to leave the country immediately to avoid potential international embarrassment.
	ABCs refers to our alphabet soup — CIA, FBI, NSA.
	Check means sever all contacts with target and/or our agents. Destroy all links.
Action:	**Exceptional, grave damage to national security — IMMEDIATE ACTION REQUIRED.**

CHAPTER TWENTY-FOUR

Steve stood at the window in the president's suite high in the Chicago Conrad Hilton. Scanning the horizon, he could see for miles — Grant Park sprawling to the east, Navy Pier to the north and Soldier's Field to the south. Peering down from the twenty-sixth floor, he watched the traffic jam inch along and hundreds of people filling the sidewalk.

He turned to the agent standing next to him and asked, "Is it always like this?"

D. J. Busch nodded and ran his hand through thin, gray hair. A gentle smile crossed his round face, recalling the past. "A friend of mine recounted his experience here in '68. He was protecting Hubert Humphrey who was standing exactly where you are. Looking down at the scene, he described it as Dante's *Inferno* — a chaotic mix of police, hippies, and the National Guard — acrid smells of marijuana and tear gas filled this room."

"I wonder what was going through his mind."

"Like always he was praying, 'please God, don't let it happen on my watch.'"

Steve laughed. "That's hard to imagine." He turned his head toward D. J. "How do you guys manage things when the president arrives?"

"It's by the book. Fifteen minutes before she arrives all traffic will stop and the street cleared."

"How do they do that?"

"Traffic is diverted two or three blocks from here. Mounted police from Chicago's finest will form a barricade along the sidewalk across the street."

"And then?"

"I pray." Steve gave him a quizzical look. "Whenever I see the president, whether on my watch or not, I pray."

"That must be extremely stressful."

"It's stress twenty-four-seven, and it takes a toll. I'll be fifty-two in three months and plan to hang it up. My wife can hardly wait." The agent lifted his left hand and listened. "Look out the window, she's on the way."

Steve peered down at the street and watched the plan unfold — six motorcycle policemen lead the way, sirens blasting. The president's motorcade turned the corner and lumbered into sight on Michigan Avenue.

Standing straight-backed next to Steve, D. J.'s eyes sharpened, not missing a point — a baby resting in his mother's arms in the park; a teenage girl on the sidewalk waving a small American flag; a dog lifting his leg by a tree.

The president's town car turned into the hotel entrance and disappeared under the portico. Steve turned to D. J. "What do you think is happening now?"

His cheeks spread into a grin. "I can describe every detail. Right now four agents are stepping to the exact spot the town car will stop. They're ready to assume a diamond formation when she steps out of the car — an agent will be on each side, one in the front of her and one in the back carrying a bulletproof shield — there'll be another agent standing nearby with a briefcase in his hand." D. J. glanced at his watch. "The limo is slowing and just stopped at the designated location. An agent is opening the door. She's sliding out of the car into the diamond formation. The agents are closing ranks."

Shots rang out — four, five, maybe six.

"Oh my God," D. J. shouted.

Steve froze against the window frame then wilted to the floor.

Below, Tony Petrarca shoved the president into the car, landing on top of her. "Get out of here! Go! Go!" he shouted to the driver. Tires smoked. The town car squealed away.

"Men down! Men down!" filled D. J.'s airwaves. He saw an agent scramble toward a colleague lying face down on the asphalt near where the car had been. The agent with the briefcase lay in a pool of blood, an unfired Uzi in his hand. He never had a chance to raise the powerful 9mm submachine gun.

***

Sometime later, Steve pulled a wet washcloth from his forehead, blinked a couple of times and wiped his face. Lying on the sofa, he heard sirens blaring, red lights flashing through the room. The loud thumps of several helicopters hovering, filled his ears.

Stumbling to the window, Steve pulled open the drapes and looked below — gas fumes filled his nostrils — police cars, fire trucks and emergency vehicles jammed the street. He saw a police officer chasing a person in Grant Park. A rescue person gave oxygen to a gray-haired man lying in the grass. Mounted policed ringed the backside of Grant Park. *How is Janet? Is she okay?*

He rushed to the television and clicked it on. "Hurry up," he said, impatiently.

Dan Rather's face filled the screen. His mind whirling; Steve listened carefully.

Rather spoke deliberately, choosing each word with care. "The President of the United States has been shot." Steve's face flushed. "At 3:41 p.m. Central Standard Time at least six shots were fired as President Stetson returned to the Conrad Hilton Hotel in downtown Chicago." A video of her motorcade flashed on the screen. "She was returning from a speech at McCormack Place."

The video on the screen was replaced with: NEWS FLASH — NEWS FLASH — NEWS FLASH!

Steve held his breath, waiting for a sign of good news.

Rather spoke slowing again. At 3:44 p.m. Central Standard Time, President Janet Stetson arrived at the emergency room at the University of Illinois-Chicago hospital. We have no word on her condition."

Steve fell to his knees as he had often as a boy. *Please God, don't take her away. I love her more than anything. I'll never cheat on her; never do anything wrong to spoil her trust in me.* Closing his eyes, he sobbed, recalling the other women he'd lost. *Not again, God, please don't let it happen again … please!*

He heard the door open and looked up.

D. J. walked in, looking dreadful — Steve could think of no other word for it.

"You okay," Steve asked.

D. J.'s eyes narrowed out of a concern for her.

"Do you know anything about Janet?"

"She's in surgery," D. J. finally answered. The agent opened a bottle of water and took a slug, catching his breath. "She took one, maybe two bullets."

"Oh my God. How's she doing?"

"Tony said her right side was blood-soaked when he removed her bullet-proof chest protector."

"Was she alert?"

"Barely. The head nurse kept shouting her name — 'Madam President. Janet. Madam President ...'"

"Did she respond?"

D. J. shook his head. "According to Tony, not a word."

"How about the agents who were shot?"

"One was hit in the shoulder. If he hadn't stepped in the way, the bullet would have struck her in the head. The agent with the Uzi was shot twice."

"Uzi?"

"The one carrying the briefcase. He took hits in the right hip and right arm. Obviously, the shooters knew what they were doing."

"Anything else?"

"The hotel is locked down. It's possible some of the shots came from inside. You have to stay in the room. The phones are off. If you want something to eat let one of the guards outside know. "They'll have room service bring you something."

"I'm not hungry ... couldn't eat a bite right now."

"I'm going back downstairs," D. J. said.

"How can I find out the latest about Janet?"

"Stay by the television; they'll be on top of it." The weary agent moved toward the door.

"Thanks," Steve said, walking into the bathroom. He took a leak then stared at his five o'clock shadow. *You dumb bastard. Why didn't you call the FBI about the telephone message and the note? Maybe Art was right ... maybe Kim was a setup, part of the Kuratong*

Baleleng all along. "Crap, how can I be so stupid?" A vision of Elena flashed. *A Russian interpreter? How do you know? Maybe she's screwing me to find out information. Shit, maybe I told her something … Oh my God, no.* Confused, he sobbed.

***

At eight o'clock the next morning Tony appeared at Steve's door. "Have you had breakfast yet?" he asked.

"No, I tossed and turned all night. I'm not hungry."

"Put on your shoes and sox. I'm picking up an Egg McMuffin on the way to the hospital. I have special clearance for you to see Janet."

"Really?" Steve's droopy eyes lifted. "Is she doing better?"

"She's over the hump. She asked for you. The doctor thinks you might give her a boost."

"I'll be just a moment." Steve slipped on his shoes and buttoned his shirt. The two men hurried downstairs then slid into the backseat of a Lincoln Town Car.

"How are *you* doing?" Steve asked Tony as they drove away from the hotel.

"I'm doing fine … even though I haven't slept in twenty-four hours." Tony shook his head. "I can't believe it happened on my watch. It was orchestrated. It happened like clockwork."

"Any ideas on who may have done it?"

"Leads are flooding in from across the world. I'm positive it was an outside group."

Steve felt sick inside, thinking he may have contributed. He felt like vomiting.

The car pulled into a McDonald's. "Are you positive you don't want anything?"

"Nothing … I'm half sick."

Tony told the driver, "Two sausage biscuits, a large coffee, and buy something for yourself." He handed the driver a twenty.

Grabbing the twenty, the driver repeated Tony's order, and they soon headed for the hospital.

Steve sat on pins and needles, the next two minutes to the hospital seeming like an eternity; then waited for the driver to open the door. The media surrounding the emergency entrance turned their way. Tony grabbed Steve's arm and pulled him through the crowd.

Reporters shouted all the way. "Is the president okay? How is she doing? Can you tell us anything?"

Tony shoved his way through the pack, yanked opened the side door and hustled Steve down the hallway. Slowing at her door, Tony said something to the agents standing on each side. They looked at Steve and nodded.

Stepping inside, Steve felt like he'd been there before — monitors beeping, tubes running in all directions — two doctors watched each screen.

Her eyes were closed, a breathing tube down her throat.

Tony motioned Steve to step forward. He eased next to her bedside and gently squeezed her hand. Leaning over, he whispered in her ear, "I love you sweetheart."

Her left eyelid fluttered and cracked open. Her lips opened, ever so slightly, then closed.

A doctor raised his fist in the air and said quietly but with elation, "She's going to make it!"

A collective sigh filled the room, followed by a muffled cheer.

"Hail to the chief."

***

FBI Headquarters
935 Pennsylvania Avenue NW
Washington, D.C.

November 18, 1998

Louis Freeh, Director of the FBI, threw the copy of an encrypted "Top Secret" email on the conference table:

To:	Elena Vishneva
From:	Family Member
Subject:	Кот выпущен из мешка. Проверь алфавит
Translation:	Cat out of bag. Check ABCs
Meaning:	Family Member has been decoded before. It is the Russian Foreign Intelligence Service. They're the counterpart to our CIA. CONFIRMED—SHE IS A RUSSIAN SPY.
	Cat is out of bag means her cover has been compromised. Normally, that's a directive for the agent to leave the country immediately to avoid potential international embarrassment.
	ABCs refers to our alphabet soup—CIA, FBI, NSA.
	Check means sever all contacts with target and/or our agents. Destroy all documents and links.
Action:	Exceptional, grave damage to national security.
	IMMEDIATE ACTION REQUIRED.

"When did you receive this?" he asked the CIA director.

"About two months ago?"

His face reddened. "When I ask a question I want an *exact* answer."

The director lowered his head. "October 17, 1998 at 4:42 a.m."

"Thirty-four days before the president was shot. And when did you send it to me?"

"Three hours after she was shot."

"Damn." He slammed his first on the table. "What the hell were you thinking?"

The director didn't raise his head.

The FBI director demanded, "When was it sent to the other agencies?"

"The next day."

"Three days ago." Director Freeh looked around the table. "If it wouldn't create a national crisis, I'd have someone's ass fired. I want every shred of evidence, piece of paper, email shared with everyone around this table since this was first received. Is that clear?"

"Yes sir," rang around the table.

"Good. We'll meet here Wednesday at ten. Meeting adjourned."

***

On November 27th Louis Freeh walked into the FBI conference room without cracking a smile or giving his fellow directors a glance. He introduced Thomas Constantine, Director of the Drug Enforcement Agency. "I asked Tom to join us in light of one of the reports that was finally shared." He peered at the others with cold, icy eyes. "Do we have everything now?"

He looked every director in the eye, extracting a nod from each. Opening his notepad, he asked, "Who wants to start?"

"I do." CIA Director Tenet said. "We've done considerable more digging on Hannah Lieberman and her husband. It looks like she was in the wrong place at the wrong time."

"Sounds like that's a common problem for her," the general chimed.

NAS Director, Lt. General Kenneth Minihan, nodded in agreement. "We're positive there's something going on with her husband and the diamond cartel. He's had a lot more activity in Antwerp during the last eighteen months."

"Maybe it's the dark-haired chickie-babe in the file who's the leak."

"That too." Minihan grinned and continued. "With his increased sales we think his smuggling business is on the upswing."

"Anything that might connect him to the president?"

"Not yet ... we're pursuing every lead."

The general opened another file. "Let's go on to the Kuratong Baleleng."

"They're going full bore in the Philippines — bank robberies, extortion, drugs — they're out of control." CIA Director Tenet said.

"How about their international activity?" Minihan asked.

"We haven't found anything specific yet."

"Crap, they're sitting in the middle of the 'Golden Triangle' corridor," Freeh said, in frustration. "Someone other than the Chinese must be processing drugs from Burma, Laos and Thailand," the DEA director added. "We've shut down several sources in Mexico and South America over the past five years. More stuff is coming in on the West Coast."

"Do you think there's any connection with the Chinese fast-food probe?" Freeh asked Constantine.

Blank looks appeared around the table.

"Fast-food probe?" the general asked.

"You recall the 'Pizza Connection' I busted in the 1980's?" Freeh said.

"Right. The DEA and us have a joint ongoing investigation on the Chinese fast-food restaurants on the West Coast. We've found evidence of drug trafficking in L. A., San Francisco and Seattle. We've expanded the investigation to ten other major cities."

"Do you think the Kuratong Baleleng is involved?"

"It's too early to say but they're prime suspects. We know drugs are coming from other than the traditional Chinese sources."

"Shit, the Kuratong Baleleng is a simple connection," the general said. "My kid could figure that out."

No one looked up.

"They know about the 'Pizza Connection' Freeh shut down. If you want him out of your 'Chinese Food Connection,' what do you do?" The general looked around the table. "Well?"

Not a head moved.

"You can't go after him — that'd be too obvious. So what do you think they would do?" The general answered his own question. "You do the same thing they do in their country — assassinate the president. We have to think like them. Kill the president, throw the country into turmoil. The new president selects a new cabinet, and all of us are gone. The Chinese Food Connection thrives."

Director Freeh shook his head in irritation. "Let's move on to Miss Hot Pants. Other than her big tits, what do we know about her?"

"She left the country two days after we intercepted the email."

The frustrated director asked. "That was five weeks ago."

"I can't explain that."

Freeh's cold eyes returned. "It has to be explained."

"Not much in drugs," the DEA director said. "The Russian society is experiencing many of the same social problems we're having."

"So what?" Freeh said. "They're still Russians."

"There has been a dramatic worsening of our relationship with the Soviets since 1995. The old partnering metaphor has been replaced by rivalry," Director Tenet pointed out.

All of the heads agreed around the table.

Freeh's face reddened. "Kosovo is more than an irritant; there are growing tensions between us. Some Russian diplomats are now describing our foreign policy as purely inimical, outright hostile. They describe recent breakthroughs as setbacks. Others are saying we are backsliding into another Cold War. I don't care *what* it is called," Freeh shouted. "There's real trouble ahead. Our president is in the hospital. The Russians are playing it cool, showing sympathy, and gaining political strength. The VP ... anyone of us ... could be next."

"We need to redouble our efforts on the Kuratong Baleleng and the Russians. There's no time to waste," Tenet announced.

"My sentiments exactly," Freeh agreed. "We'll meet every other day, including weekends, until we have those responsible in hand."

CHAPTER TWENTY-FIVE

The early arrivals sat in the Roosevelt Room waiting for the president. It'd been a month to the day since she'd been shot, six days before Thanksgiving. Sympathy cards, letters and tributes had poured in from all over the world. Congress had even taken action, passing her Kennedy-Enzi High School Reform Bill with ease. The president's survival had created a good feeling throughout the administration.

Looking across the table at Tony Petrarca, Steve thought he must have aged ten years in the past few weeks. Other than a few breaks and catnaps in W-16, the Secret Service office, under the Oval Office he'd been by the president's side through the entire ordeal.

"How would you describe the three-minute ride to the hospital?" someone in the room asked.

Looking tired and drawn, with dark circles under his eyes, Tony shook his head. "Think clearly … follow the book. All I can recall is shouting 'Get out of here. Go. Go.' Thank God for our training — cover and evacuate — there was no time to waste. I was on automatic pilot. 'University of Illinois-Chicago Hospital,' I shouted without a thought. Less than five seconds after the shots we were on our way to the hospital and I was sliding off her, pulling her from the floor of the car. She was gasping. I thought she might have cracked a rib when the two of us crashed onto the floor."

"That was quick thinking," another member said.

"That's what our training is all about — act without having to think. Within seconds I was propping her up on the seat, following our 'ten-minute medicine' drill — keep the president alive for ten minutes.

All I could think about was to follow protocol, determine if she'd been hit, minimize blood loss, if any was present.

"It must have been unreal," Steve said.

Tony winced. "Pulling off her bulletproof vest left little doubt; I jammed my left index finger in the wound on her right shoulder, and continued to search with my right hand."

"Did you find anything?" Steve asked.

"At first I thought not then I saw blood still dripping from her right hand. I ripped off half of her blouse and wrapped it around her upper arm, and held it tight like a tourniquet. Thank God, it took less than the projected three minutes to arrive at the hospital."

Tony continued to describe the event. Steve's thoughts shifted to the hours he'd spent with Janet in the hospital room. He recalled the first time she was aware of him. *It was special — her eyes had a soft glow. She cracked a partial smile — it was beautiful, she was beautiful.* He had caressed her hand all night, and never felt so close to a woman before. *A miracle!*

In the blink of an eye, Steve glanced across the table at Sherry, sitting somberly next to Art. *I know she's hurting.*

He recalled that night at his place. He had tried to let her down as gently as possible ... it hadn't worked. At first she simply stared at him as if her world had ended. *I tried everything imaginable — nothing worked. Finally, I offered to take her home. She refused.* After crying and sobbing for another hour, she stood and walked out without saying a word. *I wished there had been something else I could have said or done.*

After that, he'd paid special notice to her in the office — she'd been polite and courteous, going through the motions, but never making eye contact. *Those three weeks must have been hell for her. I was so happy for her when it was announced that she'll be the new Inspector General.*

President Stetson joined the group. Everyone stood and applauded.

She nodded with a smile then looked at Tony. "I'll never find sufficient words to thanks Tony Petrarca. Without his timely action, it's likely I wouldn't be here today."

He smiled. The team gave him a round of cheers.

She rambled several minutes thanking others involved in her recovery. She nodded to Will Chandler, recognizing his congressional leadership in getting phase three passed, then turned to Steve. "I'd be remiss if I didn't give credit where credit is due. The reform package I'm signing into law today is the brainwork of Dr. Steve Schilling. Thanks to you for your hard work and dedication. The young people of our country will be better served because of you. Thanks, again."

He wanted to hug and kiss her; instead he gave her a polite wave.

She nodded then tucked a handful of pens into her sling and began to scribble her name.

***

Carrying his bag into the Aspen lodge at Camp David, Steve realized Janet and he hadn't had sex since Atlanta, the night before the tragedy. More than a month ago he mused. Somehow that didn't matter now. She was alive; that's all that he cared about. He was looking forward to spending Christmas with her, watching movies, taking long walks, and talking about family and personal things they'd never really discussed.

After a late dinner, the two of them laid in their robes on the sofa. He looked into her hazel eyes. "How are you feeling, dear?"

"I was tired at dinner but I've caught a second breath."

"It's important to get plenty of rest this week."

Her look gave him pause. She murmured, "I could hug and kiss you all over."

Their eyes connected. He gave her a sly, sexy look. "We'll have plenty of time for that," he said, surprising himself.

"Your eyes told me something else is on your mind."

He leaned back. "I didn't want to disappoint you and your libido, Janet, but there's no reason to rush things."

"Was that Steve Schilling I just heard?" She giggled. "I'm so proud of you. The way you were in the hospital … giving my speeches … wearing that infernal red fedora. I can't believe how people ate that up."

He grinned. "As I've said before, it makes me as approachable as any guy on the street."

"Approachable? I think you look sexy as hell when you wear it."

"Now you tell me. I left it at my apartment."

"Another night." She giggled. "Let's slip on our clothes and take a walk."

"Do you think you'll be warm enough?"

"I'll put on a heavy sweater under my coat."

"Maybe you should add a scarf too."

She agreed, wrapping her neck before they left.

The two slowly walked the wooded grounds of Camp David for over an hour. "We ought to go back. There's no use wearing you out."

She flashed a sensual, impish smile. "Are you expecting something more from me?"

He ignored the signal. "I was thinking about a hot fudge sundae."

She hit him with her left hand. "You ratfink. We haven't done it since Atlanta."

"So?"

"Just because I have one arm in a sling doesn't mean the rest of the parts don't work."

"I know sweetheart. I just don't want to rush you ..."

"Rush me hell, before I was shot you were stripping me before I got in the room."

"Things have changed."

"You mean you don't want to have sex?"

"No, it's more complex."

"Complex? What does that mean?" she said, stepping into the Aspen Lodge and marching to the sofa. "Come on, let's hear it."

He closed the door and walked slowly to the sofa. Settling in beside her, he squeezed her good hand. "There's something I've wanted to say for a long time."

She looked at his lips, her impatience growing. "Well?"

"Seeing you in the hospital bed made me realize how much I love you."

"That's it?"

He pecked her on the cheek. "No, that's the beginning. Lean back and relax. I'll tell you ... the rest of the story."

Looking up into his soft dark eyes, she eased back on the sofa.

He shot her a meaningful gaze. "The first time I saw you ..."

"In North Carolina?" she interrupted.

He placed his fingers over her lips. "I watched you parade around the ballroom, like an elegant goddess dressed in modern day attire. I couldn't keep my eyes off of you."

A smile lit up her face.

"And when you called asking me to come to Washington, it was like a dream come true. We met formally, and I wanted to *jump* you right there."

She started to speak.

He held a finger to her lips. "There's more ... please hear me out. When you touched me in the secret room, I thought I was going to explode. I could hardly wait until I was in your bedroom."

She pulled him close and kissed him on the lips. "I love you, Steve."

He waved his hand. "You stole my line. "I love you, Janet, more than I've ever loved anyone."

"You're so sweet," she said. "I'll take a rain check on the sundae."

***

Long walks and chats consumed most of the next few days, and increasingly, spontaneous sex crept in — Steve still looking for the right time to tell her the truth. Following an extended afternoon delight on the last day, the two lay naked in bed. She ran her fingertip over and around his lips. "Tell me more about phase four."

"Phase four, *now*?"

"Yes, I want to hear about it — how, when and why."

"Are you positive?"

"Yes, I'm the president, I want to know."

"Well, if you put it that way ..." He straightened up in bed and saluted. "Yes madam. There are three or four major points. It'll take some time."

She arched her naked body. "Do I look like I'm going anywhere?"

"Not unless you want to be in the *National Enquirer*." He laughed.

Getting *the look,* he wasted no time. "First, I need to share a few facts."

Not one for unnecessary chit chat, she waited impatiently. "Well?"

"It's complex ... I'm thinking." He pursed his lips before he spoke. "To start there are two trends running contrary to your goal of enhancing college attendance."

Janet turned on her side giving him her full attention. "Okay, let's hear them."

"When Pell Grants were established twenty years ago, they paid 72 percent of the total college costs for a student. That was a good deal. Today, grants cover only 36 percent."

"Appropriations have been increasing on a regular basis. How come?"

"Right, almost 9 percent a year. Inflation has eaten up some but the real culprit has been the increasing cost of college tuition. Tuition for public universities has skyrocketed at a rate double that of inflation. Pell Grants are now simply a pass-through."

Light lines crossed her forehead as she considered his numbers.

"At this rate, colleges will close out significant numbers of students; those who do attend will have a heavy student loan debt when they graduate."

"Is there anything we can do?"

"The real problem is higher education spending — it's out of control. There are no checks and balances. The university system is like a big, old dinosaur lumbering along — unwilling to change, consuming more and more green — passing the costs onto students."

"Doesn't anyone care?"

"I've asked that question a thousand times. State legislatures and the feds don't seem to care. University boards don't want to upset the financial apple cart. Most college presidents don't know a hill of beans about budgeting or higher education finance. Employees want more, so the universities want more, so the old dinosaur slowly plods along. There's no commitment to changing how universities are operated. For all practical purposes they're run like they were a hundred years ago."

"That's deplorable."

"I don't understand it," Steve continued, on a roll, "Congress is concerned about medical costs, but university costs are skyrocketing at a rate double that of medical costs — presidential compensation, athletic coaches' salaries, athletic spending, excessive department expenditures, more staff, you name it. They spend like money grows on trees."

"I want to talk more about this."

"Anytime. There're lots of university boondoggle spending examples I can share."

"What thoughts do you have about Pell Grants?"

"Oh yes, I guess I got sidetracked on higher education."

"I'm glad you did. It'll be a good topic for us to discuss in the future."

"I have two thoughts. The first is an extension of the conversation we just had. You could use your bully pulpit to publicly raise the issue. Show how the costs of higher education are outstripping medical costs. Point to the growing student loan debt. There are several ways you can draw public attention to the problem. It's important for you to make it a public issue!"

"I like that."

"My other thought deals directly with Pell Grants."

"I'm all ears." She giggled, stretching her arms above her head suggestively.

Steve eyed her naked body. "Couldn't prove it by me."

Sitting up, she pulled her robe from the nearby chair and slipped it on. "I'm making a pot of coffee. Let's talk more at the kitchen table."

"Good idea. I'll get a pad of paper so I can show you the numbers." Steve jumped out of bed, pulled on a pair of loungers, slid into his slippers and ambled into the kitchen. Watching Janet flit around the kitchen reminded him of the first time she had seduced him.

His heart twitterpated.

Janet poured two cups of coffee and settled into the chair across from him. "Tell me about the numbers you mentioned."

Steve jotted a few statements on his pad. "There are a half-dozen figures that tell it all." He turned the pad so she could read his notes. "First, the facts about Pell Grants. When they were initiated twenty years ago, Congress appropriated roughly $1.3 billion. This year the funding went over $6 billion."

"Wow. That's a significant increase."

"Yes, that's over 450 percent. But ... wait until you hear the rest of the facts." She cocked her head to the side, listening intently. Steve repeated his earlier stats, "In 1977, Pell Grants covered 72 percent of the costs at public universities. This year they covered only 36 percent of the costs."

With coffee, Janet better absorbed his numbers. "No, that's not possible. How could that happen?"

"Two things contributed. First, more students are enrolled in Pell Grants. And most important, the tuition costs at public universities have escalated five-fold."

"Five-fold? I can't believe that."

"It's even worse when you see the actual amounts covered for students." Steve made a couple of calculations. "Look at these numbers." He pointed to his pad. "For a student attending a public university in 1977, federal grants paid roughly $460 and the student paid $190 for the full year. In 1997, the feds paid $1,190 and the student paid $2,110."

"Oh my God, the students have to pay over ten times more now."

"Right, and it's only going to get worse. As I said earlier, there are no checks and balances on higher education. Federal support for students is a university pass-through. If this continues uncontrolled, it's easy to project huge amounts of student debt in the future."

"We need to do something. Do you have any ideas?"

"More money won't do it — the old dinosaur will eat up the greenbacks faster than you can print them. We need to think of ways to limit the growth of tuition."

"But we don't have any control over higher education."

"That's part of the reason why the challenge is so daunting. First and foremost, you must make it a public issue. Universities won't act on their own. People will need to be to be riled up. Maybe then legislators, politicians, and university boards will take action."

Janet thought decisively. "I'll have my speech writers draft some thoughts we can discuss after the first of the year."

"I'll be glad to work with them if you want."

"Perfect. That way I can work a few key phrases into my public addresses in the weeks ahead." She stroked her chin contemplating her options. "Do you have any thoughts on legislation that might curtail or slow the escalation of costs?"

"Two or three ideas come to mind ..."

"Let's hear them." She refilled their cups as Steve warmed to his ideas.

"I haven't worked out the details yet ..."

"Don't worry about that. I'll have my staff fill in the blanks."

"The simplest one connects back to the public school reforms you've already passed." He paused making sure he had her full attention. "Roughly 50 percent of all freshmen entering colleges today are deficient in reading, writing or mathematics."

"Half?! No way."

"I'm sorry but it's true. Many students use most of their first year taking remedial courses. That's about the most expensive way to correct the problem. Students have to live in dorms or rent low-income apartments, and support highly paid professors."

"You're right. The local high schools should be educating them better."

"Absolutely. So here's the proposal: 1) Over the next five years phase out Pell Grant funding for all remedial or developmental courses taught at the university level. Without funding, universities will drop the courses like hotcakes. 2) Place added pressure on local high school officials to produce quality graduates. With their reliance on federal aid you hold the big stick."

"Great idea, I'm ready to go. Give me another one."

"We need to come up with something that connects Pell Grants and student loans to the tuition levels. Maybe we could do an indexing system so students attending institutions with lower tuitions would receive larger grants. There could be an incentive plan that increases the percentage of costs covered by grants if universities hold or reduce tuition rates."

"I like both of those," the president said. She played with her hair, deep in thought. "I'll ask some of the creative people in financial aids to see what they can come up with."

"Good. Nine out of ten students on Pell Grants are also taking out loans. Pumping more money into work-study programs would reduce the amount students have to borrow. It could also be a cost-saving measure for universities."

"Absolutely, Steve. There are lots of students who are more capable than current staff members. There may be a way to funnel more funding to schools who take advantage of this option."

"Yes. I think, too, we could add cost-saving criteria for the awarding of grants and contracts. That's another area where thousands more students could be hired as laboratory or teaching assistants."

"Excellent. I'm sure staff can generate lots of proposals in this regard."

"I have two additional thoughts." Steve paused and ran his fingers through his hair. "The default rate on paying back student loans is growing at an astronomical rate. Some in Congress are talking about a forgiveness plan."

"Forgiveness, hell!" She threw her arms in the air. "Forgiving student loans is crazy. It goes contrary to all of our values. Nothing like that will pass on my watch."

"I'm with you on that. And I have a better way to clean up the entire mess."

Janet looked skeptical. "Let's hear it."

Steve flashed his trademark smile. "When a student is delinquent one year on his or her student loan payment, turn it over to the IRS. If they are to receive a tax refund the loan payment comes off the top. If he or she owes money, the delinquent amount is added to the tax bill."

"I love it. One way or another students will pay the tab — no need for defaults, forgiveness, or another agency to collect money." Janet stirred, looking into Steve's soft brown eyes for a long moment, then headed for the bedroom. "Enough about numbers. It's my turn to be on top."

***

After a long walk that afternoon, Janet poured the drinks and placed them on the coffee table in front of the fireplace and eased onto the sofa with Steve.

"I like your sales promo. Who will we be taking on?"

"The higher education establishment — and they won't like it," Steve said. "Other than that you'll have most everyone on your side. Leaders in higher education have been arrogant bastards for such a long time that no one is going to come to their defense."

"They'll scream bloody murder."

"It doesn't matter. Most of them have never had to face reality."

"Why do you say that?" she asked.

"They've had recessions and cutbacks, but rarely have they taken a hard look at what their departments are doing. As I said before, universities are managed like they were a hundred years ago. Tell them the federal government is downsizing by 20 percent. And that, you know they could do the same without affecting the quality of education."

"Do you really believe that?"

"Yes. I did it at two universities and things went on as usual; there was no change in the quality of education. In fact, I think staff members had a more positive attitude."

Janet twirled the tips of her short dark hair. "I'll call our educational advisors together after the first of the year. You can make the proposal, and we'll see how it flies." She reached across the table and squeezed his hand. "I love to watch you get fired up about an issue. You're so exciting, full of energy …" She paused, flipped open her robe, and teased him with her breasts. "Anything else you can get excited about?"

Steve jumped up and planted a wet kiss on her lips. "You bet!"

CHAPTER TWENTY-SIX

President Stetson sat at the head of the conference table in the Roosevelt Room as the advisors walked in. Precisely at eleven o'clock she called the meeting to order. "I trust you all had a most enjoyable holiday season."

Heads bobbed around the room.

"Good. As you all know Sherry Holmgren was promoted over the holidays. Steve tells me she made numerous contributions to our reform effort. And being the architect of our 20 percent reduction was a significant accomplishment. She'll be missed. What more can I say."

"Here … here," the grouped echoed.

"I'm pleased to welcome another highly qualified person; Sherry's replacement, Fran Gather." Steve glanced at her. *Slender with gray-streaked hair and, he already knew, smart as hell.*

"As you know I'm working on a reduced schedule," the president said. "So I've asked Bradley to run today's meeting. Steve will present phase four of our reform package. I'm most interested in hearing your thoughts and advice on how we can take the next step forward."

She stood and left the room.

Bradley motioned to Steve. "The floor is yours."

Steve walked the group through the plan then handed out his one-pager outlining federal cost-saving measures that could reduce costs in higher education.

"That's good to hear, Steve. I don't see much of that type of thinking from leaders in government," Ira Magaziner said. "A little carrot and stick, I like that.

Will Chandler leaned forward on the table. "I'm for anything that will rein in the spiraling costs of tuition. This ought to get the attention of higher education officials across the country. Maybe some of them will see the gravy train has run dry."

"I agree," Secretary Cohen said. "Right now universities raise tuitions without paying the consequence — increase the tab and the feds cough up more funds — it's a vicious cycle. At least with your plan they'll have to give some thought to the actions they're taking. If universities aren't careful, students will vote with their feet, and be off to another school."

"Forcing campuses to cut expenses will receive lots of votes. The country is in a cost-cutting mood. It's about time higher education received a touch of reality," Will said.

"Short term, you can't depend on the president leading the call. Her travel will be restricted until late spring," Bradley announced.

"I don't see the need for a nationwide campaign on this one," another member chimed in.

"Sounds like Will on the hill and Steve's red fedora out with the troops," Ira quipped.

Chuckles cracked around the room.

Steve's face turned red. "I hope those laughs were for my hat," he jested.

"I'll set up a short speaking tour in key cities for Steve, so we can test the waters — Richmond, Charlotte and Atlanta," Ira said.

"Sounds good," Bradley said, "Anything else for the good of the order?"

Ms. Gather timidly raised her hand. "I have a small concern."

All eyes shifted to her.

"The entire conversation has been focused on cost-saving measures and efficiency. That's certainly a timely message. I think we ought to do more. When I hear about higher education, I think of quality."

"Good point," Bradley said.

She nodded his way and continued. "We ought to throw higher education a crumb or two. Maybe a national incentive program that rewards academic excellence and efficiency, and follows the Baldrige quality performance award for business."

"Outstanding idea," Secretary Chandler agreed. "I can sell that."

Everyone around the table nodded in agreement.

Bradley glanced at Will then looked at Steve. "Let's have the two of you work up something we can look at next week?"

Steve easily agreed. "We'll be glad to."

***

That afternoon Fran and Steve joined Secretary Chandler at his conference table. "I appreciate your suggestion that we add some incentives for higher education," he said. "That'll give the legislation some pizzazz."

"Thank you. It'll take some of the focus off the cost-cutting measures, too."

"I like that … a little icing on the cake," Steve said.

Will nodded. "What kind of thoughts do you have for the incentive proposal?"

"As I mentioned I'd take a page straight out of the Baldrige awards for corporate excellence," Fran started. "We can reward excellence and efficiency by developing criteria focused on improving performance, demonstrating value-added measures, and sharing best practices."

"Perfect," Steve said.

"The awards could be made annually by the governor and limited to no more than 10 percent of the colleges and universities in the state. I'd suggest we call it the governor's something-or-other. That'll give it some real appeal in the states."

"The Republicans can't complain about that," Will said. "Prepare a one-page draft for Steve and me to look at."

"Will do," she said.

"Do you have any other ideas?"

Fran hesitated. "As a matter of fact I do."

"Let's hear it," the secretary requested.

"I read about the Governor's Scholars Program Steve set up while he was in North Carolina — giving more academic scholarships than athletic awards."

"I'm not familiar with that," Will said, "But go ahead."

"Using his model we could create the Senator Scholars Program."

"That's an oxymoron," Steve jested.

"I thought of that too." She grinned. "Each senator could appoint one during his or her term. That would provide an opportunity for a hundred students at any one time. We might have two or three conferences each year where these students and senators could discuss national policy issues."

Will glanced at Steve. "What do you think of that?"

"I like it. It'll send another quality signal."

"Good. The two of you can draft a proposal. We'll discuss it at our next meeting."

***

Waiting in the department cafeteria for Art to return with his coffee, Steve watched a tight-skirt pass by. *Jesus Christ, what an ass.* He fantasized about jumping her.

Art sat down across from him. "How's it going," he asked.

"Great … up to a minute ago."

Art wrinkled his brow. "Why?"

The stretched-sweater view of the tight-ass walked by and smiled.

"Holy shit, that's why. Did you see how she smiled at me?"

"I thought she was smiling at me," Art quipped.

"How can you say that? It was a real come-on smile."

Art's grin beckoned the hot-looking woman their way. She stood and sashayed toward the two men. Steve watched her hips, gyrating, trying to seduce him.

Art stood. "Steve, I'd like you to meet my daughter, Cadence."

"I'm glad to meet you," Steve said, sheepishly.

"Did you receive the message?" She winked, then giggled.

Steve gave her one of his mega-smiles. "I sure did."

She held out her left hand and flashed her diamond ring. "Think again. I'm happily married with two kids." She turned to Art. "Did I do okay, daddy?"

"You were perfect."

"Nice to meet you Dr. Schilling." She grinned and walked away. Art laughed. "It was a setup. Dr. Pritts and I worked it out to prove a point."

Steve was flustered and confused.

"He thought it was important for you to understand how vulnerable you are."

"My antennas are always up."

"It's more than that, Steve. It's your perception of things. When she smiled your addiction told you she was smiling at *you*. She wasn't; she was simply giving me a fatherly smile. Your sex urges played a trick on you."

Steve pursed his lips. "You made the point."

"That's why Dr. Pritts wants us to continue our lunches on Wednesdays."

"I guess I have a ways to go yet."

Art nodded. "How are things going with the mystery woman?"

"Couldn't be better. We were together for an extended stay over the holidays. I've never felt this close to a woman in my life."

"Good for you." Satisfied, Art changed the subject. "Anything you want to discuss about your upcoming speeches?"

"Hmm, not really." He gave his remark a second thought. "I plan to start with the Governor's Excellence Program, move into cost-cutting measures, and wrap it up with the Senator's scholars. Would you do it differently?"

Art hesitated for a moment. "Not at all; it sounds fine to me … put the meat in the middle. I'd stress the good public policy point. And make sure you stress President Stetson's 20 percent federal reduction plan."

"Oh yes, good point."

***

Steve sat patiently on the stage of the Grand Ballroom in Richmond's Thomas Jefferson Hotel — the city's finest and one of the nation's best. As the glowing introduction continued, he noticed the sparkling chandeliers, ornately painted ceiling and voluminous draperies, and then smiled to himself seeing that the standing-room only crowd had spilled into the hallway.

The head of the Richmond's Business Roundtable turned to him. "It is my privilege to welcome Dr. Steve Schilling."

Steve stepped to the podium and without delay moved into his speech. "On behalf of President Stetson I am proud to announce her plans to recognize excellence in higher education and end the uncontrolled spiraling costs of tuition."

His initial comments about the two concepts quickly captured the attention of the audience. Over the next thirty minutes, he expanded on both, and presented compelling rationale why Congress should pass the proposal. "Enough of that," he perked up. "I've made my points; now it's time for me to hear what you have to say."

The business leaders gave him a standing ovation, knowing his good ol' boy red fedora was on the way. Steve pulled his hat from under the podium, adjusted it on his head, and moved to the small table on his right. A murmur filled the room.

"Who has the first question," he asked, as he slid onto the table and raised the handheld microphone.

The Q and A session went like clockwork; most of the questions sounded more like endorsements rather than concerns. After forty-five minutes, Steve stood and tipped his hat. "Thank you very much for you attention."

The audience stood and gave him another standing ovation.

RICHMOND TIMES-DISPATCH

EDITORIAL

March 15, 1999

Deputy Secretary of Education Steve Schilling delivered a sterling speech at this month's Business Roundtable. Announcing a series of direly needed reforms for higher education, he received several standing ovations. A plan to introduce awards of excellence patterned after the Baldrige Awards, received broad support as did the plan to slow the spiraling costs of higher education.

We applaud the president's efforts to reform higher education.

Steve followed the same format in Charlotte and Atlanta. The results were the identical, including pictures of him sporting his red fedora.

CHARLOTTE OBSERVER

OPINION

March 16, 1999

Finally some common sense comes out of Washington.

At today's Regional Economic Committee meeting former Mountain State University president Steve Schilling outlined administration plans to cut the spiraling costs of higher education. Wearing his traditional red fedora, Dr. Schilling stated it's time for colleges and universities to bite the bullet. "We cut costs by 20 percent when I was at MSU. And, we expect institutions across the nation can do the same."

It sounds like more North Carolina thinking is needed in Washington, D.C.

THE ATLANTA JOURNAL-CONSTITUTION

EDITORIAL

March 17, 1999

Hats off to President Stetson!

Today Deputy Secretary of Education, Steve Schilling, announced sweeping plans aimed at

cutting spiraling costs of college tuition. Coupled with a series of strategies to reward excellence, the administration has proposed policies that are a must.

It's time for Congress to play ball!

***

After hearing a half hour of accolades about Steve's performance on the tour, President Stetson concluded her educational advisory meeting. "Obviously, Steve did a great job." She paused and smiled at him. "I'd be remiss if I did not thank all of you for your hard work. And to you, Ms. Gather, a special thanks. The additional emphasis on quality made a real difference."

Her rosy cheeks broadened. "Thank you, Madam President."

The president nodded. "This meeting is adjourned," she said, with a gesture toward Steve to follow her into the Oval Office.

He walked in behind her and took his usual position in the wingback chair to the left of the fireplace. She hurried to her desk, scribed a note on a pad of paper and handed it to Steve:

I'm having a rush, want to go upstairs?

Steve gave her his mega-watt smile. She waved to her personal secretary on the way out then led the way out the door, down the promenade, to the White House residence. She waited patiently at the elevator for the usher staff member to open the door.

Almost before the door closed on the second floor, Janet began shedding her clothes. Reaching the bedroom, she motioned him in and slammed the door.

Standing in front of him, Janet stripped to her black bra, panties and high heels. Sashaying to the recorder, she turned on *the song* and began to strut her stuff, of which she had plenty.

Already turned on, Steve stripped naked and slid into bed, not missing one of her moves. She stepped to the beat of the music, made a quick move and tossed her panties at him. Kicking off her shoes, she threw her body on the bed.

Wrestling on top of Steve, she showed no side effects from the shooting, only a couple of barely noticeable scars remained.

As her arms pulled him tight, her voluminous breasts heaved; her hot body pulsated against his chest.

Steve slipped on a condom, grabbed her ass and pulling her tight. Easing inside, he joined her pace. She gasped then rose on her arms and looked him in the eye. "I'm so proud of you. I could have jumped you the minute you walked in."

"Without your decisions none of this would have happened," he panted.

"You're terrific. When you're wearing that darn red hat I can't keep my eyes off you."

"Damn," Steve shouted. "Once again I left my hat at home."

"Maybe I can make up for that." She straddled him, shifted into gear flinging her bra to the floor and pushing her breasts in his face, smothering him. Steve lapped at her nipples like a thirsty puppy. Her firm breasts teased him unmercifully.

He gasped for a breath, trying not to come too soon. She pressed harder, pushing her body against his pelvis again and again. Steve gulped, unable to stop his body from shooting out of control. She slowed for a moment then hammered him into submission.

CHAPTER TWENTY-SEVEN

FBI Headquarters
935 Pennsylvania Avenue NW
Washington, D. C.

March 22, 1999

Louis Freeh joined his security colleagues then stared around the table. "Who wants to go first this week?"

Not an eye looked up.

"What? No one?" he snarled. "We're investigating the possible assassination of the President of the United States, and there is nothing new from the world's most sophisticated intelligence gathering agencies. Give me a break!"

"I've never seen anything like it before," CIA's Tenet interjected. "There's no chatter; it's like an international lockdown."

"Someone out there knows something. I want you to stop everything you're doing and put every agent on this."

The eyes of the directors around the table focused on him.

"We must locate and eliminate the bastards responsible for this cowardly attack on freedom." Freeh covered his face with his hands, taking time to gather his thoughts. "We're starting over. There must be a lead in the material we've compiled. Open up your files, we're going through every shred of information again."

One by one the directors described the facts listed in their files.

An hour later Director Freeh stroked his jaw. "We have one common thread." Everyone looked up at him. "Steve Schilling. One more time. I want to hear everything we know about him."

The other directors meticulously reported what they had on Steve. Freeh turned his attention to Secret Service head Lewis Merletti.

Merletti didn't look up, continuing to stare at his notepad.

"Can you add anything?" the director asked, pointedly.

"I have nothing more."

"Nothing!" Freeh gave him a disgusting look. "Not acceptable. I want to hear everything you know about Steve Schilling. Do you understand?" he asked in a harsh tone.

Lewis fiddled with his pen.

"Mr. Merletti, I'm waiting."

He looked up. "You know I cannot divulge any personal information about the president."

Freeh's face flushed. "We're not talking about some fly-by-night hanky-panky; we're investigating the possible assassination of the President of the United States. Is he sleeping with her?"

Merletti grimaced then nodded. "For the last year and a half."

"Shit," Freeh said, the rest of the group likely thinking the same thing. "We have to take the gamble. We need to interview Steve Schilling. Anyone disagree?"

With a scan of the room, Tenet said, "The decision is unanimous."

"Call Schilling on my speaker line," Freeh said to his aide.

"Yes sir." He leafed through Steve's file then dialed his office.

"Office of the Deputy Secretary," the receptionist said.

"Yes, thank you. May I speak with Dr. Schilling?"

She hesitated. "I'm sorry Dr. Schilling is on medical leave. His assistant Art Wallhollister is taking his calls, may I connect you?"

"Yes," a startled Freeh said.

Following a series of bleeps and buzzes, Art picked up the phone. "Wallhollister."

The FBI director cleared his throat. "This is Louis Freeh, I'm trying to reach Steve Schilling."

Art was slow to respond. "The FBI Freeh?"

"Yes, may I speak with him?"

"Dr. Schilling was admitted to Georgetown University Hospital on Friday. He's been in the ICU ever since."

"What happened?"

"We were debriefing his latest trip when he asked me to take him home. Next thing I know, he collapsed on the floor. I called 911 and the medics rushed him to the hospital. I followed them there."

"What time was this Friday?"

"About four-thirty. An hour later they had him wired up, and then suddenly all of the bells and whistles went off. His heart rate dropped below thirty. I think his body was shutting down. Finally, they stabilized him and determined that he has sepsis."

"Sepsis?"

"It occurs when a foreign substance enters the blood stream — in his case millions of E. coli bacteria — cascading through his body. It can be life-threatening. If it progresses into sepsis shock, one's blood pressure can drop dramatically, and death can occur."

"How is he now?"

"He's turned the corner. They figure he'll recover."

"Good for him. Do you have any idea when he'll be back?"

"Not really, maybe a week or so."

"Would you ask him to call me as soon as he can?"

"Yes, of course." He ended the call and Freeh turned to the group. "Anyone know anything about sepsis?"

"A good friend's father died from it. It has a 40 percent mortality rate," Tenet said.

"Is it possible for something like this to be placed in someone's bloodstream?" Shoulders shrugged. No one answered. "I want to know everything there is to know about sepsis," Freeh demanded.

***

Two weeks later Steve walked slowly into the FBI conference room. Director Freeh shook his hand and introduced him to the others around the table. Steve sat in the vacant chair next to him. He glanced at Steve, then said, "Dr. Schilling, I want to thank you for meeting with us as soon as possible. We are most concerned for your health."

"I appreciate that … I'm doing much better, thank you."

"Do they know the source of your problem?"

"Not yet." Steve shook his head. "The infection control doctors are baffled."

"Well, let's get right to it. We'd appreciate whatever assistance you might provide regarding the attempted assassination."

"Yes, of course, I'll do whatever I can."

"Thank you," Freeh said. "We've pulled together all of the government's resources to uncover anything that might help us locate the would-be killers." He paused trying to measure Steve's composure. "We're aware of your involvement with Hannah Liebermann. Could you explain that?"

Steve's eyes opened wide. "Hannah and I spent four nights together last summer."

"What did you do, talk about?" the director continued.

"Ah … nothing special. We went to the theatre and out to dinner a couple of times."

"Did you talk to her about the Bilderberg's?"

"She mentioned them once, said her husband was a big shot then she dropped the subject like it was something she wasn't supposed to talk about."

"Do you know anything about them?"

"I read an article in the paper about their undue influence in the selection of our presidents."

"Anything else?"

"Not that I can recall."

"Did you talk about educational reform?"

"Yeah, she was really interested in that."

"How about your travel plans?"

"Hmm … we hadn't gotten to that stage then."

"When were you in Bar Harbor with her?"

"The week before Labor Day."

"Did you talk about her husband's business?"

Steve shook his head. "No."

We have some pictures we'd like to share to see if you recognize anyone."

"Okay."

Freeh flashed a series of pictures — Hannah, her husband and known associates. "Do you recognize any of these people other than Hannah?"

Steve studied each photo. "Nope."

CIA Director Tenet shifted the discussion, flashing an eight-by-ten-inch photo of Elena. "Do you know this woman?"

"Yes."

"She's spent several nights at your place and you've been at her flat many times?"

"Yes, sir."

"Did you talk about the president?"

"I guess." Steve shrugged. "We talked about everything."

Frowns formed on the faces around the table. He continued. "Trips you planned to take with the president?"

"I'm sure I did; it was the most important thing on my mind at the time."

"Did you mention dates and hotels you might stay in?"

"I can't recall specifically but ... yes I probably did. I was with her before and after every trip."

"I have some photos, would you mind looking at them?"

"Of course."

"Here are some of Elena's known associates." He tossed a half-dozen photos across the table. "Have you ever seen any of these people?"

Steve flipped though the pictures then held up the last one. "Yes, this one. He's a backup drummer at Blues Alley, Patrick Ridelman."

"Did you ever see him play?"

Steve thought for a moment. "No, why?

Freeh grinned. "He doesn't play the drums; he's a low-level Russian agent."

"Holy shit, I thought he was a really nice guy."

"How did you meet Elena?"

"Patrick came up with the idea," Steve said, then realized that he'd been conned.

Freeh motioned to Steve. "I have several recent photos taken in the Philippines. Would you take a look at these?"

Steve nodded and slid closer to him.

"Here's a picture of a protest march in Manila. Anyone you've ever seen?"

He studied each person. "Nope."

"How about these guys standing by the car?"

"Not that one," Steve said, looking at the tall one in the center. He peered at the pudgy one on the right. "Hmm, I'm not positive. Maybe. Is there a clearer picture?"

"How about this one?" Tenet handed Steve a close-up shot.

"Yes, that's Felix, Kim's driver. She is another friend of mine; and he was decapitated in a mass murder last fall."

The individuals around the table gave him a blank look.

"How about the big guy on the left?"

Steve squinted at the photo.

"Yes, that's Rodrigo, Kim's personal body guard. He was decapitated at the same time."

"I have three more from the Manila federal court. How about this one?"

"No."

"Here's another photo."

Steve stared for the longest moment then wiped a tear from his eye. "It's Kim. She was mutilated when Rodrigo and Felix were decapitated last October." Steve paused, and gave the general a questioning look. "*When* did you say these pictures were taken?"

Freeh nodded. "You were duped."

Steve cocked his head to the side. "Duped?"

"It was a setup. They're still alive. Who told you they were dead?"

"Margo."

Freeh opened another file, pulled out a photo and held it up. Is this Kim?"

"Yes, she was killed several months ago."

Freeh's grin broadened. "The photos were taken in the Philippines last week."

"No, that can't be. Margo said ..."

Freeh interrupted. "She's connected with them too."

Steve cupped his hands over his face and slouched down in his chair. "Oh my God."

"Where did you meet Kim?"

"At … at one of Margo's parties."

"Margo and her husband Freddie are on our subversive list. The parties were part of the overall scheme. It's likely most of the people in the room are connected with one or another subversive group."

Steve sobbed with the realization. "I could have had something to do with the shooting."

"Absolutely," Freeh said. "Is it okay if I send out a team to debug your apartment?"

"Yes, of course. Do whatever you need to do."

***

At the next meeting Director Freeh laid the debugging report on the table. "We may have narrowed our investigation by one third." The individuals around the table gave him their full attention. "Bugs used by the Russians and those used throughout Asia were found. For the time being I want all available agents shifted to these two venues."

"Any plans for Schilling?" General Minihan asked. "The other guys could figure out the same thing we've learned … and go after him."

Freeh nodded. "We'll give him twenty-four-hour protection. Anything else?"

The CIA director cleared his throat and said, "Our handwriting experts suspect the threatening letter sent to Steve was written by a person in their sixties or seventies, likely a woman."

"The mother or grandmother of someone," Freeh interjected. "Maybe it's Kim's mother."

"Could be … why?"

"I never know." Freeh shook his head. "When dealing with people from different cultures … I'm never sure. They think differently than we do."

"It's possible and certainly worth exploring."

"How about Russia?" Director Tenet asked, changing the subject. "Anything new there?"

"Yes," Freeh said. "Elena has a sister who lives in Chicago. She teaches political science at one of the universities there. We have the entire Chicago office checking her out."

CHAPTER TWENTY-EIGHT

Ellen waved at Steve as he passed through security at the Asheville Airport. "There she is," Ellen whispered to Charlie.

"How could I miss her?" Charlie asked. "A real looker."

The two old friends welcomed Steve with open arms. He smiled and turned to her.

"Charlie and Ellen, I want you to meet Hope Lawson."

"Nice to meet you," the two chimed.

"Thank you so much," she said. "Steve has told me so much about the two of you and how important you are to him. It's so nice to meet you, too."

Ellen complimented Hope on her sporty green outfit. Charlie eyed her silky blonde hair, recording his thoughts about her shape for a future conversation with Steve. The two men picked up their bags and lugged them to short-term parking, Ellen and Hope chatting all the way.

"Steve, sit up front with me," Charlie directed. "Looks like the women have plenty to talk about."

After placing their luggage in the trunk, Steve slid in on the passenger side. The women were already in the back seat gabbing like old friends. Before they were out of the parking lot, Steve let loose a barrage of questions on Charlie about his old university. Charlie delighted in rehashing Provost La Russa's successful transition in becoming the head man. Charlie mused. "All that aside … we miss the red fedora."

"It's a big hit in Washington," Hope piped in. "Steve slips it on after his speeches for the Q and A session. People eat it up."

"You're just jealous because you don't have one," he quipped.

"Any place around here where I might buy one?" she shot back at him.

"This is Midville." Charlie groaned. "The only hat you can buy in Midville is a John Deere ball cap."

"Fine," Hope countered. "I'll settle for that."

Ellen chuckled, as if Hope didn't have any idea of what she was in for.

Charlie glanced in the rearview mirror. "I don't think it will compliment your outfit."

"Darn, I'll have to buy some jeans too."

"That we have," Charlie said.

By the time, the four arrived at McBride's it was obvious Hope was not someone Steve had picked up in a local bar — a classy lady with a bright head on her shoulders. Charlie and Steve put their bags in the guest bedroom and hung up Hope's dress bag.

"Hope, why don't you change into something more casual," Ellen said. "It's pretty informal around here."

"Sounds great, it'll be good to take off my heels and kick back," she said, heading for the guest bedroom.

Ellen anxiously waited for her to close the door. "Where did you find *her*?"

Steve spun his yarn. "A friend in the department told me about this attractive lawyer who worked across town. Next thing I know I'm asking her out for dinner and … the rest is history."

"Does she have a particular specialty?" Charlie asked.

"Yes …" Steve said, as Hope opened the door. "Here's … my corporate takeover lawyer."

She paraded into the kitchen with looks fit to kill.

"I love your purple and teal sweatsuit."

"Thank you," she said to Ellen. "They're my favorite colors."

"I can see why," Charlie popped, glimpsing at her out of the corner of his eye then turning to open a bottle of merlot. Ellen pulled a platter of hors d'oeuvres out of the fridge.

Hope stepped into the kitchen and offered a hand. "How can I help?"

"There's some cheese in the fridge if you'd like to slice it."

"Sure." Heading her way, Hope appeared reserved, almost shy.

"Where are the crackers?" Steve asked.

"In the corner cabinet." Charlie pointed.

It wasn't long before the team had filled the table with a stack of food. Steve dug in. Enjoying several rounds of hors d'oeuvres and a couple bottles of red wine, the group settled in for an extended dinner of Ellen's special zucchini and pepperoni casserole.

Steve cleaned his plate then pushed away from the table. "I couldn't eat one more bite."

A dreary-eyed Hope looked at Ellen. "That was wonderful, Ellen. I want your recipe." She stood. "I'm really tuckered out. I hope you don't mind if I hit the hay early."

"Not at all," Charlie exclaimed. "Steve and I have plenty of catching up to do."

***

Charlie poured himself a port and filled a glass of ice for Steve with amaretto. Kicking back on his lounger, Charlie grinned. "Now for the rest of the story."

Holding onto the stem, Steve gently swirled the last of his wine. "Think you're pretty smart, don't you?"

"Corporate lawyer … I don't know."

"Charlie, it's true … she is a lawyer."

"How long have you been banging her?"

"Geez, Charlie, I just got here."

"I thought we might as well put all of the cards on the table." He took a long sip.

"We'd been working on a project for some time and all of a sudden she planted one on me."

"Now that sounds more like it."

"You mentioned on the phone that things had really turned around."

"You won't believe it Charlie; I've really turned the corner."

"Just like that?"

"No it's been a long time coming. Long story short. Dr. Pritts did a little shock-therapy."

"Shock therapy?" Charlie envisioned a full frontal lobotomy for Steve.

Seeing the look on Charlie's face, Steve assured him, "Not that kind."

"He said he was at the end of the line and couldn't do a thing for me."

"How'd you react to that?"

"I about crapped my pants. I thought if he can't help me, who could? After a while I came to realize that Dr. Benderman, you, and all of the others who've tried to help me have been right the whole time — nothing was going to change unless I made it happen."

"After all you've gone through, I can't believe he got through to you. Just like that?"

"It didn't happen overnight. I don't know what it was. Maybe I was just scared of being on my own."

"Whatever it was ... it sounds like you're finally on the right track."

"I've been working on it and actually making progress ever since. I'm trying to make the therapy part of my lifestyle."

"Good for you. Does Hope know about all of this?"

"I started to tell her once but she changed the subject. I know I need to share it with her."

Charlie's brow furrowed. "Are the two of you that serious?"

"Yes," Steve said, his mood optimistic. "I've never met a person like her."

"And you've ended it with Charisse, Sherry and the others?"

"Absolutely. Sherry was the toughest. I finally realized that I'd have to make a choice."

"That's quite a change from before."

"I knew I'd end up hurting Sherry, and the longer I put it off the worse it would be."

"Are you positive you won't hurt Hope?"

"I'm positive, Charlie. She's the only one for me. There's no one else."

Charlie shook his head, still questioning Steve's sincerity. "I hope so. She seems like a really fine woman."

***

In anticipation of her "talking head" shows Sunday morning, Ellen placed her coffee mug and a napkin holding a warm croissant, on the end table, and eased into her favorite comfy chair. She flicked on her favorite television channel — Tim Russert's pudgy face appeared.

Hope strolled into the living room wearing a light blue robe, refreshed by being out of Washington.

Ellen glanced up and said, "The coffee is ready, pour yourself a cup and join me."

Without saying a word, Hope filled a mug and slipped into the other chair and waited until the first commercial. "Do you watch *Meet the Press* all the time?"

Ellen gripped her mug and smiled smugly. "I wouldn't miss it."

"I'm the same."

"Do you have a favorite person you like to see interviewed?"

"Steve was really good."

"Good? He's wonderful. He's always been good upfront with a mike in his hand."

"You're telling me ... I've seen him perform several times. He's superb." Hope sipped her hot coffee. "Anyone else?"

"Of course, President Stetson. She's the best," Ellen announced, obviously unaware of the special pointers Janet had been given by an artist on how to apply her makeup differently so as to disguise her facial features. "Anyone you *don't* like?"

"No. How about you?"

Without hesitation, Ellen said, "I don't like Secretary Chandler."

"Secretary Chandler? Why do you say that?"

"Steve has asked me the same thing. I can't put my finger on it." Ellen fussed with her robe, considering the question. "I just don't like him. There's something about his eyes; he doesn't seem to be sincere."

"His interactions with Congress are excellent."

"So I've heard. I've told Steve to keep an eye on him, though. There's just something ..."

***

Over breakfast on the last morning, long before it was time to leave for the airport, Steve rose from the kitchen table. "Ellen, you've outdone yourself again. The Spanish omelet was wonderful. I can't recall when I've eaten so much."

Charlie eyed Steve's loose sweatshirt. "How much weight have you lost?"

"Twenty-two pounds."

Hope leaned over and pecked him on the cheek. "Doesn't he look terrific?" She winked at Steve. "Do you think we should tell them?"

Steve shrugged in a manner suggesting she should have the honor. "It's up to you."

"Thanks, Ellen, for another fabulous meal." Hope stood and turned for the bedroom then stopped and looked back. "Please excuse me, there's something I want to show you."

Charlie gave Steve a puzzled look. "What's that all about?"

"It's about our conversation the other night."

"Come on, you guys, let me in on the secret," Ellen pleaded.

"The two of them are really serious," Charlie said.

"Is she going to spill the beans?" Ellen asked. "Are they getting engaged?"

Steve laughed. "I never know what she's going to do."

A little later, Janet walked out of the bedroom no longer sporting her blonde wig, sharply dressed in a dark blue suit.

Charlie tried to speak, but nothing came out. Steve placed his finger over his lips. "Sh." The men waited for Ellen to notice.

"Sh?" Ellen asked, turning away from the sink.

Steve's mega-smile exploded. "Who do we have here ... a guest from *Meet the Press*?"

Ellen froze, dumbfounded. Unable to move, she mumbled, "Prez ... President Stetson."

Charlie stared at Steve. "You didn't say it was *her*."

Looking like a kid caught with his hand in the cookie jar, he pecked Janet on the cheek and turned to Ellen. "Better sit down, this is going to take a while."

"I guess so," Charlie erupted.

Ellen lurched toward her chair and flopped down; still, unable to take her eyes off the president.

"I have to make a toast on this," Charlie shouted, and was off to the kitchen. Returning in short order, he popped the cork and filled four glasses of Champagne. Staring at the president, Charlie hesitated. "I don't know how to say it, I've never toasted the President of the United States."

Holding her glass high, Janet stood with a grin. "Like always with good friends … here's to old and new friends."

"Here, here," the group echoed.

Ellen took a sip without saying a word.

"We confess," Steve said, the two lovebirds caressing each other. "The two of you are the only ones who know."

Ellen shook her head. "I can't believe it; how you've been able to fool everyone — the press … the country, the whole world?"

Steve sat down in the chair across from her. "It all began when the chief of staff insisted Janet have a double. From there it unfolded; it became a game for us."

"How do you get around the Secret Service?" Charlie asked.

"We don't," Janet interjected. "They need to be in on everything; they plan, organize and control the whole charade. They can limit the number of people involved to maybe a hundred or so, and keep my double at a distance. You can't imagine the number of functions that have to go on, that I need immediate access to — there are 'hotlines' and countless other tasks to be maintained for this to work."

"How do you keep the media from knowing," Ellen probed.

"That's the biggest challenge," Steve said. "It's called off the record travel. Like today, you saw us leave baggage claim. There's no way Janet could be on a commercial plane, even wearing a wig. Since she hadn't decided whether or not she was going to tell you, she played it safe."

"Safe?"

Steve grinned. "During the night her staff drove us to Asheville then delivered us on the tarmac and we walked inside the airport. Undercover Secret Service agents ushered us into the baggage claim area."

"I suppose they're outside too," Charlie ventured.

"Absolutely," Janet said. "They've cased everything around here."

"Wow." Charlie said. "This whole thing is unbelievable."

***

Sherry walked into Art's office. "Have an extra cup of coffee hanging around?" she asked.

"Sure." He turned toward the coffee pot with a wrinkled brow knowing she had not stopped by his office for a casual visit. She hadn't been there since being named Inspector General, almost five months ago.

Art wiped the inside of a mug with a paper towel, then asked, "Want something in it?"

"Black will be fine." She slid onto the side chair by his desk and laid a black binder on the corner of his desk.

He grinned. "Guess I should have remembered that."

She didn't respond. Art handed her a steaming mug.

"Thanks," she said, sounding pensive.

"I've been meaning to stop by but the time slipped away. How's your new job going?"

"It's okay," she said, staring away without emotion.

Art hesitated. "I thought this was your dream job."

"It was … I mean … it is."

"Are you all right?"

She looked pale and not dressed in her usual impeccable style. "I guess."

Art slipped forward to the edge of his chair and folded his hands on his desk. "Okay, let's hear it."

Sherry's eyes moistened. "It's awful. I shouldn't have done it." She wiped a tear from her cheek.

"It can't be that bad. Come on, were good friends. Relax and tell me."

Sherry sniffled, blew her nose and started to sob.

"Come on, Sherry, from the beginning."

She stuffed a half-used tissue back in her pocket. "It started right after Steve was appointed."

Art interrupted. "Two and a half years ago?"

She closed her eyes, her thoughts seemingly elsewhere. "Secretary Chandler called me into his office, and asked if I wanted to be the next Inspector General. I said, 'Of course.' He looked at me with a big smile knowing that was my lifelong goal. 'I can make that happen if you want to play ball.' I thought he wanted me to sleep with him or something and I was ready to tell him off and say I'd file a discrimination complaint if he said one more word."

"And?"

"It was almost as bad."

"As bad as sleeping with the guy? I don't understand."

"Well, maybe not as bad as sleeping with him ... he wanted me to compromise my values."

"Compromise your values ... I'm still behind."

"He said he'd appoint me as Steve's Senior Advisor if I was willing to be a team player."

"A team player?" Art asked.

Sherry nodded. "He said, 'the two of us could meet monthly to keep track of things.'"

"Did he offer you the Inspector General job?"

"No, he's too smart for that but I knew the deal. You scratch my back and I'll take care of you."

"What did you do?"

"I caved. I've second-guessed myself ever since. It was wrong and I knew it."

"So you had meetings with him?"

"Every month. At first it didn't seem too bad. I told him what was happening with Steve. There was nothing secretive. He could have learned most of it by looking at Steve's calendar."

"Did you tell him about Steve's personal life?"

"Mostly things I heard in the rumor mill. All of the single women and half of the married ones in the building had the hots for him. He must have been sleeping with three or four different ones a week."

"And then?"

"Next thing I know I was falling for him. The more I saw him the more I wanted him. He must have sensed it; kept stringing me along. You know, taking his time, making me want him. He was really cool about it. By the time we went to bed for the first time, I was practically begging for it ..." Sherry blushed.

"Did you tell Will about your feelings for Steve?"

"I tried but it wouldn't come out. I ended up lying and used other women to describe things I was doing. Chandler became extremely jealous. Sometimes I wouldn't say ten words before he'd go into a rage for the rest of the meeting, and then shit would hit the fan."

Art rubbed his sloped forehead then ran his fingers through his frizzy gray hair.

"There was a dinner meeting with the president at the White House. Will thought he was going to be promoted, in terms of responsibility. Turns out he got the word — Steve was taking the lead on the reform and he was left to deal with Congress."

"He's really good at that."

"I know but it shattered his ego. From then on Will ranted and raved as soon as he closed the door for our meetings. Twice he ended up bawling most of the session. Finally, I told him 'I can't take this anymore. I don't think you're being fair to me.'"

"What happened after that?"

"He stared at me, as if he hadn't heard a word."

"That's unbelievable."

"After that our meetings became infrequent and finally stopped. Everything was fine until Steve and I broke up — the word was out — two days later Chandler called me into his office and said, 'the position of Inspector General is yours. Do you want it?'"

"And?"

"I was hurting ... and he knew I'd do anything to get even with Steve."

"What did you do?" Art began to be concerned.

"We shook hands, and I agreed to do a full-scale investigation of Steve."

"A full-scale investigation? What did that mean?"

"He wanted me to destroy Steve, said, 'Do whatever it takes.' I'm so ashamed. I've never done anything like this in my entire life. Sometimes I want to kill myself."

"I'm sure it can't be that bad." Art reached across his desk and squeezed her hand.

"I betrayed my own values, along with him," she whimpered softly.

"Slow down," Art said. "Who have you betrayed?"

"It's all in this report." She pointed to the two-inch thick, black three-ring binder she'd laid on his desk earlier. "I deleted all of the computer links, shredded each piece of paper. This is the only record left."

"Why did you do that?"

"It's part of my legal background. I knew what could happen if any of this gets out."

"Happen?"

"If a federal prosecutor comes in and starts digging ..."

"Digging?" Art interrupted. "Why would a federal prosecutor be digging about Steve? I don't understand." Art paused, his brow furrowed and his analytical brain went into overtime. "You said it was about him ..." Art stopped midstream. "Steve is ..."

"Sh." Sherry placed her fingers over her lips. "Don't say it. You don't know anything."

Blood drained from Art's face; he turned white. "You've documented it, you have the evidence. What are you going to do?"

"I'm taking reasoned and prudent action," she said cryptically.

"Sorry, I still don't get it. It's my legalist mind again. Let's assume the minority party picks up a scent of some hanky-panky in the White House. Whataya think they would do?"

"They'd probably name a special prosecutor, someone like Ken Starr. His staff would be pilfering every possible file on the hill. Next thing you know, they call me to the witness stand. How do I react?"

Art scrunched his shoulders. "How the hell do I know."

"If I told them I destroyed the files they'll slap me with an obstruction of justice case. I can't lie. I can't take the Fifth Amendment — I'd have egg on my face the rest of my life. So what do I do?"

Using her words, "What any 'reasonable and prudent' person would do," Art ventured.

She smiled. "Right."

Art felt like he'd trapped himself. "And ...?"

"I send the report up the ladder."

Art paused then grimaced. "You're giving that report to ... me?"

"The legislation that created my position says I serve at the will of the Secretary of Education. In his absence I report to the deputy secretary. Since both are in my report, I can't do that. You're next ... you're his assistant."

"So you take that reasonable and prudent approach ... thanks ... now *I* go to jail."

"Art, you're the only one in the department I trust. And I know you'll do what is right."

"Thanks, a lot."

"You're old friends with Bradley Welton, so I assumed you'll send it up, like a good bureaucrat would do."

"You've thought this through, haven't you? What if someone asked if I read it?"

She snapped the wires crisscrossing the four edges of the binder then pointed. "See? The sealed square where the wires cross — it hasn't been broken."

CHAPTER TWENTY-NINE

While still not quite at full strength, Steve was back on the road before the doctors' estimates — New Orleans, Houston, Oklahoma City and Topeka. His recovery from sepsis had progressed surprisingly well, but it was his red fedora that carried every day.

In Washington, the president's health was nearly back to normal, with practically a full schedule in the office. Staff still soft-pedaled her public appearances, but her likability rate rose. Chatter on all intel sources reached the highest peak ever, putting the country on full alert; the NSA and other security agencies worked overtime.

Knowing he couldn't put off his agenda any longer, Bradley Welton paced his office waiting for a free moment on the president's schedule. He had to confront her today.

At 2:40, he knocked softly on her door and walked into the Oval office. "Do you have a minute?" he asked.

"Who does?" she said curtly without looking up, then pointed to the chair in front of her desk. "What's so important?"

"I'd like to have your undivided attention, please."

Knowing he seldom used those words, she pushed the report she was reading aside. "You have it."

Easing onto the chair, he placed a black three-ring binder — tied with a fine wire and sealed — on the edge of her desk.

She glimpsed at the binder then looked him in the eye. "Another report?"

"We have a situation."

"Again … today." Her nerves showing, she took a deep breath and tried to relax her shoulders. "Go ahead."

"Last Friday an old friend stopped by my office …"

"Does he have a name?" she interrupted.

"I'd rather not say. I'll tell you later if you think it's important to know." She looked at him skeptically. "He handed me this report and said he was doing as he had been asked."

The president raised an eyebrow. "Hold on Bradley, I'm not with you."

"Sherry Holmgren prepared this report at the request of Secretary Chandler," he said, pointing to the document he'd laid on her desk.

"She did it since becoming Inspector General?"

"Yes, that's a part of the story too. As you can see, it's sealed. Before I talk about the report, I'd like to share the events that led to its preparation."

"Fine." She gestured for him to move on.

"When Steve Schilling was appointed, Will invited Sherry into his office and told her that he'd work it out for her to be appointed as Steve's Senior Advisor if she would report monthly on Steve's activities."

The president cocked her head to the side. "Why?"

"Will was extremely paranoid about Steve's appointment and wanted to keep an eye on him."

Janet shook her head.

"He said if she would do that for him, he offered her the Inspector General position when it came available."

"Did he put it in writing?"

"No, but she got the gist of it. She met with Will monthly to share basic information about Steve."

"Personal information too?"

"Mostly things she'd heard through the grapevine."

"Was there a lot of that?"

Bradley adjusted his gray herringbone suit coat. "Apparently so ... he was a hot item — there was a 'Steve-a-mania' epidemic."

The president bit her tongue, nearly laughing aloud.

"As it turns out, the meetings between Sherry and Will developed into frequent crying jags. He became so distraught over your decision to have Steve lead the reform effort that he about lost it.

It got so bad that finally she stopped meeting with him. About the same time, Sherry fell in love with Steve."

"Sherry? ... and Steve Schilling?" The president straightened in her chair and glared. "I don't believe it."

"My source confirmed it. They were hot and heavy for a year or so. It ended last fall."

Janet's face flushed, her shoulders sagged and she took a deep breath.

"You okay?"

The president cleared her throat. "Had something caught ... go ahead, please."

"Steve dumped her before the holidays, and Will reissued the offer. Sherry felt so spiteful that she took the offer and conducted the investigation. Somewhere along the way her values crept back into the picture and she realized what she had done. She purged everything from her office — computer and paper files — and gave this report to a friend who turned it over to me."

"Why did he give the report to you?"

"He's an old Washington pro with a good head on his shoulders, figured it'd be best for us deal with it."

"Us? What do you mean by that?"

"Well, it's a little more complex."

"Let me get this straight. I have a vindictive Secretary of Education who is conniving to get the Deputy Secretary ousted. And a report that incriminates the Deputy of wrong doing, correct?"

"Ah ... it's a little more than that."

The president looked angry; her eyes dark as midnight. "Am I missing something?"

"My source said the report had national security implications."

"National security? How could that be?"

"National security can only mean it's about you."

"Me?"

"The source implied that the report reveals Steve and you were having an affair."

"An affair?" She bolted out of her chair and stormed around her desk.

He threw his arms over his head. "Hey, don't shoot me, I'm just the messenger."

Janet gritted her teeth, barely able to open her lips as she spoke. "Have you read it?"

"No." He flipped the wire band with his index finger. "It's sealed. Do you want me to?"

She took a deep breath. "I don't know. What are your thoughts?"

"Right now, there's nothing but hearsay and innuendo," Bradley said. "If I read it, I know the facts. I'm a potential witness. I think we should deep-six it."

The president eased back into her chair, folded her hands under her chin, and stared across the room. "I can't tell you what to do, Bradley. If I say deep-six it, that leaves it open for a likely obstruction of justice charge against me. You will need to decide for yourself."

Receiving the message, he grinned. "Any thoughts about Secretary Chandler?"

Her mouth quivered. "We don't have a choice. He's a virtual loose cannon. We have to ask for his resignation."

"Do you want me to handle it?"

"Hmm, yes, but the timing is not good. We're almost home free on the higher education bill. Wait until after I sign it."

"What about Steve?"

She looked warily. "What about him?"

"Both sides of the aisle will probably ask you to appoint him as the interim. And then clamor for a quick confirmation as Secretary of Education."

"I'll think about it."

Bradley cocked his head. "Think about it?"

The president stared steadily at him. "You heard me. That'll be all."

He didn't move.

"Bradley, I said that'll be all," she said in a sharp tone.

He stared at her, didn't flinch.

"Is there something else?"

"As chief of staff I'm supposed to advise you on political matters."

Her eyes drifted away, her mouth contorted into a quirky grimace.

Bradley waited until she looked back at him.

When her eyes focused back on him she asked, "Is there something else you have to say?"

"Yes." He cleared his throat. "I can't tell Janet Stetson how she should act."

A wrinkle crossed her forehead as she waited for him to continue.

"But I can advise President Stetson how she should act."

Janet took a deep breath and sighed. "Okay, let's hear it."

"Steve Schilling is highly popular, his stock is on the rise — big time. He has broad support and lots of Republicans will come on board. You shouldn't wait, but nominate him immediately after Chandler's dismissal, for the Secretary's position."

Her mouth curled downward.

"Hear me out before you say a word."

Growing impatient with the conversation, her piercing eyes could have cut steel.

"As president, you have no choice. If you don't appoint him all eyes will be on you for a damn good excuse as to why not. We could lose all of your momentum. There'll be all kinds of speculation. Rumors will fly … it could be worse than if you were …" He stopped for effect. "You need to name Steve as the Secretary."

Janet stood and paced across the room, turning back to him abruptly. "Fine. Put the wheels in motion."

***

A week later, FBI Director Freeh walked into the Oval Office for his regular meeting. "How's the investigation going?" she asked.

"We're zeroing in on the target. Steve Schilling has given us some valuable information."

"Steve? How is he connected to all of this?"

Knowing there was no way out, the director plowed forward. "He was involved with two foreign operatives." Pausing, he waited for her response. She didn't disappoint him.

"Involved? Are you saying you think he was …"

"Yes. He's given us the details and has been quite helpful."

"Helpful about what?"

"His affairs with them, things he might have said. Agents from the Philippines and Russia bugged his apartment and had wire taps on his phone."

"Did he divulge any secret information?"

"Nothing top secret. We're positive he unknowingly revealed information about your travel plans, well in advance of the dates."

"Oh my God. You mean he could have divulged our travel route where the shooting took place?"

"It's possible."

"Do you know much about these ..."

"Yes, one is a Russian spy, Elena Vishneva. Would you like to see a photo of her?"

She swallowed hard. "I-I ... I don't know. Is she attractive?"

"She's over the top."

Janet looked at him with glaring eyes. "Over the top?"

The director slid Elena's picture across her desk, face down.

The president picked it up and slowly turned the photo over. She gulped; her eyes glazed over. Looking away from it, she flipped the picture back to him.

"How long were they involved?"

"Five or six months. It ended in October."

The president bristled, unwilling to let her feelings show. "And the other one?"

"Kim Fernando, a Filipino, who posed as an administrative aid in the Philippines' embassy. She's involved with the Kuratong Baleleng — that's their counterpart to our mafia. They're big-time international drug traffickers."

"And I assume she's attractive too?

"Very ... built like you know what."

She grit her teeth. "Damn," she said under her breath.

"I have a photo of her, too." He started to open a large brown envelope.

"No, that won't be necessary."

"I'm sorry, Madam President. We didn't know about this until recently."

"It isn't your fault." The president walked across her office, her hand brushing across the secret panel. "Damn," she mumbled. Returning to her desk, she sat heavily down on the chair and straightened her shoulders. "Tell me about the investigation."

"We've made significant progress in the past few days. We're close. I hope to be asking for your authorization to strike within the week."

"Good." She forced a partial grin. "I'll be glad to see all of this come to an end."

***

Steve walked into his office after a series of meetings on the hill.

His secretary rushed to his desk. "The president called two hours ago. She wants to see you ASAP."

"The president, you're positive?"

"Yes. She called personally."

"She's never done that. Call her secretary and tell her I'm on the way," Steve said, rushing for the door.

On his arrival in the West Wing, the president motioned him directly into the Oval Office. She looked up with a sneer and headed for the door. Sensing her unusual behavior, Steve walked cautiously inside and took his customary place on the loveseat. She closed the door and marched toward him then stopped, towering over him, icy-cold eyes glaring.

"I have three questions. The answer for each is 'yes' or 'no.'"

Steve looked up at her nervously.

"Were you screwing Sherry last year at the same time you were seeing me?"

Steve's guilty eyes looked away.

"Yes or no?"

He hung his head then sighed. "Yes."

"Were you banging Elena, the Russian spy too?"

"Yes, but …"

"No buts. And Kim, the Filipino woman?"

He bit his lip. "Yes." Even though her security detail had all the facts, she had hoped he wouldn't need to know.

Shaking her head, she sneered at him. "You bastard ... all the things you said ... the things we did. You treated me like I was the *only* one. All of it a lie. How, could you do that?"

"You have things out of context. It isn't that way."

"I want to spit on you."

"Please, Janet, let me explain."

"Explain. I don't want to hear any more lies."

"Please don't close me out of your life. Five minutes. Please hear me out."

She shook her head disgustedly. "I can't believe you ... okay ... five minutes."

"I've had a sex addiction problem all of my life. I tried to tell you when we were at Camp David. I told Charlie in North Carolina that I was going to tell you.

"And when were you going to tell me about the others?"

"I was going to tell you about them too. And how I've changed."

"Here we go again. Another pack of lies."

"No, Janet, I'm not lying. Last fall my doctor made the right call. With his therapy and support, I stopped seeing Sherry and the others. I told him *you* were the only one, and that I was dedicating my life to making it work. I haven't been with or touched another woman for the last six months."

"Ha ... and after all of this, you expect me to believe that."

"Janet, you have to ... it's the truth. I love you."

"Proof, the only thing you love is what's between your legs."

"That isn't fair." Steve's eyes glazed over. "I love you," he repeated in anguish.

"Don't give me that puppy-dog look. I've seen your kind before."

"Will you at least consider that what I'm saying is true ... at least think about it?"

"I can't stand the sight of you." She shook her head. "Please leave before this gets ugly."

***

THE WASHINGTON POST

May 12, 1999

CONGRESS PASSES HIGHER EDUCATION ACT — PRESIDENT WILL SIGN

The Higher Education Act of 1999 has gained overwhelming bipartisan Congressional support and will be signed into law at a White House ceremony tomorrow.

THE WASHINGTON POST

May 15, 1999

CHANDLER OUT — SCHILLING IN AS SECRETARY

In a long anticipated move, Secretary of Education Chandler's resignation was accepted by President Stetson. On the same day, Steve Schilling was confirmed by the Senate as Secretary of Education in the shortest hearings in history.

CHAPTER THIRTY

Steve poured himself a double gin with extra olives and leaned back in his recliner, thinking about Janet as he had each night since she had ended it, three weeks ago. *Why doesn't she want to understand? All of those things happened before my addiction was under control. Besides, I'd always meant to be faithful to her. My intentions were good. Then I'd meet someone — I was attracted to them — I couldn't help it. They weren't like affairs; they just happened.*

For the past ten nights he had followed the same routine, thinking about Janet, sliding his boxer shorts down, caressing his private parts, and watching his erection grow. His fingertips had circled and teased the tip until it stood tall. Then he fondled and stroked himself, slowly, gradually picking up the pace until he climaxed. Tonight was no different.

Lying there totally spent, he thought about the doctor's advice. *Take care of yourself — don't do any excessive drinking or eating. Avoid places and situations that bring back old memories. Be logical; think with your brain not your cock. Don't make leading remarks to women. Avoid glances that say more than should be intended.* He thought about Charlie and Art and how much they had helped him. He dozed off.

It was midnight when he stepped in and closed the shower door. Half awake, he felt the hot shower pelting his body. He washed his hair and lathered up. Unable to resist the urge, he fantasized about Elena, feeling her body pressed against him, grabbing her ass; he came.

Through the night he fondled himself over and over. Was he punishing his body for being so stupid? By Saturday morning he could hardly move. Blurry-eyed, he staggered to the fridge, made a Bloody Mary and plopped down in the kitchen booth to read the paper. He flipped through the various sections, but nothing made sense. *Big deal, who the shit cares about Kosovo?*

He dumped the last of the vodka into his glass, added olives, Bloody Mary mix, and walked to the sofa. Flopping down, he flicked on the television and surfed the channels — cartoons, old movies and workout sessions. *I hate being alone. It's like it's always been; no one gives a shit about me.* Sliding off the sofa, Steve opened the cabinet below the television and pulled out a handful of porno tapes. Losing his grip on them, they scattered across the carpet. *What's wrong with me? I need to talk to Art … shit, he's on vacation all week. Dr. Pritts is gone too. Crap!*

He pulled himself up and stumbled around the room, picking up the porno tapes. Looking at the boobs on one cover, he pulled it out of the stack and slipped it into the player. Twenty minutes later, he gasped. Lying on the sofa, his hand was still wrapped around his fading erection.

Steve emptied a bottle of gin and the remaining vodka then watched a porno flick for good measure.

Sunday morning his fantasies started over, this time Charisse played the leading role. Over the rest of the day, he thought about whatever woman came to mind, fondling himself as often and as long as he could.

Totally smashed, he fell asleep.

***

Steve took off the next few days then went through motions at work on Thursday, returning congratulatory calls and notes. By the time he arrived home, the same old feelings had settled in. *I have to get out of here.* He slipped on a pair of casual slacks and a polo shirt, and took a walk. Passing several of his old watering holes, he paused outside Blues Alley then stepped inside.

Gino waved from the bar. "Steve, it's good to see you again. I thought you were too much of a big shot for us."

"I've been traveling a lot."

"Yeah, your name has been all over the paper. Hey, congratulations on your promotion."

"Thanks, I'm really looking forward to the challenge."

The bartender slid his usual in front of Steve. "It's on the house."

"Thanks, Gino. Have you seen any of that old crowd around here?"

"Everyone is still coming in except Elena and the backup drummer. It's like they fell off the face of the earth."

"Did you ever see him perform?"

The old bartender scratched his head. "Now that you mention it, I don't believe I did."

Counting his woes over a second drink, Steve felt something warm press firmly against his shoulder. He turned to the side. His old friend, Deb, draped her breasts over his arm. "Long time no see," he said.

"You're the one who took a leave of absence. Everyone except Elena has been coming here on our regular schedule for several months."

"That's quite a record." He looked at the table where they used to camp out — it was vacant. "Whatever happened to Elena?"

"Vanished. One day she was the life of the party, and the next thing we know she was gone. No one ever heard a thing from her. Weird!"

"Where's the rest of your group?"

"We moved to the other side, it's a better view. Want to join us?"

"Nah … I'll buy you a drink?"

"That'd be nice." She eased onto the stool next to him. "Tequila with a twist of lime, on the rocks."

"Comin' up," Gino said.

"So what brings you back to this place?"

"Memories, I guess. I took a walk and the next thing I knew I was sitting here."

"I'm glad you are," she said, placing her hand on his thigh.

Steve continued as if nothing had happened. "Anything new with you?"

"Nothing like I've been reading about you."

"Come on, I want to know."

"We've expanded our mission to Africa."

"Hold it." He raised his hand. "I forgot where you work."

"Department of Agriculture. For years we've been sending millions of dollars' worth of food to Africa. It was an endless process. President Stetson came up with the idea of teaching them how to farm."

"Makes sense."

"So now we'll be going to various countries as interpreters. I'm really excited."

"Good for you."

"Other than being the new Secretary of Education what's on your agenda?"

"I want to wrap up the final stage of the president's reform package."

"Can you talk about it? Or, is it top secret?"

Glancing over his shoulder, Steve smirked. "Nothing is top secret in Washington. Everyone knows something."

"Ha, you're right about that."

"It's our biggest agenda yet."

"I can't believe that. You've passed elementary-school testing, made all of the changes in the middle schools and passed new high school graduation requirements. Cutting costs of higher education, what's left?"

Feeling more comfortable, Steve flashed his trademark smile. "The future is all about technology."

"Technology?"

"You know, computers and all that stuff."

"I have a good friend at Georgetown. She's world renowned, knows Bill Gates and Steve Jobs personally."

"Really, I'd like to meet someone like her. I don't know shit about technology."

"Just a minute. I'll give you her name and number." Deb keyed her phone. "Here it is — Irene Golden. And here's her phone number."

"Super. That'll be a real jumpstart. It'll make the changes we've passed thus far look like stopgap measures."

"Stopgap measures? You've already turned the educational community upside down."

"We need to ramp up for the twenty-first century; educationally we're light years away."

"I can hardly wait to hear more." She slid closer and inched her hands up his thigh. Steve pushed his stool nearer, inviting her to go further.

She accommodated, grazing across his erection. The two made eye contact.

She must be twenty-five pounds overweight but her boobs won't quit. I can't recall when I've had something like this. "Want a bite to eat?" he asked.

"Hmm, maybe something light. I'm on a constant diet."

"Aren't we all?" He looked down. Her breasts seemed to elevate. His mood became more optimistic.

The two split an order of Jean Carnes spinach and artichoke dip. Steve ordered a bowl of seafood gumbo and she opted for mixed greens. Steve ordered two more rounds. The liquor was getting to him. Pressing his fingers against his cheeks, Steve couldn't feel a thing. *Numb … who gives a shit, I haven't had a piece of ass like this since who knows when.*

The two played footsy and lovey-dovey games through the second musical performance. Eventually, Steve's urges took control. "Do you have a way home?"

She glanced over her shoulder. "My friends are gone. Looks like you're stuck with me for the night."

"I couldn't imagine anything better."

He gave Gino his credit card and signed the bill.

Deb smiled and extended her hand. Steve followed her lead the rest of the night.

***

Unfolding the napkin he'd written the phone number down on for the contact at Georgetown University, Steve dialed. He listened to the ring then heard the message. "This is Professor Irene Golden. Please leave your name and a brief message. If I'm interested I'll call you back."

Steve followed directions and hung up. *That's quite an ego. She must really be smart or think she's hot stuff.*

Three days later, a frail voice called. "I'm returning the call of Dr. Steve Schilling."

He held the receiver close. "Yes, this is Steve Schilling."

"I'm interested in your question. Is this the Dr. Schilling who's the new Secretary of Education?"

"Yes, it is," he said, then waited for a response.

After a considerable pause, she responded. "Are you really serious about using technology to change the landscape of our public schools?"

"Yes I am."

"How about meeting in the university center for a Coke at ten tomorrow morning."

He jumped at the opportunity. "That will be fine. How will I recognize you?"

"Don't worry, I've seen your picture."

The next morning, a few minutes before ten, Steve strolled into the cafeteria at Georgetown University, and gazed at the empty tables. A short, slender, straggly-haired blonde, looking like a fifteen-year old, stepped his way. "Hi, I'm Irene Golden. I have a table over by the windows." She walked that way.

Steve paid for a cup of coffee and joined her at a small round table with wire-back chairs. Wasting no time, her eyes checked him out.

He felt like she was seducing him. Not that he was bothered by it.

She leaned over the table, her loose blouse showing off modest breasts, no bra. "We have to put all of our cards on the table."

"I'm for that."

"I can deliver everything you want," she continued. "Personal meetings with Gates and Jobs, procedures to translate textbooks into computer software, and a ten-year plan to computerize the entire public school experience."

"What's being taught in our schools is pathetic. Content is dated. Student expectations are at an all-time low. How do you turn all of that around in one swoop?"

She explained, "It isn't all me. Discussions are already underway between the Council of Chief State School Officers and the

National Governors Association to create state standards that will ensure every student graduates from high school and will be prepared to enter college or the workforce."

Steve listened with skeptical interest, "That sounds incredibly optimistic."

"It is ... but a couple years ago leaders from the two groups formed a bipartisan organization to raise academic standards and graduation requirements, improve assessments, and strengthen accountability in all fifty states. It's a grass-roots, bottom-up effort which has made great progress in developing a common core of state standards. I tell you, it's going to happen."

"Sounds terrific, how do we get started?"

She pursed her lips then blurted out, "It'll take more than dollars!"

Steve gulped. "I'm sorry ...?"

"You heard me. Either you want to make a deal or not."

"That's part of it but ..."

She cut him off. "I figure it'll take two hundred grand to create the models, timetables, and arrange the necessary meetings. I want a Request for a Proposal for that." Eyeing him closely, she paused. "In addition, I want a twenty-five thousand dollar incentive check and a weekend at my place."

"That's it?"

"Yep, in that order. I have to feel good about you and the deal. "

"Good feeling?" Steve leaned back. "Are you serious?"

She looked at him lustily. "Are you?"

"I'll have to think about it."

"Fine." She scribbled on a piece of paper. "Here's my address. Give me a call three nights before you're ready to come over."

She stood and walked away.

Dumfounded, Steve sat motionless for a few minutes, then walked slowly to his car and drove back to the office. Without a second thought, he processed the paperwork for a RFP, had a check drawn, and called her.

***

That weekend Steve pulled into a visitor spot and cut the engine. Grabbing a brown paper bag full of wine, he headed for the front door of the old apartment building on a side street in Georgetown. He had second thoughts for the first time since he agreed to see her. *Why the hell am I here? If I'm going to screw someone it should be Deb. At least she has big boobs.* Seeing a speaker box on the right side of the door, he pressed the button.

A response came back. "Yes, who is it?"

"I'm Steve Schilling to see Irene Golden."

"Come in."

A buzzer sounded.

He opened the door and walked into the tired lobby — two tattered, worn-out chairs with flowered upholstery sat on the right with an old coffee table and a plastic plant. A scruffy, gray-haired man pointed down the hall, and grunted, "The elevator is on the left."

Steve walked slowly down the hallway, stepped in the elevator and hit the button for the fourth floor, hoping the 1940s elevator had one more lift in it. When the door opened he checked the apartment signage then headed down the worn out carpet of a dimly lit hallway. He stopped in front of 423, and knocked.

The door opened. Unable to believe his eyes, he paused. The short blonde's hair was swept back in a sleek ponytail. Her black tights accentuated every aspect of her sexy, petite body.

"Irene," he said in a questioning tone.

She smiled and turned both ways, flaunting her slender figure. "Who'd you expect?"

"Nothing like this," he said, eyeing her again.

"The deal is the same." She extended her hand. "We start with the check."

He handed her a white envelope then held up the bag of booze. "I brought four bottles of wine — two whites and two reds — not knowing which you prefer."

"Perfect," she said, pulling the check out of the envelope. "You can put them in the fridge. I'll cut some cheese."

He watched her small, firm ass bounce toward the kitchen.

"Red or white?" he inquired.

"Hmm, let's do white now. We'll have red later with the New York strips I'm preparing."

"My favorite."

"We're also having Caesar salad and pecan pie."

"You must have read my mind."

She grinned. "Deb told me all about you."

Steve gave her a sly look out of the corner of his eye. "All?"

She glanced down at his zipper and smiled. "Everything!"

Steve poured two glasses of wine and placed them on the tiny kitchen bar. Looking around the apartment, he asked. "I really like the vivid colors in the pieces of art."

"I've collected twenty-seven pieces so far. They're all computer generated by top-notch artists."

"Your place looks like an art gallery. Very nice." He gazed at her firm body once more, unable to keep his eyes off her. "I don't understand."

"Understand what?" She looked confused.

"It's like you're two different people — a dumpy professor by day and a beautiful woman by night."

She picked up her glass and pressed her breasts against him. "Something you don't like?"

He shook his head and pulled back, eyeing her again. "I like everything ..."

She cut him off. "It started in college. Deb and I were the best of friends. With her body and my looks, we had our pick of guys. I got into computers big-time, and didn't have time for all of that girlie makeup and fashion stuff. One Sunday I got up, looked in the mirror and said, 'Crap. Who needs it?' I left my hair a mess, dug into computers and made something of myself."

"And that's it?"

"When I feel like it or Deb calls about someone like you, I go for it." She gulped the rest of her wine then ran her fingers around his chin. "Ready for the second part of the deal?"

Steve slid off the barstool and pulled her tight. "I can't imagine anything better."

She gave him a sly, sexy smile and pulled him down the short hallway. "My bust is not as big as Debs, but I'll give you more action than you've ever dreamed of."

I'm for that. Steve's eyes opened wide. "I'll have to see about that," he quipped.

CHAPTER THIRTY-ONE

Dr. Pritts stepped boldly toward Steve and extended a hand. "Congratulations, Mr. Secretary."

"Thanks, Doc. It's humbling to know I have a huge leadership responsibility to improve our public schools. Growing up in a coal mining town in Kentucky, I have to pinch myself as the good ol' boys would have said, 'who would have ever thunk it?'"

"Good for you."

"How was your trip?"

"Fabulous, absolutely fabulous. My wife loved the safari."

"I don't know, camping out for six weeks in Africa ..."

"It wasn't like that at all ... nights we stayed in a lodge."

"Now that's my style of camping."

The doctor laughed then skimmed down Steve's file. "Are you still seeing the same woman?"

Steve wondered anew, *why?* "She dumped me last month."

"I'm sorry to hear that. How many times did you cheat on her?"

"Not one time since I made the pact with you."

Doc looked surprised. "Not once?"

"Right, I looked at a lot of stuff but I didn't touch it."

The old doctor tapped his notepad. "Anything you want to share about her?"

"She found out about the women I'd been seeing while I was dating her. Before I made the new resolve."

"Hmm, have you talked to her since then?"

"Are you kidding? It's been like a firestorm. I've tried, but she hasn't forgiven me."

"Hmm, maybe she'll come around. More importantly, how are you doing?"

"I'm in deep-shit city."

"Tell me about it."

Steve described his drinking binge, picking up Deb at the Blues Alley and the weekend with the young professor. "I guess that's it, Doc."

"That's all?"

"Isn't that enough?"

The doctor folded his hands on his desk. "Quite frankly, I would have expected more. The things you've described are quite normal, almost textbook."

"Textbook? I fell off the wagon."

"You're not the first one. Getting smashed after you've been dumped, masturbating, having a rebound fling or two — it happens. It's understandable."

"Understandable?"

"It happens to people without compulsive disorder problems all the time. Your body sees an opportunity to feed your addiction. The urges have been there waiting for some action. It's a good lesson."

"Lesson? I don't understand, where do I go to from here?"

"Like I've said before, you can control your fantasies, drinking, and masturbating. It's no different than it was for the last five months. And now you know what'll happen if you don't avoid situations in which you're vulnerable. We've talked about it — you need to work hard, constantly be on guard."

"I've tried hard, Doc ... one slip then whamo."

"That's all it takes." Dr. Pritts shook his head. "What happened was classic."

"How can you say that?"

"Okay, let's analyze the situation. You planned the first one while you were getting dressed to go out."

"I didn't plan it. I wanted some fresh air, to relax and unwind."

"Bullshit. Your subconscious planned each step."

Two furrows filled Steve's brow.

"You put on a nice-looking causal outfit and 'happened' to walk into the Blues Alley. Think about it, Steve. There are a hundred restaurants in walking distance of your place and you picked Blues Alley. How could that happen by chance?"

Steve shrugged his shoulders; his eyes narrowed.

"The first Thursday of the month. You knew the women would be there. She placed her hand on your leg, which you had conveniently positioned there. And you slid your stool closer. Come on, Steve."

"Maybe you're right, but I can't imagine a person I've never met coming on the way the professor did."

"Think about it, Steve, it's almost the same. She's Deb's best friend. Obviously they had talked about you. It was like Irene knew you and if she liked what she saw she was going for it."

"Maybe ... you might be right."

"Steve, people don't talk the way she did without some encouragement or previous knowledge. Add in the tone of your voice and she knew sex with you was a slam dunk."

"Do you really think that's possible?"

"Possible? It's likely as all hell. Your sex antennas were up — maybe hers were too — you were sending powerful signals to her psyche. Your sex addiction was calling, 'I'm here, take me.'"

"Wow. I never realized subconscious signals could be so strong."

"Sometimes I think they are stronger than our conscious ones. They're based on firsthand experiences that have been repeated numerous times throughout our lives."

"So where to now, Doc?"

"It's back to business as usual. Work hard and be on constant guard, avoid situations where you're vulnerable; be careful what you say and be aware of your body language."

"Hmm, I don't know."

"Steve, you've had one setback ... there maybe another one or two coming yet. Look at it this way ... you've been on the straight and narrow for almost six months, that's twenty-four weeks. One week you screwed up — 4 percent — that's a great record, compared to where you started. Remember, it's one step at a time."

"I got it."

***

"Damn, I can't believe it," Art said, plopping down at Steve's conference table. "I take a vacation and the next thing I know you're the Secretary of Education. How'd that happen?"

"Bradley called and said the president had accepted Chandler's resignation, was skipping the interim stage and going directly to confirmation. Next thing I know, I'm shaking her hand."

"That's amazing. So what's next on your agenda?"

"I want to name you as my chief of staff. Will you take it?"

Art laughed. "Sure. I don't have anything else to do."

"Great. I need a crash course on dealing with Congress and who I should talk with; I don't have a clue how to get them to pass the final reform package."

Art responded with enthusiasm. "First thing, I want to read an overview of the proposed legislation; then I'll be able to develop a game plan."

Two days later Art handed Steve a draft document. "Here's a start — seven pages of who to see, the points to make; and the sequence of meetings."

Steve leafed through the handout. "I never heard of these names. Are all of these people in Congress?"

"Absolutely. And by the first of June you need to be on a first name basis with each one."

"How can I do that? The president expects me to be trucking around the country giving speeches," Steve said, his eyes skimming down the list. "Could you at least tell me why I'm meeting with some of these people?"

"Pick a name."

"This one." Steve pointed. "Conyers from Michigan."

"He's a powerful black rep from Detroit — a big union man."

"Unions?"

"Teachers unions ... the American Federation of Teachers. They have over a million members. He has to be on board."

Steve turned the page. "Okay, how about this one? A representative from Manhattan, New York."

"That's where the major publishing houses are located. If you're moving to Microsoft and other software packages, they're going to lose a lot of business. Big time!"

He flipped a couple more sheets. "What about the representative from Austin, Texas?"

"Good point. It happens to be that Round Rock is part of that metropolitan area."

"So?"

"Round Rock is the headquarters for Dell Computer. Do you think they'd have any interest in Steve Jobs's offer to discount Apple computers to schools across the country?"

"I got it."

***

AP NEWS BULLETIN

Manila, Philippines

May 20, 1999

2:17 a.m. PHT

The National Intelligence Coordinating Agency (NCIA) in close coordination with the CIA (USA) conducted a covert action in Quezon City resulting in the capture or killing of twenty-three top Kuratong Baleleng officials.

THE MANILA TIMES

ENGLISH EDITION

May 20, 1999

NCIA DESTROYS KURATONG BALELENG STRONGHOLD

Quezon City – Early this morning over a hundred NCIA agents stormed the national headquarters of Kuratong Baleleng. Twenty-three leaders were captured. Queen Bee Kim Fernando and her personal lieutenant Rodrigo Guimatao were

killed. The NCIA reports another seventy-two officials are in custody. A nationwide sweep continues.

The clandestine operation was coordinated by the United States of America's CIA, and is suspected to be a part of the United States efforts to locate the persons or groups responsible for the attempted assassin of US President Stetson last fall.

The intense investigation has been underway for six months and had become the single focus of the US intelligence community.

CHAPTER THIRTY-TWO

THE WASHINGTON POST

May 21, 1999

CIA CAPTURES SUSPECTED ASSASSINS

Six months to the day, the CIA is totally confident they have captured those responsible for last fall's attempted assassination of President Stetson. Pictured below are Kim Ferdinando and Rodrigo Guimatao, top leaders of the Philippines' Kuratong Baleleng, killed in the CIA's sting operation.

Yesterday's early morning raid of the Kuratong Baleleng stronghold resulted in the arrest of twenty-one other top officials, and rounded up over one hundred and twenty-five suspected gang members. The National intelligence Coordinating Agency (NICA) in the Philippines projects over one hundred and fifty suspected mob members nationwide have already been arrested. Warrants have been issued for another two hundred individuals.

Quezon City trucks with armed guards are now transporting thousands of tons of heroin and cocaine to the city dump. No estimate has been

made of the street value of these drugs, but their projected value will be in the billions of dollars.

Steve stared at Kim's picture then tossed the paper aside. Art looked across Steve's conference table and shook his head. "I can't believe you were a part of this whole thing. Had not the security boys worked together they would have never pulled it off."

"Sometimes they take flak, but most people don't realize how different their missions are, and how much they work together."

"Right. And when it comes down to brass tacks, they're all on the same page."

Steve refilled his mug.

Art glanced at the headlines one more time. "Did the agents give you any details?"

"Yes … but it's still all hard to believe everything they've uncovered."

"Tell me about Kim."

"I was a real sucker. Kim told me her sister had been kidnapped by the Kuratong Baleleng and was forced into prostitution. In fact, she was the one who was drugged for three years then worked her way to the top of the organization."

"She's not the first one to sleep her way to the top."

"She became so powerful, they called her Queen Bee."

"Did he say anything about that letter you received?"

"Yes, it was authentic, from Kim's mother."

"Her mother? How did that happen?"

"Kim told her mother that she was falling in love with me. Her mother knew the Kuratong Baleleng would never let her out."

"So she wrote the note to you in hopes you'd break it off."

"Yeah. Interesting."

"One strong lady, I'd say."

"You can say that again."

"One last question. Why did the Kuratong Baleleng try to assassinate the president?"

"It's all about drugs."

"Drugs?"

"In the last three years, the DEA has established a half dozen new field offices in Mexico and South America. That put a severe crimp into the flow of drugs into the US. As a result, drug trafficking from Asia shifted to the West Coast."

"I still don't see the connection."

"The Kuratong Baleleng had established a network to deliver drugs to fast-food Chinese restaurants on the West Coast and planned to expand nationwide. They were following the same approach the Sicilian mafia used with pizza parlors back in the 80's."

"Yes, I remember. That's the case where FBI director Freeh made his name as the prosecutor."

"Now you have it."

Art urged Steve to continue, with a quizzical look.

"The Kuratong Baleleng wanted Freeh out. They figured that if they assassinated the president, the new president would appoint a new FBI Director."

"That's possible but our system doesn't work that way."

"I know but that's how it works in the Philippines. When a president goes there, the entire central government changes."

"Ah, and they thought it works the same way here."

***

Following Art's advice, Steve made his rounds on the hill. It didn't take long for his charisma to take control. The numbers grew quickly in his favor, and by the time he met with the president's educational advisory group, the decision was clear.

"Dr. Schilling, as secretary we're pleased to welcome you back," the president said, without making eye contact or showing any emotion.

The group applauded. Steve smiled.

"Thank you, Madam President."

She gave him a fake smile. "Dr. Schilling, we've all heard the essence of your computerization plan. Are there other nuances that you'd like to share with the group?"

"Yes." He displayed his mega-watt smile. "As a matter of fact there is. Microsoft and Apple have agreed to be a part of our learning community."

"Learning community?" Bradley asked.

"Over the next few years, each of them will clamp down on spelling. If a word is not spelled properly the email won't be sent."

"They can do that?" a member of the group said.

"Don't be so quick in your judgment," Steve pointed out. "Dell and Texas Instruments are on board as well. And all of them are committed to extending the learning concept to all aspects of their business."

"How so?" someone asked.

"They're working on a procedure where documents won't print if they contain spelling errors. And the same will be true for their websites — if they contain errors they won't open."

"I can already hear the freedom of speech complaints from the ACLU," the president said.

"It'll be interesting … you can say what you want, but it better be spelled properly."

"I didn't read that in the legislation," the chief of staff said.

"It isn't in the legislation." Steve winked. "Trust me, it's going to happen!"

***

Dr. Pritts placed his hands behind his head and leaned back in the swivel-rocker. Steve sat relaxed in his favorite chair. "So, what do you think, Doc, five consecutive months?"

"I am absolutely amazed. I've read about success stories — none equal to what you have accomplished. The only thing I can say is to keep your guard up."

"Don't worry, Doc. I'll never let you down. I've been at the bottom. The top is a helluva lot better. Thanks, again."

"You earned it." He glanced at his watch, fifteen minutes before five o'clock. "Since we have a few moments, how about an update from the hill."

"We've had a truly amazing run. A lot of people have worked hard … I have to give all of the credit to President Stetson — it was her vision."

"Sounds like you contributed a little too."

"Early on we passed several stopgap measures, in case we were unable to accomplish the entire package. Turns out Congress is about to pass the entire computerization plan. It's going to be exciting to see our schools in 2010 when the full computerization package is implemented. It'll free up teachers so they can focus on teaching kids — helping them learn, think critically, analyze problems, and understand the hows and whys — instead of babysitting. Classrooms will be exciting places where computers are the primary source for delivering content. It'll be like night and day in comparison to what we have now."

***

CHARLOTTE OBSERVER

OPINION

November 10, 1999

SCHILLING DEMONSTRATES OUTSTANDING LEADERSHIP

LOS ANGELES TIMES

November 10, 1999

CONGRESS PASSES MASSIVE COMPUTER PLAN

SECRETARY OF EDUCATION SCHILLING DRIVING FORCE

Secretary Steve Schilling ushered in the most massive educational reform package in history. By 2010 teaching in our schools will be a dynamic process.

THE ATLANTA JOURNAL-CONSTITUTION

EDITORIAL

November 11, 1999

STEVE SCHILLING IS THE NATION'S TOP EDUCATION LEADER!

THE WASHINGTON POST

EDITORIAL

November 11, 1999

Less than two years ago, President Janet Stetson announced what we called an overly ambitious plan to reshape public education. We were wrong.

Congratulations to her — and thanks to hard-charging Steve Schilling — our schools will be dramatically better!

***

President Stetson stood at the podium in the Rose Garden highlighting the Computerization of Public Schools Act. She recognized Steve for his outstanding leadership and the Georgetown professor for her professional direction. Each taking their bows for the media.

She then turned to the group standing behind her and introduced each. Referencing them personally, she gave examples of how each of their lives would have been different had they experienced schooling under the new legislation. The mouths of the people in the audience fell open, each one trying to imagine the scope of what was ahead for our youth.

Taking a moment for it to sink-in, the crowd fell into spontaneous cheering and applause. President Stetson relished the moment, at first smiling broadly then jumping up and down in jubilation.

Following her formal remarks, she moved to a small table on the right where she used numerous pens to sign the bill. Standing up, she raised her arms in the air celebratory fashion. "I'm proud these changes will enable our youth to regain the top spot internationally. Please join me in a reception." She pointed to the large white tent on the left.

Over the next hour she shook virtually everyone's hand. Steve worked the other side of the tent, making sure to avoid direct contact with her. Near the end of the reception the president made her way to Steve and handed him an envelope.

A crease lined his forehead. "What's this?"

"An invitation for dinner. You can open it now."

He wanted to give her his patented Cheshire-smile but settled for a partial grin. He opened the uniquely embossed invitation for tonight and read:

THE PRESIDENT OF THE UNITED STATES
INVITES YOU TO A
SPECIAL CELEBRATION DINNER

"Can you attend?" she asked.

"Yes, of course."

***

Steve stood in front of the White House elevator. Glancing at the agents stationed on each side, he winked at the one he recognized on the right. The eyes of the agent didn't move. He looked straight ahead, staring through Steve.

The doors opened and Steve stepped in. The agent pushed the button and he waited. Moments later, the doors opened.

Janet stood before him in the sexiest black floor-length negligée he'd ever seen. He stared at her perfectly shaped body, silhouetted by the light shining from behind her, unable to speak.

She extended her arms. "Welcome home, dear!"

###

SHARE AN AFFAIR CONTEST

ShareAnAffair and WIN!!

Get published

Write about an "affair"

Your story might be included in my upcoming book

Share an affair, tell me your memories. They can be real or just a fantasy. Sound interesting?

How many times have you thought about that special love affair you'll never forget? It could have been a night. Maybe a weekend, or something that lasted a lifetime. It doesn't matter. It's a memory lodged deep in your heart and soul that will never be lost.

Or, maybe it isn't real at all. Perhaps it's a fantasy that you've replayed countless times in your mind.

Have you ever thought about sharing your affair with others? ShareAnAffair may be perfect for you. It's an opportunity to tell others your story.

There are no gimmicks or cost. Simply write about your love affair using the format below:

- Limit your story to four pages—1000 words maximum

- Use Times New Roman font, 12 point, double-spaced, one inch margins.

- Send your manuscript to affairs@LesCochran.com.

If your story is selected for publication, your affair will be woven into one of my future books. Winners will be notified, and recognized by name in the acknowledgements. Or, if preferred you'll remain anonymous. Either way, you'll receive a free autographed copy of the book.

Episodes may be changed or modified to fit the particular story. Winners must agree to waive all literary rights. ShareAnAffair does not accept material that may be considered depraved or illegal, pedophilia, rape, incest, necrophilia, bestiality, racially intolerant or sexually explicit. All characters must be eighteen or older.

CONTEST INFORMATION: www.LesCochran.com